Eden's Angel

"It is beyond me, sir," Alena said indignantly, "why I continue to give you credit for manners you do not possess. I would consider it a gentleman's courtesy if you would kindly turn your back."

Zach simply grinned. "I never claimed to be a gentleman, you know." He started toward her. "There are no rules of etiquette here, Angelface. So what do you say to dispensing with all this pretension. You like me. I like you—"

"I most certainly do not like you . . . not the way you say it."

He moved steadily forward.

"Dr. Summerfield, I—"

"Zach," he whispered hoarsely. "Call me Zach." He lowered his face to hers . . .

Eden's Angel

KATHERINE COMPTON

AVON BOOKS 🔷 NEW YORK

EDEN'S ANGEL is an original publication of Avon Books. This work has never before appeared in book form. This work is a novel. Any similarity to actual persons or events is purely coincidental.

AVON BOOKS
A division of
The Hearst Corporation
105 Madison Avenue
New York, New York 10016

Copyright © 1990 by Katherine Compton
Inside cover author photograph by Johnny W. Demkowich
Published by arrangement with the author
Library of Congress Catalog Card Number: 90-92981
ISBN: 0-380-76121-1

First Avon Books Printing: July 1990

AVON TRADEMARK REG. U.S. PAT. OFF. AND IN OTHER COUNTRIES, MARCA REGISTRADA, HECHO EN U.S.A.

Printed in the U.S.A.

RA 10 9 8 7 6 5 4 3 2 1

To Ron, my husband, my heart,
Descendant of a Cherokee chief.
For the warrior on the surface,
And the sensitive man beneath.

Also, to Courtney, Chris, Emma, and Brittany,
four true treasures in my life.

And a heartfelt thanks to
M. Bullinger, B. Hamilton, P. Bly, K. Crane,
and my editor, N. Yost,
for their generous gifts of advice and insight.

Author's Note

Dear reader,

One of the things I love best about writing historical fiction is the author's freedom to dabble with the time elements of history. In order to enhance my story, I've taken the liberty of doing just that.

Sir Arthur Evans, the acclaimed British archeologist of the late nineteenth century, was not actually knighted until 1911. He purchased the Kephala site at Knossos on the island of Crete in 1899. According to conflicting research, he did not begin excavation of the Minoan palace until either late that year or early in 1900.

The Philadelphia Orchestra was also pulled into the past a little. It was not formed until 1900.

And for those of you who raise a brow at the mention of H. G. Wells' *The War of the Worlds*—believe it or not, the work was indeed published in 1898.

I wish you all the treasures in life that your heart can hold.

Happy reading,
K.C.

Chapter 1

Philadelphia
October 19, 1898

Presumed dead. The words echoed in Alena Sutton's head once again. Bracing a hand against her spine, she concentrated firmly on the brownstone residence, and breathed in the crisp autumn air.

"Presumed dead, indeed," she murmured to no one but the quiet morning. Why, in all her twenty-one years she'd never heard of anything so preposterous.

Alena gave her jade bolero jacket an unnecessary, tidying tug and hurried across the street. The chime of a distant church bell tweaked her conscience. *I should be back home*, she mused, *back home at morning Mass instead of here in this godforsaken country*.

On that thought, she turned down the leaf-scattered walk of the stately home and veered toward the side entrance where a sign marked LAW OFFICE swung above the door. Without breaking her stride, she hiked the hem of her fluted skirt and climbed the steps.

Atop the stoop, a brass lion's head glared at her from the center of the heavy oak door, as if to protest her presence. Not in the least intimidated, she glared boldly back. A sudden blast of October wind caused a cyclone of red-gold leaves to spiral around her feet. *Shh ... shh ... should leave it alone*, they whispered, and were gone.

Alena exhaled slowly, fighting the urge to run back to London, to Mistress Stephens' School for Young Ladies. There, her duties had kept her mind occupied. She hadn't had time to dwell on memories too precious to forget totally, yet too painful to openly ponder. Beyond the door, those memories would most definitely be resurrected. After all, despite past grievances, she had once dearly loved the man.

She checked the tilt of her hat and squared her shoulders. Although she dreaded the prospect of such tender feelings surfacing, curiosity won out over the butterflies in her stomach. So she dusted her sleeve, and, paying no heed to the tremor of her spotlessly white-gloved hand, reached for the pull. A clattering commotion, followed by a series of muffled curses, prompted her to give the pull another persistent yank.

"All right! All right! I'm coming!" bellowed an irritated voice. The door was jerked open by a tall, elderly gentleman with mussed gray hair. He squinted against the bright sunlight then, quivering with indignation, looked down his long nose at Alena. "This is the Sabbath, young lady," he snapped, giving the belt of his striped dressing robe a sharp tug. "I don't conduct business on the Lord's day."

Upon that note, he began to close the huge door. Alena thrust her parasol forward, bracing the tip against it. She'd never done anything so vulgar in her life. Nevertheless, she'd come too far to be put off now. Resolutely, she lifted her chin and held the parasol in place. "Are you George Dalton, solicitor for Howard Sutton?"

"Solicitor? For Howard?" The man furrowed his bushy silver brows and pushed his spectacles back up on his nose. "Well, yes, I—"

"Then with all due respect, sir, I must insist you see me. I promise not to take too much of your time." The drop of his jaw gave Alena an unfair advantage which she immediately took. Pushing the door wider, she forced the bewildered man to retreat a step, and swept through the small entry into the office beyond.

Alena stopped just inside to calculate her next move. The monotonous ticking of a pendulum clock gave the huge room a hollow, foreboding ambience. The essence of fine Cuban cigars lingered heavily in the air. Cluttered bookshelves lined the walls. At the far end of the office, muted light shone through a dirty, cross-paned window, illuminating the dust particles that hovered above a massive oak desk placed before it. Facing the desk, side by side, were two large, brown leather chairs, their tall winged backs to the door.

"Now see here, young lady—"

Alena spun to face the man as he entered the room. With a flick of her wrist she snapped open the folded letter she held, and raised it for his inspection before he could say another word. "Mr. Dalton," she said, her clipped British accent ringing an octave higher than normal, "would you please explain the meaning of 'presumed dead'?"

His pale gray eyes roved over the paper briefly, then lifted to hers. He stared at her for a long moment, then, aggravation draining from his face, he stepped forward. "Forgive me, Miss—"

"Sutton. Alena Sutton."

"Yes, of course, Howard's—"

"Daughter," she stated flatly.

He smiled sympathetically. "Forgive me, Miss Sutton, for my abruptness at the door. I didn't expect you until next week. You favor your mother so much, I should have seen the resemblance immediately." He tilted his head to one side and his smile of commiseration changed to one tinged with admiration. "I can't get over it. You're the very likeness of Marion. The same golden hair . . . same heart-shaped face."

An impatient sigh escaped Alena before she could stop it. Weeks of rough seas, close quarters, and meddling old biddies aboard ship had exhausted her good manners. "About my father—"

Quickly closing the distance between them, Mr. Dalton took her elbow and guided her to one of the leather chairs. "Please sit down. I was very sorry to hear the news about your father," he said, then rounded the desk and seated himself. "Howard was not only my client, but a very dear friend."

Alena stiffened, gathering what precious little patience she had left. "Mr. Dalton, I haven't come all the way from London to receive your sympathy. While I'm sure it's well meant, I'm not quite certain if it's warranted yet." She glanced at her hands clasped tightly in her lap, then steadily, determinedly, lifted her gaze. "Is my father dead or isn't he?"

The old solicitor cleared his throat, his brows settling into a frown as he tapped steepled fingers against his lips. "Miss Sutton," he said at long last, "it is my considered opinion, and that of the local authorities in the area where your father was last seen, that Howard Sutton is indeed . . . deceased."

Alena braced a hand against her corset, steeling herself against the rising turbulence inside. She'd expected something like this to happen. Feelings were bothersome, always cropping up spontaneously, serving solely to make one's life difficult. Which was precisely why she'd learned long ago to detach her head from her heart. Taking a firm rein on the uninvited emotions, she folded her hands in her lap and fixed what she hoped was a controlled expression on her face. "On what grounds do the authorities base this opinion, sir?"

"According to reliable sources, my dear, the Venezuelan government has thoroughly investigated Howard's disappearance."

"Disappearance? You made no mention of a disappearance in your summons. In fact, you made very little reference to anything, except that my father was 'presumed dead.' What, pray tell, was he doing in Venezuela?"

"As I understand it, Howard was researching a possible expedition into the Amazon at the time. Witnesses say he wandered from camp one day and simply vanished without a trace. He's been missing for quite some time . . ."

Mr. Dalton's voice faded into the distance. The word "missing" struck an all too familiar chord. Howard Sutton had been "missing" from her life since she was six years old. It seemed like an age since her father had kissed her cheek, made promises he'd never kept, and left her in Mistress Stephens' care. Time had crawled those first few years, until she'd stopped waiting, stopped worrying, stopped wondering if he would ever return. She'd simply evaded the issue, as children often do, by pretending.

Her father, a most distinguished archeologist, had met with an unfortunate accident. At least, that was what she'd told schoolmates when the subject had arisen. In her imagination, she'd buried Howard Sutton long ago.

". . . so you see, my dear, almost anything could have happened. Savage natives or wild animals could have . . . ah . . . nevertheless, Howard's body has yet to be found. To be quite frank, Miss Sutton, under the circumstances, there may not be a body left to find. At this point, the local authorities believe it would be useless to continue their search."

George Dalton tugged a nose cloth from his robe pocket and dabbed the beads of perspiration from his upper lip, searching the girl's face for signs of lamentation. The poor little thing was more than likely in shock. "I know this must be difficult for you," he said sincerely. "I regret with all my heart that I should be the bearer of such ill news. But as Howard's only living relative, you had to be informed."

He laid a hand against his top desk drawer where he always kept a clean hanky for just such occasions. It had been his experience that ladies fainted just about now. He waited patiently. The clock ticked loudly in the prolonged silence. Alena Sutton's reaction, or lack of it, puzzled him. Expressionless, she sat starch-stiff, void of a single tear. If not for her wan color or the brief flashes of emotion in her forest-green eyes, he would have sworn the young woman was completely made of stone.

When a respectful amount of time had passed without incident, he thought it best to carry on in a businesslike manner. "Your father's possessions have not yet been retrieved, but I have asked that they be sent to this office. Will this arrangement be satisfactory? Miss Sutton?"

"Yes. Yes, of course." Alena's gaze fell to her new kid oxfords. Scooted back in the chair as she was, they barely brushed the floor. She'd thus far been able to disregard the fact that the recently purchased shoes still pinched her toes. Now the pain that plagued her feet moved up the full length of her body and settled in her head. There were so many questions left unanswered.

"Mr. Dalton?" The attorney stopped writing and looked up from his notes. "Is it not possible," she asked, fingering the ivory lace of her high collar, "that my father might still be alive?"

The solicitor contemplated the question for only a moment. "Possible, but highly doubtful, my dear. You see, I believe Howard may have had a premonition of his death. He contacted me a few months before his disappearance, and entrusted me to transfer all of his holdings at the Girard National Bank into your name. I was also instructed to give you something in case anything happened to him." He turned to the safe behind him, spun the black numbered knob this way and that, then clicked it open. Swiveling back around, he held out a large, sealed envelope. "I was asked to deliver this safely into your hands."

Alena reached for the envelope, unable to control a shiver. There, in bold black lettering, was the same hurried scrawl that had written the brief greeting received upon her seventh birthday. A hellish battle to maintain her indifference ignited within her.

The man meant nothing to her, *nothing*, she told herself as she stared at the envelope. It was addressed to *My beloved daughter, Alena*. Why, after all this time, would he acknowledge her? Was this an explanation? An attempt to appease his guilty conscience? Could apologies for abandonment be made so easily?

Reserving further judgment, she bit her bottom lip and broke the wax seal. A folded yellowed parchment of what appeared to be thin, brittle animal skin was the sole contents. No letter. No regrets. Unfolding the document, she secretly hoped something, anything, had been penned inside.

In dire disappointment, she spied nothing more than a torn section of some ancient writing, the likes of which she remembered well from early youth. Dozens of similar items had been carelessly scattered about her father's library.

Alena furrowed her brows and focused harder on the faded symbols upon the parchment. Primitive, painted stick figures danced motionless across the surface and were interwoven with meaningless scribbles. None of it made any sense. Unless . . . just perhaps, there was a hidden message. She set her mind to work, lightly tracing the drawings with her fingertips.

Somewhere amid her concentrated effort it suddenly dawned on her that this was a map of some sort. But in heaven's name to *what?* Why would her father send her a map she couldn't make heads or tails of? And why was part of it missing? She lifted her gaze to Mr. Dalton, a score of questions on the tip of her tongue. His bewildered look told her he had no answers.

"I'm afraid I can tell you very little," he confessed, then tugged his upper lip. "Except . . . there is a second envelope. It's addressed to the curator of a small museum. Dr. Summerfield is a former colleague of Howard's." He rubbed his chin thoughtfully. "Perhaps he could be of some help. Though, I must warn you, he tends to be . . . well, at times he—"

A gust of wind swept into the office, rustling the papers on the desk. Following the old attorney's startled gaze, Alena peered around the winged back of her chair to see a tall, broad-shouldered, lean-hipped silhouette filling the doorway. Sunlight beamed into the room around the figure, outlining it in a bright white aura. The man wore a strange, foreign-looking hat, one side of the wide brim folded up alongside the crown. Dust flew from his weathered, rugged clothing as he strode through the entry and into the office like some ruthless hunter emerging from the depths of an African jungle.

Though he seemed oblivious to her presence, Alena ducked back behind the protective cover of her chair as he neared. His footsteps halted just behind her and a swishing paper sailed above her head to alight on Mr. Dalton's desk. A heavy fist landed forcefully on the top back of her chair, with a vibration that jarred her teeth. Covering her mouth to muffle a startled gasp, she shrank back, desperately trying to disappear.

"What the hell," the man thundered, "just what in the hell is this?"

"Now, calm down, boy," Mr. Dalton began.

"Howard Sutton's not dead, dammit. He can't

be! We were on the brink of the greatest discovery of the century!"

The distinctive accent conclusively branded the man a Yankee. Acute curiosity as to why a Yankee would mention her father in such terms triumphed over Alena's wariness. At the sound of weighted heels striding away from her, she braved another peek in his direction. He was pacing back and forth, raising his voice in an ardent curse. The wide brim of his exotic hat shadowed everything above the bridge of an aquiline nose. His whisker-shaded jaw was prominent, his chin strong. His sulking, full lower lip, was set in a hard line. He wore a leather waist-length jacket over a tattered, tan shirt that gaped open, obscenely exposing a sprinkle of dark hair across his chest. For the sake of decency, Alena tried to avert her gaze from such immodesty, yet her eyes seemed to have a will of their own. Without permission, they persisted on a downward course, taking in the snug dungarees and well-defined hip and thigh muscles that flexed as he strode to and fro.

Of a sudden, she realized her transgression, and heat stung her cheeks. Imagine ogling the man as if he were on display at a circus sideshow. She was abashed and, indeed, rightfully so. Still, rather than look away completely, she focused on the pacing knee-high boots that had obviously seen better days, and considered the owner's identity. *Who was he?* What possible connection could there be between her father and this unkempt American?

Alena's thoughts on the matter ended as the boots stopped abruptly and pivoted toward Mr. Dalton's desk. She lifted her gaze to see a slow smile curve the stranger's lips. Not wishing to catch his attention, she eased back into the safety of her chair. And none too soon. Seconds later, he barreled past her, braced his hands upon the desk, and leaned face to face with the solicitor.

"Oh, I get it," he said, then chuckled in a way that made Alena wonder if he had all his wits about him. "It's another one of Howie's crazy stunts . . . just to get me back here, right? He's found it, hasn't he? Somehow he's gotten his hands on the map!" He straightened, arms akimbo, and nodded knowingly. "Okay, Howie, you old coot," he proclaimed, "the game's up. You can come out now."

Mr. Dalton sighed wearily. "Zach—"

"Come on, How—" As if sensing a presence behind him, the tall stranger spun around, obviously expecting Howard Sutton.

She sat very still, wary, feeling his hat-shaded eyes rake her. His wide smile deteriorated by degrees until the corners of his mouth were downturned. Then, in lightning succession, surprise, confusion, embarrassment, and a number of other expressions Alena couldn't quite assess flitted across his face. However, within a matter of moments, he evidently regained his composure for he smiled again. Oh, no ordinary smile, mind you. Rather, a dashing smile, all white and bright in contrast to his deeply tanned skin—a smile that, in spite of the shadowy beard surrounding it, could have made a more simpleminded lady swoon.

Alena, of course, didn't swoon. Nor did she return the smile. She'd seen a rake smile a time or two, and had never been particularly impressed. She was unsettled, though, when he nudged up his hat, revealing the clearest silver-blue eyes that heaven must ever have bestowed. Even the faint circles beneath them did nothing to diminish their striking appeal.

"I sincerely apologize for the intrusion, ma'am," he said with a precise, scholarly air that had been noticeably lacking in the tirade of a moment ago. "My uncle doesn't generally entertain—"

Mr. Dalton cleared his throat. "Zach, I believe I should make the proper introductions."

"Please do," Zach said, his intense stare making Alena extremely uncomfortable.

The solicitor stood and, leaning to one side, peered around the bigger man. "Miss Sutton, may I present Dr. Zachariah Summerfield?"

Alena arched a brow with a surprise she made no pretense at concealing. *This* was Dr. Summerfield? This ranting, profane man? For some reason, she'd imagined him . . . well, more dignified . . . not quite so large . . . more timid . . . and much older, at least her father's age, perhaps even balding. As it was, he couldn't be much more than . . . a full score and ten? He certainly didn't look old enough to have achieved a doctorate, nor did he agree with her image of a museum curator. Surely, museum curators didn't smile like that.

"Dr. Summerfield is . . . ah, unfortunately my nephew," Mr. Dalton peered pointedly above the brim of his spectacles at the man, "and a constant embarrassment to the family. I hope you can overlook his barbarous manners. He often—"

"Uncle George, I believe the young lady has me at a disadvantage. If you'd be so kind as to finish the introductions, I'm sure we can continue the topic of my lack of civility later."

"Humph. He's also very disrespectful of his elders," Mr. Dalton grumbled, and rounded his desk. He gave his nephew a disapproving glare before turning a pleasant smile Alena's way. "Zachariah, this is Miss Alena Sutton, Howard's daughter."

"Howard's—?" As if suddenly remembering himself, the curator doffed his hat and combed a hand through longish, dark mahogany hair. "It's a pleasure, Miss Sutton, a sheer pleasure to make your acquaintance."

Without waiting for Alena to offer, he bent, took her hand, and pressed it to his lips. The transaction was brief and awkwardly performed, yet a peculiar warmth from his touch lingered beneath her glove, leaving her with an uneasiness she didn't quite know how to cope with. Under the scrutiny of those blue eyes, suitable words evaded her, so she merely nodded, and tried to project one of her typically unruffled guises.

Her cool greeting wasn't lost on Zach. He didn't know what he'd expected, but it certainly wasn't this chilly, detached young lady. When he'd first turned around and seen her, he'd been struck by a strong sense of familiarity, an overpowering feeling that he knew her from somewhere before, though he was sure he'd never met the woman. He would have remembered if he had.

When his uncle had finally gotten around to introducing her, he'd suddenly recalled the photograph of a laughing, curly-headed cherub Howard had carried inside his pocket watch.

Could that picture have set off his sensation of déjà vu? Nah. This poker-faced young lady bore not even a vague resemblance to that engaging tot.

It had to be the eyes—definitely the almond-shaped eyes, a unique shade of green he had encountered only once in his life. They were Howie's eyes. That same steady, clover-colored gaze must have been what had given him the uncanny feeling that he'd known her in another lifetime. Be that as it may, that was where the similarity between father and daughter ended. Now that Zach looked closer, it was no wonder he hadn't immediately noticed her presence. Howard was a big man. Miss Sutton was so small that the huge chair almost swallowed her slight form. And there was another distinct difference that had nothing to do with physical character-istics. Howie was jovial, about as easygoing as they came, and it showed in his every manner-ism. Something in his daughter's erect posture and the tilt of her chin suggested a strictly en-forced self-discipline. Yes sirree. From the toque hat perched just so upon her head, right down to the unscuffed tips of those practical shoes, she was every inch a by-the-book lady.

Despite her stiff upper lip, Zach couldn't help but note that she was also an exquisite example of the feminine species. Even unsmiling, her fea-tures possessed an angelic quality. Her flawless skin, the color of fresh cream, was tinted peach along fine, high cheekbones. The artfully slanted brows and full, pouty lips almost looked painted on, but at a second glance, weren't.

Save for the golden ringlets framing her deli-cate face, he would have placed her in the same category as the fragile china dolls he had seen in the Orient. A bit too perfect for his taste. She sat so straight and still under his inspection, her gaze intent on the small, slender fingers entwined in her lap, that he had a sudden itch to touch her just to see if she was real.

Instead of giving in to the urge, he took the chair beside her, turning his attention to his uncle and the business at hand. "Well, now that we've dispensed with introductions, suppose you tell me why you summoned me from my work in Crete. What's all this about Howard? Where is he?" Zach glanced from the solicitor's sober expression to Alena's solemn one and back again. "This fool talk about Howie being presumed dead *is* a prank . . . isn't it?"

Alena listened with only half an ear while Mr. Dalton repeated the circumstances of her father's disappearance. Having no wish to hear the gruesome details again, she set her mind adrift. The strange symbols on the map played over and over in her head. She tried to make some sense of it all. Why had her father sent only part of a map? He had to have known she lacked proper training to interpret ancient writings.

Her train of thought was quickly drawn back to the conversation when the solicitor handed an envelope exactly like hers to Dr. Summerfield. Inside that envelope, perhaps, was the key that could unlock the puzzle.

Much to Alena's disappointment, the archeologist didn't open the parcel instantly. For what seemed like an eternity, he admired it as one besotted with a beautiful woman. Finally, he tilted his head to stare unseeingly at the ceiling.

"Howie," he whispered in his rich, mellow

baritone, "if this is what I think it is . . . I'm eternally in your debt, old boy." Then he planted an exaggerated kiss on the envelope and ripped it open.

"Hot damn, this is it!" Jumping up, he all but danced a jig around his chair. Deep, throaty laughter escaped him and once again he spoke into the air. "Oh, God bless ya, Howie, wherever you are! This is—" His enthusiasm died a quick death as he eyed the map more closely. "This . . . this is only half of the map." He sank into his chair, clearly despondent, his eyes silently pleading with his uncle for some response.

The solicitor jutted his chin toward Alena. "If I've guessed correctly, Howard saw fit to give the other part to Miss Sutton here. Now, maybe you should tell us what this all means. How about it, Zach?"

Alena caught a glimpse of ill-concealed ire as Zach looked from his uncle to her and back again.

"How should I know?" he replied with a shrug of his broad shoulders.

"Come now, Zach." Mr. Dalton propped his forearms on the desk and squinted dangerously. "You know more about this than you're saying. Miss Sutton is legal owner of the rest of that map. Howard must have given it to her for a reason. She has every right to an explanation."

Dr. Summerfield dropped his head and massaged the bridge of his nose. Alena watched his chest expand with a deep breath. She was taken back when he abruptly cocked his vivid eyes her way. "Miss Sutton," he said, giving her a quick, bland smile that was gone a moment after it appeared, "may I be permitted to examine your part of the map?"

Alena nodded, unable to find any harm in his request. Yet when she offered him the parcel, her hands were reluctant to let go.

With a gentle tug, Zach broke Miss Sutton's hold on the envelope. Her gaze met his briefly, then skittered away. She was a bashful little thing, he decided, as he stood and took the divided writing to the window behind the desk. Taking great care to keep them out of direct sunlight, he laid both sections on a small table next to the safe, and reached inside his jacket for his glasses. He fogged the wire-rimmed lenses with a puff of warm breath and cleaned them on his shirttail, relishing the thought of what this archeological find could mean to the museum: prestige, recognition, and, most importantly, the funds to clear its debts.

Skeptical scholars had called Howard a fool. They'd said the treasure was nothing more than folklore. Well, in Zach's experience, archaic people didn't bother drafting a map unless it led to something. The sound of his heart pounding echoed in his ears as he placed his glasses on his nose. He wiped his perspiring palms against his thighs, then flexed his fingers, and, with great precision, pieced the map together.

"Fascinating," he murmured. Hardly aware he'd spoken aloud, he ran his forefinger along the ancient symbols translating significant sections. Howie had been right all along. It *did* exist! The lost tribe did exist! And in all probability, so did the fabled riches. Captivated by this newfound evidence of the ancient civilization, he was drawn into another time, another place . . . until his uncle's counterfeit cough broke into his reverie.

Returning to the present, Zach took a deep breath and smiled inwardly. He slipped his glasses back into his pocket, then turned to face the anxious stares of his uncle and Miss Sutton. Tucking both pieces of the map under his arm, he skirted the desk to join them.

Dr. Summerfield's impressive height struck her anew when he stopped by Alena's chair and looked down at her. "In my opinion, the map is authentic," he announced. He raised a brow. "Pardon my suspicious nature, Miss Sutton, but do *you* have any credentials that prove you are who you say you are?"

"I can vouch for Miss Sutton, Zach," Mr. Dalton cut in before Alena could utter a reply. "I knew her mother. The girl is the spitting image . . . except for the eyes. Now, will you stop stalling and tell us what the devil all this folderol means?"

The curator regarded her a moment longer, then dropped into his chair, running a hand over his face in apparent exhaustion. "I apologize, Miss Sutton," he said in a tired voice. "I had no call to doubt you like that. But I had to be sure. You see, Howard and I searched for this map for almost six years. We weren't even sure if it really existed." He propped his elbow on the arm of the chair, cupping his chin, and stared off into the distance at some vision only he could see. "The tales we'd heard on previous excavations in South America were incredible. Some of the friendlier natives told us stories of a legendary princess and a lost Amazonian culture said to be quite a wealthy lot. No one knows the name of the tribe. Apparently they are an ancient clan the outside world has yet to discover. At first, it all sounded a bit farfetched to me. But you know Howie. He was intrigued by the whole thing. He said he had a 'hunch' about it. And when old Howie had a hunch about something . . ." Dr. Summerfield paused, rubbed his stubbled chin, and smiled to himself. "To make a long story short, he finally conned me into a partnership. In the beginning, I think I agreed just to pacify him, but when we started researching the possibilities, sure enough, we found evidence that substantiated the old legend."

"The map, Zachariah," Mr. Dalton urged impatiently. "What about the map?"

His nephew's gaze dropped to the pieces of primitive writing he still held. "The map was supposedly written by the elders of the lost tribe. Only the high priests were allowed to see it. It was used during certain ceremonies to guide them through a secret passage into the treasure chamber."

"And what, pray tell," Alena interrupted, unable to hold her tongue any longer, "does any of this have to do with the fact that my father is missing?"

The curator looked pensive. "I would guess Howard's disappearance has something to do with the alleged treasure."

"Treasure?"

"Treasure?" Mr. Dalton echoed.

Dr. Summerfield raised his eyebrows high, and a wry smile lifted one side of his face. He eased uncomfortably close to Alena and whispered, "You know—gold, priceless relics, and jewels, my dear," making the tiny wisps of hair around her ear flutter. "Never-before-seen artifacts and precious gems. In particular, the solid gold headdress of Mahrakimba, an ancient Amazonian princess."

Stunned at his boldness, Alena pulled back and marked his lack of decorum with a frown. Keeping his incorrigible smile, he winked, seemingly unaware that he'd just been overly audacious.

A thread of giddiness rippled through Alena, though she couldn't imagine why. The man was totally absurd, and for him to subject her to such a frivolous feeling, even if it was for only a split second, irritated her immensely. Nevertheless, she held her stern expression, not about to give him the slightest inclination that he had disturbed her in the least.

"While I've no doubt whatsoever that this treasure is quite remarkable," she said, addressing him in a calm, even tone, "I have no interest in such things. I am, however, extremely interested in discovering what has happened to my father. Obviously, the map does indeed have something to do with his disappearance. Inasmuch as we've each received part of it, it seems to me the only logical recourse is to join forces. Now, how soon, do you suppose, could we arrange for passage to South America?"

Zach dangled halfway between amazement and amusement as he searched the woman's cool, apathetic green eyes and realized she wasn't jesting. Forcibly curtailing the twinges at the corners of his mouth, he called forth his professional demeanor. "I believe you've misunderstood me, Miss Sutton. *We* aren't going anywhere. Of course, I'll do everything possible to find out what has happened to Howard. I'm sure I can turn up something, given time." Sliding a hand along his jawline, he peered at her beneath his brows and decided now was as good a time as any to approach the next subject. "In addition, for the use of your section of the map, I'll split the proceeds with you, fifty-fifty, just as Howie and I intended."

"Why, that's ever so considerate of you, Dr. Summerfield," Alena said, "but I believe *you* misunderstand *me*, sir. As I have already stated, I care naught for the treasure." She paused and gripped her parasol tighter, trying to subdue her rising temper. "Furthermore, I have no intention of handing my part of the map over to you, or to anyone else, for that matter."

Zach's feigned smile tightened a muscle in his cheek. "Miss Sutton, you can't be serious about actively participating in this venture. The Amazon jungle is no place for a woman. Why, a dainty little thing such as yourself wouldn't last a day there. Besides, unless I miss my guess, you have no idea how to read an ancient writing. Of what possible use could it be to you?"

"This document, sir," Alena countered, hard-pressed to keep from slapping that smirk off his face, "is the only news I've received of my father in fourteen years. If he is still alive, then the map may be my only link to him. I do not intend to be cheated out of the pleasure of seeing him face to face when he tells me why he never bothered to contact me before. What I don't know about the jungle *or* the map, I'm sure I can learn." She leaned forward, giving him a small, complacent smile of her own. "Rest assured, sir, when that treasure is discovered, I *will* be there . . . with or without the likes of you."

A distinct hardening of Dr. Summerfield's features jarred Alena's confidence. Perhaps she had been too rash in the way she'd handled the situation. In fact, she was more than a bit regretful that she'd spoken so harshly when, with slow, deliberate care, he laid both sections of the map on the solicitor's desk and rose to tower above her like a Titan. What was left of her smile expired completely as he drew near, so close that his boots grazed her skirt, his steel-blue eyes promising trouble.

"Zachariah!" his uncle bellowed. "In the name of heaven, have you gone mad? Stop this tom-foolery!" Mr. Dalton came around his desk and caught the younger man's coat sleeve. "Stop it this instant, do you hear?"

Ignoring his uncle, Dr. Summerfield easily broke his hold, bent forward, and gripped the arms of Alena's chair, pinning her in. His face moved inexorably, menacingly toward her own. She shrank back in her chair and tucked her chin. Scant inches away, he halted. With a suppressed gasp, her eyes dipped to a silver religious medal dangling in the center of the thick mat of hair on his chest. Her gaze skittered down, observing the buttons missing from his shirt, then rose to meet his intense glimmering stare. At such close range he appeared to have the ability to see beyond human capacity. His saturnine smile brought to mind the very devil, and Alena fought to regulate the frenzied beating of her heart. *Stay calm, stay calm*, her logic urged, yet all rationality was slipping away and she was rapidly becoming powerless to move . . . to speak . . . to look away.

"Did you know, Miss Sutton," he purred in a deep, rumbling voice, "that there are alligators and poisonous snakes and all sorts of wild, ferocious animals in the Amazon jungle?" He moved a tad closer and the musky scent of his leather jacket infiltrated her senses. "Not to mention stark-naked savages, vicious headhunters, and cannibals that would absolutely *delight* in having a tender morsel like you . . . for breakfast!"

Like a sudden clap of thunder, fury at the man's bullying overcame Alena. He was trying to intimidate her, and she simply refused to sit there like a scared rabbit. Narrowing her eyes, she compressed her lips into a tight straight line and lifted her chin. "Really, Dr. Summerfield. Do you honestly think me some mindless nitwit to be frightened off by such childish tales?"

"Oh, I assure you, Miss Sutton, I tell no tales."

"Excuse me," she said with a curt smile and purposely poked his chest with the end of her parasol. He bolted upright, as she suspected he might, and she promptly came to her feet. "I daresay I have a good many better things to do than listen to your prankish prattle." Giving him a patronizing glare, she tugged down her jacket, then sidestepped his tall, rigid form, and retrieved her portion of the map from the desk.

The solicitor glanced from Alena to Zach with a mixture of worry and exasperation. "Miss Sutton, I'm terribly sorry," he began.

"'Twas certainly no fault of yours, Mr. Dalton," Alena told the poor, flustered man and graciously offered him her hand. "Thank you for all you've done. I shall call again to conclude these affairs when I return from South America. Good day to you, sir."

She fairly glided to the door, but paused as she grasped the brass knob. "Whether you realize it now or not, Dr. Summerfield," she said without a backward glance, "we need each other's help. When, or if, you're willing to discuss this sensibly, I can be contacted at the Philadelphia House Inn on Market Street."

Chapter 2

A puff of brisk air lingered in the room after Miss Sutton swept out the door in what Zach clearly termed a royal huff.

"Jeez almighty," he muttered, amazed that Howard could have sired such a straitlaced little snit. Assuming a pinched, British accent, he threw the back of his hand against his forehead and declaimed, *"I shall call again when I return from the Amazon."* His terse laugh broke the end of the sentence. "Yes, of course, Miss Sutton, I can just see you now—strutting through the jungle, thumping poor alligators on the head with that treacherous parasol." Smirking, he turned to his uncle and rolled his eyes. "Did you notice how tight her hair was pulled back? It must have affected her ability to think rationally."

The old attorney's glower could have frozen the sun in August. Zach had seen that look often enough to know what would follow. He tried the beguiling smile that usually got him out of trouble. But that maneuver had never worked on good old Uncle George and it certainly didn't appear to be working now.

"For crying out loud, Zachariah!" The words exploded from George Dalton's mouth. He threw up his arms and glanced heavenward, apparently appealing for strength. "Why did you have to go and pull a foolhardy stunt like that? Well? Answer me," he bellowed, without really giving Zach a chance to do so. "You had quite enough to say to that poor, innocent girl, didn't you? Have you nothing at all to say now? Go on. I'm waiting."

Zach sighed heavily and spread his arms wide. "Aw, come on, Uncle George. You know as well as I do—"

"Don't use that tone with me, young man. I'll tell you what I know: I know you were raised in a respectable household; I know my dear sister did not neglect your instruction in simple etiquette—nor did I, after you came to live with me! I know your parents, God rest their souls, would have been appalled at the way you tried to terrorize that young woman. You should be ashamed, Zachariah. Ashamed," he repeated, wagging a long, thin finger in his nephew's face.

Zach tensed, ears on fire, subconsciously grinding his teeth. "All right, I'm ashamed," he said in a low, subdued tone. "Is that what you want to hear?" His voice rose. "I'm ashamed of myself for not succeeding in scaring the living daylights out of Miss Hoity-toity. The South American jungle is no place for a woman, especially *that* one. Hell, the tropical heat alone would do her in. What's the matter with her anyway? Is she dense?"

"She is not dense." George seated himself and clasped his hands upon his desk, maintaining his severe expression while tempering his tone.

"Quite the contrary, as I understand. She well exceeded the best of her class in one of the most accredited schools in London and, upon finishing her schooling, was awarded a teaching post there."

"A schoolmarm. I might have guessed." Zach ran a hand over his face and widened his eyes in an attempt to keep them open a little longer. In the process, a heretofore forgotten thought struck him. "You know, Howie only mentioned having a daughter a few times, but from what little he said, I got the impression he was talking about a six-year-old kid in pigtails."

"For the life of me, I've never understood Howard's motives," the attorney said, pensively stroking his chin. "He never wanted any contact with the child . . . just had me forward money for her expenses. Several times, I tried to convince him to visit, or at least write to his daughter, but he refused to listen, told me to mind my own business."

Zach furrowed his brows, trying to picture his old colleague in the light his uncle was painting. "That doesn't sound like the man I knew. Howard was a good man, Uncle George. Oh, he drank a bit more than he should've now and then, but don't we all?"

The memory of a bottle being liberally passed around the campfire filled Zach's mind. Countless evenings, he and Howie had talked long into the night after everyone else had retired, discussing things they'd done, things they yearned to do. They'd roared with laughter at one another's misadventures and hair-brained escapes. Sometimes they'd debated on philosophy, legends, and myths, or speculated about the future

of the world to come. On the rare occasions Howard had spoken of his daughter, he'd grown mel-
ancholy, misty-eyed, and would finally drift into
a pitiful silence that ended the evening.

Zach's chest tightened as the severity of the
current situation dawned on him. Howie must
have been in trouble, *real trouble*, to part with the
map he'd pursued for half a decade. As long as
Howard Sutton had breath left in his body, he
would have found some way of sending word
by now. Zach felt the floor shift beneath him.
There was no other conclusion, no other explanation . . .

"He's gone," he said, thinking aloud. He
searched his uncle's face for signs of denial, but
the old man's silence and dismal expression confirmed his own verdict.

Dropping into a chair, Zach slapped his hat
against his thigh. "Damn him! I told him not to
take off by himself on any unsubstantiated leads.
He wasn't a spring chicken anymore. I came right
out and told him he needed to slow down. You
know what he did? He laughed at me, the old
fool. Told me he could still beat me in an arm-
wrestling match any day of the week." In spite
of his anguish, Zach smiled a little. "Damned
old fool. I used to let him win . . . and he knew
it."

Weeks of stress taking their toll, Zach rubbed
the nape of his neck, then peered beneath his
brows at his uncle. "He's finally done it this time,
hasn't he? He's gone and gotten himself into
something he couldn't get out of."

George Dalton nodded. "I'm afraid so, son.
Now . . . suppose you tell me the rest of it."

"The rest of it?"

The attorney eyed his nephew suspiciously. "You do know more about this than you've let on."

"Not much. Howie left the expedition in Crete six months ago after receiving some documentation he'd inquired about previously. We'd just uncovered the Minoan palace and were working different shifts at the time." Zach shook his head slowly. "While I was directing the excavation of the king's chambers, Howie just took off in the middle of the night. He left me a message, but it was brief—a lot of shady characters hang around the site, and information can sometimes fall into the wrong hands. All he had jotted down was that the papers had something to do with locating the lost tribe of Mahrakimba and he'd be in touch soon to let me know where to meet him. He didn't say where he was going or who his contact was."

Zach's mind drifted back to the last time he'd spoken with his old friend. Being intrigued by the past himself, he could understand Howie's enthusiasm. The discovery of the lost city would have meant the realization of a long-held dream for the aging archeologist. Howard Sutton had researched every minute detail of the fables about the Amazonian princess. Howie and he had spent years searching for the lost tribe. Zach dropped his head and massaged the bridge of his nose. It wasn't fair for all that hard work to fall by the wayside now. Although he had to wonder how Alena Sutton fit into the puzzle, he had no doubt whatsoever as to why Howard had sent him the map. Nor did he have any qualms about the course that lay ahead of him.

"If it's the last thing I do," he told his uncle

as he reached for his worn section of the ancient writing and tucked it under his arm, "I'm going to find Howie's lost civilization. I owe him that much." Zach leaned forward, bracing a hand on the desk. "All I need is Alena Sutton's piece of the map. Now, if you could just apply some legal remedy to secure her part—"

"My advice to you, young man, is to get cleaned up and go over to the Philadelphia House Inn and try to negotiate with Miss Sutton yourself." The attorney shifted his attention to the piles of paperwork before him. "She's a clever young woman," he said without looking up. "I think she'll be reasonable if you go about it in the right way. Perhaps you should ask her to supper." He dipped his pen in the inkwell, pausing long enough to glance at Zach above his spectacles. "And act like a gentleman, boy. Women like Miss Sutton respond far better to good manners than they do to the bullheaded tactics *you're* apt to use."

Zach ran a hand down his ragtag shirt, digesting the older man's suggestion. His uncle was right. Miss Sutton hadn't been too receptive to his previous strategy. Perhaps a touch of charm was the answer. A nap and a long hot soak in an epsom-salt bath would make a new man of him, then he'd spruce up and put his best foot forward. After all, he'd been said to have a way with the ladies.

Zach looked affectionately at the fuzzy gray head bent over the disorderly piles of paper. His uncle's voice always sounded harsh, but beneath all his gruffness, the old man had a tender heart. Zach had known the moment he'd shown up on George Dalton's doorstep, cold and hungry, that the elderly gentleman's bark was much worse than his bite. "You're a wise man, Uncle George."

The aged attorney, absorbed in his labor, just gave him a nonchalant wave of his hand. Zach smiled at the dismissal. "I'll be around to see you before I leave town," he said, well aware that his uncle merely pretended to ignore him. "Maybe we'll play a game of checkers."

As he made his way to the door, Zach donned his hat and tugged it low on his forehead, pondering the mission ahead. Winning Alena Sutton's favor wouldn't be an easy task. Of that much, he could be sure.

Ah, but the prospect of a challenge always had enticed him.

Alena entered the small but adequate hotel room, asking herself for the hundredth time what she was doing here. Of course, she already knew. The answer had been unearthed in Mr. Dalton's office. The traces of emotions still trembling within her seemed strange and awkward after so many years of detachment. Yet they were there and very real—proof of something she'd tried to deny, something she wasn't quite ready to face.

She tossed the brown envelope containing her map on the bed. Relaxing her shoulders and the stern tilt of her chin, she slipped out of her jacket and hung it by habit in the wardrobe, placed her parasol beside it, then turned to the bureau to remove her hat. A careless jerk of the pearl hat pin caught a strand of hair and she winced, laying full blame for her negligence on that horrid creature, Dr. Zachariah Summerfield.

Alena took a deep breath, determined not to let the man upset her. He was a grave-robber, a rover—just like her father. He probably never stayed in one place long enough to let the dust gather on his boots. She picked up her button-hook and seated herself on the edge of the wrought-iron bed. It was obvious, she decided as she reached down to unhook her shoes, that he was virtually without scruples. His conduct had been disgraceful. It was totally beyond her why anyone, including her father, would will-ingly associate with such riffraff. Then again, how could *she* possibly judge Howard Sutton's taste in companions? She hadn't seen the man in over fourteen years.

Although her feet felt better once she'd re-moved her shoes, the dull ache in her head remained. She reclined on the bed, hoping the pain would go away. She closed her eyes and waited for blessed sleep to temporarily solve all her problems. Instead, the past invaded her thoughts.

In her youth she'd often thought of running away from school. Countless times, she'd imag-ined what her father would do if she showed up unannounced at the site of his current expedition and demanded to assist him in his work. His reaction had changed from daydream to day-dream. Sometimes he'd been elated to see her. Sometimes not. Alena dwelled on the memory for a while, with indifference now, unable to recall exactly when she'd dismissed the idea as sentimental foolishness.

She rolled over on her side, opened her eyes, and saw the briefly forgotten envelope. Slowly, a smile curved her lips. *The map*. She reached out and pulled it to her. The map changed everything. It gave new life to those dusty, shelved dreams she'd assumed were lost forever, didn't it? The very center of her being suddenly swelled with hope of confronting Howard Sutton. Even if half of Summerfield's wild tales about the jungle *were* true, the possibility of locating her father—forcing him to answer her lifelong questions—would be something worth dying for. She clasped the map tighter against her breast. The ancient writing would lead her to him. Somehow she *knew* it would. Nothing, she vowed, would stop her from going to South America. *Nothing*.

Alena squeezed her eyes shut and, for the first time in years, tried to remember what her father looked like. The face she conjured was veiled, shadowy, and quickly replaced by the same bittersweet vision that had haunted her throughout childhood. It came like rolling clouds of a summer storm, clearer, more explicit than ever before.

The cozy cottage set against the lush, green English countryside drew nearer and nearer . . . so close this time that the scent of the wild mountain heather growing along the cobblestone fence filled her nostrils. A cool, morning mist gently caressed her face as she peered through the ivy-trellised window. Inside, the fireplace glowed warm and secure. Spiraling backwards to a place where it was safe to love . . . safe to care . . . safe to feel, she snuggled on Papa's lap while he told wonderful tales of his latest expedition and Mama's soft laughter filled the room . . .

Alena's heart rose to the base of her throat. *Why had Papa left her?* Why had he never returned as he'd promised he would? What had she done to make him hate her so? Tears brimmed in her eyes, but a cold determination from within stopped them from spilling over. She hugged her ribs, striving to feel the imagined warmth of her mother's arms around her. She listened for the tenderly whispered words, confident that soon the gentle specter of a woman she'd scarcely known would come and spread her faithful wings of comfort.

As always, the apparition did indeed appear, and once sedated with calmness, Alena saw things as they really were. As much as she wanted to hate Howard Sutton—something deep inside wouldn't let her. There, behind the wall of bitterness she'd so carefully constructed in the past, remained all the loyal devotion of the vulnerable seven-year-old she'd once been.

With that revelation, weariness washed over her like a warm blanket on a cold day. Before sleep could drown her, however, she made herself a solemn promise. A confrontation with her father was the only hope of ever achieving peace. She knew that now. She would find Howard Sutton with or without the help of that vulgar Dr. Summerfield. She *would* find him ... *alive*, God willing.

Faint shafts of sunlight streamed through the leafy canopy. Alena wove her way through the fog that engulfed the dark emerald foliage. Chattering calls, rustling branches, and dreadful screeches jerked her attention this way and that. She quickened her pace.

Her mind fogged as she struggled to maintain some sort of direction. Was she moving in circles? Everything looked the same. Anxiously parting the fronds of a large palm, she found herself in a small clearing. A tiny splash of pink on the ground moved her forward in slow motion and upon reaching the object, she found it to be an exquisite orchid.

In a strange daze, she stooped to touch the blossom, halting her hand halfway as the jungle's constant symphony abruptly grew silent. The tiny hairs on the back of her neck prickled. She straightened, slowly turning to inspect the vine-covered trees that surrounded her.

A bloodcurdling howl broke the stillness and a hideously masked being sprang from the shrubs.

Alena stood paralyzed as the creature started forward, his dark eyes gleaming through two holes in the mask. After what seemed like an eternity, her heart began to beat again, threatening to burst from her chest. *Run*, her brain somehow managed to command. Her feet took flight at the order.

A second savage leaped into her path. In a frenzy, she tried another route, only to be blocked again and again by more natives wearing the same demonlike masks until they completely surrounded her.

The heathens circled, taunting, touching her with the tips of their spears, pushing her closer and closer to the edge of hysteria.

"*I told you so, Miss Sutton*," came a hauntingly familiar voice.

Alena's gaze was propelled to a nearby cliff. Zachariah Summerfield stood on the ledge, the dark purple sky flashing with lightning behind him. "*I told you so*," he repeated. His eyes blazed like a madman's as he raised an enormous, writhing snake above his head. Horrible, echoing laughter broke from his throat and ran down Alena's spine, splintering her nerves into a thousand pieces . . .

Alena bolted upright in bed and gasped for breath. She pushed damp ringlets from her face and blinked, half-expecting a painted savage to spring from the wardrobe.

Gradually, she remembered where she was. She felt utterly foolish peeking beneath the bed. Nevertheless, she couldn't put her feet on the floor until she did.

With quivery legs, she crossed the room to the washstand and bathed her feverish cheeks. The ice-cold water stabilized her heartbeat. It was just a nightmare, she assured herself, patting her face dry. As she returned the towel to its proper place, a folded paper, apparently slipped beneath the door while she'd slept, caught her eye.

The note was addressed to her in bold yet neat handwriting. Curious, Alena opened it.

My dear Miss Sutton,
    Please forgive my deplorable conduct in my uncle's office. I attribute my ill manners to the upset I suffered upon receiving the news about your father.
    Allow me to redeem myself in your favor by requesting the pleasure of your company at dinner this evening. I will call for you at your hotel at precisely seven o'clock.
                            Kind regards,
                            Dr. Zachariah Summerfield

Alena smiled and arched a brow. So the good doctor had come to his senses. Of course, she'd known all along he would eventually have to see

the logic in forming some sort of an alliance.
From his display of irrational behavior in Mr.
Dalton's office, she hadn't expected him to come
around so soon.

She glanced back over the note and observed
that he'd neglected to provide a return address.
Had that been an oversight? Or was it deliberate?
Had he purposely omitted that particular information for fear she would refuse his invitation?

Either way, it didn't matter, she decided, and
slipped the note into her skirt pocket. She
wouldn't have declined even if she had been
given the option. After all, the meeting would
be for the sake of mutual gain.

Her thoughts veering to a more immediate issue, she opened the wardrobe, assessed the contents, and frowned. Now, *whatever* should she
wear?

The last of the day's soft pink sunlight danced
through the sheer curtains of the hotel window
and shimmered across the dressing table where
Alena sat, tucking the final hairpin into place.
She'd finally given up trying to copy the coiffure
of the Gibson girl in the *Harper's* magazine that
she'd propped against the mirror. Her hair was
simply too curly. In the end, she had opted for
her usual style and pulled her tresses into a tight
bun at the nape of her neck, leaving a few spiraling wisps at her temples.

She pondered her reflection, silently chastising
herself for wasting so much time with such sil-
liness. She'd never fussed with her appearance
before. What on earth had gotten into her? The
pale blue taffeta dress, while not of the latest
fashion, was serviceable for the occasion: not that

she gave a flip whether Dr. Summerfield would
think so or not. 'Twas a matter of important business she was attending, not a cotillion. It was
ridiculous to be so nervous.

Still, it never hurt to look one's best, Alena
thought as she pinned a gold heart-shaped locket
in the center of her high valenciennes collar. Dr.
Summerfield's note had been polite enough. Perhaps he possessed some admirable qualities after
all. People often did things when overwrought
that they wouldn't do otherwise. Straightening
the bodice of her dress, she examined the locket
to make sure it wasn't crooked. The poor man
had most definitely been upset. Truth to tell, she
hadn't quite been herself either. In such a state,
it was possible that she might have misjudged
him.

Alena rose and pulled on her gloves, remembering the way he'd smiled at her. He did have
a nice smile . . . and splendid features. Beneath
all that grime, she suspected he might be rather
comely. Not, of course, that his comeliness
should matter to her in the least.

Uncomfortable with such notions, she picked
up her shawl and quit the room, thinking all the
way down the stairs that she had a perfectly good
reason for considering the man's looks. It was
very simply to assure herself that she wouldn't
be too ashamed to be seen on his arm this evening, especially if he had bathed, and would
mind his manners.

Upon reaching the lobby, she noted that Dr.
Summerfield had not yet arrived. The vestibule
buzzed with activity. Grandly dressed men and
women greeted each other graciously. Alena
spotted an unoccupied reception chair beside a

large palm and retreated to the comfortable corner to wait.

Gradually, the crowd thinned. The clock above the clerk's desk chimed fifteen past the hour. Its monotonous ticking set the rhythm for Alena's foot tapping against the hardwood floor. Promptness, she decided, could be struck from the list of any virtues Dr. Summerfield might possess. Periodically, her gaze wandered from the entrance to the clock, then fell to her hands, which were neatly folded in her lap. She was beginning to feel conspicuous.

Her attention had lighted once again on her twiddling thumbs when an odd sensation crept upon her. She had the strangest feeling that someone was watching her. Without lifting her head, she scanned the room beneath the cover of her lashes.

Her glance halted on a tall, mid-thirtyish, blond stranger across the room, who was regarding her intently. Her eyes opened fully, and he lifted a glass of Madeira and smiled. Naturally, she looked away, not wishing to encourage any advances. Yet, curious to see if he'd heeded her obvious declination of his attention, she glanced his way again. Evidently mistaking the gesture, he straightened his vest and smoothed his hair, then started toward her.

Aghast, Alena pressed her spine against the back of her chair. The sweet smell of hair tonic preceded him as he moved toward her. She nearly jumped out of her skin when he stopped before her and clicked his heels in military fashion.

"You are, I believe, the daughter of Howard

Sutton," he said with an accent that identified him as one of her own countrymen. "Am I correct?"

Not having been properly introduced, Alena hesitated to speak to the man. Then it occurred to her that he might carry a message explaining Dr. Summerfield's tardiness. "I . . . I am Alena Sutton," she replied after an awkward pause.

"Ah, good. Allow me to introduce myself, Miss Sutton. I am Richard Blythe, an old friend of your father's." He extended his hand, and she reluctantly gave him hers. He bent gallantly from the waist and pressed a kiss upon her fingertips, lingering longer than was strictly respectable. He then raised his lids slowly to meet her gaze. "Please accept my condolences."

His expression, as well as his languor, made Alena's cheeks burn. He was not unattractive— quite the opposite really—and very well groomed. Yet there was something about the way his smile failed to reach his warm brown eyes that unnerved her. She tugged her fingers from his grasp, and he straightened abruptly.

"I'm not yet convinced, Mr. Blythe, that condolences are in order. However, it is most gracious of you to offer them. May I presume you know my father well?"

"You may indeed. Howard and I worked together on a project in Egypt several years ago, and have had numerous dealings since. Of course, it has been quite some time since I last saw him."

Mr. Blythe went on and on about his association with her father. His speech was cultured, his voice hypnotically relaxing. Eager to learn more of her father's affairs, Alena listened with great interest as he praised Howard Sutton's participation in the reopening of the plundered tomb of Rameses II. Indeed, despite her earlier reservations, Mr. Blythe proved most entertaining until he mentioned a legendary map leading to a treasure in South America.

Alena went rigid again. "Map?"

"Yes." Richard Blythe's expression took on a faraway look as he stroked his smooth, square chin. "If I recall, it had something to do with a princess and a lost tribe in the Amazon." He raised a brow and gave her a pleasant smile. "Did he ever find it?"

Alena inspected the man's face for guile, but could find no ill intent in his handsome features. He was merely curious, she decided. He appeared more than trustworthy, and being closely associated with her father, she reasoned there could be no harm in divulging what little she knew of the matter. In return, he might be able to provide some useful tidbit of information that could shed some light on the mystery of her father's disappearance. She leaned forward and motioned for him to come closer. "Well," she said confidentially, "as a matter of fact—" Strong warm hands seized her shoulders from behind, sitting her upright.

"Is this ruffian bothering you, my dear?"

Alena recognized the deep voice immediately and swerved her head to see Zachariah Summerfield. He grinned down at her, blue eyes sparkling with mischief.

She glowered and opened her mouth to give him an adequate dressing-down, but the words caught in her throat as he began fondling her shoulders in a much too familiar way. The bold caress sent a shock wave through her entire body, while his spiced-wood cologne swirled about her nostrils to further daze her senses. Decorum demanded she pull away, yet, painfully aware that she must look like a baby bird waiting to be fed, she could only gawk at him.

"Hello, Zach." At the other man's greeting, Dr. Summerfield's hands stilled, but stayed where they were. His engaging smile transformed itself into a sardonic one. His eyes turned a cool gray before he dragged them from Alena's and focused them on Richard Blythe.

"What hole did you crawl out of, Blythe?" His tone was as hostile as his glare.

Alena checked the tall blond man's reaction and was surprised to see that his lips were curved slightly upward.

"I can see," Richard said, nonchalantly tugging down his cuffs, "that you still harbor ill feelings."

Dr. Summerfield's grip tightened on her arms. "Yes, well, I'd say I have a few hard feelings, all right. Four good men died in that explosion."

Blythe looked at him levelly. "I told you before that I had nothing to do with that incident."

"And I told you that it was just a matter of time before I proved that you did."

The animosity between the two men emanated from one to the other. Feeling caught in the cross fire, Alena found the fortitude to pry the unwanted hands from her person and use her voice. "Really, Dr. Summerfield. This is all quite uncalled for. Mr. Blythe was simply—"

"Oh, I know what he was doing," Zach cut in, his unwavering gaze narrowing on the other man.

"This is getting us nowhere, Summerfield."
Mr. Blythe shifted his attention to Alena. "I'm
sure that the lady finds public quarrels offen-
sive." He gave her a polite nod. "If you'll excuse
me, Miss Sutton, I find I'm late for an appointment." He reached for her hand, and she gave
it willingly this time, glancing askance at Dr.
Summerfield. "It has been charming to make
your acquaintance," he said and lowered his lids
seductively. "I do hope we meet again in the
very near future."

As soon as he'd left the hotel, Alena came to
her feet and turned on the man standing behind
her chair. "How dare you," she said in a harsh
whisper. "You were incredibly rude just now.
And to come here, a common area, and put your
hands on me as if we were—" Alena felt her
color deepen. Her voice automatically rose in
pitch as well as volume. "To insinuate that you
and I were more than casual acquaintances was
. . . was totally . . . outlandish!"

"Totally outlandish?" Zach's brows formed a
hard line. "Me? Totally outlandish? Oh, yeah?
Well, what about you, huh?" He lifted his chin
at an angle comparable to hers. "Hasn't anyone
ever told you not to speak to strangers?"

"I'll have you know, Mr. Blythe displayed all
the traits of a true gentleman when he introduced
himself. It just so happens that he is a very good
friend of my father's, and is therefore no complete stranger at all."

"Gentleman? Friend of your father's? Hah! Is
that what he told you?" Zach rolled his eyes.
"Howie detested the man." He glared at her for
a long moment, then sighed and dropped his
head. When he raised it, the anger in his eyes

had been replaced with grave seriousness. "I'm sorry, Miss Sutton, but I must insist that you keep your distance from Richard Blythe. Believe me, it's for your own good. Now, if you don't mind, we're late. We need to be on our way." Without ceremony, he snatched up her shawl, tossed it around her shoulders, and steered her toward the door. Seemingly unconscious of his long stride, he moved her outside at an uncivilized pace.

Alena dug her heels into the boardwalk and jerked her elbow from his grasp. She'd had enough of his bullying and fully intended to get a few things settled before the evening went any further. Tilting her head way back, she looked up at him, no longer able to control her indignation. "*Insist? You insist?* I am not a child, Dr. Summerfield. And you are certainly not my guardian. I shall see whomever I wish, whenever I wish. Do I make myself clear?"

"Perfectly. Now can we—"

"Furthermore, *we* are not late, it's *you* who . . ."

Miss Sutton's voice droned in Zach's ears, though he blocked out the words. He'd learned long ago that it was best, at times, to let a woman have her say and get it out of her system. Stuffing his hands into his pants pockets, he rocked back on his heels and glanced idly across the way. The other side of the street was deserted except for a big, burly fellow leaning against the lamppost, his face half-covered by the newspaper he read. The man met Zach's gaze and lifted the paper higher. Zach quickly reverted his attention to Howie's daughter, and pretended to listen as she gave him a piece of her mind. He even nodded now and then, but was acutely aware that the man across the street was peering at them again over the top of his paper.

It could have been that the fellow enjoyed eavesdropping on little spats between couples, but Zach didn't think so. He was a seedy-looking character, and was out of place on this side of town. It was a sure bet that he was up to no good. A pickpocket? Maybe. Whatever the big bruiser's plans, a gut feeling told Zach that he and Miss Sutton were the targeted prey. Deciding there was only one sure way to find out, Zach refocused on the complaining female before him.

"... And I have *never*," Alena persisted, "in all my life—"

"Oh, I'm quite sure you haven't, Miss Sutton." Zach flashed the smile he'd found most effective in curbing ladies' tempers. "Have I told you how lovely you look this evening?"

Alena was totally caught off guard by the compliment. Not used to flattery, she closed her mouth abruptly.

With a dawning realization that she'd stood there publicly harping like a fishwife, her gaze fell to a small dark space between two boards in the sidewalk. She wished she could slip through the crack. Too ashamed to glance about and determine whether anyone had heard her or not, she took a deep breath. It was all Dr. Summerfield's fault. She'd never have resorted to such irrational behavior had he not driven her to it. Feeling somewhat absolved, she lifted her head with as much dignity as she could muster.

Dr. Summerfield's eyes twinkled as she met them. He still wore that incorrigible smile that made one want to blush. She noticed then that he'd shaved. Indeed, he'd even made a genuine, if unsuccessful, attempt to tame his dark hair. Alas, though, unruly tendrils had escaped from beneath the black fedora, and fell where they would across his forehead. Grinning down at her with his hat cocked slightly forward, he put her in mind of a wayward child that needed special consideration.

Dr. Summerfield, however, was no child. He was well aware of the effect his good looks generated. The man was utterly disconcerting. On the one hand, he was undeniably clever, on the other, prone to fits of insanity. Crass one moment, charming the next. His mood changed so fast, it made her dizzy.

She didn't like how he made her feel: uncomfortable. Confused. She wasn't used to feeling either way. In any given situation, she'd always managed to keep a tight hold on her emotions. Dealing with the conflicting ones she encountered each time she looked at Dr. Summerfield was most disturbing. He was too much like her father, she continually reminded herself, the sort who made promises they'd never keep. She didn't trust him, *or* those come-hither eyes. And if it wasn't for the fact that she needed his help, she wouldn't have had anything more to do with him.

"I've made reservations at my favorite restaurant," he said, distracting her from her thoughts. "It's just around the next corner. Should I call for a carriage or would you care to walk?"

"I'd prefer to walk, if you don't object," she replied flatly.

"Not at all. Just look at those stars. It's a fine night for a stroll, don't you think?"

Alena had no inclination to gaze at the stars.

She glanced at both his agreeable expression and the arm he offered. Some of her objections to his rude conduct must have hit home since, for the time being, he appeared in control of all his faculties. Still, she was more than a bit wary as she slipped her hand into the crook of his elbow.

The slight tremor in the fingertips that barely touched his sleeve made Zach remorseful. The evening had started all wrong—not at all as he'd planned. He'd fully intended to be the perfect gentleman; to win Miss Sutton's undying esteem.

As they promenaded down the lamplit walk, it occurred to him that the warning of impending doom inscribed upon the Minoan casket they'd opened last month might hold some truth. He banished the idea almost as soon as it came. If curses had any effect on him, he would have perished a long time ago. Still, he hadn't had so much trouble charming a member of the female gender since puberty. What was it about Miss Alena Sutton that made her so damnably unaffected?

He stole a glance at his companion. Her proud profile and her smooth complexion were like a Greek goddess, perfect in every way. Yet there was a sternness around her rosebud mouth, a hard gleam in those fascinating green eyes that detracted from her beauty.

He had to give her one thing, though. She had a flair for conjuring up the fool in him. She'd done so, not once, but twice in a single day.

Zach frowned and focused straight ahead. Just as the woman had brought out the fool in him, Blythe had brought out the beast. It irked him to no end that Richard had managed to wheedle his way into Miss Sutton's good graces, especially before Zach had had the opportunity to do so himself.

Blythe could only have been after one thing. And if *he* knew about the map, no telling how many other glory-seekers and black-market art dealers knew of its existence.

There was trouble brewing, all right. It was in the air. In fact, at the moment, it was right across the street, stalking their every move. From the corner of his eye, Zach checked the shadow again that slithered along the dark adjacent storefronts. The burly fellow that had watched them outside the hotel had taken the bait. He was no doubt tailing them. But what did he want? They were nearing the eating house. If the big oaf was going to try to pick their pockets or rob them, he would have to make his move soon.

Alena studied her escort on the sly. He was in such serious contemplation of some subject that she earnestly believed he'd forgotten her. He looked very distinguished lost in thought, almost studious. Half absentmindedly, he tipped his hat to passersby and, for all the world, gave the impression that he was quite respectable. Indeed, he played the part well. His navy cheviot suit fit impeccably without the need for padded shoulders. His black dress boots had been polished to a lustrous shine. The clean smell of his freshly laundered shirt mingled with that of soap and the spicy scent she had noticed before. Not at all awkward or out of his element as she would have suspected he might be, he projected a picture of aristocracy. She couldn't blame the two giggling young girls who had just passed, eyeing him with interest and blushing profusely when he'd flashed them a smile. He truly was a fine figure of a man—the most handsome, in fact, that she'd ever seen.

Alena glanced sideways at him once more and frowned at the opinions her mind had been forming. Handsome or not, he was a lunatic. Granted, a wily lunatic, but a lunatic just the same. She would do well not to forget that.

A whiff of fresh-baked bread blended into the cool, night breeze when they turned the corner, interrupting Alena's thoughts. The delicious aroma made her realize she'd neglected to eat all day. As they neared the restaurant, her stomach grumbled at the sight of a sign boasting authentic French cuisine. Thankfully, the sound was drowned out by the chatter of patrons leaving the establishment. The departing customers were obviously from the upper crust of society. The gentlemen were decked out in top hats and tuxedoes, while the ladies in the group wore rustling, ruffled gowns, and jewels that sparkled in the light of the street lamp.

Alena fingered the simple filigree heart locket that had once belonged to her mother. She wasn't properly dressed to set foot in such an elegant eatery. Her hope that she and Dr. Summerfield might only be passing by on their way to another restaurant died when she was steered through the double doors of this grand establishment.

A stout man with coal-black hair parted in the middle rushed forward to greet them, stroking a long, curled mustache. "Ah, Dr. Zummerfield," he said, then turned to Alena and swept into a low bow. "Mademoiselle."

"Good evening, Pierre," Zach said, handing

his hat and Alena's shawl to the cloak attendant. "Is our table ready?"

"*Oui*, monsieur, your usual. If you will follow me."

The maitre d' led them through the lavishly furnished dining room with glittering chandeliers and a quartet of violinists. They proceeded up an opulently wallpapered stairway. Stopping at one of many dimly lit tables draped with red and gold flocked curtains, Pierre pulled out Alena's chair.

Disturbed by the seclusion and the soft music that drifted from below, Alena hesitated slightly before taking her seat. A solicitous waiter materialized to take their order, then disappeared, leaving them to their privacy. Alena's attention was drawn to the like compartments across the way. Between the drapes, she caught glimpses of other twosomes. Some brazenly held hands above the tables, while others openly mooned at the person across from them, making intimate kissy faces and the like.

"I thought we might talk privately here."

Alena's gaze snapped back to Dr. Summerfield. She felt as if she'd been caught window peeping. Soft candlelight flickered across his face, accenting his strong, chiseled features. His eyes held a touch of amusement. And there was that smile again. Only marauders smiled like that. She had no doubt whatsoever that the man was indeed a marauder—a marauder of ladies' hearts, she'd wager. That choir-boy smile had most likely been the undoing of many fine young women.

Dropping her lashes, she focused on the single red rosebud in the crystal vase upon the white linen tablecloth. Frantically, she searched her brain for something to say that would bar her thoughts from the scandalous behavior going on around them. "Tell me, Dr. Summerfield," she said at length, "how is it you came to choose your profession? Pardon me for saying so, but you don't appear the sort that would be overly interested in museums."

"Oh, I don't, do I?" Zach laughed. It was a nice laugh, deep, husky. Leaning back in his chair, he looked thoughtful, as if he were contemplating the question for the first time himself. "I suppose I would have to give good old Uncle George credit for my interest in museums. I know you'll find this hard to believe, but I wasn't exactly a mild, well-mannered young man when I came to live with Uncle George. In fact, 'hellion' would have been a good one-word description of me in those days."

"Mr. Dalton raised you?" Alena asked, this tidbit of information sparking her interest for some reason.

Zach shrugged. "I wouldn't say he raised me exactly. I ran away from home at the age of sixteen. Worked my way back east. When I got to Philadelphia and couldn't find anyone willing to hire me, I remembered my mother had a brother here. So I looked him up, actually just planning to con him out of a meal. He glared at me over the top of his spectacles, the way he does to everyone when he first meets them, then hauled me inside. After a thorough tongue-lashing, he fed me more food than I'd seen in a week and insisted I stay."

Zach smiled to himself, then directed a smile tinged with embarrassment her way. "To answer your original question, I guess my interest in archeology could be traced back to my youth. My father's ranch in Texas bordered an old Indian burial ground. When my father and I got into—well, I was forever hanging around those ruins, searching for arrowheads, turning up bits and pieces of the tribe's civilization. I used to stand there for hours at a time, wondering what it had been like to live back then.

"Not too long after I moved in with him, Uncle George came across some arrowheads I had stuffed into my pocket when I'd left home. He asked me about them, and all through my explanation he nodded and stroked his chin. I knew he was up to something, but I never expected him to take me to a primitive Indian exhibit. I was fascinated, and he was overjoyed to find anything that held my attention for more than three minutes. He took me to three other museums and observed me falling into a trance over each mystery of the past I encountered. A couple of weeks after he'd introduced me to my first exhibit, he suggested I study archeology. Of course, my age raised the dean of the university's brow, but Uncle George, being very persistent, used his connections to get me admitted."

"I see," Alena commented, though it was easier for her to visualize a young Dr. Summerfield stealing other boys' marbles rather than collecting arrowheads.

"That's where I met Howie. He was lecturing one evening at the university." Zach peered into the flickering candle flame, recalling the past. "He held my steadfast interest with his indignant account of the plundering of King Rameses II's tomb by Giovanni Belzoni and his band of thieves. I had the opportunity to speak with Howie afterwards and found we had a mutual infatuation with past civilizations. When he asked if I might be interested in accompanying him and a team of archeologists on an expedition to Egypt the following summer, I jumped at the chance. From then on, I hired on every summer to pay my tuition." A certain pride filled Zach's gaze as he looked up at Alena. "Howie was brilliant, you know, a natural in his field. To see the past through his eyes was like reliving it. I learned more from him that first summer than I did in all my years at the university."

It was Alena's turn to stare at the dancing candlelight. The tenderness in the man's voice implied a father-and-son relationship between the two. She ached at the thought that her father would have lavished attention that by all rights should have been hers on someone else.

Determined to ignore the tightness in her chest, she clasped her hands tightly in her lap, and viewed her rival with a steady gaze. "Your life must be very adventurous," she commented dryly, for lack of anything else to say.

Zach gave her a lopsided smile. "My line of work allows me to indulge in the wise philosophy of an old friend of my father's, Colonel Teddy 'Rough Rider' Roosevelt. In his words, 'I like to drink the wine of life with brandy in it.'"

The waiter arrived with their plates, and Alena was grateful to be saved from commenting upon such a ridiculous philosophy.

Zach dove heartily into his steak and potatoes, explaining he'd never acquired a taste for French cooking.

Alena nibbled her *poulet Veronique*, savoring each bite.

Each surreptitiously contemplated the other.

Zach viewed Miss Sutton's meticulous eating habits above the rim of his wineglass. It amused him the way she dabbed her mouth after each tiny bite and sipped her tea at precise intervals, taking the utmost care to extend her pinkie. How could anyone be so damned proper? Hell, she was so stiff, he would lay ten to one she starched her unmentionables.

From behind her raised teacup, Alena studied him demurely, when she was sure he wasn't looking. She considered his expressed motive for bringing her to such an intimate setting. She suspected he was a man who stopped at nothing to get what he wanted. Did he hope to entice the map from her with charm? Did he really think her so foolish? Or had he finally conceded defeat and was planning to take her with him to the Amazon? She refolded her napkin and placed it neatly by her plate, deciding it was high time she ended the suspense.

Alena's gaze clashed with his and held steady. He had finished his third piece of pie and was leaning back in his chair, arms folded across his chest, staring at her as if he were admiring a fine painting. His eyes brightened as the room seemed to grow darker. The romantic tune the musicians played accented the silence. And intuition told Alena she was about to find out what he was up to.

Chapter 3

Dr. Summerfield leaned forward in a suave, lithe movement that reminded Alena of a cat, and braced his forearms on the table. His lids lowered to half-mast. "You know, Miss Sutton, you have fantastic eyes. The color makes me think of a field of spring barley."

He really was quite good at it, Alena promptly decided. She felt certain that, had she been younger, more naive, or perhaps simpleminded, he would have completely swept her away. As she claimed none of those frailties, *thank heaven*, she merely smiled complacently and said, "Give it up, Dr. Summerfield. Your flattery won't work on me. I am all too aware of my attributes. Mistress Stephens has often commented on my plainness, and my looking glass has confirmed the fact. While I may not be a raving beauty, I do possess the intelligence to know when I'm being hoodwinked."

Frowning, Zach abruptly sat back in his chair and ran a finger around the inside of his high, starched collar. "You don't have to be, you know. Plain, I mean."

"I beg your pardon?"

Zach peered at the woman and struggled with the wisdom of silence as he took in her stiff attire and mannerisms. Hell, he could be doing her a favor. "Well, for instance," he blurted out, "why do you wear your hair like that? And your clothes. You dress like—" *A spinster*, he was going to say, but quickly thought better of it. "—like a woman twice your age."

Alena should have been shocked. Indeed, she *would* have been stunned witless, had someone else spoken to her thus. As it was, she was simply exasperated. Closing her eyes, she absorbed the fact that she must be getting used to this barbaric creature's crude manners. It would be senseless to argue the issue. The man would probably just go into another one of his fits. Pressing her lips into a tight line, she opened her eyes. "You, my good man, and I *do* use the term loosely, are incredible."

Zach smiled brightly. "Why, thank you."

" 'Twas not a compliment."

"Yes, I know."

Alena sighed inwardly. "Might I remind you, Dr. Summerfield, that we came here this evening to discuss business, not my appearance?"

"Ah, yes. Business." Zach sat up straight and tugged at his lapels. "You're right, of course. The whole purpose of our meeting *is* to form some sort of agreement, isn't it?" He smiled blandly. "I have, in fact, given the matter a great deal of consideration and feel I may have reached a solution that could be satisfactory to us both."

"Do go on," Alena said dryly, clasping her hands in her lap. Actually, she was rather looking forward to his next ploy. She was gripped by the same anticipation one experiences when a theater curtain is about to open.

"Yes, well." Zach cleared his throat. "While I am not a wealthy man, Miss Sutton, I do have a substantial holding in a New York bank and I'm sure I could secure a loan—"

"Excuse me." Zach and Alena turned their heads to see a small, scholarly-looking man standing beside their table. "Dr. Summerfield, I believe."

Zach took the man's offered hand somewhat reluctantly.

"Of course, we've never met," the stranger went on, "but I know you well by reputation, sir. Your work in Crete under the direction of Sir Arthur Evans is to be commended. Arthur raves about your brilliance, you know. Oh, but where are my manners? Allow me to introduce myself." The odd little man produced a card from his pocket and gave it to Zach. "Nigel Flemming, sir. I represent the British Museum of Antiquities."

Zach scanned the card briefly and passed it to Alena.

"And this lovely young lady must be Howard Sutton's daughter. Miss Sutton, what an honor. I met your father once. Remarkable man, truly remarkable. Howard revolutionized the field of archeology with his new techniques, he did. Dear, but I do rattle on. Terribly sorry. I don't wish to intrude for any longer than necessary, so let me come straight to the point. I understand the two of you may have possession of a map that could lead to the treasure chamber of the lost tribe of the Amazon. Is there any truth to the rumor?"

Zach and Alena exchanged glances, but said nothing.

"Ah. I can see your reluctance to discuss the matter. Well, let me just say the British Museum of Antiquities is prepared to offer a considerable sum for a share of the map, perhaps even finance the expedition, if *indeed* the ancient writing does—"

"The map," Zach said in a stoic tone, "even if it existed, would not be for sale, Mr. Flemming."

"Indeed it wouldn't," Alena put in, pointedly looking at Zach. "Not to you, nor anyone, sir."

Mr. Flemming fingered the brown derby he held at his waist. "Very well," he said curtly. The corners of his mouth twitched in a disgusted fashion. "I had hoped you might see clear to combine our efforts. As you quite plainly refuse any affiliation with us, I feel obliged to tell you that we have already acquired a great deal of information concerning the lost tribe and shall therefore conduct a separate search of our own in all due haste. Good evening, Miss Sutton." He gave Alena a quick smile, then directed a glare Zach's way. "May the best man win, Dr. Summerfield," he said through clenched teeth, and nodded in farewell.

As soon as he was out of earshot, Zach expelled a long-held breath. "Dammit. I knew it," he muttered, then looked at Alena accusingly. "Just what in the hell did you tell Blythe before I got there?"

"Nothing." Becoming vexed, Alena raised her chin. "I told him nothing at all about the map."

Zach eyed her suspiciously, took a sizable swig of wine, then frowned at the door Flemming had just exited. "The nerve of that guy—walking in here and openly making an offer like that. He could have at least approached us in private."

"If I recall correctly, Dr. Summerfield, you were about to make me a similar offer."

"Yes, but—"

"Yes, but nothing, sir. You were about to make a proposal which I would not have accepted. Now, if we may dispense with all this chicanery, I shall tell you what terms *are* acceptable."

Zach was sure he wasn't going to like what she had to say. But from the impression he'd gotten so far, she wasn't going to rest until she told him. Reaching into his pocket, he pulled out his pipe. "Very well, Miss Sutton. I'm listening."

"I suggest we join forces," Alena stated. She watched him strike a match and puff on the stem of his pipe until the end glowed orange. "I shall fund a goodly portion of the expedition. You will make arrangements for transportation, as I am not knowledgeable about such things. Any rare or valuable objects and antiquities that we find shall naturally be yours to do with as you please. I, on the other hand, would want to make inquiries about my father—with your help, of course."

Dense smoke swirled about Dr. Summerfield's head, making him appear sinister. His face was hidden by the shadows. Alena couldn't assess what he might be thinking until he shifted forward into the glow of the candlelight. His expression quite grim, he laid down his pipe.

"Miss Sutton, I don't know how to tell you this, except to just say it." He drained his glass of wine, refilled the goblet, and took another generous swallow. "Howard's . . . he can't be . . . alive. He would have found some way to contact me by now if he wasn't— Look, I knew the man too well. I generally escape disaster by the seat of my pants, but Howard was a wizard when it came to getting out of a tight spot." Zach combed his fingers through his hair, irritably surveying the woman's blank stare. "I'm putting this all wrong. I guess what I'm trying to say is that it would be useless for you to trek through the wilds looking for him. He won't be there."

"Are you sure, Dr. Summerfield? Absolutely, positively, one hundred percent sure?"

Zach furrowed his brows. "I'm damned near sure."

Thoughtful, Alena took a sip of tea, then set the china cup carefully down on the saucer and gave him a small smile. "I shall take the chance then, however slight, that he may still be amongst the living. And if he is, I *will* find him."

Staring at her incredulously, Zach decided she had to be the most stubborn female he had ever encountered. "Let me be blunt, Miss Sutton," he said when he found his voice. "There is no way in Hades I'm going to have a woman tailing me through the jungle. No offense intended toward you personally. It's just not done."

The set of her mouth told him she was taking none of this to heart. So he tried another approach. Putting a fierce gleam in his eyes, he squinted like a pirate and moved closer. "I attract trouble, dear lady. I live on the edge. Hell, I carry death in my hip pocket!" Zach leaned back, folded his arms across his chest, and regarded her impassive features. Jeez almighty, hadn't she heard a single word he'd said? "Let me put it to you this way, Miss Sutton. Under no circumstances am I taking you to the Amazon. Not now.

Not ever. And there is nothing—I repeat, nothing—you can do or say to make me change my mind. Understand?"

Alena lowered her lashes and brushed a crumb from the tablecloth. "I'm terribly afraid you've forgotten something, sir."

Zach swallowed the remainder of his wine, set the glass down with a clink, and arched a brow. "Oh? And what is that?"

Alena smiled triumphantly. "I have the other part of the map."

A muscle in Zach's jaw clenched involuntarily. Damn her. She had a point. She had the vital portion of the map. She couldn't be seduced. Wouldn't be bought off. Impulsively, he pressed one forearm against the table, ready to offer her anything.

As if she read his mind, she matched his pose and said unblinkingly, "Take me with you and it's yours."

The moment hung suspended in silence as neither backed down from the other's intense gaze.

"You'd be on your own," Zach grumbled at last. "I wouldn't coddle you."

"Dr. Summerfield, I've been on my own for quite some time now, and quite frankly, I would prefer *not* to be coddled by the likes of you."

Zach straightened, pressing his shoulders against the chair. She left him no choice. If he wanted the balance of the map, it looked like he was going to have to take Alena Sutton right along with it. He exhaled a long breath that fluttered the hair on his forehead. Maybe he could come up with another course of action later. Meeting her hopeful expression, he grimaced. "Okay. Okay, Angelface. You win." He re-

signedly offered her his hand. "We're full partners. Satisfied?"

Alena toyed with her locket and looked from
his blue eyes to his outstretched hand and back
again. "And does being partners mean we shall
be traveling to South America . . . together?"

"Right, Miss Sutton, *together*." Zach made an
honest attempt to return her enthusiastic handshake. He tried his best to equal her radiant
smile, but suspected he looked more like he'd
just been stung by a bumblebee. That was sure
as hell how he felt.

Alena stepped from the millinery shop, more
than a bit perturbed with herself. She shifted the
hatbox from one hand to the other and started
down the walk, wondering if all Americans were
so cunning. It amazed her, simply amazed her,
how cleverly the shopkeeper had talked her into
buying a hat she wasn't particularly fond of.
Alena increased her stride. She'd always been so
levelheaded. Being coerced verbally was a completely new experience. Then again, she decided, as she took in the strangers bustling about
the busy Philadelphia streets, everything here
was a new experience. Just as going to the Amazon would be.

The Amazon. The thought added a jaunty
bounce to her walk. In two days they'd be on
their way. Dr. Summerfield had purchased their
train tickets to New York City. From New York,
they would sail to Venezuela, he'd told her.

The prospect of a possible reconciliation with
her father sent shivers all through her system.
What if . . . oh, but she didn't have time to day-
dream now. She had far too many things to do

before their departure. Hurrying along, she made a mental list of other items she needed to locate.

As Alena rounded the corner, she found her way blocked by a horde of people gathered on the sidewalk. She noted that traffic from both directions had been stopped by something going on in the middle of the street. Curiosity caused her to stand on tiptoe and peer between and around the multitude of bobbing heads.

Several women dressed in black marched in a circle carrying signs. Some had bawling babies perched on their hips or small children clinging to their skirts. Other women stood on the edge of the circle and called out encouragement, while the majority of men sprinkled throughout the crowd heckled the women and shouted obscenities.

"Why, Miss Sutton. What a pleasant surprise."

Alena turned from the commotion to find Richard Blythe beside her.

"Are you for or against?" he asked, gesturing toward the rowdy assemblage.

Alena blinked. "Am I for or against what? Mr. Blythe, what in heaven's name are all these people going on about?"

"Why, the emancipation of women, of course," he replied with a smile.

"The emancipation of women?"

"They want the right to vote." Richard viewed the marchers, a gleam of respect glowing in his warm brown eyes. "America's wonderful, don't you agree? Where else on earth can a person openly oppose the government? In England, the bobbies would have hauled them all off to the clink. Not here. Here, you have freedom of speech. Here, these brave women, the backbone of America, are standing up for what they believe."

Alena's gaze followed his to a woman on a platform. Chin held high, her voice was loud, clear, and filled with fierce determination. "Again I say, sisters," she shouted, and jabbed the air with a pointed finger, "we will not hold ourselves bound by any laws in which we have no voice or representation . . ."

Alena listened with great admiration for these courageous women. Standing in their midst made her proud to be of the same gender. She wanted to cheer with them, for them.

And yet, she couldn't quite identify with them. The whisperings of her strict upbringing would not be silenced. Proper young English misses were reared to become wives and mothers, not march about the streets when they should be at home attending to their duties. Though the turn of the century was nearly at hand, for Alena that old-fashioned idea still clung. Something inside made her long for a day when she'd have a home and family of her own. It seemed inevitable that someday the right man would come along. A good man. One who'd not go gallivanting off all the time. Not a man like her father. Not one like Zachariah Summerfield. A man who would be reliable and sensitive to a woman's need to express herself. A man like . . .

Alena looked up at Richard Blythe and returned the smile he was giving her. The October breeze caught a strand of blond hair that had slipped from beneath his bowler hat. Now here was a man who understood women. He was striking, truly striking...in both appearance and opinion.

"It's getting late, Miss Sutton. Might I walk you to your hotel? An unescorted lady shouldn't be about this section of Philadelphia after dark." Richard offered his arm, and Alena took it, allowing him to lead her through the crowd.

"It must have been a stroke of good luck that we chanced to meet today," he said as they broke away from the confusion and started down the walk. "Actually, I must confess I had planned on coming round to speak with you this evening. I wanted to offer my apologies."

"Offer your apologies?" Alena raised a brow.

"Yes, indeed." Richard glanced at her, then lowered his lids. "I've felt simply horrid about subjecting you to that little disagreement the other night between Dr. Summerfield and myself. I didn't intend to cause such a stir."

Alena halted and turned to face him. "I assure you, sir, no apologies are due on your part. You did not provoke Dr. Summerfield."

"My mere presence provokes him, dear lady." Richard smiled halfheartedly. "Zach is very intense when it comes to his work. When something goes wrong on an expedition, he becomes a bit irrational, I'm afraid. At times, he tends to blame others for his own careless—ah, but I won't bore you with the details of our differences." Taking her elbow, he steered her forward at a leisurely pace. "By no means do I wish to insinuate the man is a bad sort, really. Still, it's well known among his colleagues that he does have a nasty temper."

"Yes, I've noticed that about him," Alena commented dryly.

"I fear Zach and I have somehow become rivals in our field," Richard continued as they neared the hotel. "While I don't possess the title of an archeologist, I do, however, have extensive experience in the area. You see, Miss Sutton, I am quite simply a dealer of antiquities and rare objects. I own a modest establishment here in Philadelphia. Until a few years ago, most of my clients were private collectors. I think Zach understandably resents the fact that, recently, more and more prestigious museums have sought my services. Ah, here we are."

On the steps of her hotel, Richard took Alena's hands. His thumbs brushed her knuckles while he stared at her for a long moment, his brown eyes conveying he wished to do more. Feeling ill at ease and awkward, Alena withdrew her hands and looked away.

"Forgive me, Miss Sutton," Richard said, then cleared his throat and took a step back. "I meant no disrespect. I . . . I've truly enjoyed your company. I haven't ruined my opportunity of getting to know you better, have I?"

"No." Alena gave him a shy smile. "Of course not." She was quickly growing fond of Richard. He was kind and considerate and undeniably handsome. She couldn't imagine why Dr. Summerfield had warned her off him.

"Good. Then I wonder if you might consider accompanying me to a concert of the Philadelphia Orchestra next week. Fritz Scheel will be conducting. Afterwards, perhaps, we could take a stroll through Fairmount Park."

Alena glanced at her hands folded against her waist. "It sounds wonderful . . . it truly does, and I would like very much to attend the concert with you, but I'm afraid I must decline. You see, Mr. Blythe, I shall be on my way to South America by then."

"South America, did you say? Well, this is a coincidence. I shall be journeying to South America myself, the week after next. A British museum has employed me to head their expedition. Perhaps we'll have another stroke of good fortune and our paths will cross. If not, will you be returning to Philadelphia?"

"Why, yes. Yes, I will." Alena was suddenly anxious to see him again. She hadn't realized until now how much she missed her fellow countrymen, missed simple conversation with a civil-tongued Englishman. "As soon as my business abroad is finished, I shall return to attend my father's legal affairs."

"Splendid," Richard said with a wide, enchanting smile. "You will look me up then, won't you? If I'm in town, we'll have a nice spot of tea."

"I would enjoy that ever so much." Alena ducked her head, hoping she didn't appear too eager.

"Well, mustn't let you stand out in the chill and catch your death." He touched the brim of his hat. "I shan't say good-bye, but rather, until we meet again."

Alena watched him walk out of sight. Dr. Summerfield had been terribly wrong about Richard Blythe, she quickly decided. Richard hadn't once mentioned the map. He'd been nothing but a perfect gentleman all afternoon. He had even been reluctant to speak ill of Zachariah Summerfield when the opportunity had arisen. Shaking her head, Alena made her way up the steps

of the Philadelphia House Inn. Men and their
petty rivalries. Did that portion of God's creation
ever really grow up, or did they merely get bigger
in size?

The sound of New York City's evening activ-
ities dwindled as Alena settled beneath her cov-
erlet. The softly whistled tune of a lamplighter
drifted from the street below as he went about
his business of dousing the lights one by one.
Somewhere in the distance, a chorus of cats sang
until someone bellowed and shooed them away.
Alena watched the moonbeams playing across
yet another far-from-home hotel ceiling, listened
for footsteps in the hallway, and waited for the
unwelcome visitor who was sure to arrive.

The past week had flown by like a March
whirlwind. Dr. Summerfield had been most
helpful in assisting her with the purchase of a
sturdy pair of ladies' boots. The day before
they'd left Philadelphia he'd treated her to her
first egg-cream soda. He'd been almost polite
and very attentive on the train from Philadelphia
to New York. Too attentive, she now realized.

She should've known something was amiss.

Alena rolled over and stared at the door. She
hadn't seen Richard again, though she'd thought
of him often enough. He had awakened a spark
of feminine interest she hadn't known she possessed. For the first time in her life, she was
honestly taking note of a man's physical attributes. She'd caught herself several times noticing attractive strangers on the street. Somehow,
that peculiar little quirk she'd picked up had mi-
grated to Zachariah Summerfield.

Twisting her mouth at the thought, she

punched her pillow. Feelings. What a nuisance. She should've kept them in check. She shouldn't have observed how Dr. Summerfield's eyes twinkled when he teased her . . . or the way his lids lowered a little as he regarded her in conversation. She should have completely ignored that heart-stopping smile. She shouldn't have considered the width of his shoulders, the trimness of his waist, or how he stood much taller than most men. She shouldn't have noticed how female passersby stared at him as if he were a particularly appealing bunch of ribbons at a May fair.

Above all, she should have trusted her original impression that he was a good-for-nothing, two-faced—

Alena's thoughts jerked to a halt. She opened her eyes wide. What was that? Pricking her ears, she listened intently. There it was again. A faint clicking outside her door.

Aha!

In great haste, yet careful not to make the bedsprings creak, Alena arose and slipped on her wrapper. She stooped to fetch the parasol she'd placed beneath the bed, then quickly but silently moved into position by the lamp. Breath held, she peered through the darkness at the brass doorknob. It wriggled and turned, then the door creaked slowly open.

From the shadows, Alena saw a dark figure creep stealthily into the room and close the door without a sound. She would have known that brawny build anywhere. She allowed the crouched silhouette to tiptoe halfway across the room before she jabbed her parasol into his back and lit the lamp. "Pardon me, Dr. Summerfield, have you lost the way to your room?"

Hands held high, Zach turned at a snail's pace, his face stark white against the backdrop of the dimly lit room. Focusing on the parasol, he expelled a long heavy sigh that turned into a chuckle. Then he straightened to his full height, looking for all the world as if he had been invited, and gave Alena a smile that would have lit up all of London. "Good evening, Miss Sutton. I didn't mean to frighten you."

Alena was frightened, all right, though not, she suddenly realized, for the reason he thought. Her fear was more of herself than of him—of what that smile did to her. Indeed, she was much more afraid of the feelings his nearness evoked. Much more afraid of the way his softly whispered words seeped into her, warming her blood. Afraid of the way his manly essence reached out and wrapped around her. She was terrified by the sensuous low-lidded gaze that seemed to probe her thoughts.

She hated that thing he did with his eyes. She *did*, she silently swore with greater conviction. He knew very well it made women feel that way.

Zach took a step forward.

Bracing the end of her parasol against his chest, Alena stopped him in his tracks. "What, may I ask, are you doing here?"

"Business, Miss Sutton," he replied, his cheeky grin still intact. "I'm here on legitimate business. Honest." He glanced at the makeshift weapon aimed at his heart and his smile twisted to one side of his face. "You can put your umbrella away now. Or do you plan to run me through?"

Alena dropped her gaze to where her sunshade poked into his furry chest and noted with dismay that his shirt hung completely open. With a will of their own, her eyes followed the dark trail of hair down the flat ridge of his stomach, and halted on the top button of his fly, which was undone.

She promptly closed her eyes, sucked in her breath, and dropped the parasol. "*Please*, Dr. Summerfield, button yourself up."

Zach looked down, and, seeing the cause of her mortification, quickly fastened his pants and the last three buttons on his shirt, then raked a hand through his hair. "You can look now. I'm decent."

Hardly, Alena thought, her eyes still squeezed shut.

"Ah, sorry. I didn't know—"

"You didn't know I'd be awake," Alena said, peering through one eye to inspect him briefly before opening the other. "Now kindly tell me what you are doing here half-naked in the middle of the night."

"Look, I really am sorry about my state of dress. Sometimes I forget myself, that's all. I was lying in bed thinking and it suddenly occurred to me that this might be our last opportunity to view the map in privacy until we reach Venezuela." He leaned his weight on one hip and hooked his thumbs in his belt loops. "I had every intention of waking you."

"Oh? Then why did you pick my lock?"

"Pick your lock?" He looked shocked. "I didn't pick your lock. The door was open."

"No. It wasn't."

"You must be mistaken."

She wasn't mistaken. She distinctly remembered securing the latch. Yet he stood there, looking perfectly harmless in his big stockinged feet, almost convincing her that she'd forgotten to lock the door. She pressed her fingertips to her temples, wondering what kind of magic the man possessed. Odd—her father had had the same uncanny ability to make her believe fabrications that were patently untrue. Her mind whirled as she watched Summerfield pad across the room and drag the overstuffed chair over to the one at the desk. He lit the other lamp, turned up the wick, then glanced over his shoulder and said, "Uh, I'll need your part of the map."

Alena stared at his back as he produced his half and spread it open on the desk. How should she proceed? A plan brewed in her head as she stood, watching every move he made. Perhaps the best way to outfox Dr. Oh-so-smart was to let him think he was winning.

Zach turned to find her standing motionless in the middle of the room, her face pale, her fists clenched at her sides. "Come on, Angelface. This could take all night." When she didn't budge, he added, "Look what I've got." He pulled a folded paper from his shirt pocket and held it up enticingly. "Aren't you the least bit interested in the exact route we'll be taking to the Amazon? I've charted it all out here. Come on, bring me your section of the map and I'll show you the itinerary."

Alena wanted to scream at him, rake her nails across his impossibly guileless face. Yet her gaze kept sliding to the folded piece of paper he held. She needed that information—needed it desperately—just in case her hastily formulated plans failed.

Calling forth her reserves of discipline, she

walked to the bed and tugged the envelope from under her pillow. Zach met her halfway, took the map and her arm, and guided her to the overstuffed chair.

Alena watched him put on his wire-rimmed spectacles, wishing they made him look old and crotchety instead of so damnably distinguished. Forcing herself to focus on the hand-drawn diagram that he unfolded and laid atop his part of the treasure map, she listened intently.

"Okay, now, this is Venezuela," he said, pointing to the northern tip of the South American continent. "We should dock somewhere around Caracas here, move south across the Venezuelan foothills until we reach the Orinoco River. We'll be able to use pack mules on the first part of the trek, but the closer we get to the Orinoco, the denser the vegetation becomes. Right about here, on the other side of the foothills, we'll have to go afoot. I'm arranging for an old acquaintance to meet us at the river with his dugout. The Orinoco runs right into the Amazon."

Alena tried to memorize every detail, though it wasn't easy, because Zach quickly stuffed the chart back into his pocket, then pieced her segment of the ancient writing together with his. Her attention was drawn by his long fingers as he traced the symbols on the yellowed parchment. "Ah, here it is. Right here," he said, tapping the brittle page. "This is the part I'm having trouble deciphering. The text is so faded . . ."

Absorbed in his work, he looked so serious, so intense—she could almost picture him as a young, enthusiastic student. He mumbled phrases now and then in a language Alena couldn't understand. Occasionally, he repeated them in English, but more, she thought, for his own benefit than hers. In fact, she thought, smiling, he had totally forgotten her presence.

The night ticked away while he continued his examination. Finally, Alena gave in to her heavy lids, tucked her feet beneath her, and laid her head against the padded wing of the chair.

A good hour passed before Zach noted her relaxed, even breathing. He smiled and glanced sideways, then cocked his head to view Howard's daughter fully, when he realized she was fast asleep.

Her unbound curls cascaded like spun gold over her shoulders, over her breasts. Sooty lashes fanned her high cheekbones. She reminded him of a porcelain angel on top of a Christmas tree. Once again, as he had during the past days, he felt the urge to touch her flawless face, yet his hand stopped just short of its destination.

He looked back at the map pieced together before him and was suddenly nauseated. He was doing the right thing, dammit. So why in the hell did he feel sick?

Okay, granted, maybe he wasn't handling the situation in a very honorable way. But confound it, it was too late to come up with anything else. It would be in Alena Sutton's best interest. It would, dammit!

He rose quietly from his chair. Hesitating only a moment, he rolled up both sections of the map and tucked them under his arm. He headed for the door, telling himself not to look back, knowing if he caught a glimpse of that too-trusting face, he might waver in his decision. With an iron will, he slipped out the door and was gone.

Alena opened one eye at the slight click of her door closing, and smiled. "Gloat while you can, Dr. Summerfield," she whispered. "The game is not yet over."

Hudson Bay dissolved into the horizon as Zach leaned against the rail of the freighter and watched the morning sky change from dusty pink to a pale shade of blue. A cool breeze ruffled his hair. He turned his coat collar up around his ears to ward off not only the chill, but the green eyes that had haunted him since he'd left Alena's room early that morning. Try as he might, he couldn't forget how the stuffy schoolmarm had been transformed into an enchantress over the past ten days by doing nothing more than smiling. He couldn't stop the sound of her laughter— when she'd first tasted her egg cream; when she'd tried on her boots; he could go on and on— from playing over and over in his head. Worst of all, he couldn't shake the vision of how she had looked when he'd left her sleeping in her New York hotel room.

He tried to concentrate on other things, tried to convince himself it was only the swaying of the boat that made his stomach churn. But he knew differently; he knew what had really caused his nausea. He felt every inch the louse the woman would no doubt label him when she awoke and found him, and the map, gone.

"Beautiful morning, is it not, Dr. Summerfield?"

The voice behind him grated across his ragged nerves like fingernails on a chalkboard. It couldn't be! It was his imagination, nagged on by a guilty conscience, aided by the whispering sea winds.

Just to prove he was right, Zach glanced over his shoulder. His mouth fell open at the sight of Alena Sutton, large as life, standing on the deck. He closed his eyes, reopened them, then whirled to face her.

"Is that a look of surprise, I see, Doctor?" Alena placed her hands on her hips, examining him with feigned concern. "I must say, you look positively green. I'd get out of the sun if I were you. Maybe you should go below and take a nap."

Zach tried to speak but nothing came out.

"To be quite honest, I never did trust you, sir." Alena stepped forward. "I became even more suspicious yesterday morning when I asked if I might accompany you on your outing. You didn't truly expect me to believe you were visiting a club where they didn't allow women, did you? Really, Dr. Summerfield. This is America. The twentieth century is right around the corner." Peering into his face, she noted his color was coming back. "You were acting quite odd, you know. That's why I followed you to the docks. When I saw you talking to the captain, I thought it wise to confirm our reservations. You can well imagine my astonishment when I found only your name on the passenger list."

Zach hung his head. "Miss Sutton, I swear by all that's holy . . . I was only worried about your welfare."

"Welfare? You were only seeing to my welfare?" Alena pressed a hand to the base of her throat. "I shudder to think what you might do, sir, if you set your mind against me. I ask you, does seeing to my welfare mean leaving me stranded in foreign land where I know not a soul?"

"I never intended to leave you there alone."

"I beg your pardon?"

Zach raised his head. "I wasn't going to leave you by yourself. I'd paid someone to collect you this morning at nine o'clock. Molly McGregor, an actress I know, was to deliver a note and take you back to her place until I returned."

"I don't believe you," Alena said, eyeing his tall form skeptically.

"Miss Sutton, at the moment, I don't give a tweedle-damn whether you believe me or not. It's the truth."

Smirking, Alena held out her hand. "I'll have my part of the map back now."

For the benefit of the curious sailors who were beginning to mill about the deck, Zach smiled. He reached into his pocket, pulled out the parchment, and laid it in her open palm.

"You, sir, are sorely lacking in moral fiber," Alena said as she tucked the map into her waist-band. "Nevertheless, the fact remains, we are partners. If you will recall, we shook hands—a legally binding gesture in any court, I believe. I assure you, if you try to doublecross me again, I shan't hesitate to have you incarcerated." She took a giant step backwards and tugged her jacket down. "As far as my stolen property is concerned, I shall be lenient this once. It has, after all, been retrieved."

"Miss Sutton, I can see this little ... misunderstanding, shall we call it, has caused a strain on our relationship. As you've said, you have your part of the map back. No real harm has been done. I see no reason why we can't just let bygones be bygones." Putting on his best smile, Zach extended his hand. "Shall we call a truce?"

Alena stared at him for a long moment. "A truce, Dr. Summerfield? Whatever for? You see, I have no regard for you whatsoever. Though I'm certain you have enough for yourself to go around. Furthermore, I do not trust you. And so, a truce would be futile in this case, don't you agree?" She paused, but his only response was the deterioration of his smile. "Just the same, I feel it only fair to warn you that once we get to Venezuela, I don't intend to take my eyes off you. Until then, I suggest you seek companionship elsewhere."

Zach was struck speechless for the second time that day. Unable to utter a word, he stood there watching while Miss Holier-than-thou whirled and marched off, heels clicking, her back as stiff as any soldier in Her Majesty's royal brigade. Shoving his hands into his pockets, he glared after her until she disappeared below deck.

"Lacking in moral fiber, indeed," he grumbled, then turned toward the sea. He crossed his arms over the rail. A lot of women could testify he wasn't lacking in anything.

Something strange had seized him the past day or so. He'd never been troubled by what people thought of him before. *Why now?* he beseeched the blue waters below. People had called him names in a hundred different languages. What difference did it make if some snooty little schoolmarm told him he lacked moral fiber?

He stood on the deck for hours, oblivious to the north wind that had picked up and now whipped furiously at his hair and clothes. His

face was cold and chafed, his hands were numb
when he finally arrived at the disturbing conclusion that Alena Sutton's opinion of him did matter. For some idiotic reason he couldn't quite
grasp, her approval held significance.

It wasn't what she'd said, or how she'd said
it, that bothered him. No—it was the way she
had looked at him, her eyes filled with animosity,
distrust, and something resembling hurt, that
even now, cut him to the quick. Shifting his
weight, he wrapped his coat tighter around him.
The chill had suddenly begun to seep into his
bones.

Chapter 4

Upon the third morning at sea, Alena awoke in the small, windowless cabin that had hastily been converted from a storeroom, and cautiously rose on her elbows, testing her queasiness.

What a blessed relief to find her stomach back where it belonged.

After washing thoroughly, she wove her hair into a long plait that hung down her back, and slipped into a white lawn dress. Then she left the stuffy confines of her room as fast as her legs could carry her, in search of a badly needed breath of fresh air.

A breeze teased the stray curls around her face as she stepped onto the sunny deck. She inhaled deeply, then moved to the rail. In every direction she looked, blue, rippling water blended into the sky. She let her mind go blank, feeling nothing but tranquility as the summer-soft rays drove away the chill that had occupied her body and kept her abed since they'd first put to sea. It was heaven to be out in the open air. Sheer heaven.

"Good morning, Angelface."

Alena whirled, her braid flying over her shoulder.

Dr. Summerfield, dressed in the same exotic manner as when she'd first seen him, smiled and tipped his bush hat. "Feeling better?" he asked.

"I was, until you showed up," she commented dryly, then turned back to the rail. "And stop calling me—"

"Angelface? Now, why should I do that?"

Alena angled her head over her shoulder and glared at him. "Because I don't like it, that's why."

"Ah, but it suits you so well." He sidled next to her, caught her braid, and rolled it between his thumb and finger. "You're such a saint."

"And you, sir, are absurd," she countered, snatching her hair from his grasp. She took a big step sideways and regarded the blue waters once more, trying to recapture her erstwhile peacefulness and hoping he'd go away.

Not to be ignored, he moved near to her again, this time so close that their sleeves touched. Knowing he did so deliberately, she stood completely still, staring out to sea.

"I'd be willing to bet," he whispered, his breath warm against her ear, "that you are so unworldly that you've never even been kissed."

Alena stiffened. Needless to say, his madness had returned. In no mood to put up with such nonsense, she started to go around him, bent on retreating to her cabin. She'd no sooner taken a step when he caught her arms and pulled her to him, his face barely an inch away from hers.

"What's your hurry, Angelface?"

"Unhand me this instant, you madman." Alena tried to wrench free, but his hold was unbreakable.

Zach cocked his head, studied her a moment,

then widened his eyes. "Good Lord. I've hit a nerve, haven't I? You really haven't ever been kissed, have you, Miss Sutton?"

Alena stared up into that gaze the color of the sky for the longest instant before she blinked and said, "I . . . I have so." She had no unearthly idea why she felt compelled to lie, but once the fib was out, she raised her chin to make it more convincing. "I have," she insisted, "many times, by several gentlemen, if you must know."

The notion that he was peering into her very soul made her back away from him—a dreadful mistake, for he held her so firmly that only her upper half moved backwards. Her lower half bumped his. Shock waves rippled through every square inch of her body, and left her cheeks blazing.

She might have died then and there, had it not been for the man's irritating grin. The cad. She'd box his ears if she could get loose. "Let . . . me . . . go," she ground out between her teeth.

"What's the matter, Angelface, aren't you having fun? *I'm* having fun. Just think how much fun we'll have all alone in the jungle together."

Observing that the more she squirmed, the wider he smiled, she ceased her useless struggles. Of a sudden, she changed her strategy, stood rigid and gave him a glare full of contempt. "Dr. Summerfield, is there some reason for this ludicrous sport or have you completely taken leave of your senses?"

"Actually," he said with a wiggle of his brow, "at the moment I am seriously considering kissing you."

He was baiting her, of course, trying to scare

her off again. She dare not let him know he affected her in the least, else he would think he could torment her the entire way to the Amazon. Upon that conclusion, she swallowed hard, her eyes never leaving his face. "Then do so and get it over with," she blurted out with much more confidence than she felt. "I fear I grow weary of this ridiculous game." Closing her eyes, she presented her upturned face, determined not to feel a thing.

Zach took in her tightly puckered lips, squelching the chuckle that rose in his throat. It was as if she was offering herself for some supreme sacrifice. God. How could someone so young and adorable be so damned cold?

Cold. The thought made him grim. A few minutes ago, he'd been childishly antagonizing her, playing a practical joke to rattle her composure— but now . . .

Now, as she waited with cool aplomb for him to give her a peck and turn her loose, he wanted more than anything to provoke a response from her, stir some hidden emotion he was sure existed below the surface. He smiled. *Well, Miss Sutton, let's just see if you won't thaw a degree or two.*

Not one of Mistress Stephens' four-hour oratories on the trials of marriage could have prepared Alena for what happened next.

As soft as a feather, his mouth coasted over hers, barely touching at first. Then, in a manner that exceeded her wildest dreams, he nibbled at her sealed lips, courting, teasing them with the tip of his tongue. Second by second, his kiss grew more persuasive, more insistent. His arms slipped about her waist, gripping her more securely while his hands did marvelous things to her back.

And the world spun round and round.

All on their own, her lips parted and her spine melted like snow in the sun. Losing her balance, she clung to him for support. He tightened his hold, deepened the kiss, and she was only barely aware of being lifted off the deck.

Zach had half-expected her to smack him a good one when he released her arms to encircle her waist. What he hadn't anticipated was his own reaction to the kiss. But then, he hadn't anticipated her hands gliding up his chest and curling around his neck either. And he sure as hell hadn't counted on the woman molding her soft curves against him and making him burn with an urgency he hadn't felt since puberty.

Somewhere along the way, his plan to coax a response from her had backfired. Damn her. If she hadn't acted so blasted unobtainable, he wouldn't have felt pressed to break down her icy barrier. Yet the scientist in him had needed to test that cool indifference, and the result of his little experiment had proved she was human all right.

And so was he. It was perfectly logical to be feeling what he was feeling. He was a healthy, normal male. The intensity of his desire, he theorized, stemmed not from the kiss, but from the conquest. A simple deduction.

Still, even with that obvious conclusion clear in his mind, it was damned difficult to make himself pry Miss Sutton's arms from his neck and set her down on deck. In fact, he did so with such abruptness that she teetered on her heels.

Something besides the movement of the boat

made Alena sway. She had to catch the rail behind her to steady herself while her wits re-
grouped. Dizzy, dazed and confused, she
pressed cold fingers against one side of her
scorching face, and focused on the lips that had
just ravished hers. While she watched that fine-
formed mouth curve into a Cheshire-cat grin, she
had the sensation of awakening from a deep
trance.

Merciful Mary. It was broad daylight. What
had she done? What— What had *he* done? What
had that wretched man done to her now?

Alena gradually raised her gaze to Dr. Summerfield's and he winked, sending her into a
flabbergasted state all over again.

"Why, Miss Sutton, you look positively green.
I'd get out of the sun if I were you. Maybe you
should go below and take a nap." Winking once
more, Zach tipped his hat. "Good day, Miss Sutton. Pleasant dreams."

With that, he strode away, whistling, of all
things. Alena leaned against the rail, watching
him go, waiting for her equilibrium to return,
and trying to sort out the strange mishmash of
emotions that whirled in her head.

The night was deathly quiet, save the steady
clank of the steam engine vibrating the floorboards beneath Alena's cot. Wide awake, she
stared into the darkness, hands laced across her
middle.

She'd tried hard not to think about the episode
on deck that morning. She'd also tried not to
think about Zach. Yet it seemed she could think
of nothing else.

Absently, she traced her lower lip with a single

fingertip. The simple touch made her quiver, and she quickly locked her hand with the other on her abdomen.

Kissing hadn't been nearly as atrocious as Mistress Stephens had warned. Quite the contrary, in fact.

It was, however, dangerous.

She still couldn't remember how long she'd stood on deck or how she'd gotten back to her cabin. For the better part of the day, she'd moved about feeling all fuzzy. It was indeed perilous business, this . . . *kissing*. In the condition she'd been in, she might have very well fallen overboard.

She gave the stifling covers a sharp kick, imagining they were Dr. Summerfield's shin. How dare he put her in a position of losing her facilities! How dare he leave her dizzy while he diddled off down the deck, whistling as if he owned the world!

Alena flung her forearm across her eyes and moaned, knowing full well the incident was not entirely Zach's fault. Kiss me and get it over with, she'd told him, as if it was a subject she discussed every day. What on earth had she been thinking of?

Conflicting thoughts bumped against each other in her brain and made her head hurt.

Air. She needed air to sort this all out properly.

Throwing the covers back, she grabbed her shawl, and peeked out her door. Once she was certain everyone had retired for the evening, she padded barefoot down the dimly lit corridor. After checking to make sure no one was stirring, she ventured onto the deserted deck.

Against the jet-black sky, the moon was as

round and bright as a white china plate, lighting
the deck with a soft, hazy glow. A cool breeze
blew off the sea and whipped Alena's nightgown
around her legs. She wrapped her shawl tighter,
chilled by the mist spraying her face and hair.
With a deep breath, she wondered why no one
had ever tried to kiss her before. Perhaps if they
had, she wouldn't have been so giddy this morning.

Of course, the opportunity of being properly
introduced to someone who might kiss her had
simply not arisen at Mistress Stephens' School
for Young Ladies. The only gentlemen callers,
who were few and far between, had been the
students' fathers. Besides being ineligible, all of
them had been elderly, and usually profoundly
angry at having their daughters' misdeeds called
to their attention. Alena braced her forearms
against the rail and clasped her hands, wishing
Zach could be as easily dismissed from her
thoughts as those old fogies had been.

Things at school may have been dull, but they
were also uncomplicated. She'd never needed to
worry about restraining secret yearnings before,
and she wasn't particularly fond of having to do
so now.

She frowned at the rippled reflection of the
moon upon the water. What had come over her?
She wasn't some silly, swooning girl. Why, even
when the handsomest dandy in the park had
tipped his hat, she'd merely turned her head.
What could make Zachariah Summerfield, with
all his faults, so appealing?

Now that she contemplated it, there were lots
of attributes in his favor. His smile alone was
enough to arouse any healthy young woman's

interest. Aside from his being a learned scholar, he possessed a cleverness all his own. She had to give him that much.

Then, too, there was that thing he did with his eyes. Whether he was raging, or teasing, or laughing, or stricken with one of his fits of lunacy, a magnetic force seemed to generate from those too-blue eyes.

Alena sighed deeply, and inspected the brightness of the full moon. There was also something special about the way he moved. His tall, superbly fit form had the swift graceful movements and sturdy assurance of a thoroughbred stallion. There was a certain aura about him that could make one feel safe and sound and protected, or quiver beneath his wrath.

All in all, she could honestly say he possessed the charisma of a snake charmer—if she believed in such things, which she didn't.

Nor, she thought as she straightened her spine, did she believe in standing here mooning over a man. Especially one who, on the down side, she highly suspected partook of spirits, and also cursed like a sailor, was rude, disrespectful, untrustworthy, forward, and obviously knew his way around the ladies.

She gathered her shawl in a tight knot beneath her chin. This fuzzy feeling she got inside when she looked at him was nothing more than petty attraction. 'Twas something all young women were prone to go through sooner or later, she supposed. Had she paid more attention to the dandies in the park in her youth, perhaps she would have already gotten over this idiotic phase of her life.

The one thing she had in her favor was that

she was no longer a witless child of sixteen, but a woman full grown. She would deal with this enigma rationally, as an adult. She would simply ignore it until it passed.

Alena stretched her arms above her head. Heavens, it felt good to have this dilemma settled. She could get a proper night's rest now.

She started back to her cabin, intending to return to bed and forget all about Zach's come-hither insinuations, but a tiny flash of light caught her eye. Stopping, she squinted in the direction of the flash. A conglomeration of boxes, barrels, and crates were stacked against the dark wall overshadowed by the upper deck.

She had almost decided it was her imagination, when she saw it again . . . a moonbeam reflecting off something in the shadows. Then, grisly laughter, low in someone's throat, made the hair at the base of her neck stand on end.

Alena made a mad dash for the corridor. A few feet from the brightly lit door of the passageway, she skidded to a halt.

Something massive moved to block the light—block her path.

Stricken with increasing panic, she watched the form lumber forward. Retreating, she covered a gasp as the light of the moon fell upon a broad, balding forehead and haggard features. Her gaze traced a long red scar that ran from his bushy brow, down the right side of his face, and then disappeared into a scraggly beard.

"So, you've finally come out to play, have you, my pretty?" His grin displayed rotted teeth.

Hugging her ribs, Alena glanced wildly about for a means of escape.

"I wouldn't try it, sweetheart." The same glim-

mer she'd seen earlier came from the folds of his
coat. She froze as a bright moonbeam glinted off
the edge of a knife half as long as her arm.

Chuckling, the vile man deliberately shimmied
the blade so it beamed in the moonlight. In her
head, she heard herself scream like a banshee,
though try as she would, no sound would come
forth.

In the next instant, he snared her in a viselike
grip, crushing her against his chest, pinning her
arms between them. His rancid stench stung her
nostrils. She swallowed the nausea that rose in
her stomach. From the corner of her eye, she
saw the knife move toward her face, felt the cold
steel touch her cheek. She ceased her struggles.

"You're a sweet little morsel, ain't you now?"
Hot, liquor-soured breath grazed the top of her
head. "'Twould be a cryin' shame to mess up
that pretty face afore I had a taste of your
charms."

Alena's heart constricted. Beginning to shake
violently, uncontrollably, she tried her voice
again, but all that came out was a pitiful whimper. Oh, God, she prayed, let me die. Let me
die before this foul man— Squeezing her eyes
shut, she tried not to think about the unspeak-
able things he could do.

"Ah, but we got some business to attend to
first, now don't we, luv?" Keeping a tight grip
on her arm, he pushed her away from him, his
fingers biting into her flesh. With the point of
the knife still at her cheek, her other arm fell
uselessly to her side. "The map, dearie, where
is it?" When she remained silent, he jerked hard,
lifting her shoulder up to her ear till she feared
her collarbone would pop from the socket. "I'll

ask you nicely one more time. Where is it?"

"I . . . in . . . my . . . c-cabin," she choked out.

Humiliation shot through her like wildfire when she heard herself stutter. Opening her eyes, she took a good, hard look at the evil face that loomed over her . . . and something occurred to her. The worst that could happen if she fought him was death. Death would be a blessing compared to what this horrid beast had insinuated he would do to her.

A source of strength greater than her own balled her free hand into a fist, and she rammed it with all her might into his stomach.

The surprise blow caught him lower, in a more delicate spot than she'd intended, and jarred the knife from his hand. Stunned, he doubled over. His backside bumped an upturned mop propped against the wall and the damp stringy end plopped down on his head. For the moment, he forgot all about Alena, expending his attention on the monster behind him.

Alena dashed off before he knew it, her bare feet slapping the wet, slippery deck. If she could only make it to the other passageway . . .

Her heart pounded in her ears at the thunder of heavy footsteps behind her. She tried to increase her speed, but her legs would move no faster. Her breath was ragged, drying the inside of her mouth, closing her throat. Her side ached. Her eyes stung.

The thumping that followed her grew louder . . . came closer. She could hear his rapid breathing . . . *feel* it on her back.

Alena yelped as her arm was jerked backwards. Her sleeve ripped off in his hand. Propelled forward, she caught her foot on the edge of a coiled rope.

The moments stretching in distorted time, she toppled to the deck with all the sensation of falling off a cliff.

The hulk slid into her, catching the toe of his boot on her side. Her cry of pain was stifled as his weight slammed atop her and knocked the breath out of her.

Covered by his body, Alena lay with her face pressed against the cold, hard surface. She closed her eyes and saw her entire life pass before her in a split second. Dutifully, she began her last confession.

As she lay there making her peace with God, something warm and sticky beneath her oozed onto the deck and made her open her eyes. How much time had passed since the brute had fallen on her? Five, ten minutes? Yet he hadn't moved, had not twitched even once. Cautiously, she wiggled. Still no movement came from the surly beast.

Unconscious. Dear, sweet God, he was unconscious.

With great effort, she managed to struggle onto her back. When she pushed up on his arm and found it dead weight, adrenaline surged through her veins. She wriggled and squirmed and pushed, until she finally half-crawled, half-slithered out from under his enormous bulk.

She came to her knees panting, sat back on her heels, and glanced warily at the man.

Her gaze froze on his back.

There, angling between his shoulder blades, protruded the sharp point of the knife.

A knot formed in Alena's abdomen and rose to her chest. She swallowed it down and slowly, very slowly, pressed her hands to her cheeks.

As her wet, tacky fingers met her face, she jerked them away, then stared in horror at her palms. Even in the dark, she recognized the stains for what they were. Frantically, she started wiping them off on her gown, but her hands stilled at the sight of the crimson blotches that already soiled the once-white fabric.

Numb and cold, so cold, she focused on the pool of blood that seeped onto the deck from the lifeless body . . .

Chapter 5

Zach's eyelids fluttered drowsily. From somewhere, maybe inside his brain, came a hollow
tapping. He made a lazy attempt to listen harder,
then lifted his head slightly off the pillow.

It was no dream. Someone was knocking with
a quiet urgency at his cabin door.

Muttering, he planted his feet on the floor,
yawned, and raked a hand through his hair.
"Hold your horses," he grumbled, then grabbed
his trousers and tugged them on. "I said just a
minute, dammit." Still fastening his fly, he
opened the door a crack.

The sight that greeted him shocked him into
full consciousness.

Alena stood glassy-eyed, like a store manne-
quin in the soft golden glow of the hall. Her hair
streamed wildly about her face, her bloodstained
gown hung half-off her shoulder.

Zach glanced both ways down the corridor,
scooped her into his arms, and carried her into
the room, kicking the door shut behind him.

He deposited her gently on his cot, knelt beside her, and vigorously rubbed her icy hands
between his. "God in heaven, woman, what's
happened?"

When she didn't respond, he tried to make contact with the blank, expressionless eyes that looked right through him. "Alena?" Cupping her chin, he angled her face to his. "It's okay, Angelface. Do you hear me? You're here with me now. You're safe. I won't let anyone hurt you. Alena? Alena, look at me, dammit! Aw, jeez, come on, sweetheart, talk to me."

Alena heard the emotion in his voice first: the concern, the fury, and, in the end, a resigned helplessness. Then she saw his face, so very close, his forehead creased with worry. But it was the feel of his thumb absently stroking her cheek that finally broke hell's hold and brought her, tumbling back, from somewhere far away. "D-Dr. Summerfield?"

"Thank God! Are you hurt, sweetheart?" His hands skimmed down her body, feeling for broken bones or open wounds. When he touched her ribs, she winced. Without a second thought, he started to lift her gown.

Alena's eyes flew open. She caught her hem as he raised it to her thigh. "No . . . no, I'm sure it's only bruised."

Zach frowned, but decided he'd best comply with her modesty, given her overwrought condition. "Can you sit up?" When she nodded, he caught her shoulders and helped her get situated.

Alena met his eyes, knowing he awaited an explanation. "I shouldn't have come here. I just didn't know where else to go."

"Alena, what the hell happened to you?"

She hung her head, and her chin began to quiver at the sight of her bloody palms lying face-up on her lap. "M-may I please . . . wash my hands?"

Zach stood abruptly, irritated with her, irritated with himself for being irritated. Looking down at her, he strove for patience. She was so pitiful, like a tiny, wilted flower that needed tending.

He'd wished a hundred times in the past couple of weeks she would break. He'd wanted to see that uppity little chin of hers quake, see her unyielding disposition bend just a little.

But not like this. God, not like *this*.

He combed his fingers through his hair. He wasn't good at these situations. He was inclined to hold her, just hold her. But what if she misinterpreted his intentions? It could upset her all the more. Trying to quell his uneasiness with concrete action, he turned and emptied the water pitcher into the small basin.

When he stood before her, washbowl in hand, she made no move to take it. She sat motionless, seemingly entranced by her hands. Going down on one knee, Zach set the basin on the floor. He took the handkerchief from his back pocket, dipped it in the water, crooked two fingers beneath her chin, and lifted her head. Her eyes stayed downcast for a long moment before she raised her thick lashes and he noted the unspilled tears brimming in her forest-green eyes. He prayed to God she'd hold them at bay as he concentrated on a grimy spot on her forehead. He didn't think he could stand to see her cry. Taking her jaw between his thumb and forefinger, he proceeded to wipe her face.

"You've obviously had a bad upset," he said, keeping his voice nice and smooth. "Let's see if we can clean you up a bit and then you can tell me all about it." He turned her head to the side

and went to work on a smudge near her cheekbone, hard put to avoid those emerald eyes he
knew watched his every move.

Alena's apprehension slowly melted away.
There was something about him washing her
face as if she were a child that was immensely
comforting. Perhaps it was some lost memory of
her mother doing the same. Whatever it was that
transpired between them made her forget for a
few serene minutes that this was the same man
who'd done his best to bamboozle her only a few
days before.

Reaching up, she hesitantly touched the back
of his hand. The wet handkerchief froze where
it was on her jaw and his gaze met hers. His
heavy brows were pinched and there was a com-
passion in the depths of his eyes that Alena
would have never believed him capable of feeling.

She looked down at his chin and absently noticed that his beard grew extremely fast. "Thank
you," she murmured. "I'm all right now. Really.
I can finish by myself." To verify her statement,
she picked up the washbowl and set it on her
lap.

She scrubbed her hands so hard Zach
thought for sure she would scrape off the hide.
"That's good enough," he said. Capturing both
her small hands in one of his, he gave them a
gentle squeeze, laid them in her lap, and set
the bowl back on the floor. "You know, I think
I have just the thing to help loosen your
tongue, my dear lady." He sat down on the cot
next to her, reached between the mattress and
bed board, and pulled out a bottle of rum.

After downing a generous swig himself, he offered her the bottle.

Alena glanced from the spirits to him and back again. "Oh, no . . . no, thank you. I don't—"

"Drink it," he commanded in a tone that brooked no refusal. His face broke into a lopsided grin, and he added, "For medicinal purposes only, of course. It'll make talking easier." Seeing her hesitation, he nudged her with the bottle. "Go on, take it."

Something in his challenging expression made Alena wrap both hands around the flask. She took a deep breath, then before she could change her mind, tilted the bottle all the way up.

She was sorry the instant she did it. Liquid fire scalded her insides. She gagged, coughed, and sputtered till tears sprang to her eyes. Zach slapped her on the back so hard she almost flew off the bed. The impact stopped her conniption, which was replaced by a warm furry glow.

The intoxicating drink worked its magic, bolstering her, making her suddenly bold. She looked Zach right in the eye and with an extraordinary amount of calmness said, "Dr. Summerfield, there's a dead man on the deck." Rambling on, she began to recount the entire event.

As she neared the end of her story, her artificial courage was fading. By the time she finished, she was gazing unseeingly at the wall. Reality seemed to have a sobering affect, she noted, and warily awaited Zach's reaction.

He sat silent, elbows propped on his knees and fingers steepled against his lips, apparently lost in thought. After a moment, he took a deep breath, looked at her, and brushed a stray strand of hair from her eyes. "It'll be all right, Angelface."

He smiled in a way that made Alena believe him. Her gaze followed that smile when he rose and grabbed his shirt from a ladder-back chair. "I'll take care of everything," he promised, pulling the garment over his broad shoulders. "You stay put till I get back, you hear?"

Alena watched him tug on his tall black boots and all at once felt overly heated. She'd been in the man's room for she didn't know how long, and had just noticed he'd been half-naked. "Dr. Summerfield," she said, studying the plank-board floor, "I believe I should return to my own room."

"You're going to stay right here."

His adamant tone brought Alena's head up. Hands on hips, feet planted wide, he reminded her of an ancient Roman warrior. "You're not to take one step out of this room until I return. Do I make myself clear?"

"W-what are you going to do?"

Zach glanced at the ceiling as if completely exasperated, then looked her way, his features somewhat relaxed. "I'm going to go up on deck, get rid of the body, and clean up the mess."

"Get rid of the b-body?"

"Yes, Miss Sutton. I'm going to throw it overboard. That is, of course, unless you would like to perform that honor yourself."

Alena crossed her hands upon her heart. "Oh! Oh, Dr. Summerfield, that just doesn't seem right. I mean . . . after all, he was a human being. He deserves a Christian—"

She was jerked to her feet so fast she dropped her jaw.

"Save your puritanical morality for someone who deserves it, Angelface. You probably did humanity a favor tonight. Do you have any idea what that scum had in mind for you?" He gave her a shake and cocked his head. "Do you? I can guaran-damn-tee you he wasn't planning on taking you to a Sunday ice-cream social!" He released her with such energy that she plopped back onto the cot, still openmouthed. He held up his forefinger. "Lesson number one. Don't *ever* sympathize with your enemy. Where we're going, my dear, *that* can get you killed."

Remorse stopped Zach at the door. Hell, the girl had been through enough tonight. She hadn't needed him to manhandle her. Dropping his head against the doorjamb, he exhaled slowly. He half-turned, his gaze meeting hers for only a brief second as he glanced around the room. "Miss Sutton . . . look, I'm sorry, I—"

"It's all right. Go. Go . . . do whatever you have to do. I'll be here when you get back. I promise I shan't take one step out of this room until you return."

Their eyes held briefly.

In that short moment, Zach noted how tall and straight she sat, chin held high. That was more like the woman he'd come to know. Somehow that rigid-back pose of hers made leaving a little easier. He slipped outside, then poked his head back in the door and said, "Lock the latch behind me and don't open it to anyone but me. Understand? And have another sip of rum, Angelface. It'll do you good."

The moon shone eerily on deck as Zach approached the body. He knelt on one knee to examine the still, cold form, his back muscles straining as he rolled the dead man over.

Recognition was immediate. Zach never forgot a face, and he would have remembered this ugly mug even if Alena's description hadn't brought the man to mind. Just as he'd suspected, it was the same seedy character that had followed them to the restaurant in Philadelphia.

Staring at the man's pale death mask, Zach searched for explanations. It just didn't make sense. This poor wretch wouldn't have known what to do with the map if he had gotten it. There had to be someone else involved. But who? Surely the British Museum of Antiquities wouldn't go to such lengths to obtain the map. Or would they? Something about Fielding, or Flemming, or whatever his name was, bothered Zach.

He didn't trust Richard Blythe, either. Blythe was like a bloodhound—always showing up and sniffing around every time he caught a whiff of something cooking. Those were two angles Zach could explore, but he'd have to ponder it all later when he had more time. Right now he had work to do.

Dragging the lifeless bulk to the edge of the boat, Zach hoisted it up, rolled it off his shoulder, and let it fall into the depths of the sea. Probably a stowaway, he thought, as he watched the body splash into the water. Regardless, none of the crew would be missed in these parts. Sailors deserted ship frequently in this area, in search of the perfect island paradise.

He turned to survey the dark red blotches that stained the deck and grimaced. Hell, this could take half the night. And he still had to figure out what to do with the distraught girl who waited in his cabin.

* * *

Alena leaned her head against the beam that supported the bunk, her nerves pulled as taut as corset laces. What was taking him so long?

Maybe he'd gotten caught. At this very moment he could be telling the captain everything. What if he told them she'd done it on purpose, just to be rid of her once and for all? Her stomach lurched, threatening to give up the day's ration.

No. He wouldn't. Merciful Mother, he couldn't. No. *Everything is going to be all right. He promised*. She closed her eyes, recalling his kindness, the gentleness with which he tended her.

Miraculously, her queasiness subsided.

Unfortunately, her limbs still twitched. She looked at the bottle of rum lying on the bed. *No . . . I shouldn't*. One shouldn't have to rely on spirits to bolster stamina. Still, these were special circumstances . . .

In no time at all, the magic liquid soared through her veins with a warmth that soothed her jitters. Just to ensure that the wonderful feeling remained, she took another generous swig . . . and another. Each swallow burned a little less, numbed a little more.

She was examining the silver flask with great concentration when a knock at the door made her raise her too-heavy head. "Come in," she called, then returned her attention to the intricately engraved *S* in the center of the small decanter.

"Alena! Quit fooling around and open up. It's Zach." His voice was low but fierce enough to make her bob her way over to undo the latch.

He slipped through the door, locked it behind him, and turned on her like a mad hornet. "Come *in*? I thought I told you—"

Zach narrowed his eyes on her ridiculous smile, then raised them to her glittering gaze. "Good Lord, you're soused." He sidestepped her weaving form, snatched the flask from the bed, opened it, and turned it upside down. A single drop trickled out. "Jeez almighty! You little lush! You've downed two dollars' worth of my best rum."

"For medi...medishinal purposes, I ash-shure you, s-sir." Alena had only a moment to wonder why her tongue was at such odds with her brain before she hiccuped. She frowned and pressed her fingertips to her lips. Beneath her brows, she took in Zach's expression and couldn't, for the life of her, suppress a giggle.

"Here," he grumbled at last, shoving a garment of some sort at her. "I stopped by your cabin and got you a clean gown. We'll have to dispose of the one you're wearing."

"Y-you went through my things?"

"Now is not the time for modesty, Miss Sutton. If the captain suspects us of anything, he won't hesitate to drop us off at the next port we pass." He jerked the blanket off the bed and held it up to shield her from view. "Do you think you can change now?"

"Of course I can change." She hiccuped once more as she wrestled the soiled gown over her head. "I'm nau-hot the idiot you think I am, s-sir. I don't need...anybody. I can take care of my"—she hiccuped again—"myself, th-thank you very much."

"I never implied you were an idiot, Miss Sut—"

"Oh, you implied, all right, several times, and in several ways, you have—"

"Okay, okay. Just get dressed, will you?"

The lamp behind her cast her shadow on the blanket. Zach caught a glimpse of her nude silhouette. Though he rolled his eyes to the ceiling, the image stuck in his mind.

"Oops. I put it on backwards."

"Dammit! Will you hurry up?"

In what felt like an eternity to Zach, she pulled the blanket down and hooked her chin over it. "I'm done," she announced, beaming as if she'd just accomplished the greatest feat of her life.

"Good," he commented dryly, and tossed the blanket on the cot. Taking her arm, he turned her toward the door. "Now we can get you back to your room." He started to move, but she didn't.

"Oh, dear." Alena pressed a hand against her forehead. "I feel all woozy."

"Well, hell, I'm not surprised," Zach grumbled, perching her on the edge of the cot. "What on earth possessed you to sit here and get riproaring drunk while I—"

"I'm *not* dr—" Alena covered her mouth to hold down the bile that rose from her stomach to her chest.

"Lord." Zach glanced up, shook his head, and put a hand on her back, forcing her forward. "Lean over and put your head between your knees."

Her upper half hanging upside down, she muttered into her gown, "I feel like I'm spinning in circles."

"Yes, I know. Just take some deep breaths in through your nose, out through your mouth." He rubbed the taut muscles of her back. "You'll feel better in a bit."

As if by his command the dizziness stopped almost immediately. She sat up slowly with Zach's help. She checked her nausea, and found it gone, too. Now all that was left was a dreadful embarrassment.

"All better?" Zach smoothed the hair from her face.

She nodded, keeping her eyes downcast in shame. "I . . . I don't know how to thank you for all you've done tonight. I had no one else to turn to, you know. That m-man was so awful . . . he said such aw-awful things. But I didn't mean to hurt him. Truly, I didn't." Of its own accord, her lower lip puckered. She promptly bit it back. "And I am sorry about your rum and for the horrible things I've said to you and for getting—"

Zach crooked two fingers beneath her chin and raised her face to his. The single tear that rolled down her cheek caused something to clench behind his sternum. He reached out and enfolded her protectively in his arms. "Shh, sweet angel, don't cry," he said, nuzzling her temple. "Everything looks brighter in the morning light."

Alena had no strength left to struggle. She let him snuggle her close, not caring that his shirt gaped half-open and her cheek was pressed against the soft fur of his chest. His heart beat sure and steady and strong in her ear. She closed her eyes, filling her senses with his essence: the mingled scent of spice, leather, pipe tobacco, and rum. Never had she felt so safe, so secure. When she'd finally given up hope of her father ever returning to collect her, she'd held others at arm's length. She had vowed never again to let anyone close enough to hurt her. Never again.

Yet, at the moment, being nestled against Zach's sturdy chest felt so good, so right. The soft kisses and soothing words he whispered against her hair sedated her, and for the first time in a long, long while, she didn't fight the illusion of feeling cared for . . . feeling loved.

Just for a moment or two longer, she promised herself, she would indulge in this fool's paradise and the wondrous sensation it evoked. Just for a moment longer . . .

But as the moment passed and the next stretched on, she drifted farther and farther into a euphoric peacefulness and, finally, into oblivion.

"Alena?" The lack of response made Zach pull slightly away from her. Her head lolled and he smiled at the contentment in her sleeping face.

He laid her in his bed, wondering what it was about the woman that tugged at him . . . tugged at a conscience he'd thought was long dead . . . tugged at a heart he'd thought was stone-cold and bulletproof. She was a complication that contradicted his rule about emotional involvement where women were concerned. He couldn't afford to get emotionally involved with this little nymph. Didn't want to. She was the type he'd made a point of staying away from in the past— the type who'd require a commitment. He was the kind of man who couldn't give one.

Even with that thought still warm in his mind, on a wild impulse, he bent and kissed her forehead. "Good night, Angelface," he whispered. A slight smile curved her lips, then faded, and he tucked the covers beneath her chin.

Taking the extra blanket, Zach settled himself on the floor by the door. It had been one hell of a night, he mused as he set his hat over his face and folded his arms across his chest.

A not-so-unwilling guardian, he dozed on and off, never allowing sleep to fully take him. In the meantime, the questions he asked himself about his feelings for Howard Sutton's daughter were constantly interrupted by a single phrase that kept running through his mind. *Where there is one snake in the grass, another usually slithers nearby.*

"You cheated!" Alena pointed at Zach and lifted her chin indignantly. For such a scoundrel, Zach looked amazingly innocent.

"I did not."

"You most certainly did," Alena insisted. "I saw you pull that ace from your sleeve." She scowled at the man across from her.

For a matter of minutes, Zach scowled right back, then, straightening in his chair, he grinned slowly. "You're very observant, Miss Sutton. Just testing you." He tossed his cards on the table. "You are now officially a full-fledged black-jack player. I do believe you're ready for any dealer employed by the finest gambling halls in New Orleans."

Alena's lips twitched, then broke into a smile. "I think I'd prefer some fresh air, actually."

Something had happened between them since the night Alena had sought refuge in Zach's arms. Something had changed. Whether it was a truce or true camaraderie, Alena couldn't say. Whatever it was called, it and their shared secret had bound them together like clasped hands. In the month that had followed, Alena had ceased to think about the new alliance in terms of good or bad.

"Well, if it's air you want," Zach said as he pushed away from the table, stood, and donned his hat, "it's air you'll get—that is, if you're sure you don't need any more tips on how to become the reigning queen of blackjack."

"Quite sure." Alena rose, took the arm he offered, and let him lead her from the small cabin. Since they had ceased their bickering, they'd spent almost all their waking hours in each other's company. They had taken meals together, strolled about the deck, chatted, and played chess or cards in Zach's quarters.

These had been serene days for Alena, the happiest she could clearly remember. Somewhere along the way, she had set aside her customary dictum against becoming too chummy with another human being—set aside the consequences of doing so.

The sun was blindingly bright as they stepped from the dark confines below and onto the deck. The farther south they journeyed, the warmer, more sultry the climate became. Zach guided Alena to the bow of the freighter where the air coming off the water was cooler.

They stood in companionable silence, the wind whipping their hair and clothes. Thinking about the complex man beside her, Alena closed her eyes and tilted her face to the sun. The only thing she truly knew about him was that he was much more tenderhearted than he appeared. She'd glimpsed his hidden gentleness. It was there, lodged far beneath that coarse exterior he presented to the world. Perhaps he merely pretended to be a cynic, merely acted like a lunatic at times to hide his sensitivity.

Alena opened her eyes and angled them

Zach's way to find him contemplating her seriously. Though she'd caught him doing so before, she couldn't yet keep from blushing. To avoid his intense gaze, she lowered her lashes. "Is something the matter?" she asked.

"No." He gave her a small, fleeting smile. "It's just . . . well, I like your hair down. It makes you look—" *Years younger*, he was going to say, but before he could think of a tactful way to phrase it, Alena filled in the blank.

"A bit like Alice in Wonderland, I'm afraid." Touching the wide ribbon she'd used to keep her hairline curls from falling in her face, she bit back a smile. "Too childish."

"Not at all. Though, now that you mention it, you do resemble Alice a little." His lips twitched. "Seriously, the style is very becoming on you. And it doesn't make you look childish, just less reserved, very . . . pretty."

Warmth surged to Alena's cheeks all over again. Her lashes fluttered involuntarily as she tried to decide how best to deal the blandishments he'd been showering her with of late. "You're teasing me again," she said, glancing up at him.

"No, really. I like it." Thankfully, he seemed to sense her uneasiness, and dropped the issue. "You must take after your mother. I mean, in terms of characteristics, you and your father, well, you're very different."

"I wouldn't know about that." Alena smiled, trying to quell the sudden melancholia that washed over her. "As you well know, I haven't seen my father in years. People change, and the memories I have of him are vague, as are those of my mother. I hardly remember her at all. She died when I was but four."

Zach was silent, contemplative for a moment. "It must have been awful growing up in that dreary old school. It couldn't have been easy. From the little you've said about Mrs. What's-her-name . . ."

"Mistress Stephens."

"Yeah, Mistress Stephens." Zach narrowed his eyes and made a face. "I keep picturing her wearing a tall, black hat, with a wart on the end of her nose. She didn't happen to carry a broom around, did she?"

Alena shook her head, her lips curving upward. "No, but she did have a timing stick that was probably just as efficient."

They both laughed.

As their mirth dwindled, Alena stared at some point beyond the sea. "She wasn't all that bad. Not really. As long as her rules were followed, one didn't have to worry about coming face to face with Mistress Stephens. She didn't bother with you overmuch. Actually, there was only one thing that disturbed her equanimity." Alena brushed a stray curl from her eyes. "Tears. She couldn't abide sniveling. Sent her into a rage, it did."

As much as she'd tried, Alena could never forget those first few years spent in Mistress Stephens' care. They were the basis for her reserve, her coolness toward others, as she was only now beginning to realize. They were the transitional years in which she had grown from a warm-hearted, trusting little girl into a detached creature who'd closed the door on feelings.

Something pressed Alena to go on—a need to discuss it openly, purge her system—prove in her own mind that she could still express herself without emotion.

"Yes, Mistress Stephens most assuredly hated tears. She'd stand the offender on a chair in the middle of the room and line up the lot of us to learn by example. 'You are *not* babies', she used to say." Alena ignored the sting behind her lids that made her blink. She glanced at Zach, afraid she'd gone too far, said too much. Trying to smile at his obvious pity, she cleared her throat. "Well, enough of that. What about you?"

Zach's expression turned blank. "What about me?"

"Dr. Summerfield—"

"Zach. I've asked you to call me Zach, remember?"

Alena rolled her eyes. "Please don't start that again. We've thoroughly discussed my views on the intimacy of calling you by your first name. You are simply trying to change the subject."

"Me? Change the subject?" He looked shocked. "I'm wounded that you could think I'd do such a thing."

Having learned to appreciate his frequent satire, Alena good-naturedly countered, "You madman. I've just made a complete ninny of myself, sputtering on the way I did. It's only fair that you should tell me a little about yourself."

Zach pressed his lips into a tight, straight line. After a moment's consideration, he braced his forearms on the rail. "Okay. Fair's fair. Now let's see, I could tell you about the time . . . uh, no, that one might offend your tender sensibilities. Wait a minute." He squinted one eye. "I've got it! I could tell you how I barely escaped the good citizens of Baalbek with my"—he glanced sideways, then smiled—"with my head intact. Of course, I was much younger and lighter on my feet in those days—"

"Pardon me, I'm sure that's all very interesting, and I should very much like to hear it . . . someday . . . but actually I've been curious about something a little more personal." Alena clasped her hands against her waist, weighing how best to put her question. It wasn't one a lady should ask. However, Dr. Summerfield was not exactly conventional when it came to such formalities. Considering that, she decided she would simply blurt it out. "Why is it that you've never married?"

Zach appeared dumbstruck for a split second before he broke into a one-sided grin. "Well, if you must know, Angelface, I disapprove of matrimony as a matter of principle. At least, for myself. While I'm sure some men find wedlock to be satisfactory, my present style of life and my work doesn't exactly allow me room for a lasting relationship. I mean, it would be rather unrealistic of me to expect a spouse to live half her married life alone, don't you agree?"

Studying the railing, Alena ran her finger along it. "Oh, I don't know. I suppose there are women who are willing to sacrifice their monopoly on an adventurous man's time . . . for the sake of love."

"My mother, for one." Zach grimaced and set his attention on something in the distance. "I've seen what love like that can do to a woman, Miss Sutton. I watched my mother wither because of my father's adventurous bouts . . . heard her crying herself to sleep while he was off on some African safari or a wild buffalo hunt for months at a time. They claimed a bad heart killed her. I was only a boy at the time, but I knew different. Her heart wasn't bad. It was broken." Zach glanced at Alena with an earnest expression she'd never seen before. "As you might have guessed, Miss Sutton, my parents didn't exactly have a blissfully content marriage. Theirs was a high-society marriage of convenience formed to keep my father's family business from going under. Only, my mother made the mistake of falling in love." Zach paused and looked directly at her. "Hah—love. I'm not sure I completely understand the meaning of that word. So you'll have to excuse me if I don't believe in 'happily ever after.'"

Alena turned from the resentment etched on his face, and thought for a moment as she searched the blue waters before her. "Is your father still alive?" she asked in a quiet voice, turning back to him.

"No." Zach stared straight ahead. "He died a few years ago while I was working in Egypt."

"I'm sorry."

"No need to be," Zach replied without a tremor of emotion. "We weren't close. I was nothing more than a nuisance to him after my mother died. Something he had to tend to before he took off on another expedition. For years I tried to make the old man notice I was alive, but the only attention I received was applied to the seat of my pants for what he'd term 'some fool-crazy stunt.' That was about the extent of our relationship. In fact, he cut me out of his will, probably the very day I ran off." Taking a deep breath, Zach continued his study of the sea. "And God help me, I'm just like him. Just like my father. The urge to wander the earth in search of . . . who knows what . . . is in my blood. And I'm just as selfish as he ever was. The one big difference between us lies in a promise I've made myself. My father never loved my mother, or me. I'll never subject a wife and family to that kind of life. Never."

After a moment of silence, Zach flashed an unexpected smile Alena's way. It was almost as if he was trying to invalidate all he'd just told her. "So," he said with a wiggle of his brows, "you want to hear about the little misunderstanding in Baalbek now?"

Alena returned his smile, her heart going out to him for the effort he had expended to recover his composure so quickly. "If you must tell me a story, Dr. Summerfield, I'd rather hear the legend of the Amazonian princess. I can't recall her name."

"Mahrakimba." Zach's eyes lit up and he moved closer. "Well, it's a bizarre tale. I didn't believe it myself at first. Let's see, where do I begin?"

"At the beginning," Alena said, catching his enthusiasm.

"Then I suppose I should mention Mahrakimba's oddity. You see, she was said to be albinic."

"Albinic?"

"Lacking pigment in the eyes, hair, and skin. She allegedly was a true beauty, and being the seventh daughter of the chief, she was held in the highest esteem. The whole village revered her because of her long white hair, a rare sight in the Amazon. The people believed her to have a pure heart and claimed she was a great being, sent from heaven. I'm told she performed many miracles and cured every ailment brought before her. Unfortunately, she fell in love with a young warrior from another clan."

Alena frowned. "What could be the harm in that?"

"Well, it was understood that blood should not be mixed between tribes. This law applied to the princess in a special way because the priests declared she would lose her power when she lost her virtue. The priests themselves were to choose an appropriate husband for her at the appointed time.

"As the legend goes, the young buck turned out to be Mahrakimba's undoing. The lovers were discovered together by the shaman of the village. I imagine the old witch doctor had always been jealous of Mahrakimba and was delighted to tell the high priests all about her indiscretion. It is said that the priests were so angry that they sealed the princess alive in the treasure chamber to repent her sin for the rest of eternity."

"How dreadful!" Alena scrunched her nose, then whispered, "What happened to the warrior?"

Zach adopted her secretive tone. "Though he was sentenced to share Mahrakimba's fate, he somehow managed to free himself. He was chased into the rain forest, but mysteriously disappeared. Some believe Mahrakimba used the last of her powers to hide him. Others swear he fell beneath the vines that line the jungle floor and justly vanished into the netherworld."

Skeptical, Alena raised a brow.

"I know, I know," Zach said, nodding. "It's a hard story to swallow. I felt the same way the first time I heard it." He lifted his gaze to the dark puffy clouds gathering above them, then settled it back on her. "Looks like rain. You want to go below and play cards? I promise not to cheat."

Chapter 6

The Venezuelan coast materialized through a cloudy mist on the horizon. Alena stood on deck, heart drumming, and watched the landscape take form as the freighter glided nearer and nearer its destination.

Only in picture books had she ever seen the likes of such exotic places. Yet no artist's illustration, no poet's skilled tongue could have captured the breathtaking beauty she not only saw, but felt. Celadon tops of palm trees swayed, waving in silent greeting. Beyond the golden beaches, mountainous highlands rose to meet billowing white clouds in the bluest sky she'd ever seen.

Zach leaned against the doorjamb a few feet away, observing the schoolmarm's reaction. She viewed the coastline with childlike fascination, her mouth slightly parted in awe. A warm breeze blew across the deck, billowing her white lawn dress and fluttering the halo of curls around her face. Zach shoved his hands into his pockets and sighed. Why the hell did she have to look like she ought to own wings?

Dammit, she had no business being here.

116

He'd known that all along, but since the evening she'd sought his protection, the real world had somehow slipped away. He'd forgotten where they were going, completely disregarded the risks that lay ahead. He'd spent too many days enjoying the pleasure of her company, too many nights lying awake thinking about her in ways he shouldn't have.

Zach grimaced at what a little voice in his head nagged him to do. He didn't want to lose that twinkle of admiration he'd seen in her eyes recently. He wasn't ready to give up the friendship that had started to bud between them.

His sixth sense tingled again. Trouble. Something sinister. Something or someone altogether unrelated to the jungle.

Zach closed his eyes, the feeling intensifying with each notch closer they came to the shoreline. In all good conscience, he was honor-bound to make one last attempt to dissuade the woman. Howie would never forgive him if he let something happen to her. Howie, hell. He would never forgive himself. He still carried the burden of what had happened in Egypt.

The explosion hadn't been his fault. He had told himself that over and over again. But he'd been in charge of that sector and still felt responsible for the family that one of the dead men had left behind. He'd tried to ease his own guilt with the knowledge that excavating a tomb could be dangerous at times and that all four men killed had known the risks when they'd hired on. But the vision of a tearful widow at the graveside with three small children clutching her skirt had never left his mind. That was yet another very strong reason why he had always been of the opinion that the work he did was no way for a family man to make a living.

Zach nudged up his hat, wiped the sweat from his forehead, and set his sights on Alena. Moving soundlessly behind her, close enough to brush her skirt, he said, "Beyond the splendor at which you now gaze awaits danger that exceeds your worst nightmare."

Alena whirled, placing a hand to her throat. "Dr. Summerfield, you startled me."

"Did I? I didn't mean to. I meant to scare you into going home where you belong."

There'd been no measure of jesting in his voice. His features were hard, expressionless, giving Alena no clue to this sudden reversal of attitude. It was as if the past several weeks had never been. A pain behind her sternum made her turn from him and feign great interest in the view. "As you must know by now," she said in a monotone, "I'm not that easily frightened." Lifting her chin, she squared her shoulders. "I'm not afraid of you or the Amazon."

"You should be. You should be very, very afraid . . . of us *both*." His breath grazed the top of her head.

She pulled herself closer to the rail, putting as much space between them as possible.

"In two days' time this freighter returns to New York, Angelface. I suggest you be on it."

Alena glared at him over her shoulder. "You're wasting your time and mine, sir. I came here to find my father, and find my father I shall. Or at least have proof that he is indeed—" Too close to tears, she looked again to the shore.

Zach moved beside her, fidgeted briefly, then

leaned forward and cocked his head, trying to catch her misty gaze. "You're hell-bent on this, aren't you?"

Staring right past him, she nodded. "I am."

Zach straightened and exhaled deeply. "Dammit," he muttered. "Damn it all to hell and back again." He jerked his hat low on his forehead. "And you'd follow me, wouldn't you, if I left you behind."

"I would."

Zach narrowed his eyes on the mountains as the freighter docked a quarter of a mile from the beach and the crew bustled about the deck. "Very well, Miss Sutton. Since your mind is made up, we may as well get a few things settled here and now. As I've mentioned before, it's every man—or woman in this case—for themselves in the jungle. It's not an easy trek. If you insist on coming along, you're going to have to keep up. You'll carry your own weight. Understand?"

"Of course."

Zach shifted his weight. "And I'll be dog-tied if I'll play nursemaid."

"Dr. Summerfield," Alena said, tilting her head slowly to look at him, "as you can plainly see, I am a woman full grown. I do not need a nanny. When I set upon a goal, I accomplish it. I gave you my assurance in Philadelphia that I would be no burden, and I shan't. While I may not look sturdy, you have my word as a lady that I am perfectly capable of enduring whatever hardships I must."

Zach stared long and hard into her earnest green eyes, needing to believe her, hoping for her sake and his that there was indeed a source of strength he couldn't see beneath her fragile daintiness.

Regardless, he was stuck with her, saddled with yet another responsibility he didn't want, and there wasn't a damn thing he could do about it. Like it or not, the two of them were going to be in close proximity for the next few months. "Alena Sutton, you have a nasty way of bending a man to your will," he murmured half to himself and in grave seriousness.

Alena smiled. "Why, thank you."

"It wasn't a compliment."

"Yes, I know."

Zach shook his head, unable to hide a slight grin of his own. "Since there's no talking you out of this fiasco, we'd better get a move on. They'll be shuffling exports back and forth most of the morning. I'll speak to the captain about borrowing a boat. How soon can you be ready to go ashore?"

"Would a matter of minutes be too long?"

She was beaming, absolutely beaming, and Zach had the strongest urge to kiss her again. He might have indulged his whim had a sailor not bumped him in passing and distracted his gaze from those sweetly curved lips.

It was just as well, he decided on second thought, and cleared his throat *and* his mind. "Take your time, Angelface. It'll take at least a half hour to hoist the boat into the water."

Alena glanced around the small cabin, grabbed her bag, and started for the door, then stopped, her hand flying to her head. Good heavens, she must be getting lax. Where was her hat? It wouldn't do at all to disembark without a hat.

Returning to the bed, she sat on the edge and retrieved the only hat she'd packed from the one small bag Zach had allowed her to bring. It was the hat she'd bought in Philadelphia. She eyed the conglomeration of bird's nest, feathers, and flowers, once again thinking it a bit . . . excessive as she straightened the big straw brim. Nevertheless, it would have to suffice, as the trunk containing all her other hats had been sent to Mr. Dalton's office for safekeeping.

She recalled the shopkeeper at the Philadelphia millinery had said it was a hat that could be worn upon any occasion. Without further ado, she perched it atop her head and tied the wide blue scarf into a bow beneath her chin, and promptly quit the room.

Dr. Summerfield was waiting on deck. She noted with some dismay that he could hardly tear his eyes from her hat as she approached, though he was kind enough not to make a comment. "May we proceed to the boarding plank now?" she asked, hoping her question would divert his attention.

"The boarding plank?" His gaze finally settled on hers. "Ah, sorry, Miss Sutton, but the water is too shallow here for this freighter to get any closer to shore." Zach pointed over the side of the ship. "We'll use the ladder to climb down to the boat."

Craning her neck, she looked over the rail. "That's . . . a ladder? Why, it's nothing more than bits of rope tied together."

Zach just smiled, threw his pack over his shoulder, and hooked her bag on his arm. "Look, I'll go down first and steady the boat. Just watch me and do what I do."

Alena observed him scamper down the rope and alight in the boat with ease. It didn't look so difficult. Still, she automatically made the sign of the cross before gathering up her skirts.

Below, Zach leaned back comfortably in the boat, clasping his hands behind his head. The boat hadn't really needed steadying. The sea was calm. He just hadn't been able to resist this angle of view. Besides, someone ought to be nearby in case the lady lost her footing. He pushed his hat down over his eyes, but not so far he couldn't watch Miss Priss climb over the rail. "Just take it one step at a time," he hollered, cupping his hands around his mouth.

She did. Placing one foot down and then the other, she waited until the rope stabilized before moving on to the next step. Zach chuckled under his hat. It looked like this was going to take longer than he'd originally thought. He wasn't at all perturbed, though. Glimpses of shapely white-stockinged calves made the wait worthwhile.

When at long last, she neared the bottom of the ladder, Zach stood, feet apart, leveling the boat. He caught her around the waist and swung her into the small craft. She teetered. The boat swayed. "Sit down, Miss Sutton," he commanded, sinking onto the seat opposite her.

Alena had every intention of doing just that when a wave sloshed against the side. Completely missing the plank board, her backside landed right behind the seat. Her legs and feet dangled over the board in a most audacious display. To make matters worse, somewhere during the course of action, her hat had slipped down over her eyes. For a moment she simply sat there

trying to collect herself. Beyond humiliation, totally exasperated, she tilted her head way back
and peered at Dr. Summerfield from under her
wide brim.

The man was near bursting with the effort to
keep a straight face. The quivers at the corners
of his tightly closed mouth made her instantly
realize what a sight she must be. Doing all she
could to hold back a sputter of laughter herself,
she arched a brow. "Well, are you going to simply sit there gawking," she asked, extending her
hand, "or are you going to help me up?"

Ignoring her hand, Zach caught her under the
arms and plopped her onto the seat.

Alena set her attention on smoothing her skirt.
"I believe we may proceed now, sir."

"By all means," Zach agreed, his voice an octave higher than usual. He rotated in his seat
and shook in silent mirth momentarily before
rolling up his sleeves and taking hold of the oars.

A sea gull cried overhead, and the small craft
launched forward. Water swishing gently, Zach
dipped the paddles in and out of the blue Ca-
ribbean with steady, graceful strokes. Alena
watched his tan shirt pull taut across the rippling
of his back muscles as he rowed. Idly, she wondered how that skin might feel moving beneath
her hand.

The thought brought her up short. She quickly
shifted her gaze from his broad shoulders to the
dark, windblown curls at his collar and was
thankful for the sudden breeze.

"Is it always so sultry here?" she asked, pluck-
ing at her warm, sticky bodice.

"It's even hotter in the jungle, Angelface. And
if I may be so bold, if I were you, I'd consider

retiring your corset for the duration of our stay here."

He'd spoken matter-of-factly, never missing a stroke, while the blood had drained from Alena's face at the mention of such a tender subject.

"You needn't ask my permission to be bold, Dr. Summerfield," she said upon gathering her composure. "You seem to have a knack for it, regardless. And if I were you, sir, and a gentleman of any sort, I'd keep any illicit suggestions to myself the next time I thought of one." She drew herself erect. "Rest assured, I'm perfectly capable of caring for my own person, thank you."

Zach shrugged. "Whatever you say, Miss Sutton. I was just trying to help."

"Well, don't."

"I won't."

"Good."

They made their way wordlessly to shore, Alena dismissing Zach's coarse manners as she took in the exotic surroundings at close range. The bright sun reflected off the sand, making it look like gold dust. The feeling that she was about to embark upon a land filled with enchantment overcame her. It was the same initial excitement that had rushed through her the moment the mist had cleared, making the continent visible. She barely even noticed that Zach's thumb brushed the side of her breast when he lifted her from the boat and set her on the sandy beach.

"We're just outside Caracas," he commented as if he'd read her mind. "Come on. We'll be meeting an old friend of mine here." Grabbing her hand, he towed her along. "I wired Slim Johnson before we left the States and asked him to meet us. Slim and I go way back. His father owned the spread next to ours in Texas. I ran into him again in Mexico a few years ago. Since I'd last seen him, he'd been wildcatting all over the world. He got to know some pretty desolate places rather well, started doing some unchartered exploring on his own, and figured out he could make a heck of a lot more money as a guide. We've worked together several times now. These days, he's the best guide there is, and one of the few men I know who've journeyed as far as he has into the Amazon and lived to tell about it."

They trudged through the sand, up a slight incline, then wove between the thick green-topped palms. It was shady there, cooler, the wind rustling the broad leaves above. Alena cocked her ear to the pleasant, lilting sound of a lone guitar that drifted from somewhere beyond and became louder with each step.

Upon leaving the grove, a small village appeared. Caramel-skinned children came running from everywhere. One grasped Alena's hand, while another pushed her along. Eyes and hair shining black as night, they laughed, and chattered in a language that Zach told her was Portuguese. He gave her a wink of assurance while two small boys dragged him forward by his shirttail.

The town was a charming example of early Spanish influence, its buildings ensconced in iron scrollwork. Brightly painted gourds, clattering in the breeze, hung from every portico.

When they approached the middle of town, Zach tossed a handful of coins into the street. The children squealed and scattered, deserting their visitors for the treasure.

"Where are you dragging me now?" Alena demanded.

"To my friend, Hussong's, cantina," Zach answered. "We're meeting Slim there."

"Hussong?" Alena raised her brow. "That—"

"Yes, I know," interrupted Zach. "The name sounds Oriental, but it's not. And don't let Hussong hear you say that. It's a very old and respected name in South America."

Zach guided Alena through swinging doors and she found herself in a questionable establishment that suspiciously resembled a saloon. A metal fan suspended from the ceiling clanked round and round. The place was deserted except for an old-timer snoring in a chair in the corner, and a short, round man drying a glass behind the bar.

"Hussong!" Zach threw his arms wide in greeting.

The plump bartender looked up, and a wide, white smile cracked his dark-complected face. He set the glass down so fast it vibrated, tossed the towel over his shoulder, and hurried forward. He and Zach embraced, whacked each other's back soundly, then parted, laughing.

"It is good to see you, Dr. Zach," Hussong said. "It has been a long time, *sí?*"

"*Sí*, a long time, my friend." Zach nodded at the aged man still dozing in the corner. "I see *Abuelo* hasn't changed much."

"He's getting old. Sometimes he remembers. Sometimes he does not. Sometimes he thinks he is a conquistador and fights *inadvertido* enemies with the broom." Hussong rolled his eyes. "Most of the time now, he is as you see him, taking a long siesta, many thanks to the Holy Mother."

Zach smiled, a little sadly Alena thought, then he turned to her and winked. "Welcome to Hussong's cantina, Angelface. Hussong, I'd like you to meet—"

A high, reverberating caterwaul pierced the air, directing everyone's startled gaze to the stairway at the rear of the room. A girl of no more than sixteen, Alena guessed, came charging toward them. Bounding into Zach's arms, she wrapped her legs around his waist, her red skirt hiking up past her knees, and proceeded to dispense loud kisses all over his face.

Alena had the oddest urge to pinch her. She was young, of course, but very curvaceous, and well past the age for such rousting about.

Shortly, Zach pried the girl off and swung her down beside him. "Miss Sutton, this is Carmelita, Hussong's daughter. Carmelita, Miss Alena Sutton."

"How do you do," Alena managed, observing how low Carmelita's white, ruffled blouse hung off her smooth brown shoulders.

Hands on hips, Carmelita flung her long midnight-black hair to one side with a toss of her head and raked Alena from head to toe with her dark eyes.

"Well, I'll be damned if it ain't Zachariah Summerfield!" A tall, sandy-haired man stood grinning atop the stairs. He lifted a half-empty bottle and started down the steps, his plaid shirt gaping open. "Took your sweet-lovin' time about gettin' here, you son of—"

"Ach! Watch the language, old buddy, there's a lady present." Zach reached around behind him and pulled Alena forward. "Slim, I'd like you to meet Alena Sutton, Howard's daughter. Miss Sutton, this is Slim Johnson, the friend I told you about."

Slim was already tucking in his shirt. He smoothed back his hair and self-consciously ran a hand over the whiskers he could do nothing about. His gaze warmed at the sight of the pint-sized blonde, but turned quizzical when it flickered Zach's way. "How do, ma'am," he drawled.

Zach shifted under the Texan's scrutiny. "Carmelita, we're going to need a couple of rooms. I'm sure Miss Sutton would like to rest. Could you show her to her room now?" He turned to Alena and winked again. "Try to take a nap, Angelface. We'll be leaving at the crack of dawn tomorrow. Right, Slim?"

"Uh . . . yeah, sure, first thing in the mornin'."

With a jerk of her head, Carmelita indicated that Alena accompany her, and swayed up the stairs.

Alena followed, overhearing Slim mutter, "Hellfire, Zach, your wire didn't say nothin' about no female."

"There's been an unavoidable change in plans," Zach whispered back.

"But you didn't say nothin' about—"

"I'll tell you all about it later."

Alena stopped at the landing, glancing down at them from the balcony. The two men stood, smiling up like marble statues.

"Come," Carmelita snapped. "Thees is where you stay." She leaned back against an open door.

Alena set her bag on the crisply made bed, noting how tidy the room was. The only other piece of furniture was a small table which held a pitcher and bowl. Her gaze settled on a crucifix hanging above the shuttered window.

"Your man is not pleased with you," Carmelita stated from the doorway. "Thees is not so good for you, but is good for Carmelita, no?"

Alena whirled and quirked a brow. "I beg your pardon?"

The girl cocked her head to the side. "He asks for *dos* rooms, no?" She held up two fingers. "Thees can only mean . . . he will not sleep with you."

Alena went rigid. Crossing the room in three long strides, she stood eye to eye with the ill-mannered little trollop. Hands on hips, she bent slowly forward at the waist. "Young woman, in the first place, he is not my . . . my *man*. Furthermore, it is certainly no concern of yours whom I do or do not sleep with. Now, if you don't mind, I should like very much to be alone."

Carmelita shrugged past her. With one last sweep of her lashes, she hugged the doorjamb, then sashayed out.

Satisfying a deep need to slam the door, Alena barely missed that bright red skirt.

Late afternoon brought an unbearable heat. Even with the window open, the air hung heavy, making a nap impossible. Alena dabbed perspiration from her neck and face with a wet hanky. She'd tried reading, but had ended up fanning herself with the book.

The clinking of glasses downstairs made her think again how good a cool drink would taste. Yet she stubbornly stayed where she was. She had no wish to join the trio below. Occasional laughter drifted up through the floorboards.

Zach's, deep and easy; Carmelita's, shrill; Slim's rumbling. Alena had no doubt they were inebriated. They'd been at it all afternoon, toasting and guffawing like baboons.

She moved to the windowsill, longing for a breeze. The sea air smelled so sweet, it gave her an idea. She quickly refastened the top two buttons of her blouse, smoothed her hair, and left the stifling room.

Downstairs, Zach and Slim were constructing a pyramid from empty bottles. Carmelita stood between them, one hand massaging Zach's shoulder, the other tickling Slim's ear. The latter shrugged.

"Come on, Carmelita, stop it. You're breakin' my concentration."

Zach looked up just as Alena reached the bottom of the stairs. "Well, well. Will you take a gander at this? Her royal highness has consented to grace us with her presence. I was wondering when it would get too hot up there for you, Angelface."

Alena lifted her chin, planning to walk right past the lot of them and out the door. Unfortunately, as she whisked past the table, Zach grabbed her skirt.

"Not so fast. Just where do you think you're going in such a hurry?" His speech was slow and slurred, his blue eyes . . . too bright.

"To the beach to cool myself," she said curtly, and yanked her skirt from his grasp.

He leaned back in his chair, a smile curling his mouth. "Lady, if you get any cooler, you're going to turn blue."

With a glare, Alena spun on her heel, then plowed through the café doors and left them flapping on their hinges.

"Hey!" Zach's booming voice came from behind her. She kept walking, but a backward glance placed his head and shoulders above the slatted doors. "Don't go too far. Alena! Do you hear me? And get your tail back here before dark. Sharks move into shallow water when the sun goes down."

Sharks, indeed. Alena picked up her pace, fists swinging at her side. The man was truly quite creative when his noggin was swollen with libation.

After combing the beach for a short time, Alena found a quaint little cove. It was very private, surrounded by a thicket of palms and exotic plants she couldn't identify. She removed her shoes and stockings and cooled her feet in the small pool of water. It was so soothing that she was soon struck with a fancy to submerge herself completely.

She glanced around the secluded cove again. Disrobing would be a very daring thing to do. Mistress Stephens wouldn't at all be pleased to know Alena was even thinking about it. Still, there was something about this place, she decided as she picked up a shell and examined it, that made one impetuous . . . daring. The feeling had claimed her the instant she'd climbed over the freighter's rail.

Alena bit her bottom lip, then smiled. Mistress Stephens wasn't here, was she? Neither was anyone else.

Ignoring the little voices that told her not to, Alena pulled the pins from her hair and shed her clothes quickly before she could change her mind. Clad only in chemise and bloomers, feeling positively wicked and wonderful, she waded in. Cool water crept up her fevered body until it was waist-high. With a quick dip, she dunked entirely under. Unable to hold her breath any longer, she plunged up with a sensation of being baptismally reborn. She swished slowly in a circle, rippling the water into rings around her. Everything was so beautiful here ... so ... exalted. The sea and sky were bluer ... the sun, brighter, hotter ... the lush greenery, greener. Her gaze rose to the patch of sky fringed with feathery foliage above her. Mesmerized, she watched it fade into breathtaking pastels of pink and violet.

Leaves rustled behind her, startling Alena out of her reverie. She swirled about as fast as the water would allow, then ducked neck-high at the sight of Zach. He stood barefoot on the shore, naked from the waist up.

"Ah, there you are. Sorry to spoil your outing, Angelface." His eyes narrowed on a point past her in the open sea. "I think you'd better get out of the water ... *now*, Miss Sutton."

The way he said "now" made her follow his gaze. Looking over her shoulder, she gasped. A cluster of shark fins circled in the water, not thirty yards away!

Fear pushed her at an amazing pace through the resistant water. By the time she reached the sandy shore, she was panting from exertion. Falling to her knees, she pressed a hand to her swiftly beating heart to contain it. As her breathing resumed some semblance of normality, she peered from behind her soggy stands of hair at Zach.

He was grinning like a village idiot. Yet his eyes were narrowed on her with an altogether

different look that made her feel as if she hadn't
a stitch on—

Good Lord. Alena glanced down and felt the
blood leave her face. Her wet, clinging under-
wear left little to the imagination. She dove for
her clothes and attempted to hide behind them,
though that feat, she soon realized, was nigh
impossible.

"It is beyond me, sir," she said indignantly
when Zach made no move to allow her any privacy, "why I continue to give you credit for manners you do not possess." He simply grinned all
the wider, and she closed her eyes a moment,
praying for patience. "I would consider it a
gentleman's courtesy if you would kindly turn
your back."

Zach's grin quirked to one side. "I never
claimed to be a gentleman, you know."

"Oh, I'm quite sure I've misused the term in
your case. Nevertheless, you *will* turn around
... *this instant!*"

"Okay, okay," he said, complying with her
wish. "Jeez almighty, woman, don't work yourself into such a tizzy."

Alena turned as well. She'd donned her petticoat and was fastening her skirt, when a strange
feeling crept up her spine. On impulse, she
peeked over her shoulder.

She shouldn't have been surprised. There he
stood, as big as you please, turned full around,
watching her. "Dr. Summerfield!"

"Ah, Alena," he said, arms widespread.
"Don't you think now that I've seen you in your
unmentionables, you should call me Zach?"

"I should say not!" She jammed her arms into
her blouse and wrapped it tightly across her

front, not having time to button it when he started toward her.

"But why not? Since fate has seen fit to throw us together, don't you think we should be on a little friendlier terms?"

"Under the present circumstances, it would be most improper for me to call you by your first name. And as far as friendliness goes . . . you may be friendly from where you are." His steps slowed to that of a hunter stalking his prey. In a like stance, Alena crouched, ready to retreat.

"There are no rules of etiquette here, Angelface. So what do you say to dispensing with all this pretension?"

Alena backed away, leery of the gleam in his eyes. "You, sir, are talking like a drunken fool."

"Ah, well, a fool I may be, but I'm far from drunk. Just had a nip or two"—he smiled—"for medicinal purposes. I have a bum knee that acts up now and then."

His bad knee didn't seem to stop him from taking a bold step forward, and Alena skittered back.

"Oh, come now, Alena. You like me. I like you—"

"I most certainly do not like you . . . not the way you say it."

He moved steadily closer.

She steadily kept a proper distance between them.

"Of course, you would never say you did," he went on. "But you do. Why don't you just break down and face it? You've had designs on me from the very first day we met."

"Why, of all the gall! You arrogant . . . conceited . . . *ass*—"

"Ooh, *Miss Sutton*, you have no idea what it does to me to hear you talk that way." He lunged forward.

Alena jumped back, and, stumbling over something protruding from the sand, sat smack-dab down in no less than two feet of water. She sat quiet for a moment, recovering from shock, then looked up and saw Zach through a red haze. "You . . . *madman*! You pompous toad! You're mean and hateful and rude and I *despise* you! Do you hear? I *loathe* you." Wishing his head was closer, she whacked the water so hard it sprayed his chest.

"Ah, jeez, Angelface. I'm really sorry. I was just fooling around. I didn't mean . . . here, let me help you up."

Alena sniffed at his pained expression. He wasn't sorry, the big galoot. On an impulse, she grabbed his extended arm and jerked with all her might.

Caught off guard, Zach splashed face-down beside her.

Whatever had possessed her to do such a thing, she would never know. She'd never in her life done anything so malicious. She eyed him askance. Though he would surely be in a dander, she felt absolutely splendid.

Moonbeams danced on the water where he lay sprawled flat. His head slowly lifted, craning like a tortoise. He sputtered, blew water out his mouth, and shook his head.

Despite his probable fury, laughter bubbled inside Alena. It rose to her throat, and once it broke loose, was uncontrollable.

Zach rolled over, sat up, and propped his fore-arms on his knees. Cocking his head her way, he frowned. The more he scowled, the harder she giggled. Finally, his mouth began to quiver and he snickered, chuckled, then burst out laughing.

Their mirth gradually dying down, Zach raked his fingers through his damp hair and glanced at her sideways. "I suppose I deserved that."

"You most certainly did."

He rose from the water and stretched out his hand. "No tricks now," he warned, pulling back a little when she reached out. "I'm ready for you this time."

"A truce, Dr. Summerfield. Shall we have a truce for the time being?"

He nodded in agreement and tugged her to her feet.

When she tried to relinquish her hand, his grip tightened.

"It's an old American custom for a truce between genders to be sealed with a kiss." He pulled her close, his free arm catching her waist and drawing her flat against him.

Alena was aware then that when she'd fallen, her blouse must have gaped open, for only her thin wet camisole separated them. "Dr. Summerfield, I—"

"Zach," he whispered hoarsely. "Call me Zach." His smoky blue eyes illuminated his intention: he lowered his face to hers.

Alena turned, and his soft lips landed on her earlobe. With a maddening slowness, he trailed feather-light kisses down the side of her neck. Her hand relaxed on his chest when his tongue seared across her collarbone. His heartbeat pumping sure and strong beneath her palm provoked her own heart to thunder painfully. She made a feeble attempt to object, but his mouth muffled her words. Tasting of rum, sweet and intoxicating, his warm moist lips moved over hers in a way that made her toes curl into the sand. *This is insanity*, her mind screamed, but when his hips began to move slowly against her, hers followed suit by their own accord.

Gathering the last of her morals, she broke the kiss and flung her head back. "Please . . . please stop . . . stop."

Zach stood rigid, his muscles straining taut against her, his eyes blazing with something she couldn't name. "*You* stop it, dammit. *I* can't. I *can't*, dammit." He devoured her lips once more, daring her to try.

Blame the full moon . . . the heat . . . the sea breeze that rustled the palms . . . or the rush of the incoming tide. But Alena couldn't stop the madness that made her lace her fingers through the wet silky curls at the nape of his neck. Shivers of delight pricked her veins as he teased and tickled the corners of her mouth. A sliver of moonlight couldn't have passed between them. Yet, with a desperate urgency, she wanted him . . . needed him . . . closer.

Slowly, slowly his hands glided up her spine, gently massaging, till they reached her shoulders. He gripped her shoulders loosely, his thumbs circling, caressing, then slipped his fingers under the fabric. She quivered as he touched her bare skin. Deepening the kiss, he grasped her blouse and slid it down her arms, his thumbs sensually brushing the forbidden fullness above her chemise.

Zach whisked her off her feet and Alena heedlessly let the blouse fall to the beach. She could merely stare at him as he carried her with a swift stride toward a nearby cluster of palms. He lowered her tenderly onto sand still warm from the day's sun. The dark sky twinkled with stars, the full moon silhouetted Zach's form and the palm leaves above him. He bent nearer, and, lost in the blue of his eyes, Alena curled her hand around his neck and pulled him to her. His breath came hot and labored against her skin as he whispered endearments between kisses.

She let his hands wander where they would, weaving their magic spell. She knew it was wrong. Yet the sensuality he aroused in her eclipsed everything she'd ever believed in. She knew she shouldn't allow him to tug at the ties of her camisole . . . shouldn't allow him to inch her petticoat higher . . . shouldn't let his hand . . .

As if rendered senseless, she trembled with every touch. A submission too long restrained burned within her. And like the opening of a floodgate, a need burst forth . . . the need to cherish, and be cherished.

The roaring came nearer, grew louder in her ears. Alena felt the sand shift beneath her as Zach molded his body full atop hers. Then, as if from nowhere, a great, frothing wave crashed over them.

Zach grabbed hold of the roots of a palm and caught Alena's wrist to keep her from washing away with the tide. As the mighty wave rolled back to the sea, she jerked free and scrambled to her feet, coughing.

The spell was broken. The magic, gone. Alena hugged her ribs in disbelief at what had almost happened. Positive the hand of God had stopped something that never should have started, she took one look at Zach, and ran. She ran from him. She ran from the shame that was creeping upon her fast. She ran from herself.

She skidded to an abrupt halt just outside the cantina. Music and merriment came from inside, making her self-consciously pluck at her soggy chemise. She couldn't go in there looking like this!

"Alena! You hold up right there, woman! We need to talk."

Jerking around, she saw Zach emerge from the row of palms. Long purposeful steps carried a face scowling blacker than night toward her. The breath caught in her throat. She looked from him to the door and back again. In a state of panic and confusion, she chose the lesser of two evils, and made a dash for the café doors.

Once inside, she quickly folded her arms across her bosom. Then, holding her head high, she swept through the room, completely ignoring the gawking patrons. She wanted to reach out and close Carmelita's mouth as she passed her. However, she merely smiled and said, "Good evening, Carmelita," then took the stairs two at a time.

Zach hit the café doors and left them swinging as he came to a dead standstill just inside the cantina. He narrowed his eyes, watching the door at the top of the stairs slam shut. Damn her. She'd taken him halfway to heaven, then skittered off without a word. *Women!* Who the hell needed them?

Dropping his head, he kneaded the tight muscles in the back of his neck and noticed the music had stopped. He peered under his brows to see everyone in the whole blasted room staring at him.

Zach raised his head slowly, expanded his chest, and squared his shoulders. Not a single soul in the cantina would meet his glare. The guitarist struck up a tune and one by one, the patrons returned to their carousing. Carmelita started forward, but when Zach glowered at her, she veered off in another direction.

"Hussong!" he hollered above the noise as he sauntered over to where Slim sat and took the chair opposite him. "Bring me a bottle!"

Hussong hastily set his best rum in front of Zach and scurried off. Zach popped the cork, took a lethal swallow, then pointed at Slim's wide grin. "Don't you say a damn word."

Slim raised his hands and shook his head, but kept his smile. Leaning back in his chair, he crossed his arms, then propped his boots on the table. He didn't have to ask. The way Zach was hitting that bottle, he'd be spouting off at the mouth any minute. Nope. He didn't figure he'd have long to wait.

"Hell, Slim. I'm not a bad fellow . . . *am I?* I mean, I could have my pick of . . . of a hundred women. Couldn't I?" Zach glanced at Alena's door again and frowned. "Well, almost a hundred. Don't you think?"

"Oh, I'd say at least a hundred, ol' buddy." Slim tugged his Stetson down, watching Zach chug another quarter of the bottle in a single swig.

In deep thought, Zach dragged a knuckle across his mouth. "I tell you, Slim, there's something about *that* woman that makes me sweat. Look at this, Slim." He pointed to the beads of perspiration on his forehead. "I've never sweat over a woman in all my life." Slamming the bottle down on the table, he leaned halfway across the wooden top. "What the hell's wrong with me?"

Slim hid a chuckle behind a cough.

"I mean, hell, Slim, you and I go back a long ways. Be honest with me. Am I losing my touch? I've heard men sometimes do that," he lowered his voice, "when they get on in years." Keeping one eye on the Texan, Zach tipped the bottle again.

Slim shook his head slowly, hard put to keep a straight face. Lowering his gaze to his shot glass, he ran a finger around the edge. "First off, Zach, thirty-five ain't that old—"

"Thirty-six."

"Okay, so you're thirty-six. That ain't that old neither. Only a couple of years older than me. And as you can plain well see, I ain't ready for the old folks' home yet."

Zach's brows drew together in concentration.

"I tell you what I think, and you can take it for what it's worth." Slim stared hard at the amber liquid in his glass, not real sure whether his buddy would swallow what he was fixing to say. He glanced at Zach again, then back at his whiskey, deciding he'd best not look him in the eye when he said it. "Tarnation, Zach, I ain't no romance columnist from back East or nothin', but any fool could see that you and that little gal up there . . . well, hellfire, boy, if I didn't know you better, I'd think you were fallin' head-over-heels—"

A loud thump sloshed whiskey over the rim of Slim's jigger. Slim's head popped up and he automatically went for his gun, but his hand stilled on the ivory handle.

Zach's face lay sideways on the table, his fingers still loosely curled around the empty bottle.

Slim smiled and lifted his glass to his snoozing friend. "Yeah, I know, pard. It's hell, ain't it? You don't need me to tell you that much," he mumbled, then downed his whiskey and winked. "You'll find out on your own soon enough, I reckon."

Chapter 7

Alena drummed her fingertips against the tabletop and nudged her gladstone bag with the toe of her shoe. She'd thought long and hard about what had happened the night before and had decided it was wisest to act as if the incident had never occurred. It didn't matter whether his touch made her tingle all over or not. She simply wouldn't give in to such nonsense again. She wouldn't dwell on it, either, she decided as she watched the ceiling fan go round and round. It was the heat. This awful, unbearable heat was enough to make anyone behave irrationally. That was her excuse. And very probably Dr. Summerfield's, too.

The man's tardiness this morning, however, was inexcusable. Alena lifted the wide brim of her hat a little, looked across the table at Slim, and raised a brow.

Slim squirmed in his chair. "I'm sure he'll be down directly, ma'am," he said, unable to meet her eyes.

"I simply can't understand the delay, Mr. Johnson. He was so insistent about getting an early start."

Slim pushed his hat back on the crown of his head and set his sights on Zach's closed door. "To tell the truth, ma'am, Zach was feelin' a mite under the weather last night when I took—when he went upstairs last night."

"Mmm, I'm sure he was." Alena eyed the Texan suspiciously. "No doubt, ill with ... *inebriation*, perhaps?"

Slim pulled his hat back down and cleared his throat.

"Well, I should think three and a half hours' extra sleep would be enough to cure Dr. Summerfield of his drunken bout." Alena stood, smoothed the waistband of her skirt, and started for the stairway.

Slim bolted upright in his chair. "Ah, ma'am," he said, raising one finger, "I wouldn't do that, if I were you."

"Mr. Johnson," she tossed over her shoulder, continuing up the steps, "we are never going to be on our way if Dr. Summerfield insists on lying about all day."

Upon reaching Zach's door, Alena hesitated only briefly before knocking. There was no reply. She knocked again and was answered by a low muffled groan. The third time, she rapped harder, louder. A growl came from inside the room.

"Dr. Summerfield?" she called, and had started knocking once more when the door creaked open on its own.

Alena looked both ways down the hall, then back at the door. She hadn't planned on it coming open, but it had. And since she was here ... well, *someone* had to awaken him. Lord knew, they needed to be on about their business if she was ever going to find her father.

She pushed the door wider and walked a few steps into the room. He was in bed, his back was to her, a pillow flung over his head. He was covered to his waist with a sheet, yet his lower half was well defined beneath it. She flushed, remembering how those hips had felt against hers, and wondered what she was doing here staring at them now.

The answer to that question brought her round to her purpose. After all, she could hardly place emphasis on modesty after what had passed between them on the beach.

"Dr. Summerfield, we are ready to leave. Please, wake up."

He rolled over on his back, keeping the pillow over his face, but made no sound.

Raising her voice, she tried again. "Dr. Summerfield, you simply must wake up now."

Still, she received no reply.

In a burst of frustration, she crossed the room in swift strides. Jerking the pillow off his head, she bent dangerously close to his ear and shouted, "Dr. Summerfield, wake up!"

Zach sat straight up like a jack-in-the-box, grabbed his head, and groaned. One bloodshot eye opened, then the other. He literally snarled at Alena.

She took a few steps back.

"What . . . the . . . hell?" He grimaced with each word.

Alena clasped her hands against her waist, and lifted her chin. "It is now precisely half past the hour of ten o'clock. I distinctly remember you saying we would leave at dawn. Mr. Johnson and I have been waiting—"

"Miss Sutton, *please*." He covered his eyes,

and laid back on his pillow, massaging his brow. "I know what I said, but as certain excruciating circumstances have it, I am in dire pain here."

"Excruciating circumstances? I believe the excruciating circumstances of which you speak, sir, stem from the plain and simple fact that you and Mr. Johnson indulged in too much drink last evening. Mr. Johnson does not seem to be suffering any ill effects. Mr. Johnson is downstairs at this very moment, packed and ready to go. Mr. Johnson—"

"I DON'T GIVE A HELL-HOOT—" Zach clamped his jaw shut, quivered, and took a deep breath, then continued in a much softer tone. "I could care less *what . . . Mr. Johnson . . .* is doing at the moment." He raised his hand a little and squinted one eye at her. "Now, if you don't mind—"

"Oh, but I *do* mind." She arched a brow. "I must insist you get out of that bed before the day is entirely wasted."

He covered his eyes again and his cheeks tightened. Slowly, his mouth curved into a wicked grin. "So, you insist, do you?"

"I most certainly do."

"And you want me out of bed . . . this very instant?"

"I do."

His hand slid up his forehead and combed back through his dark hair, revealing a twinkle in his eyes. "Very well, Miss Sutton. But, I must warn you, I can't rightly remember whether I left my woolies on last night or not." He sat up on the side of the bed and the covers shifted to expose his naked upper half, two big feet, and hairy calves.

Alena sucked in her breath, whirled, and was out of there in two shakes of a lamb's tail. She paused just outside, placing a hand on her heart. She closed her eyes, calmed herself, then turned and pressed an ear against the door. Hearing him stumble about, she straightened, patted her hair, and smiled. Despite her chagrin, her mission had not been in vain.

Within a half hour Zach emerged onto the balcony. He jammed his hat on and glared like the devil at the two waiting below. "Well? I thought you were both so all-fired ready to leave. What are you just sitting there for? Let's go."

Slim threw his gear over his shoulder and reached for Alena's bag.

"She carries her own, Slim," Zach bellowed.

Slim dropped the bag and stood to his full height, hooking his thumbs in his belt loops. His features lacked their usual easiness as his gaze narrowed on his friend. "Now look here, Zach—"

"It's quite all right, Mr. Johnson," Alena broke in. She glanced from one to the other. "It is very kind of you to offer, but Dr. Summerfield and I have an agreement." She stooped to grasp her bag and came back up with a smile for both of them. "I shall tote my own weight. Shall we go?"

Slim took her elbow and ushered her out, directing a remark about a horse's rear end Zach's way.

Zach rolled his eyes and followed, sincerely wishing he'd stayed in bed.

In the stable behind the cantina, Alena stood face to face with the mule Zach had said she would ride. Offering a few kind words, she stroked the beast's nose in hopes he wouldn't notice her fear of him. Then she moved alongside him to secure her bag on his back as the others were doing. Mistress Stephens' School for Young Ladies had boasted riding lessons, but Alena had never been fond of the sport. To boot, it was beyond her how she was to stay atop this animal without a sidesaddle.

When Zach had readied his own mount, he turned to examine Alena's. From the corner of his eye, he saw her gaze skitter from his hands as he tested the knots. Did he bother her the same way she bothered him? She *had* responded to him on the beach. Lord, she'd felt good in his arms. Better than any woman he'd ever held, so soft and natural, a made-to-order fit. He tugged the rope tighter. But dammit, she wasn't like the others. She wasn't the kind you could kiss good-bye and forget about in the morning. A woman like her deserved a decent proposal from an honest, upstanding man. He wasn't always honest, was far from upstanding, and a nuptial vow was more than he could offer. And to further ponder this line of thought was foolishness, plain and simple. Still, he could at least try to make her understand his actions—not that it mattered if she did . . . He glanced up to make sure Slim was out of earshot, then returned his attention to his task. "About last night—"

"Last night is best forgotten, Dr. Summerfield." Alena focused on the mule's bright blanket. "You were in an inebriated state, and I . . . I was exhausted from the trip and . . . enchanted by the environment." She let her gaze touch him briefly. "I can assure you, I will not allow it to happen again."

It *was* best forgotten, she silently swore. Though, in truth, she wondered if she could ever rid herself of the memory of his body pressed to hers. Could she completely dismiss the way the whole world had ceased to exist when he'd kissed her? She had to try.

Torn between frustration and admiration, Zach contemplated her a moment. Then he caught her waist, swung her up on the mule, and handed her the reins. "Miss Sutton," he said, forcing her to look at him from beneath that god-awful hat, "hold on tight. The hills are fairly steep in places."

The sun blazed down on the trio as their mounts sauntered up the uneven paths of the Venezuelan foothills. Sparse trees and large rocks protruding from the ground dotted the landscape. Alena opened her parasol for shade, but once out of range of the cool sea breeze, the air became still and heavy.

Zach pushed onward at brisk pace. Hours after they'd left the cantina, Alena glanced at the sun and guessed it to be about four o'clock. She shifted her position on the long-eared creature. Had it not been so crass, she would have rubbed her tender backside. Unfastening the top button of her blouse, she chastised herself again for not taking Zach's advice about the corset. She should have at least discarded one of her petticoats.

When they crested the next ridge, inviting shade trees caught her attention. A hushed rush of water grew louder as they neared. Then she saw it. The clear stream loomed before them like an oasis in the desert.

"Dr. Summerfield!"

Without halting his mule, Zach half-turned. He pushed up his hat just enough to show his annoyance and the sun pierced the slits of his eyes like daggers.

"This is such a lovely spot. Couldn't we stop . . . just for a moment?"

"We have a long way to go before sundown, Miss Sutton," he said flatly, and swiveled back around. His temples throbbed. His knee ached. And since he'd had time to think about it, Miss Sutton's casual dismissal of his amorous efforts had progressively demolished his ego.

Alena swatted her mule, moving the beast up even with Zach's mount. "But we've been traveling for quite some time," she persisted.

Zach pulled back on the reins. He angled his head her way and gave her a troubled smile. "This is no picnic, Miss Sutton. We aren't going to stop for crumpets and tea. I told you this wasn't going to be easy. I told you it was no place for the likes of you." He dropped the smile, leaned forward, and narrowed his eyes. "But would you listen? Hell, no, not you. You insisted on coming. Well, you're here now, Angelface. There's no turning back. You're just going to have to live with a little discomfort right along with the rest of us."

Alena matched his sour expression. "Now see here, I do not intend to dawdle. I simply wish to get off this dreadful animal for a moment, splash my face, remount, and be on our way."

"We're not stopping."

"But why?"

"Because I said so." Zach arched a brow, daring her to say another word.

Alena clamped her mouth closed, but looked

him straight in the eye. Then, deliberately defying him, she slid off her mule and headed for the stream.

In a flash, he was behind her. He whirled her around so fast it made her head swim.

"Aw, come on, Zach," Slim broke in, still mounted. "Let her—"

"You stay out of this!" Zach threw him a warning glance, then jerked Alena to him and bent his head so close their noses almost touched. "Get . . . your . . . fanny . . . back . . . on . . . that . . . mule."

Alena shrugged free, but stayed where she was, glaring up at him from under her hat. "Do this! Do that! You have no right to order me about like a galley slave. So far, I have tolerated your profanity, your insults, your foul manners, and . . . your . . . your *molestation*. But I will stand for no further ill treatment! Do I make myself clear?"

"Ill treatment? Hah! What about me? Huh?" He jabbed his finger toward her. "What about me? First you hold your part of the map over my head to bring you here, *assure* me you'll be no bother, and look at this! The first day out, you're nagging. Oh, and don't think I don't know what last night was all about. I wasn't born yesterday. I know when a woman is trying to get on my good side."

Alena's mouth fell open, but he didn't give her time to get a word in edgewise.

"Just let me tell you something, Miss Hoity-toity. From here on, if you want to survive, you'll do as I say. If, and when, I tell you to get off the mule, you'll get your little butt off it. If I tell you to stay on, you had damned well better stay on. Got it? Oh, and don't look so mortified. I hate it when you look at me like that. I hate it when you hack me off like this." His gaze jumped from her wide eyes to the cluster of flowers and bird's nest atop her head. "And I *hate* that damned silly hat!" He jerked the bow loose beneath her chin, swiped off the hat, and sent it sailing into the stream.

Both stock-still, they watched the hat flow rapidly downstream and disappear around the bend.

Alena turned to him slowly, her hands curling into fists.

Zach knew he'd made a big mistake. If the woman's eyes could have shot arrows, he would've been rattling the Pearly Gates at that very moment. He tried his best smile, the one that usually got him out of trouble. "Now, now, Miss Sutton, don't get—"

"You vile, despicable, black-hearted nincompoop!" With every word, she took a step forward, and he moved back. "That . . . hat . . . cost . . . me . . . *three* . . . bloody . . . American . . . dollars."

"Why, Miss Sutton, is that the kind of language they taught you in that fancy girls' school?"

Alena riveted her sight on the oh-so-prized Australian bush hat he wore and swung her doubled fist at the brim as Zach ducked backward.

Missing the hat altogether, she smashed the side of his nose.

Alena clapped her hand over her mouth. Good heavens, was she turning into a barbarian?

"Jeez almighty, Alena," Zach moaned in a nasal tone, covering his injured beak. "I think you broke my blasted nose." Wounded in more ways

than one, he sank down on the grass, tilted his
head back, closed his eyes, and pinched his nostrils to stop the bleeding.

"Oh! Oh, Dr. Summerfield, I'm so sorry,"
Alena said, flustered. She fluttered around him.
"Please, please forgive me. Why, I've never
struck another human being in all my life . . .
unless you count that awful man on the boat,
but that was a matter of life or death. He provoked me. And so did you, only I didn't mean
to actually smite you. Honestly, I didn't. Oh,
dear, you're bleeding. Here, let me help—"

Zach opened one eye to see her hovering
above him, her hand quivering as it moved toward his face. "Woman," he grumbled, "if you
truly want to help, get the hell away from me."

Alena straightened abruptly, clasping her
hands against her waist. "Very well," she said
indignantly. "'Twas your own fault, you know.
You did start the whole affair." In return for his
glare, she gave him a curt smile, then turned on
her heel and headed for the stream.

Observing all from atop his mule, Slim worked
his jaw to keep his amusement in check. "Ah,
Zach?" He fought to hold down a chuckle when
his friend turned an evil eye his way. "Does this
mean we'll be campin' here tonight?"

Zach stood, pulled a handkerchief out of his
pocket, and blew his nose. He stalked toward
his mule. Jerking the ties loose from his bedroll,
he shot a single glance at Slim and frowned. "It's
as good a place as any, isn't it?"

Hussong sat the bottle on the only occupied
table in the cantina and the Englishman sitting
there seized his wrist.

"The freighter in the bay was supposed to dock in Caracas. Do you have any idea why it didn't?"

"*Sí, señor.* The port in Caracas is juzually full this time of month. Often the bigger boats dock here." Hussong dipped his head, trying to get a peek at the stranger, but the man had kept his hat low, his eyes hidden since he'd arrived two hours before.

"I'm looking for an American, a tall fellow with dark hair and blue eyes. He may have been accompanied by a young blonde woman. Have you seen them?"

At the bartender's prolonged silence, the Englishman's grip tightened.

"*Sí!*" Hussong said at last, no longer able to endure the sharp pains shooting up his arm. "They were here. They left this morning."

"In what direction did they go?"

"South, *señor*, toward the mountains."

The man released Hussong, shoving him away.

Hussong rubbed his wrist and started for the bar, despising himself for being such a spineless coward.

"Just a minute."

Hussong halted his retreat.

"There should have been another man, perhaps asking questions, a big brute with a long scar down the right side of his face. He should have left shortly after the American did. Was he also here?"

"No, *señor*, I have not seen such an *hombre*." Hussong watched what he could see of the foreigner's face turn bright red.

"The imbecile," the stranger hissed as he rose and tossed a handful of coins on the table. He grabbed the bottle and headed for the room he'd paid for in advance. Halfway up the stairs, he paused and without looking back, said, "Get me enough supplies and ammunition to last two months and a good sturdy mule. I'll not have a sick one, understand? And be quick about it, good man. I expect to leave within the hour."

Alena hugged her knees and stared into the fire. The ground here in the Venezuelan foothills, she'd decided, was extremely hard. She'd never even stayed up late, much less spent the entire night out in the open. She was finding she didn't care for it overmuch. Insects buzzed about freely. Horribly wretched shrieks leaped forth from the all-too-near distance without warning. At least she'd finally stopped jumping and asking Slim, "What's that?" at every strange sound she heard.

Soon after sundown, Zach had told Slim he'd take first watch and disappeared into the darkness with his rifle. He hadn't spoken to Alena since the accident. Nor did he look at her as they all did their part to prepare camp. She had avoided his path while she gathered fallen branches, but had glanced at him from time to time. The hard set of his mouth had made her suspect his hat-shaded eyes were a stormy blue.

She was more at ease since he'd left camp, yet also felt very safe knowing he wasn't far, knowing he was somewhere outside the warm golden firelight that encircled her.

"You all right, ma'am?" Slim asked, stoking the fire.

"Quite." Alena gave him a smile for his concern, then focused on the tiny orange sparks that drifted upward and vanished.

"Don't pay Zach no mind. He gets like this sometimes." Slim sat down a few feet away and gandered in the direction his friend had gone. "He'll be over it by mornin'. He always feels real remorseful after he blows up like that."

The fire crackled in the silence and the faraway cry of some unknown animal brought Alena's head up. She shivered and hugged her knees tighter. Determined not to allow her fear to get the best of her, she moved a little closer to the golden blaze that lent light to the darkness around them.

"You're good friends, you and he," she stated rather than asked, and laid her face sideways on her knees to observe the Texan.

Slim nudged his hat up and smiled. "Yes, ma'am, I reckon we are." He poked at the fire again with a stick. "Zach was nigh on twelve when his folks bought the broken-down spread that bordered our ranch. Everybody thought they was plum crazy for takin' on the old Miller place. The local saloon took bets on how long it'd take 'em to go runnin' back east. The first day Zach came to school he was wearin' a fancy suit. I made the mistake of commentin' on his purty string tie and he knocked the fire outta me. When the other boys started laughin' at me, he knocked the fire outta them. We became blood brothers shortly after that. Had a ceremony like Injuns and everything. Zach was always readin' about Injuns, and knew just how it was done."

Slim stared into the flickering flames and his smile faded, leaving his face grim. "Zach's ma died less than a year later. His pa was a real adventurer. Came from some wealthy family in New York City that indulged him when he

wanted to go huntin' in Africa and such. He
wasn't around much. When he was at home, he
threw himself into makin' a real showplace outta
their ranch. Reckon he forgot he had a son. Zach
started spendin' more and more time at our
place. I don't know, maybe he and his pa never
really had gotten along before, but after Zach's
ma was gone, puttin' those two together was like
puttin' two bulls in the same pen. The old man
didn't pay Zach no never-mind unless there was
work to do. Then he'd come clamorin' down the
road to our house like Geronimo, looking for
Zach to help with brandin' or the likes." A frown
creased Slim's brow and he tugged his hat down.
"Maybe if his pa would've tried talkin' to Zach
instead of orderin' him around like a ranch hand
things could've been different between them.
Yep, maybe then Zach wouldn't't've acted so
crazy sometimes. Maybe he wouldn't't've taken
off the way he did."

It was hard to imagine Zach as a boy, though
Alena could easily identify with the way he must
have felt. She too had lost a mother; had grown
up without the affection of a father. She knew
that pain well. They were very different, she and
Zach. Or at least she'd always thought so. Yet
visualizing poor Zach's life as a youngster made
her wonder if they didn't share some common
burdens after all.

Slim glanced at her sideways and fidgeted a
little. "You're in good hands with Zach, ma'am.
Regardless of what happened today, he's a worthy companion and I cain't have you thinkin'
otherwise. Beneath that rough crust of his, he's
got a heart o' pure gold. Heck, I know better
than anybody he can be an ornery cuss at times,

and I ain't all that sure he ever outgrew that craziness. He just deals with certain situations in a more unconventional way than most people, I reckon.

"Oh, now, I ain't sayin' he ain't got faults same as the rest of us. He's got plenty. But he's also got somethin' a lot of us don't. Gumption. Yep, Zach's got gumption, all right. Why, a few years back, we was excavatin' a tomb in Egypt when there was this explosion. Zach held up a beam till everyone got out. Risked his life, he did, to go back in and search for the four that were still trapped inside."

"There was an explosion?"

"Yes, ma'am. Best we can figure was that it was set off as a diversion."

"You mean on purpose?"

"Yes, ma'am. See, sometime durin' all the ruckus the main burial room was looted. Funny thing about it was that we'd kept the discovery of that tomb quiet. Nobody even knew the chamber had been opened, except us that were doin' inventory on the contents. Zach had his suspicions, though there was no way of provin' them. There was this fellow we'd hired on, supposedly an expert on Egyption artifacts. Just seemed kinda odd that this fellow, Blythe, disappeared the night before the explosion."

"*Richard* . . . Blythe?"

"You know him?"

"I've made his acquaintance." Alena thought for a moment. "My experience with Mr. Blythe showed him to be nothing but a true gentleman. In my unbiased opinion, he is a man with a great deal of integrity. I cannot imagine him skulking about, setting off explosives. Surely Dr. Summerfield is mistaken."

Slim shrugged. "Maybe so. Zach has been known to go off on a tangent about somethin' and later find out he's been all wrong, but this is sort of a sore spot with him, Miss Sutton. You see, those four men he pulled out were already dead. One of 'em left a wife and three younguns. Zach sends what he can to help out the widow, but he's not gonna rest until he finds out who's responsible. You needn't worry though, he won't act until he's got the evidence he's after."

"And then? Then what will he do?"

Slim ran a hand over his chin. "I can't rightly say, ma'am. But I can tell you it'll be fair and just. When it gets down to it, Zach always comes around to doin' the right thing."

Long after bidding Slim good night, Alena lay awake in her hammock. She stared through the mosquito net at the stars twinkling between the overhead leaves and thought about the many facets of Zachariah Summerfield. She tugged the coarse blanket tighter around her, wishing upon the brightest star that she could recapture her original opinion of him: that he was crude and selfish and thought of no one but himself. Yet his frequent periods of kindness, concern, and sensitivity had already convinced her that wasn't the case.

She didn't want to like him. She didn't want to get too used to having him around only to have him abandon her the way her father had. She didn't particularly relish having to depend on him, yet in her immediate predicament, as uneducated as she was about her present surroundings, she had no choice. She didn't want to admire the dauntless Dr. Summerfield, or his vast knowledge of the wilds.

She did admire him though, and for some inexplicable reason, *that* very revelation frightened her . . . even more so than the howls and screeches that continued throughout the night.

Chapter 8

Alena awakened to the shrill songs of day-break in the wilderness. Bright spots of sunlight danced through the growth above. Nothing seemed real until she heard the clatter of the coffeepot. Yawning, she ducked from under her mosquito net and pushed the curls from her eyes.

"Mornin', ma'am."

"Good morning, Mr. Johnson," she said, and wrapped her hands around the warm tin cup he offered her. She nearly gagged on her first taste of the black brew. How could anything smell so wonderful and taste so bitter? Bracing herself, she took another acrid sip and wished she'd thought to bring tea. "Where is Dr. Summer-field?" she asked, glancing about camp.

"Don't rightly know." Slim doused the fire with the rest of the coffee, then turned, running a hand through his sandy hair. "He was wide awake when I got in from watch this mornin'. Still broodin', I'm afraid. Had a cup of coffee and took off. Said he had somethin' to attend to. I'm sure he'll be back directly."

The thought that Zach might still be angry with

her worried Alena. Was he the kind of man that would plot revenge? Trying not to dwell on it overmuch, she plaited her hair into a long braid, then gathered her things.

"Mr. Johnson, would it be all right if I went to the stream and washed?" she asked as she tied her bedding to the mule. "I promise I shan't be long."

Slim paused from the task of breaking camp, and nudged his hat up. "I don't think it would hurt, ma'am, if you don't wander far. I've still got a few chores to do here. But be careful now, hear? If you need anything, you just holler."

Chirps and chatters broke the stillness of the sunny morning as she wove her way through the trees. She smiled at the colorful birds that jumped from limb to limb, cocking their heads and fussing at her intrusion.

The stream was clear and shallow where she stooped to splash her face. The ice-cold water nearly stole her breath, but left her skin tingling. She'd just dipped her hands into the stream again, when a shadow fell across her and a rippled reflection formed in the water. Her heart jolted, and she came to her feet, pivoting sharply.

"Dr. Summerfield! I—" Commanding her pulse to behave, she dried her hands on her skirt. "I apologize for the delay. I was just—"

"It's all right, Miss Sutton." His tone was civil, almost too polite, his features unreadable. Alena wondered what he was hiding behind his back. Without being too conspicuous, she tried to peer around him, but he turned so she couldn't see. Surely . . . it couldn't be a stick to thrash her with. On second thought, his nose *was* still a tad red. She swallowed nervously. He wouldn't dare do such a thing. Would he?

Zach squinted into the sun. "Looks like it's going to be a real scorcher today." He lowered his gaze to hers. "I did a lot of thinking last night, and . . . well, was that the only hat you had with you?"

Alena eyed him carefully. Dear heaven. He was going to bring the subject up again.

"Well, was it?"

She nodded, bracing herself to run if he started showing signs of having another fit.

He glanced once more at the sun. "A person's brain could fry in heat like this, you know. You'll be needing another hat . . . so . . . so, here."

From behind his back came a battered hat styled like the one he was wearing. Scratched and warped, it looked as if it had been through many adventures, but Alena hardly noticed as she took in the cluster of colorful wildflowers that had been woven into the band.

"I couldn't find a blasted bird's nest," he said, shoving it forward. "I know it's not much, just my old spare, but it's the best I could do under the circumstances."

Alena clutched the simple gift against her breast, feeling somewhat like she'd just been handed the crown jewels. "It's lovely," she whispered. "Thank you."

Zach doffed his hat and fiddled with the brim. He shifted slowly from side to side, looking everywhere but directly at her. "I don't know what got into me yesterday. When you tilted your chin up, that bird's nest started bobbing up and down and . . . well, it just got to me. I guess

I've been a little on edge lately. For one thing, that big lug on the freighter who tried to get the map from you keeps nagging at me. He couldn't have been working alone, which means someone else is probably trailing— That's still no excuse for what I did yesterday." He glanced at her, then made an intent study of his boots. "Jeez, I *deserved* a punch in the nose for doing something like that."

"Oh, dear me, Dr. Summerfield, 'twas all my fault. It is I who should apologize." It was her turn to examine his scuffed boots. "I should have never defied you in the first place. And to further antagonize you by trying to knock off your hat was a dreadful error in judgment on my part. I shouldn't have let my anger—"

"My hat?" Zach's head popped up. "You were aiming for my . . . *hat*?"

"Of course I was. You can't possibly think I truly meant to strike you."

Zach grinned. "In that case, Angelface, it's a good thing you missed. I would've really been put out if you'd hit your target." He started to chuckle, and when the chuckle developed into full-fledged laughter, Alena had no choice but to join him.

The shared bit of humor eased the tension between them and Alena met his bright blue eyes with mirthful tears in her own.

"Tell you what, Angelface," he said with a wink. "I'll buy you a brand-new hat when we get back to the States."

"Oh, no . . . no, I couldn't allow you to—"

"Ah, but I insist. We'll go to the same shop and order another just like the one I . . . er . . . lost."

"No, really, Dr. Summerfield, to be honest, I—" She bit her bottom lip. "Can you keep a secret?"

Zach lifted a brow. "Cross my heart and hope to die," he proclaimed, holding up his right hand.

She stared at the ground for a long moment, then raised her head and frowned exaggeratedly. "In truth, I wasn't that fond of the hat."

Zach looked confused. "Why on earth would you buy something you disliked?"

"Well, I'm not at all proud of the fact, but quite frankly . . . I was bullied into the purchase by the shopkeeper. She assured me all my acquaintances would turn green with envy."

"Why, Miss Sutton. And here I was, all set to believe that someone would have to get up pretty early in the morning to get the best of you." He chucked her chin playfully. "Nevertheless, I owe you. And, as I always pay my debts, you're going to get a new hat . . . preferably one you like."

"Nonsense. This one shall do fine." Alena placed the too-big hat on her head. It plopped down over her eyes and she leaned way back, peeking at him from under the brim. "Quite the rage in the jungle this year. Don't you agree?"

Zach's mouth quirked, and he slid the hat back on the crown of her head. "Maybe it would fit better if you tucked all your hair up under it." His smile dimming slightly, he brushed a stray curl behind her ear and let his fingers linger on the side of her face.

Alena stood motionless, watching his lids lower a little and his eyes darken with the same expression he had worn when he'd embraced her on the beach. In spite of her resolution not to get involved with the man, her heart began to pitter-patter like a toy drum. One side of her brain was whispering, *No . . . no . . . I mustn't let him affect me this way,* the other side was pleading, *Kiss me, kiss me . . . I shan't resist this time if you do.*

"Are you two about through there?" Alena and Zach both turned to see Slim standing against the line of trees, his thumbs hooked in his belt loops. "Daylight's burnin', you know," he shouted.

As they approached him, his face stretched into a wide grin. "Nice hat, ma'am," he said, tipping his own.

"Why, thank you, Mr. Johnson." Alena tossed a shy smile over her shoulder at Zach, then started toward camp.

Slim squinted, sniffing the air as Zach passed him. "Gosh-dang, Zach, you sure do smell good."

Giving him a mind-your-own-business glare, Zach headed down the trail.

In deep thought, Slim scratched his ear for a moment, then grinned all the wider as he turned to follow.

"Hang on, Angelface. There's another steep one coming up."

Alena glanced over her shoulder at Zach, then followed his nod toward the hill ahead. Once again, she clung to the mule's neck to keep from sliding off as the poor animal scaled the rocky trail. The higher they climbed into the mountainous region, the closer together the trees grew, the thicker the foliage became.

Never in her life had a mere morning seemed so long. With each passing day, however, her riding had improved, along with the condition of her backside. Now it was only the prickly heat beneath her corset that tortured her. Just thinking of it made her ribs itch again. She knew she was being obstinate. But just because she was in an uncivilized country was certainly no excuse to act uncivilized. Though she'd given in to retiring all but one of her petticoats, by heavens she'd keep her corset, heat rash or not. It was, after all, her last vestige of decorum.

By the time they reached the highland plateau, after several spells of dizziness and nausea, she'd had to remind herself that, despite the elements, she was still a lady.

"*Ahheee!*" The cry came from the right as they crested the ridge. A boy, who appeared to be no more than eight, waved his arms, and barreled toward them.

Zach dismounted and caught the boy, swinging him around once before he set him down and ruffled his midnight-black hair. "Armando! *Buenas tardes*, my friend. Why, you've grown so much, I can hardly lift you."

"*Sí*," the boy agreed, tucking his thumbs under his arms. "Armando is almost a man now."

The corners of Zach's mouth quivered, but he maintained a serious expression. "It sure looks that way to me, pardner. Say, I'd like you to meet my friends here. This is Miss Sutton and this is Slim."

Armando gave them each a shy nod, then cocked his head up at Zach and squinted. "You bring me something, no, Dr. Zach?"

"Hmm, well, I don't know. Let me see what

I can find." Zach winked at Alena as he began to search his duffel bag. "Your *madre* and *padre*, are they well?"

"*Sí*," Armando said absently, more occupied with trying to peek into the bag.

"Wait a minute, what's this?" Zach pulled out a white wrapped bundle and held it up to his nose. "Hmm, smells like licorice. Now I wonder how that could have gotten in there. I don't even like licorice, do you?"

The boy's black eyes twinkled and he grinned as if he'd played this game before. "*Sí*, you know Armando likes leecorice."

"Well then," Zach said, handing over the treat, "I guess you better take it. I have no use for it."

Armando had the wrapper ripped open and a licorice stick hanging out the corner of his mouth before he could say, "*Muchas gracias*, Dr. Zach."

"You can thank me, young man, by saving a piece for your brothers and sisters." Zach turned, smiling, and helped Alena down. "From here on," he told her, "we'll travel by foot. Armando has come to take the mules. His family will care for them until we return."

When they'd unpacked the beasts, Zach handed the boy the reins. "You'll take good care of my mules?"

"*Sí*, Dr. Zach."

"Tell your *madre* and *padre* hello for me, will you?" Armando nodded, then started up the hill, pulling the tenacious animals behind. Just before he disappeared over the ridge, Zach cupped his hands around his mouth and shouted, "Don't forget to share that licorice, you hear?"

In the few hours it took to cross the increas-

ingly wooded plateau, Alena actually missed the
mule. Her feet ached clear up to her back. Yet
she'd not give in to the pain. She assured herself
that, just as she'd gotten used to the mule, she'd
adapt to trodding the bumpy trail. Strengthened
by that firm resolution, she set her sights ahead
on the sea of vegetation that seemed to multiply
by the thousands and diminished the path.

She felt a mixture of excitement and apprehension as they entered the jungle. The thought
that they were that much closer to finding her
father made her wonder again whether he would
be receptive to her or not. Repositioning her bag
over her shoulder, she registered the change in
the terrain. It appeared the tropical shrubbery
had suddenly moved in on them instead of the
other way around. Green canopies loomed overhead, allowing only occasional shafts of sunlight
to fall to earth. Alena glanced up at the chattering
monkeys that rustled the extremely tall trees.
The little clowns didn't worry her overmuch.
However, the unidentifiable hoots and hisses
that infested the area had her throwing glances
over her shoulder to make sure Zach was still
there.

He was. Rifle at the ready, he apparently concentrated on every movement, every noise that
came too near. His presence bolstered Alena's
courage when their route narrowed even more,
and she had to shove low-hanging vines, fronds,
and broad-leafed plants from her way to pass.

"Hold up." Zach caught her shoulder and
moved her behind him. Alena looked around for
signs of trouble. "Don't worry," he said with a
quick reassuring smile. "We only need to clear
a trail here. Just stand back."

Alena watched him draw a long, wide knife from a sheath on his belt. He and Slim hacked through the overgrown brush for nearly an hour. As the last of the thick hedge fell away, bits of sky appeared and they found themselves standing on the edge of a deep, wide ravine, high above a river. At such heights, the clouds gave the illusion of looking through a white veil. For as far as the eye could see, every imaginable shade of green carpeted the land beyond.

There, upon the cliff, a panoramic view of the emerald valley bewitched them all. The three stood in silent reverence. It was as if they had broken through into another time, into some celestial sphere . . . a place where heaven met the earth.

Though Zach had seen—or, rather, experienced—the overwhelming power of the jungle and stood on the sacred ground of such mystical places before, he had never ceased to be awed by the sensation. As far as he was concerned, this, along with every other exotic region of the world, was Eden. An ageless empire unscathed by civilization. Solitude. Serenity. A province unto itself, far removed from the hustle and bustle of society, rules, and government.

In every jungle Zach had encountered, there had always been a certain hidden spot that held this particular ambience, evoked the feeling that you'd been somehow exalted and were as close as a mere mortal could get to the King of Creation. He had that notion now. He knew Slim felt it, too. They'd discussed the effect of these special places many times. Did Alena feel it?

Zach turned his head to check the schoolmarm's reaction and his heart stopped for several beats. At that moment in time, Alena Sutton was an ethereal vision one saw only in dreams.

Entranced by the scenery, she stood completely still, enveloped in a cloudy vapor, her hat clutched to her breast. Wild ferns and lush greenery surrounded her, and a ray of sunshine fell behind her head, lighting her golden hair with a hazy glow. Zach had often likened her to an angel, but he'd never been so sure such heavenly creatures truly existed . . . until now.

As he stared at Alena's haloed form, reality slipped away. In his fantasy, this was Eden—God's mythical Garden. And she . . . was the guardian of the garden. The corners of Zach's mouth tipped upward slightly. She was Eden's Angel.

Alena stepped forward out of the stream of light, breaking the spell. She looked at Zach abruptly and smiled. "I've never seen anything so beautiful," she said. "It is truly"—she took a deep breath, then half-laughed—"magnificent. Isn't it?"

Zach blinked. He glanced toward the valley again and nodded. "Magnificent," he whispered, then looked back at her. "So magnificent it belies real life."

He was staring at Alena with such a peculiar gleam in his eyes that gooseflesh rose on her arms. As she opened her mouth to question him about his odd statement, he turned to Slim.

"Okay, pard, this is your territory," he said, gesturing to the deep ravine. "I'd gauge the river to be about sixty yards wide. Where do we cross?"

"Well, we got two choices." Slim removed his hat and wiped his forehead. "If I've guessed right about where we are, to the east here, oh, I'd say no more than a mile, there's a bridge. No telling what kind of condition it's in now, though. The last time I was here it was passable . . . but just barely." Setting his hat back on his head, he narrowed his gaze on the western horizon and nodded in that direction. "Or we could go this way but it would be about nine or ten miles till we got to a point where we could cross the river."

Zach's gaze roved over Alena. "How long would that take us out of our way? Two, maybe three days?"

Alena eased between them before Slim could answer. "May I be allowed an opinion?"

Zach looked from her to Slim and back again. "Of course."

"We can't afford a three-day delay. I say we try to cross the bridge. If Mr. Johnson says it's passable—"

"Now hold up, little lady, I said it *was* passable. That doesn't mean it is now. Zach, what do you think?"

Zach ran a hand over the nape of his neck. "Excuse us a moment, Angelface." He turned Slim around and moved him a few feet away. "I've seen how she is when she doesn't get her way," he whispered. "I think I'd just as soon take my chances on an old bridge as have her nag us to death for nine miles."

Alena was rather pleased with the decision. That is, until she spied the so-called bridge. The nearer they came, the worse it looked. It was more what she'd call a catwalk. Suspended by frayed ropes that spanned the canyon, half the planks were missing. The ones that remained appeared worm-eaten and rotted. What must have been, at the very least, a century's growth of vines entwined the rope handrail. She doubted if a dormouse could make it across the dilapidated thing.

"Well, it doesn't look any worse for wear than it did a few years back," Slim commented, running a hand over his chin. "I wouldn't count on it supportin' all three of us at once though. I'll go first."

Alena made the sign of the cross as he stepped onto the bridge. The unstable contraption creaked and groaned beneath him. Every few steps, a slat would give way, and everyone would freeze, watching it fall for a full minute till it hit the raging water below. Then Slim would ease onward.

When at last he reached the other side he turned with a wide grin. "I reckon it's safe enough," he hollered, waving his hat. "Just take 'er nice and easy, and watch your step."

Alena moved into position. Peering over the edge, her vision doubled and the view of the turbulent river below swirled. She felt herself go pale and closed her eyes. "Dr. Summerfield, I . . . I *can't* do this."

Zach caught her from behind, massaging her shoulders. His thumbs gently rubbed the tendons in her neck. "Sure you can, Angelface. It's just a case of the willies. Everybody gets them. Look, you're not alone in your fear. Don't you think Slim was scared senseless a few minutes ago? And hell, I'll be trembling when it comes my turn. Jeez almighty, I hate heights. But there comes a time in all our lives when we have to do something we're terrified of. It's good for the circulation."

His attempted humor failing, he planted a light kiss atop her head. "I can't go with you. The bridge won't hold us both. But I can tell you how it's done. Come on, take a couple of deep breaths. There, that's better, isn't it? Now, whatever you do, don't look down. Go slow and test each board with your foot before you put your full weight on it. Understand? You can do it, Angelface. I know you can."

Alena nodded, inhaling and exhaling at long intervals. She was here to find her father. She'd accepted the fact, before she'd left Philadelphia, that there could be perils along the way. *Coward*, a little voice inside her shouted, nagging her into calling forth all the determination she had in reserve. She squared her shoulders. She would cross the blooming bridge, by heaven . . . if it was bloody well the last thing she did.

Starting forward at a snail's pace, she repeated, *I can do this, I can do this*, over and over in her head. She gripped the wobbly rail and moved mechanically. She kept her eyes straight ahead, focusing on Slim, whose diminished size made her ever aware of how far away he was. Her heart battered itself against her sternum like a bird in a box as she inched onward and carefully tested each subsequent step with her toe.

Zach was experiencing a strange sense of pride while he watched her press on. He'd thought this might be her breaking point. His worry had been a little premature, he now decided. She was doing fine. Actually, she was displaying a lot more bravado than he had the first time he'd found himself in a similar predicament. She was almost halfway across when his gaze shifted to a certain spot on the rail as her hand left it—and he choked.

The rope was unraveling!

"Sweet Jesus in heaven," he murmured, as close to a prayer as he had come in years. He took a step forward, then stopped dead in his tracks. Damn his size! The bridge couldn't take his weight. Helplessly, he focused on Alena's straight, stiff back. Maybe it would hold until she could make—

The sound of a snap ended the thought.

All hell broke loose. The bridge slanted, and Alena's scream tore through Zach. She clung to the vines. Birds scattered from the trees. Monkeys shrieked, hysterically hopping from limb to limb.

The remaining handrail began to unravel.

Zach didn't think. He reacted.

Running onto the bridge, he leaped, seconds before it gave way under his feet and separated in two. He landed at the end of the break, trapping Alena's lower half beneath him. Flattened against the rotted floor, they were suspended in midair for an eternity. Alena's wail echoed into the canyon, vibrating through Zach's whole being as they swooshed toward the cliff in a span of time that seemed like forever. Zach's voice being lost somewhere in his throat, Alena screamed for both of them.

At long last, the upper part of the bridge crashed into a huge boulder that jutted out from the side of the ravine. Like the end of a whip, the lower half jolted violently from the impact. Zach braced himself against Alena, holding on to the weak boards with every ounce of strength he owned.

He didn't know how long after the bridge had slowed to a dangle that he half-came to his senses. But even for a while afterwards, he stayed motionless while bits of debris drizzled down on them. He listened to the fragile ropes strain and groan, waiting for them to settle . . . wondering if they would hold. He could hear Slim hollering, but couldn't find the energy to answer.

He eased his eyes open only long enough to glimpse the alligator-infested water and jagged rocks far, far below, then squeezed them shut again.

Jeez almighty, I hate heights.

Iridescent spots danced beneath his closed lids. Nausea gripped him. Beads of sweat popped out on his forehead. The rope groaned again, and he cringed, feeling the veins in his hands start to constrict. He was slipping . . .

"Zachariah! For God's sake," came his father's voice from somewhere beyond the whispering winds, "*get a hold on yourself, boy!*"

Zach's eyes flew open. His head was resting against something soft and round. His breath came out in a gush, then he tightened his grip, and ordered his limbs to stop shaking. When they obeyed, he realized the softness beneath his cheek still quivered. All at once, it registered that the soft round something was Alena's bottom. She was murmuring. He strained his ears.

"Hail Mary, full of grace, blessed are thou amongst women. Blessed is the fruit . . ."

"Alena?"

"Holy Mary, mother of God, pray for us sinners . . ."

"Alena, answer me! Are you hurt?" He nudged her with his shoulder and the praying stopped. "You okay?"

"No." The word was little more than a whisper.

"No, you're not hurt or no, you're not okay?"

"*No* . . . I'm *not* hurt . . . and no . . . I'm *not* okay. I'm near heart failure."

"Alena, listen to me—"

"I listened to you before and look where it got me."

"Dammit, woman, this is neither the time nor place to be contrary! We're going to have to climb up." Gathering his patience, he smoothed his voice. "Do you think you can do that?"

"I don't know. I don't think I can let go of the rope."

"Alena, you have to try. Here, I'll help." She let out a squeak as he hoisted her up on his shoulder. "You pull, I'll push."

Swallowing hard, she collected the courage to pry the fingers of one hand open. She stretched up and quickly clasped the rope above her. A pumping, a pounding, in her veins overtook her as she climbed the swaying remnants of the bridge. She did not question the propriety of Zach's hand spanning her backside to boost her when she faltered. When her palms began to throb from rawness and splinters, she blocked the pain. The same self-preservation that had guarded her heart all these years pushed her onward . . . upward . . . toward the sweet promise of solid ground.

The first glimpse of Slim's face peering over the edge was like seeing a lone, shining star on the darkest night. It prompted Alena to move faster than she'd ever thought possible. It was a blessed relief when he caught her arm.

Panting, she hugged the earth, before turning to aid Slim with Zach's ascent.

But in that moment, the joy of her deliverance shattered.

One side of the bridge gave way, and Zach lost his footing. Alena lunged for him, but Slim stopped her just short of flying off the cliff herself. "Zach!" she screamed. She struggled in Slim's arms as, helpless to do otherwise, they watched Zach's timeless spiral downward. He made wild grabs at scrub brush and the remains of the bridge. Alena's hope rose when he caught hold of a root that jutted out from the canyon wall, but it broke off in his hand. Even knowing it was futile, she reached out to him as he slipped from sight and vanished below the overhang.

Alena crumpled to her knees. "Zach," she whispered. "Oh, Zach, no. Please, God . . . no."

Slim knelt beside her and laid his arm across her shoulders. She hugged her ribs, occasionally swiping at the rush of tears that streamed down her face. She thought of every hateful thing she'd ever said to Zachariah and wished she could take them all back. She wished a thousand times she hadn't bound herself by her conviction not to get too close to others. She ached with a sense of loss that she hadn't taken the chance to know him better. In between her self-inflicted chastising, she prayed. She prayed harder than she'd ever prayed before for divine intervention—for God to somehow turn back time and save Zach.

Neither Slim nor Alena could have said how long they sat there in silent mourning and stared at the edge of the ravine as if they expected a miracle. But when the crown of that Australian bush hat appeared above the ledge, they both would have sworn that's exactly what it was. A miracle.

Each grabbed an arm, and tugged Zach up. He came lamely to his feet. Half-laughing, half-crying, Alena threw her arms around him and showered his face with kisses.

Zach winced when she squeezed his battered body. Hell, he hurt in places he hadn't known he had. "Jeez, woman, you're killing me," he said. Prying her off, he set her an arm's length away.

Alena fell solemn and wrung her hands. She'd been so ecstatic to see him alive, the fact that he must be injured had simply passed her by. Biting her bottom lip, she surveyed the damage. He was ghostly white, severely bruised and scraped. She sucked in her breath at the sight of blood seeping through his pant leg just above the left knee. Truly worried now, she met his gaze . . . surprised to see he wore that familiar cocky smile, the very one that generally ended up infuriating her.

"Why, Miss Sutton, you do care." He made his eyebrows jump, and nodded his head knowingly. "I knew it all along. You're smack-dab crazy about me, right?"

"I most certainly am not, you arrogant fool." Alena stiffened her back, and despite the pain, balled her hands into fists at her side. "I fear, sir, you must have hit your head when you fell."

"Oh, yeah, Miss-holier-than-thou?" He took a step forward and his face came down a whisper away from hers. "Well, just what was all that about? Huh? All that hugging and kissing, huh?"

His blue eyes peered into her soul. She felt cold and hot at the same time. Her head swirled and tiny white sparks blocked him from view.

Then everything went black.

"Alena?" Someone patted her wrist. Her eyes fluttered open, closed again, then she fixed a

blurred gaze on Zach's face. It registered somewhere in her fuzzy brain that she was lying on
the ground as he knelt over her.

"Hey, Angelface, you okay?" he asked, brushing the hair from her forehead. "Look, I didn't
mean all that. I was just horsing around. I—"

Her fingertips stopped his lips, and moved to
the purple swelling on his cheekbone. "You need
tending," she said, quietly.

He captured her hand, and when she winced,
turned it palm up and grimaced. "It's you who
needs tending. Lord, woman," he said, examining the other one, "your hands are torn to
shreds. We need to get something on them.
There's a plant that grows around here that will
cure—"

"I'll be fine. Your wounds are much worse and
should be cared for before infection sets in." She
raised herself to her elbows. "I do know a few
medicinal remedies. Please allow me—"

"Not on your life, Angelface. I can tend my
own wounds. They're not all that bad. Not a
single broken bone, thank God." He rolled his
shoulder. "I'm just going to be sore as the dick-
ens for a while." Giving her a wink, he slid his
hand behind her. "Now, let's just get you over
there in the shade where you can rest."

"Really, Dr. Summerfield, I'm quite capable of
managing on my own now, I assure you." She
started to rise to prove it.

"Wait a minute." His hands roved over her
back in a too-familiar fashion. *"What* is *this?"*

Alena had had enough of his nonsense for one
day. She wrestled away from him as they came
to their feet. Wearing the most awful scowl, he
reached out, caught her waist, and boldly ran
his thumbs over her ribs.

"Now, see here," she snapped, prying at his grip. "You stop that this instant!"

"Aha! Just as I thought!" He turned her loose, lowered his brows, and accusingly pointed at her torso. "You're still wearing that damned corset."

Alena lifted her chin. "That, sir, is hardly your concern."

He thrust his nose so close to hers she could see herself reflected in his eyes. His tense jaw jutted forward. "It damn sure is my concern! That blasted thing is more than likely the reason you just fainted. I can't have you passing out all over the jungle. It's entirely too hot here to wear one of those contraptions." Narrowing his eyes to slits, he added, "And you're going to march right over there behind those bushes and take it off . . . right now."

She set her jaw just as hard as he had his. "I most certainly will not."

"You will."

"I . . . will . . . not!"

"You will so." He smiled, but it wasn't a nice smile. "Or else . . . I will take the utmost pleasure in removing it for you. Got it?"

Alena glared at him for a mere moment. He meant it, every word. She could see in his eyes that he had every intention of doing exactly what he'd said he would. Perhaps he *had* hit his head. Was her corset worth testing a madman?

She thought not. "You'll turn around now, sir, or I shan't take a single step toward those bushes."

When he did, she performed yet another discourtesy that she'd never in her life considered before. She stuck her tongue out at those broad shoulders of Zach's. Then she turned on her heel, and with no small satisfaction, headed for the cover of shrubs.

Zach had insisted on no more than a night's rest following the ordeal at the old bridge. Alena was amazed that he had apparently recovered so quickly. When she'd mentioned it, he'd merely smiled and told her he mended fast. Even so, the deeper they'd moved into the jungle, the slicker the uneven moss-covered trails had become, and she'd noted that he limped. To accommodate the muddy path he'd taken to using a stick for support.

True to his word, he had produced the healing plant for her hands. A poultice made from the leaves had miraculously cured them, and within three days' time, she was more than ready to take her turn preparing the evening meal.

"What? Beans again?" Zach leaned over her shoulder and sniffed. "How about steak and fried potatoes tonight? And whip up an apple pie, too, okay?"

Alena gave him an annoyed look.

He held up his hands. "Just kidding," he said and backed off, settling himself comfortably on the ground nearby.

She added bits of dried beef, stirred the beans once more, then hung the ladle on the side of the pot. Bone-weary, she settled down on a large flat rock to relax while the pot came to a boil.

Her gaze shifting to her mud-caked skirt, she sighed. Ruined. Trudging over the muck that oozed along the trails had ruined it beyond repair. Not only that, the dried mud clinging to the hem hampered her movements. With the added weight and increasing heat, by tomorrow she'd probably not be able to walk at all.

There was only one thing to do, though propriety felt obliged to protest. She gazed up at the tiny pieces of faded sky peeking through the leaves. *Dear Father in heaven, wasn't removing my corset enough? Must I be faced with yet another decision that goes against my standards?*

She looked at her skirt once more and grimaced. Things were different here. Actions that would have been totally unacceptable among civilization were unquestioned here. She was only just beginning to understand that sometimes, they were even necessary for survival in this wild untamed land. Again, she observed the mud clumped on her skirt, but this time her mind was firmly made up. One must do what one must do.

"Dr. Summerfield, may I borrow your knife, please?"

Zach stopped whittling, and looked up with pinched brows. "My . . . what?"

"Your knife, may I borrow it?"

Hesitantly, he handed it to her, handle first. She jerked it from him so fast he flinched as the blade left his fingers. "Jeez, woman, be careful! That thing is sharp!"

"Good," she replied, then began to hack at the bottom of her skirt, patently ignoring his astonishment.

Zach wasn't just astonished. He was awestruck as he sat there in disbelief, witnessing this once-in-a-lifetime event. Heck, she was chopping that thing off mid-calf . . . all the way to the top of her boots.

She returned the knife, stood up square-shouldered, and smoothed her waistband. "Thank you," she said, dusting her hands together. Then, of all things, she pushed her sleeves right up, mind you, to her elbows, and went to tend the boiling pot.

Realizing his chin nearly touched his chest, he closed his mouth, and settled back to take up where he'd left off. Hard put to concentrate on his whittling, his gaze strayed again and again to where she stooped over the bean pot. Bathed in the golden glow of the campfire, she wiped her brow, and nonchalantly reached down and unfastened the third button of her blouse.

Zach tossed the stick over his shoulder, sheathed his knife, and stretched out on his side. The *third* button, Lord almighty. Propped on his elbow, head in hand, he stared at the hollow of her throat, remembering the soft feel of her. As bold as spiked punch, he watched the perspiration trickle down her front and dampen her blouse. He knew it seeped between full ripe breasts that by all rights should have belonged to a dance-hall girl. It was beyond him why the Creator would have bestowed such a gift on a woman that didn't want the world to know she had a bosom.

He had to admire her for one thing though. She had stamina. Since they'd left the ravine, their journey hadn't been easy. But she hadn't once complained, not even when she'd slipped or stumbled. It was hard to believe this was the same prim lady he'd met in his uncle's office.

She was wearing her hair down again this evening. He'd taken to watching her brush out that long, silky mane at the end of each day. The ritual never failed to spur a memory of how soft it was to the touch.

Alena tucked a curl behind her ear and looked up at him. Zach averted his gaze till she started stirring the beans again, then watched the slight movement of her hips that the task evoked.

How was it she attracted him in those mud-clad clothes? Hell, she even looked good in his old, oversized hat. Beneath her ragtag appearance, of course, she was still a decent woman.

Decent women. He'd always taken great pains to steer clear of them. He'd never even cast a second glance at a one before. Heck, if you took up with a decent woman, the next thing you'd know, they'd have you all spruced up, sitting in the parlor, skeining their knitting yarn. No sirree, thank you. Give him a painted lady any day. They were safe.

That thought rolled him onto his back and he jerked his hat over his eyes to keep them from wandering her way. Dammit, he had no business thinking of her like that, anyway. Nothing could ever become of this attraction. Her rigid standards wouldn't allow her to submit to him without the exchange of vows. And that, by George, was out of the question. He liked his life the way it was. No complications, no commitments. He'd been very careful over the years to avoid any attachments. He liked not having to answer to anyone, not worrying about hurting anyone. He liked being able to come and go as he—

"Dr. Summerfield, supper's ready. Should I call for Mr. Johnson?"

"Hmm?" Zach nudged his hat up. "Ah, no . . . no. He'll be coming in soon. It's almost time for me to take watch." He sat up and took the bowl she offered. When she settled down beside him, he looked at her askance, wishing she'd sit somewhere else.

"I couldn't help but notice . . . you've been limping," she said quietly. She kept her eyes on the spoonful of beans she'd lifted from her bowl. "Are you still in pain?"

Zach rubbed his thigh above his knee. "Nah, it'll heal soon. How about you? Have you recovered from your near heart failure?"

She met his gaze, smiling. "I was cured the moment I felt solid ground beneath my feet."

"Oh, come now, Angelface, look me straight in the eye and tell me you didn't find the whole thing exhilarating."

Alena almost choked on her mouthful. "*Exhilarating?* Why, we very nearly lost our lives."

"Yes, but couldn't you just feel the blood pumping through your veins . . . the old heart pounding? Haven't you ever been to the circus and wondered what it was like to swing from the flying trapeze?"

Alena set her bowl in her lap and looked at him with amazement. "Flying trapeze, indeed." She tucked in her chin and lowered her brows. "My heart was pounding all right, but certainly not from exhilaration. From sheer terror, I daresay."

"It's almost the same thing, Angelface. Either way, it sure makes you thankful you're alive, doesn't it?"

He stood, and Alena tilted her head back, captured by his gaze.

"I mean, it makes you—" Zach's attention fell to the gap of that third undone button. He took in the voluptuous view this angle provided and swallowed hard.

"It makes you what, Dr. Summerfield?"

Turning abruptly, he tugged his hat down. "Nothing," he snapped, then cupped his mouth and yelled into the darkness, "Slim! Come on in. I'll take over now."

Chapter 9

The downpour came without warning. Gushing like a river from the sky, it flattened Alena's hat against her head and streamed down her face. She could hardly see Slim moving along the trail in front of her. Yet instead of feeling vexed, she considered the cool shower a godsend.

The gully-washer stopped with the same abruptness that it had begun. In the aftermath of the blessed rain, hot steam rose from the jungle floor, making it hard to breathe. Further hindered by the weight of her drenched clothes and the sludge tugging at her boots, Alena's stride slowed, as did her companions'.

Her arm started to cramp and she shifted her bundle to the other hand. She wasn't a bit sorry now that she'd shed her corset and petticoats and altered her skirt. She couldn't imagine being any more miserable than she already was. Perspiration stung her eyes. The rain had stirred up a dreadful swarm of mosquitoes and, finding it impossible to swat them all, she gave up trying. Her entire body ached and she was so bloody tired she feared she might fall face-down in the mud.

The sole thing that kept her on her feet was the hope of finding her father. Though her resolve was growing weaker by the moment, she held that purpose firmly in her mind as she trudged onward.

"Hold it, Slim!" Zach called out from the rear guard.

Alena froze, and so did the Texan. If she'd learned anything about this desolate land, it was when someone said "Hold it" you didn't so much as wiggle a toe. Zach had stopped her only the day before from stepping on a deadly snake that had slithered onto the path.

Slowly, cautiously, she and Slim looked over their shoulders. Zach had his back to them and scanned the trail behind. He held up a hand, signaling them to be still and quiet. The hum of the jungle grew louder in the silence.

"What is it, Zach?" Slim finally asked in a low voice.

Zach shrugged. "Probably nothing. But I just can't shake the feeling someone's been tracking us all day." He turned around with a pensive expression.

"Those feelin's you get ain't usually nothin', Zach. They've saved our tails more 'n once. Besides, I've kinda had the same notions myself today." Slim frowned, surveying the thick vegetation through the fog that surrounded them. "I reckon we'll all rest a whole lot easier if I double back and check it out. I'll catch up with y'all when you stop t' break for camp."

Slim sloshed around Alena, but Zach caught the Texan's shoulder as he started past him. "Slim . . . be careful."

Slim smiled and patted his gun. "You can bet

on it, pard," he said, then disappeared into a cloud of steam.

Less than an hour after Slim's departure, Alena and Zach had climbed to higher, drier ground. Near twilight, they made camp in a small clearing.

Afterwards, Zach sat on his haunches and stared unseeingly into the fire, absently snapping twigs in two. Every so often, his head jerked toward the bush. His eyes would narrow while he made an intense inspection of the tropical shrubbery surrounding camp, then he'd look back to the fire and start his brooding ritual all over again.

"Who do you think it is?" Alena asked as she busied herself with unnecessary chores.

"Hmm?" Zach answered, still lost in his thoughts.

Alena halted the task of shaking out her blanket. "Who," she inquired again, this time in a louder voice, "do you suppose is following us?"

Zach met her gaze, pressed his lips into a tight line, and shook his head slowly. "Could be anyone, Angel. Howie talked a lot when he'd been drinking."

Sighing deeply, Alena settled on the ground beside him. "Yes, I suppose it could be anyone," she commented, looking at him, her head tilted. "However, you think you know who it is. Don't you?"

Zach gave her a one-sided smile. "You're starting to read me pretty well, aren't you, Angelface?"

"Come now, Dr. Summerfield, do stop trying to change the subject. Give over." Alena moved a little closer. "Who do you think it is?"

"Well, for one, Blythe is very high on my list of suspects. He was snooping around for information in Philadelphia." Zach tossed a stick into the fire. "Then there was that creepy little guy that claimed to be with the British Museum of Antiquities. That Flemmers, or Fielding, or whatever his name—"

"Flemming," Alena supplied. "Nigel Flemming. I remember the name because a Miss Flemming was employed to take over my teaching post until I return."

Zach lifted a brow, his expression plainly implying there could be a connection between the two Flemmings.

"Oh, I'm sure it's simply a coincidence." Alena was thoughtful a moment. "I'm positive it is. And you're wrong about Mr. Blythe, too. He didn't ask at all about the map when next I saw him."

"What?" Zach looked at her as if she'd just committed some heinous crime. "I thought I told you to stay away from him. Alena, he's a swindler if I ever saw one."

"He is not," she said, tipping her chin. "He's a dealer of antiques and rare objects. We merely happened across each other while I was finishing up my purchases for the journey here. Being the gentleman he is, he escorted me to the steps of my hotel. And he didn't broach the subject of the map even once. God's truth."

Zach twisted his mouth into a sarcastic grin. "Yeah, well, your nice Mr. Blythe had probably already gotten all the information he needed elsewhere. Regardless of whether you and old Richard-boy exchanged pleasantries in Philadelphia or not, I still say he's a weasel that can't be trusted. As for Nigel Flemming, I've never heard of him, and I've had plenty of dealings with the British Museum of Antiquities over the past several years. Don't you think it's kind of funny that I've never once heard the name Flemming mentioned?''

"Would you truly like to know what I think?''

"Yeah." Pausing, Zach glanced to the side. "Yeah, I would.''

"Very well then. I think perhaps you've overtaxed yourself. You know, been overdoing things a bit. And this place does have a tendency to play havoc with one's imagination. I think you might be suffering from—what was it you called it?—a 'case of the willies.' '' Alena bit her bottom lip, not at all liking the expression on Zach's face.

"I am not," he said flatly, "suffering from the willies.''

"But you've been so jumpy lately.''

"I have not been jumpy. I've been . . . alert. And believe me, it pays to be alert when you're in a foreign country." Leaning back on his elbows, Zach stared into the fire again. "Once when we were in Bangkok, I got this same kind of feeling—kind of like doom just hanging in the air waiting to fall. I don't know why, but I've always gotten these little tingly warnings when something was about to happen. And I'll tell you what, missy, if I hadn't have been so alert that night in Bangkok, a wily band of thieves would have slit all of our throats while we slept. Every single man in the expedition would have been—''

A sudden snapping sound outside the clearing brought Zach quickly to his feet. Grabbing his gun, he motioned Alena to stay quiet and move behind him, then aimed his rifle in the direction of rustling leaves.

"Don't shoot, Zach, it's me," came Slim's voice just before he parted a broad-leafed palm and stepped into view.

Zach eased his finger off the trigger, expelled a deep breath, and lowered the barrel of his gun to the ground. "Glad you're back, Slim." After a half-second of surveying his friend's grim expression, he asked, "How many are there?"

"Just one as far as I could tell. The rain washed away most of the tracks." Slim started for the coffeepot, but Alena hurriedly poured a cup and handed it to him. Nodding his thanks, he took a sip, then turned to Zach. "Ain't no Injun, neither. He was wearing English ridin' boots. I got a pair like 'em for Christmas once. No offense, ma'am, but they don't hold a candle to the boots they make back home in Texas."

"You're sure he's following us?" Zach asked, dropping his head and massaging the back of his neck. "Not just another hunter or explorer or missionary?"

"Oh, he's trackin' us, all right. Ain't no doubt about it." Slim sank down on the ground and rolled his shoulders. "He's being real sneaky about it, too, weavin' on and off the trail."

Focusing on the campfire, Zach set his mouth hard. The flames crackled and popped, amplified in the extended silence.

Slim's noisy, wide-mouthed yawn drew Zach's attention, making him smile. "Get some rest, Slim. You've earned it. I'll take first watch."

"Believe I'll just do that, pard." Slim stood and stretched his long arms over his head. "I'm plum tuckered. Wake me when you're ready for me to take over. 'Night, ma'am," he said, tipping his hat to Alena as he moved to the other side of the firelight and threw out his bedroll.

"Good night, Mr. Johnson." Alena shifted her gaze to Zach. She felt an impulse to reach out and smooth the worry lines etched in his forehead. To keep from doing so, she folded her arms across her chest and, as an optional remedy, said, "Dr. Summerfield, I regret accusing you of being jittery a while ago. In lieu of Mr. Johnson's discovery, I feel I owe you an apology. You had every right to be concerned."

"It's okay. No apologies are necessary." Zach's attempted smile wasn't very convincing. "You'd better try to get some sleep now. We'll be moving double-time tomorrow and won't stop to rest until we reach our next campsite."

Alena wrapped her blanket around her shoulders and pulled it tight under her chin. "Not to worry," she said reassuringly. "We'll lose this chap soon enough and everything will be all right. You'll see." She turned and, moving to her bedroll, glanced briefly back at him. "Good night."

"Sweet dreams, Angel," Zach replied, his pasted-on smile softening into a sincere one as he watched her bed down.

Zach set a hard pace to follow for the next two days. He and his machete hacked relentlessly through the dense growth of vines and tree limbs. With every swipe, sweat poured down him, dampening his shirt. He ignored the knotted muscles in his arms, refused to dwell on the fact that his fingers were cramped around the heavy knife handle. He was determined to shake whoever was tailing them. And even more determined to outrun the warning signals that kept going off in his head.

It was closer to dark than usual when they stopped to camp the second day. Pushing himself past the limits of physical exhaustion hadn't diminished Zach's cursed premonitions. Unable to sleep and irritable with everything the others did or said, he offered to stand guard first and left camp as soon as possible.

Zach leaned against a vine-covered tree on the outskirts of camp. As the balmy night grew darker, he listened to exotic birds call their mates. He watched the monkeys swing from limb to limb until they settled for the night and their chatter died down. At last the jungle stilled to the constant, serene hum and chirps of insects, and the occasional shuffle of a nocturnal creature. A soft breeze rustled the leaves overhead. Solitude. Zach closed his eyes a moment and let it seep into him. The peaceful solitude of the wilds usually cured him of any troubles. Why wasn't it working tonight?

With a deep sigh, he pulled the flask from his pocket, downed a generous swig of rum, and wondered at his uncanny knack for getting himself into such crack-brained situations. Maybe he *was* as insane as Alena Sutton seemed to think him. He took another drink and wrist-wiped his mouth. Hell, he wasn't crazy. Crazy things just happened to him, that's all. He seemed to attract trouble wherever he went. And he didn't always get into these fixes all by himself. He hadn't asked someone to follow them. He'd tried to stop Alena from tagging along. And dammit, he couldn't help it if Howie'd gotten careless and bragged about the map when he'd had a few.

Zach repositioned his rifle across his chest. Howie hadn't always socialized in the best of places. Nor had he been very choosy about his drinking partners. It was altogether possible that a lot of low-life characters knew Howie was close to obtaining the ancient writing. All Zach could be sure of was that someone knew he and Alena had the map now—and whoever it was, was stalking them for it. Zach grimaced. He didn't enjoy waiting for someone to bushwhack them. It made him extremely uneasy.

And that wasn't the only thing that had made him uneasy lately.

He was beginning to get little twinges in his chest sometimes when he looked at Alena Sutton. He could have passed it off as jungle fever if it had been no more than lust. But it wasn't just physical attraction. This was something altogether new to him. It was . . . admiration. He'd never allowed himself to get close enough to women to admire them. In fact, he'd taken great pains to avoid spending more than a day or two at a time in any female's company.

Everything had always been black or white with him. He either liked something or he didn't. But Howie's daughter had him dealing with two-sided emotions. On one hand, he was completely fascinated with her. On the other hand, it chafed him to come to the conclusion that she wasn't the ninny he'd originally taken her for. She hadn't whimpered or whined like he'd thought she would, though Lord knew he'd given her plenty of reasons to. She wasn't just soft and pretty. She was spunky and smart and he was growing more attached to her than he liked. Even being aware of that, for some damned inexplicable reason, he wanted her to like him, needed her to approve of him.

Zach jerked the brim of his hat down. He wasn't good at sorting out mixed feelings, especially the ones he had for Alena. Just thinking about it made his head hurt. He drained his flask, determined not to dwell on the matter any further tonight.

That vow ended approximately five minutes later, however, when muffled laughter drifted to him from camp. Muttering an oath, he shifted his weight and attempted to calculate how much longer it would take them to reach the Orinoco River. Instead he caught himself wondering when those two back at camp had become so chummy.

As Alena's pleasant laugh was carried on the breeze once again, Zach snapped his pocket watch open and struck a match. Good. It was time for Slim to take guard duty.

Sauntering into camp, Zach rolled his eyes at the tail end of one of Slim's famous yarns.

"Oh, Mr. Johnson, surely you jest," Alena was saying.

"No, ma'am, it's God's truth." Slim grinned at Zach. "Tell her, Zach. You remember the time old man Ferrol swallowed that gold tooth of his and—"

"Isn't it time for you to take watch?"

A frown dampened Slim's amused features. "I reckon so," he said, and came to his feet. "You okay?"

Zach reached for the coffeepot. "Oh, sure, just peachy."

"Hell, I was only askin'." Grabbing his rifle, Slim disappeared into the dark brush.

Zach took a sip of coffee and looked at Alena. "You still up? You're usually sound asleep by now."

"Yes, I suppose I am," she said, gazing into the fire. "But Mr. Johnson and I were just talking. He's such a nice man."

"Yeah, that Slim is one *hell* of a nice man, he is."

The bite in his tone made Alena cock her head. "Are you upset with Mr. Johnson about something?"

"Hell, no, I'm not upset with Mr. Johnson."

Alena believed his scowl and the way he tossed his coffee out said different. "Then why are you cursing at me?"

"I'm not cursing at you, dammit."

Alena lifted a brow, then clenched her jaw. Dropping her attention to the book in her lap, she flipped it open.

Zach swiped his hat off and ran a hand through his hair. After a slight hesitation, he walked to where Alena was seated and looked down at her. "Sorry," he said. "Guess I'm just a little edgy. Mind if I join you?"

"If you wish," Alena replied without sparing him a glance. She touched a finger to her tongue, turned the page, and concentrated on the passage as he settled on the ground beside her.

Zach leaned close and peered at her book. "What are you reading?"

"The poetical works of Elizabeth Barrett Browning." Alena regarded him a moment. "Do you like poetry, Dr. Summerfield?"

"Not really." Zach took out his pipe and began

filling it with tobacco. "Frankly, I'm partial to the writings of H. G. Wells. I've just finished his latest publication, *The War of the Worlds*. Have you read it?"

Alena tucked her chin. "I should say not."

"Well, you should, you know. It's very enlightening. Maybe even a prediction of things to come." He struck a match against the bowl of his pipe. As he lit it, he looked up at the few bright stars that peeked between the leaves above.

Alena followed his gaze. "You don't mean to say that you believe other worlds actually exist?"

"They might." He drew on his pipe, blew the smoke out slowly, and turned to assess her reaction. She was all eyes now. "Just think about it. If we're here, isn't it possible that out there somewhere, there could be others?"

Alena stared at the sky, pondering on that a moment. *Others?* How preposterous. A person would have to be daft to even consider such a thing. She watched him askance. "I'm afraid, Dr. Summerfield, that your philosophy is a bit too ridiculous."

"There are several things, Angelface, right here on this earth that are inexplainable. For instance, have you ever heard of a *curupira*?"

"No, I can't say that I have."

"I guess you could compare them to wood sprites."

"Wood sprites?"

"You know, like elves and fairies, or . . . goblins."

Alena snapped her book closed, and straightened her back. "Oh, come now, Dr. Summerfield, outside of a child's imagination, there's no such thing."

"Are you so sure?" He lifted a brow, leaning a little closer. "I'm afraid the Indians in these parts would disagree with you. They've seen these *curupiras*."

She eyed him suspiciously. "You're not serious."

"Oh, but I am." He laid his pipe aside, and closed the space between them. "You see," he whispered, "they say these *curupiras* live in the hollow trunks of trees. At night they lurk in the jungle, especially near the crossing of two trails. Then, when some unsuspecting soul walks by, they jump out and grab them. The Indians claim they've seen these malevolent spirits turn human beings into trees or animals. Haven't you noticed how some of the trees here look like tortured souls?"

Alena nodded. There had been times when a tree swathed in twisted vines had indeed resembled some poor mortal.

"You know"—Zach made a slow inspection of the pitch-black darkness outside the glow of fire, knowing that her gaze followed his—"the little creatures are probably out there watching us right now." Aware her attention was absorbed by the surroundings, he slipped his hands behind her, then grabbed her waist. "Gotcha!"

Alena jumped, landing on Zach's lap. Before she could gather her wits, he locked his arms around her and rocked backwards.

She lay atop him, half in shock until his broad grin spurred her anger. Then, his chest began to rumble, jarring her as he broke into laughter. She closed her eyes, her ire floundered, and a giggle of her own slipped out. Merciful Mary, his fits of lunacy were contagious.

As their mirth dwindled, she peered into his blue eyes tinged with humor. "You, sir, are incorrigible."

"So they say. I've never denied it. Still, you have to give me credit for my cleverness."

"What you call cleverness, I would call conniving."

"Ah, yes, but I did achieve my purpose." He made his eyebrows jump. "I have you in a most compromising position here, don't I?"

"Indeed, Dr. Summerfield." She gave him the same tolerant look she used on naughty students. " 'Tis a most devious achievement, for the likes of which I'm certain Hades has reserved you a special place."

"Mmm . . . just as sure as heaven has for you." His eyes turned to liquid silver while his mouth lost all but a trace of his former smile.

A warm glow deep inside made Alena suddenly aware of his sinewy body beneath her. She curled her fingers into fists against his chest and cleared her throat. "Very well, Dr. Summerfield, you've had your bit of fun." She started to rise, but his grip tightened around her waist. "If you'll be so kind as to let me up."

"Not yet, Angelface, I want you to do something for me first."

Alena widened her eyes in disbelief. He couldn't be about to suggest what she thought he was about to suggest.

"It's nothing dishonorable, I promise. A kiss, that's all. I just want you to put your arms around my neck, kiss me, and say, 'Zach, you're not such a bad guy, after all.' "

Alena looked at him incredulously. The tenderness in his voice, on his face, in his clear blue eyes, insinuated he wasn't teasing her. A kiss? That was all he wanted?

Alena bit her bottom lip. A kiss didn't seem like much in return for all he'd done for her. She opened her mouth, closed it, then opened it again. "You're ... not such a bad fellow, after all ... Zach," she said, giving him a small, faltering smile.

Shifting her gaze from his eyes to the base of his throat, she haltingly slipped her arms about his neck. She tilted her face an iota closer, then froze as the hollow of his throat started to pulsate. She closed her eyes, swallowed hard, and steeled herself to move slowly forward.

Zach lifted his head and his mouth met hers impatiently. Scrumptious shivers shot through her as he ran his hands up and down her spine. His tongue darted between her parted lips and the kiss increased in intensity.

Alena tightened her hold on him, plunging headlong into the embrace with as much vigor as Zach. Even as she did so, she wondered what it was about him that made her toss years of discipline and moral fortitude aside.

"Am I interruptin' somethin'?"

Alena very nearly threw her back out scrambling off of Zach. Coming to her feet, she smoothed her hair and straightened her skirt. "No ... no, not at all, Mr. Johnson. I ... ah, just tripped, and ... and Dr. Summerfield was helping me up. If you'll excuse me, I was just about to retire for the evening. Good night, gentlemen."

" 'Night, ma'am." A grin twitched at the corners of Slim's mouth as he watched her grab her blanket, move across the way, and sack out.

Snickering, he turned to where Zach lay flat on his back, staring at the dark sky.

"Slim, you have a hell of a sense of timing," Zach muttered to the stars. "Thanks a lot."

"Any time, old buddy."

Zach gave him a look to kill. "I thought you were supposed to be on guard."

Slim held up the coffeepot. "Needed some coffee. Me and Miss Sutton was havin' such a fine time visitin', I plum forgot to rest. Somethin' itchin' you, Zach?"

Zach raised himself off the ground and dusted his britches with fierce swats. "You know damned good and well what's bothering me," he whispered, moving in on Slim.

"Oh, say, look," Slim said, matching his quiet tone, "I'm really sorry about interferin' with your little wrestlin' match there, pard." He smiled into his coffee cup. "Looked to me like Miss Sutton was winnin', anyway."

"Dad-blast you, Slim—" A low growl came from Zach's throat. He thrust his hat on his head, then grabbed his rifle. "Drink your coffee. Hell, I can't sleep. I'll take double duty." Parting the leafy fronds with a thwack, he vanished.

Morning didn't diminish the warm, furry feeling that had wrapped itself around Alena's heart when she'd kissed Zach. In fact, it seemed to have doubled in intensity overnight.

Humming, she walked from the stream toward camp. Somewhere amidst her restless sleep, she'd come to the conclusion that there was more to Zachariah Summerfield than met the eye. He was different than anyone she'd ever met. He could be disarming, ruthless, and crazy, each within the span of batting a lash. Yet behind all his nonsense, he hid a great deal of sensitivity. She had thought about it, and thought about it, and had finally decided she might never again have the opportunity to make the acquaintance of such a unique man. She remembered how she'd felt when he had fallen off the cliff— how she had wished for more time to get to know him properly. Of course, that old childhood vow to stay aloof from people, keep herself emotionally separated, had naturally come to mind, but had been outweighed by the notion that by rejecting his—'friendship,' she'd elected to call it— she could very possibly be doing herself a grave injustice. She was, after all, no longer a frightened child. This bright, beautiful morning had brought her to the conclusion that it was time she put the past behind her and started opening up to the world a bit. Perhaps it was even time to start trusting again.

She wove her way through the broad-leafed, exotic plants in a lighthearted mood she couldn't recall ever having experienced before. She would find her father and his explanation for leaving her would be a perfectly reasonable one. She and Zachariah would be friends. Good friends. Alena stooped to pick an orchid, stuck it through the top buttonhole of her blouse, and, smiling, continued through the thick green foliage. Perhaps she and Zach could be more than good friends. If things progressed between them, perhaps they would travel to the far corners of the earth together seeking lost artifacts, exploring bygone civilizations—

Angry voices lifted as she came within earshot of camp, putting a quick halt to both her daydreaming and her footsteps.

"Look, Zach, if I'd had any idea you had a hankerin' for her—"

"I don't have a hankering for anyone, dammit. That's beside the point. The issue here is that we have a job to do. In case you've forgotten, someone is out there just biding their time, waiting for us to slip up. Waiting to bushwhack us. This is serious business, Slim. We can't let rational judgment be swayed by the attentions of some little filly. You know as well as I do that you have to stay on your toes in these parts. One slipup can cost you your life."

"I ain't havin' no trouble with my judgment . . . are *you?*"

Zach lowered his brows. "Just what the hell is that supposed to mean? Huh?"

Slim scratched his ear. "I gotta ask you somethin'. I reckon it's gonna make you madder than a stirred-up hornet's nest, but I gotta ask it, just the same." He squinted one eye at his friend. "Just what *are* your intentions t'wards Miss Sutton, Zach?"

Alena held her breath. Eavesdropping was a shameful, wicked thing to do. By all that was holy, she should clear her throat this very minute and make her presence known. But she couldn't utter a sound. To be perfectly honest, Slim's question was one she wanted to hear answered.

Zach's upper lip quivered, making one side of his nose twitch. "My intentions," he said in a controlled voice, "are to find out whatever I can about her father's disappearance, locate the damned treasure, then get the hell out of here."

Slim shook his head slowly and ran a hand over the back of his neck. "Sorry, buddy, but that answer just don't hold water. 'Specially after what I saw last night . . . the two of you rollin' around on the ground—"

"That . . . was nothing."

"It sure as hell didn't look like nothin' to me."

Zach threw his head back, stared at the overgrowth for a moment, then fixed a narrowed gaze on Slim. "Just what are you implying?"

"All I want to hear is that your intentions t'wards her are honorable. You just look me square in the eye and tell me that, Zach, and I won't say another damn word."

"Honorable?"

The Texan took a step forward and hooked his thumbs in his belt loops. "Don't act like you don't know what I'm talkin' about. You know it riles me when you do that."

"Oh, I get it now." Zach gave a little laugh. "You want her for yourself, is that it? Well—"

"Dammit, Zach, I'm warnin' you, quit pussyfootin' around. You know I'm promised to Sarah Beth."

"Yeah, well, Sarah Beth isn't here, is she?"

Slim cocked his head to the side and looked at him. "You're just tryin' to throw me off course. And it ain't gonna work this time, old buddy. I've never so much as touched Miss Sutton, nor do I intend to. Cain't say the same, can you?"

"Aw, come on, Slim. You know me. When it comes to women, I'm charmed. What can I say?"

"You can say you'll put a lid on that charm of yours, as you call it. Miss Sutton is a fine, decent woman, and unless you plan to propose matrimony—"

"MATRIMONY?" Zach jerked his hat off, ran a hand through his hair, and turned a full circle. He came back around with a stricken expression.

"Matrimony? Jeez almighty, Slim, how could you even suggest such a thing?"

"She'd make some man a mighty fine wife."

"Hah! That woman?" He pointed in the direction of the stream. "Are we talking about the same woman? The one who nagged, and nagged, and *nagged* me to bring her along? The same dear Miss Sutton who wears funny hats and socks people in the nose? You want *me* to propose to a woman like that? Why, I'd sooner climb on the back of the meanest bull in Texas. It would be the same thing. Suicide. She'd have me needled to death inside of six months."

The warmth around Alena's heart dissolved by degrees and was replaced by a sinking feeling in the pit of her stomach. She closed her eyes and pressed a hand to her temples. She was generally so logical. How could she have been so foolish? It must have been the heat that had made her think a man like Zach could truly care for someone like her, or anyone for that matter.

Tears stung from behind her lids, but her childhood-instilled stamina refused to let them fall. Turning away, she walked slowly toward the stream.

". . . No, sir. No, thank you, Slim. Settling down may be fine for you, but I'm a loner. Always have been, always will be. I don't need a woman telling me when to jump, and how high."

Slim tugged the brim of his hat. "Then you'll give me your word you'll leave Miss Sutton be?"

"Look, Slim, I don't know what makes you think you can tell me how to live my life, but—"

"No, you look," Slim said, bumping Zach's

shoulder with the heel of his hand. Zach gave him a warning glare, but Slim went right on. "You and I both know that little lady is as pure as fresh-fallen snow. You've made it plain enough that you want no respectable ties with her. That's all good and well, but I'm a-holdin' you to it." Slim gave him another shove for good measure, and saw Zach's nostrils flare. "As long as I'm around, you won't be warmin' your bed with her like she's some kind of two-bit—"

Whack!

Zach's fist caught Slim's jaw, sending the Texan sprawling to the ground. "Alena Sutton's no two-bit anything and you damn well know it. Don't ever let me hear you refer to her in such terms again." Nursing his knuckles, Zach stomped off into the thicket of broad green leaves.

Slim raised up on his elbow and ran a hand over his jaw. He grinned, wincing at the effort. "Damn, Zach," he murmured to himself. "I *knew* you liked her." He worked his aching jawbone once more. "Yep, by the brunt of that whallop, I'd say you liked her a lot."

Chapter 10

Pinks and pale hues of orange streaked the evening sky by the time the trio reached the Orinoco. A long dugout that Alena guessed to be some twenty-odd feet or more waited near the bank.

"Yori?" Slim shouted, nearing the boat.

A middle-aged man with straight black hair poked his head out from under the canopy stretched across the middle.

Gooseflesh rose on Alena's arms as she realized with great dismay that the person Slim called Yori was . . . an *Indian*. Barely aware she did so, she retreated a step.

"John-sen?" Yori shaded his eyes. "That you?" A broad smile brightened his face. He straightened his ill-fitting white men's clothes, then hopped over the side of the crude boat with the agility of a twelve-year-old. Clasping Slim's hand, he shook it vigorously, then grabbed Zach's and agitated it in the same manner. "How you fare, Doctu?"

"I'm faring well, Yori. And you?"

"All is good. The rains not wash away too many crops this year. The hunt is plentiful. I

have two more sons since last you were here."
Yori spread his arms wide. "I ask you, Doctu,
what more a man can ask for?" His gaze roved
curiously over Alena as she peeked around Zach,
then he elbowed Slim and spoke in a language
Alena had never heard the likes of.

"No . . . no, she's not mine," Slim answered,
apparently trying to keep a straight face.

A bit uneasy that she was being discussed in
a jargon she couldn't understand, Alena tugged
Zach's sleeve. "What did he say?" she whispered.

Zach smiled, puffed out his chest, and rubbed
it. "He says you are a very fortunate woman to
have strong, wise men like us to protect you."

Nervously, Alena tightened her grip on Zach's
shirt. "He's . . . he's an—"

"A native Indian," Zach supplied when her
voice faltered. "Don't worry. Yori's a good man.
He was virtually raised by missionaries."

Alena's tension had almost started to melt
when Yori stepped forward and caught a strand
of her hair between his thumb and forefinger. A
gasp caught in her throat. Then, fear mixing with
mortification, she frowned and snatched the lock
from his grip.

Yori threw his head back and laughed. Turning to Slim, he rattled off something else in a
rapid succession.

Alena looked askance at Zach. He appeared to
comprehend the conversation, his smile growing
wider. From the way Yori kept pointing at her,
she got the distinct impression that she was the
main topic. Unable to bear the suspense any
longer, she tugged Zach's sleeve again and
asked, "Whatever is he going on about now?"

"It seems you may add another admirer to your list, Angelface," Zach said, bending to her ear. Carefully leashed laughter played about his lips as he listened intently, then began translating. "He says . . . you have the spirit of a jaguar . . . your hair is like the sun . . . your eyes, like the forest just after the gods have blessed it with rain . . . any man with a woman like you would be envied . . . and, if I'm not mistaken, he's negotiating a very tempting trade for you."

Alena felt the blood drain from her face. Wide-eyed, she glanced from Zach to Yori and back again. "*Surely . . . you jest.*"

"Aw, cheer up, Angelface." He gave her shoulder a light squeeze. "You look like you just swallowed a live frog. He's offering an extraordinary price. You should feel honored."

"Honored? Why, you big baboon! You tell him right this minute—"

"Ach." Zach held up a hand. "Let's not call each other names in front of Yori. He's prone to pick up bad habits."

"No, Yori," Slim said with a firm shake of his head. "Sorry, but she's not for sale. She's—" The Texan glanced around as if he searched the jungle for his next words. His gaze landed on Zach and he grinned. "She's Zach's woman."

Alena couldn't believe her ears. *Zach's woman?* She took a step forward, doubling her fists in the folds of her skirt. "Now, see here, you heathen, I am not any man's—"

Zach clamped a hand over her mouth. "Shh," he whispered against her temple. "Slim knows what he's doing. Any unattached woman is considered fair game in these parts. Just play along."

Alena started to struggle, but his free arm came

around her, pinning her elbows to her waist.

With her wails muffled beneath his hand, Zach gave the Indian a feigned grimace. "See, Yori? You wouldn't want her, anyway. She's too scrawny to do much work. And . . . she's disobedient. Why, I have to beat her with a stick two, sometimes three, times a we—*eek*." Alena's heel slammed back into his shin, making his grimace authentic.

"Look, missy, see? Those white crocs." Yori pointed to the giant reptiles as they left the sunny banks. Sloshing belly-first into the water, they circled the drifting dugout as if they hoped someone would fall overboard. "No hide face, missy. Look!"

Alena peeked between her fingers at the awful creatures. In the past ten days that they'd moved downriver, she'd warmed to the Indian and his never-ending smile. Still, in his attempt to enrich her limited knowledge of the jungle, there were things he pointed out that she'd rather not know.

"Crocs. See? No worry, missy," he told her. "These all white crocs. White crocs, no worry. Black crocs bad. Black crocs eat you."

Alena closed her eyes behind her fingers, feeling a tad faint. "Thank you for telling me so, Yori," she mumbled behind her hands. "I feel so much better knowing that. All the same, I believe I've learned quite enough for one day." Sinking down on a crate, she pulled her hanky from her bodice to dab the perspiration from her throat.

Yori crouched down beside her and peered up into her face. "We read now, missy?"

Alena dropped her hands and considered how, in many ways, he was like a child. She'd no doubt, though, that here in his own domain, it was he who was cunning, and she who was ignorant. "We'll finish the book this afternoon. I must write in my journal now." She looked up to watch a flock of birds flutter across the sky. "I must preserve everything I see here. It's very important for me to bring a firsthand report home to my students." She regarded his adoring black eyes. "You do understand, don't you?"

Yori nodded, smiling as always, then left her at the back of the boat. She opened her journal to the last entry, prepared to describe the breathtaking sunsets, but her gaze strayed to the bow of the dugout.

Zach sprawled against the side, napping, his long legs stretched out in front of him. His hands were closed over the rifle across his middle, his hat lay over his face.

After overhearing his and Slim's argument and finally coming to terms with it, Alena had decided it was all good and well that the relationship between them remain businesslike. Yori's presence had apparently caused Zach and Slim to put their differences on hold. They spoke, discussed plans, but the jesting and camaraderie they'd shared before was missing, and an underlying strain lingered among the lot of them.

Zach had distanced himself from her. Of course, Alena was aware he had a lot on his mind. Late at night when they thought she was asleep, she'd heard him and the Texan discussing the possibility that they had eluded whoever was following them. Slim was certain they had. Zach, however, had disputed Mr. Johnson's thoughts on the matter, and persistently argued otherwise. Alena understood Zach's concern. He was, after all, responsible for the entire party. She had learned over the past few weeks that he took that responsibility, though sometimes begrudgingly, most seriously. She knew she was an added burden and regretted it, but her heart nearly broke whenever she caught him watching her and he looked away. It pained her sorely that when she tried to talk to him, his reply was always brief and he would soon excuse himself to attend to some task. If she was at one end of the boat, she could be certain he would find some excuse to be at the other.

Alena averted her eyes from Zachariah Summerfield and surveyed the ebony water that rippled behind the boat. If only she hadn't misinterpreted Zach's motive for pursuing her, perhaps things would have continued on a friendly basis. Mistress Stephens would say she'd been thinking with her heart instead of her head. Indeed, the shrewd old bird would have been right.

Her attention was drawn to Zach again as he sat up, stretched his arms, and blinked against the bright sun. He combed a hand through his shaggy hair, then set his hat on the crown of his head. Alena drank in every detail of Zach's profile as he stared straight ahead, one arm draped over a raised knee.

She should never have allowed him to take such liberties with her to begin with. She should have boxed his ears the very first time he kissed her, let him know right off she'd not put up with his unscrupulous advances. It was entirely her mistake not to have done so. Yet for some reason, she'd thought—

She wasn't quite sure what she'd thought. She only knew his kisses had driven her senseless, left her void of any logical thoughts, made her yearn for . . . something she couldn't name. She had assumed he'd felt the same. But it appeared she had assumed too much. Men like Zachariah Summerfield considered women no more than temporary diversions. It wasn't his fault. It was simply the way he was.

She could not be a temporary diversion. At times, she wished she could. Nevertheless, her deep-seated morals wouldn't allow such a thing to happen.

Her eyes never wavering from Zach, she absently swatted an insect on the side of her neck. She didn't want to end up like Mistress Stephens: mean, hateful, and lonely. But there was certainly a possibility that she would. When all was said and done, Zach would go his way, and she . . . she would return to her teaching post. Merciful heavens, she was going to miss him. Miss talking to him. Miss their verbal battles . . . his cocky smile . . . the mischievous twinkle in his eyes when he teased her.

Zach stood and the same force that had pulled his gaze toward Alena so many times before made him angle his head her way. Their eyes locked for a long, endless, agonizing moment. Unspoken, not quite readable messages passed between them.

Breaking the contact abruptly, Zach glanced at the dugout floor, then turned around and studied the thick underbrush that lined the far bank. He clenched his fists, fighting the urge to stride down the length of the boat and take her in his arms. Dammit, why couldn't she just let the attraction between them die? Why couldn't he?

She was trouble with a capital *T*. He'd known that from the start. Why in God's name he had pursued her, he couldn't say. Maybe, at first, he'd merely sought to draw her out into the real world, show her there was more to life than catering to spoiled little rich girls and reading books alone in her room. He'd never intended things to go this far.

But they had.

And he had initiated it all. He'd done everything in his power to make her like him, make her need him, make her want him. Now . . . now he didn't know what to do with her affection. He couldn't shake the feelings that jostled about inside him, made him ill, killed his appetite, and caused him to toss and turn in his sleep. His concentration was shot to hell. When he should have been worrying about the tracker behind them, studying the map, charting their position, crazy notions popped into his head. Instead of his work or the treasure of Mahrakimba, he thought about the sweet, remembered taste of Alena Sutton's lips. He visualized her in domestic terms—wearing an apron, holding a baby.

"You just wait, Zach," Slim had once warned him, *"someday you're gonna meet up with a little gal that'll turn your heart inside out, just like Sarah Beth did mine."* Zach had laughed and replied, "Not me, buddy. Not me."

He wasn't laughing now.

Zach tugged the brim of his hat down resolutely. It didn't matter whether Sutton's daughter was the "little gal" Slim had prophesied, or not. He had no intentions of tying the knot with anyone. He wasn't ready to give up his work. It was the only kind of life he knew. Roving was in his blood and wouldn't mix with a family. He refused to put a wife and children through the hell he and his mother had endured. Nor did he plan to spend any more time pining for things that could never be when he had more pressing complications to take care of. One of which was to settle the conflict between himself and Slim.

He shifted his gaze to Slim, who lay stretched out beneath the tarpaulin. All that was visible were his boots crossed at the ankle. Fine-grain cowhide, the Texan had pointed out often enough. Zach half-smiled, then fell pensive. The man had saved his life at least a dozen times over the years, pulled him out of impossible scrapes. And Zach had belted him. Dropping his head, he massaged the nape of his neck. He owed Slim an apology.

A heavy hand clamped Zach's shoulder. His head snapped up to find Slim regarding him with an out-of-character seriousness. "Zach, don't you think it's high time we talked this thing out?"

Zach nodded. "My very thoughts, old buddy. You were right, Slim. About Alena Sutton. About me. I should've never gone after her the way I did and I had no right to deck you for saying so."

"Aw, now hold up there, pard. Don't be so hard on yourself. If you recall, I pushed you."

"Yeah." Zach glanced up. "But I shouldn't have taken a swing at you like that. We've never fought over a woman."

"I asked for it." Slim rubbed his jaw and grinned. "As for the woman . . . well, she ain't just any woman, Zach. That punch told me as much, whether you're willin' to admit it or not."

Zach squinted at his friend. What the hell was he up to now? Slim had always had a clever way of pussyfooting all around the edges of a subject, leaving you to figure it out yourself.

"Use your head, boy. We've been on a lot of excursions together." Slim paused, dipping his brows. "You ain't never kept your face scraped clean before. And in all those times, I've never known you to pack a single extra item. You've always been a real stickler about travelin' light, yet you're totin' smell-good. Don't that tell you somethin'?"

"Hell, Slim, a man gets tired of smelling like a horse."

"Is that so?"

"Okay, Slim, I give up." Zach threw his arms out wide. "Why don't you just say whatever it is you have to say and get it over with. You and I both know you're going to, sooner or later anyway."

"All right, I will." Slim tugged down his Stetson, then hooked his thumbs in his belt loops. "But I'm a-tellin' you right here and now if you take another poke at me I'll be obliged to knock some sense into your thick skull. You hear?" He stepped closer, looking Zach right in the eye. "You blind fool, cain't you see you're fallin'—"

A single shot rang out, shattering the peacefulness of the jungle. It echoed, causing chaos. Flocks of birds scattered. Monkeys screamed.

In the horror of slow motion, Zach watched Slim's expression change to blank confusion and his face pale to a deathly white. His eyes conveying a silent plea for help, Slim fell forward and crumpled into Zach's arms.

Another bullet whizzed past Zach's ear before he could ease his friend's limp body onto the deck. "Alena! Yori!" he yelled. "Take cover!"

Making a wild grab for his rifle, Zach braced it on the dugout's edge. Aiming at the underbrush, he fired repeatedly. Two more shots whistled from the bank. He tightened his jaw as one of the bullets grazed the top of his right hand. "Dammit," he muttered, one eye sighted down the barrel, "whoever you are, you'd better prepare to meet your Maker."

This time his shots got close enough to scare the assailant, for the bushes started moving. Mindless of the sting across his knuckles, Zach quickly reloaded, and continued firing until the movement of vegetation trailed off into the jungle, out of range.

Scanning the bank, Zach rose, swiped off his hat, and slung it down on the deck. When he turned to Slim's inert form, his anger withered instantly, replaced by concern.

Alena cradled the injured man's head on her lap and looked up, tears glistening on her lashes. "H-he's... bleeding, Zach. He's bleeding... s-so... badly."

Zach set his gun aside and scooped the big man into his arms. "Yori!" he bellowed, "get us to shore. For God's sake hurry!" He carried Slim to the shade of the tarpaulin. "Alena!" he called over his shoulder as he laid him on the pallet. "I need—"

A wad of white linen was stuffed into his hand before he could finish and he looked up to find Alena beside him. All traces of her tears had vanished. She was tearing one of her discarded petticoats into strips. She met his gaze with a steady eye. "What else can I do to help?" she asked.

He hadn't the time to consider her quick response, but took the wads of cloth and pressed them to Slim's shoulder. "As soon as we get to shore, we've got to start a fire. Tell Yori."

Alena nodded, and quickly ducked from beneath the tarpaulin to do as he had bid.

Within a few minutes, the boat bumped against the bank. "Dammit, Yori, be careful," Zach uttered beneath his breath as he staunched Slim's wound again. From the corner of his eye, he saw Alena kneel beside him.

"Here," she said, offering the flask from his bag. "I took the liberty of retrieving this from your things. I thought you might need it. Yori started the fire, then darted off into the jungle— he said something about getting medicine. So I'm afraid you'll have to rely on me for whatever else must be done."

Zach took a swig of the rum. He regarded the woman next to him while he wiped his mouth, hoping like hell she wouldn't pass out. Spotting no indications of faintness in her face, he cradled the half-conscious man and poured a generous amount of the warm liquid into him. "That's it, swallow it, old buddy." He rubbed Slim's throat. "You're going to be okay."

Slim's eyes briefly fluttered open. Then he drifted back into oblivion.

Zach eased his friend face-down on the mat. "I'll have to work fast . . . remove the bullet while he's out. Here." He pulled his knife from the sheath. "Sterilize this for me while I get his shirt off."

When Alena didn't immediately respond,

Zach's head snapped up. He followed her worried gaze to the ugly gash across his knuckles.

"You're hurt," she whispered. "Your hand is shaking."

Zach tried to stabilize the vibration of his hand. But, for all his determination, the attempt was useless. He looked from Alena to Slim and back again. Time was running out. Slim's only chance was—"Take the knife, Angelface," he commanded, holding it out to her. "Go on. Stick the blade in the fire and get it good and hot."

Alena curled her fingers around the knife, biting her bottom lip. "Zach, you're hurt. You can't possibly—"

"I'm not going to. You are." Her face turned ashen and her eyes rounded as they lifted to his. Zach reached out with his good hand and touched her cheek. "Look, Angelface, I know you're scared. But we can't waste any more time. Slim is going to bleed to death if we don't get the bullet out and cauterize the wound. It'll be all right. I promise. I'll talk you through it."

A chill ran up Alena's spine. What if the knife slipped? What if she swooned? What if she couldn't hold steady? What if—

Stop it, stop it! her rational side screamed. *The man will surely die if you don't do something to help him.* She looked at Slim's pale face. Dark circles were forming beneath his eyes. God in heaven, she had no choice. She couldn't just stand idly by and watch this man die. Raising her chin, she met Zach's gaze head-on. "Get his shirt off," she said with much more bravado than she felt. "I'll be right back."

Alena was sure her legs would give way before she could sterilize the knife and return to the wounded man. Yet as she knelt beside him, intent on Zach's guidance, an inner strength she'd not known she possessed began to take over. Her trembling steadied. Her breathing relaxed. And she focused on the open gash with the single-minded goal of saving Slim's life. Zach spoke to her in an easy, even tone, almost crooning at times. He dabbed the perspiration from her brow as she searched for the bullet with the tip of the blade. She bit the inside of her cheeks so hard she could taste tart blood until, at last, she dislodged the lead from the bone.

She took a deep, recuperative breath before Zach started to tell her the next step. A queasiness gripped her as he spoke, and it must have shown, for his eyes transmitted a fear that she'd be unable to follow through. His doubt made her swallow the constriction in her throat. Without further hesitation, she nodded, and resumed the procedure.

"That's it, Angelface. You're doing just fine," Zach murmured. A mixture of astonishment and admiration welled up inside as he watched her slender fingers gently probe the laceration for the slug. Slim was right. She wasn't just any woman. He would've never believed she could perform the task he was witnessing. Truth was, he couldn't have done a better job himself.

In a matter of minutes, she extracted the bullet, and half-crying, half-laughing, held it up for his inspection.

Zach cupped her face. "Thanks, Angel." In a euphoric state of relief and elation, he almost kissed her. Stopping just short of her mouth, he pulled back and tweaked her nose instead. "I'll take over now."

Alena moved out into the open space of the dugout while Zach cauterized the wound. The stench of burning flesh that permeated the air made a badly needed deep breath impossible and she was glad when Yori returned with leaves to crush . . . glad to have something to busy her hands . . . glad to have something other than what she'd just done to occupy her mind.

From the depths of a deep dark tunnel, a haze appeared through the slits of Slim's eyes. He tried opening them a little wider but a painful brightness made him slam them shut again. Somewhere voices chanted a hymn . . . celestial voices . . . voices of . . . angels?

Where in blazes was he? Was this an honest-to-goodness bed beneath him? He tried to move, but the mere attempt sent white-hot fire shooting through his body. Hell, it hurt to breathe.

He pried his eyes open, forcing them to adjust to the light. They focused on a lone crucifix on an otherwise stark, yellowed stucco wall. A musty smell filled his nostrils. He tried to swallow, but his throat was so dry. Sweet Jesus, what had happened? Where was he? Where was Zach?

As he rolled his head to the side, one question was answered. Asleep, Zach sat in a straight-backed, uncomfortable-looking chair. Instinctively, Slim turned to the other side of the bed and saw Alena. Though her eyes were closed, her mouth moved in silent prayer as her fingers slipped from bead to bead of a rosary.

"Miss . . ." he tried to say, but the word grated his throat and came out in a whisper.

Alena's eyes flew open at the sound. Springing from her seat, she clasped her hands over her mouth.

Slim didn't rightly know if she was crying or laughing. "Water," he mouthed. She hurriedly filled a glass from the pitcher on the table behind her. Another pain gripped him when she lifted his head to help him drink.

"Oh, Mr. Johnson," she said softly, laying him back on his pillow. "I'm so glad you're better. We thought—"

Her voice roused Zach and he nearly knocked over the chair coming to his feet.

Slim managed a weak smile. "Hey, pard," he croaked, "you look like livin' hell."

Grinning, Zach ran a hand over his stubbled chin. "Yeah, probably so. But no worse than you." He sobered a little. "How do you feel?"

"Like I been dancin' with the devil." Slim furrowed his brows. "What in tarnation happened, Zach? You didn't punch me again, did you? Last thing I remember, we were driftin' downriver, you and me was talkin' . . . then here I am." He frowned again. "Where am I, anyway?"

"An old Jesuit mission. It's a convent now. Mother Superior was kind enough to take us in."

Slim's smile broadened. "That explains them singin' angels. For a minute there, I thought I'd died and gone to heaven." He squinted, trying to orient himself. "How long've I been out?"

"Three days. For a while we were afraid you weren't going to make it."

"Aw, heck, Zach, you of all people should know I'm too ornery to kick the bucket. Besides, Sarah Beth would hang my hide for breach of promise."

Zach's smile was subdued. "Some yahoo started popping off shots at us from the shore. I shouldn't have let my guard down. The feeling that we were still being tracked had never left me."

"Now don't you go blamin' yourself. I was the one tryin' to convince you we'd given him the slip. If I was you, I'd be givin' myself a pat on the back, pard. I'd sure as hell been a goner if ya hadn't been around to see to me." Slim's suffering was etched in the grin he attempted. "I s'pose you even had to dig the bullet out of me. I take it they got me in the back. That's where it pains me the most."

"In the shoulder blade. But I'm not the one who took out the slug. I was sort of out of commission myself." Zach raised his bandaged hand, then stared across the bed at Alena. "You can thank Miss Sutton. You'd have bled to death in the dugout if it wasn't for her."

Somewhat in awe, Slim shifted his gaze to the demure woman who stood silently at his bedside. "*You* took the bullet out?"

Casting her eyes downward, Alena nodded.

"Well, I'll be a donkey-eared—" Slim stopped short of being disrespectful. "I'm much obliged, ma'am. What you done wasn't an easy thing. I don't rightly know how to thank you."

"No thanks are necessary, Mr. Johnson." With a smile, she leaned forward and tucked the blanket beneath his chin. "Rest. 'Tis the best medicine for you now. I believe I'll take some air and let you two talk. But, mind you," she said, pointing a finger at Zach as she left the room, "don't tire him."

As soon as he suspected she was out of earshot, Slim chuckled, and rolled his eyes. "She's somethin', ain't she?"

Zach smiled at the empty doorway. "She's

been clucking over you like a mother hen for the past three days. We took turns sleeping, but she wouldn't leave the room."

Slim noted a strange glow in his friend's eyes. "Zach," he said, "do somethin' for me, will ya?"

Zach blinked and turned from the doorway and his own thoughts. "Sure. What?"

"Help her find out what happened to her pa. It's real important to her."

"Slim, if Howard's still alive, I'll find him. That's something I've planned to do from the start—for myself as well as her."

"I mean you can't waste any more time here worryin' about the likes of me. Soon as I'm back on my feet, I'll catch up—"

"You're going nowhere but home," Zach interrupted. "It's all been arranged. Yori's going to see you as far as the mountain range and meet us farther downriver. Armando and his father will get you back to the coast."

Slim twisted his mouth. "Doesn't sound like I got a whole lot of choice, seein' as I'm too banged up to fuss about it."

"That's right," Zach said with a wink. "Now try to get some rest before Mistress Sutton comes back in here and skins me alive for overtiring you. I'll check in on you when I get back to the States." Rubbing his whiskers, he added, "Think I need a bath and a few hours' sleep myself. Might even shave."

"Yeah, and put on some of that smell-good, too, huh?"

Zach chuckled and started to leave.

"Zach?"

Zach turned, raising an inquisitive brow.

"You watch out for that sidewinder, you hear?

He's as slippery as a catfish and may be twice as hard to snare."

"I'll be careful, Slim," Zach assured him, then headed for the door again.

"And pard, one more thing."

Zach stopped and braced a hand against the doorframe. "What's that?"

Slim fiddled with the blanket. There was a lot he wanted to say, but figured most of it'd go in one of his old pard's ears and right out the other. So he opted for "Try to be a little nicer to Miss Sutton, will you? She *is* a damn fine woman."

"Yeah, I know." Zach gave him a small smile, then took off down the hall, boot heels clicking as they faded into the distance.

Chapter 11

Apprehension had crept over Alena after the dugout had rounded the river's bend and the last glimpse of the cross atop the mission steeple had disappeared behind vast jungle greens. The thought of never seeing the tall, noble Texan again had tugged at her heart. She had reminded herself that everyone eventually parted ways, and that the sadness of final goodbyes was one of the very reasons she had always avoided friendships. Even so, she did not regret having made his acquaintance.

She did, however, have certain qualms about being alone in the wilds with Zachariah Summerfield. Not that she feared he might ravish her or the like. She'd long since learned he was a man of true integrity, not at all the dishonorable brute she'd once thought he was. The man she'd come to know, and trust with her life, would never cause her such disgrace. Actually, it was her own emotions that distressed her. She was most afraid of being unable to tether the secret yearnings she couldn't rid herself of, especially once they were without a chaperone.

As it was, in the following three weeks that

they drifted downriver, Alena found she'd had no need to worry. Zach's irritable disposition was anything but alluring. He cursed at everything. He cursed the squawking birds. He cursed the dugout for being too big for one man to handle. He cursed at Alena when she offered to help. He cursed at the water when it was too high.

At the moment, he stood on the bow, cursing because the water was too low. With a sigh, Alena laid her book aside and made her way to the front of the boat. She picked up the extra pole, braced it against the bank, as she'd often seen Slim or Yori do, and pushed with all her might.

Cocking his head, Zach leaned his weight on the long pole he had propped against the riverbed. "Just what in the hell do you think you're doing?"

"Go ahead," Alena said, paying his scowl no mind. "Curse away. I'm not listening. I'm going to help whether you like it or not. Otherwise, I fear we shall be stuck here till the moon comes out. *Then* you'll no doubt wake me in the middle of the night, cursing the stars for shining too brightly." She met his gaze, adding, "I'm tired of your terrible temper, Zachariah. 'Twould be much better if we at least tried to get along. This hatefulness of yours is getting us absolutely nowhere."

Zach tightened his jaw. He stared at her, absorbing her accusation. Then he blinked, relaxed his face muscles, and hung his head. "Gads, have I really been that bad?"

"You have."

"I have, haven't I." He glanced up from under his brows. Lifting his head, he doffed his hat.

He raked a hand through his hair, looking as if he wanted to say something important. After a moment's hesitation though, he jammed his hat back on and simply said, "Wait to push until I tell you."

Alena nodded, and as soon as they'd cleared shallow water, she wordlessly resumed her usual pastime, reading.

Once the dugout caught the current, Zach tossed his paddle aside and let the river pull them smoothly southward on its own.

He regarded Alena perched on a small crate at the back of the boat. For the first time in weeks, he didn't force himself to look away. Her skin, as flawless as ever, had tanned to a light golden-brown, and a soft peach stained her cheekbones and the bridge of her nose. The sun had woven streaks of moonlit silver through her pale gold hair. In contrast, her eyes had taken on the deep green color of the jungle and were brighter than ever. She glowed with vitality. A smile curved his lips as he took in the way the sun reflected off the water and played on the curls peeking out from under her hat. That damned old hat he'd given her, for all its wilted flowers, had found a place of honor upon her head. Only on her could it look as distinguished as a queen's crown.

His smile dwindled as he carefully considered the tremor of emotion that was taking hold of him. It hadn't been easy denying himself the simple pleasure of looking at her. He'd tried his best to alienate her from his thoughts, but ignoring her these past weeks had only aggravated the problem. Curbing his longing had added fuel to the fire, making him miserable, making her an obsession.

He had wished a hundred times she'd stayed in New York, or Philadelphia, or London. He wished she was anywhere but here alone with him. Dragging a knuckle across his clean-shaven chin, he would have laughed if he hadn't felt so pathetic about lying to himself. In truth, he wished she was sitting beside him.

Zach turned away from her to inspect his image in the dark water. Facing his feelings was a new experience, one that frightened him more than any danger he'd ever confronted. He reached down, scooped up some water, and splashed his face, hoping the deed might shock some sense into him. But it did no good. For when he turned around, his gaze went straight to the angel at the back of the boat.

She wasn't just another pretty face and this wasn't just a simple case of desire. Lord, it was more like an incurable sickness. Somehow he knew the gnawing inside him wouldn't cease with a communion of their bodies. He wanted more, needed more, to cure what ailed him. He needed to talk to her, to laugh with her. He craved her companionship, her devotion. Above all, he longed with an unquenchable yearning for a special place in her heart.

Zach plowed his fingers through his hair. God, he had finally taken that one step beyond the edge—just as Slim had always said he would. He felt suspended in midair, breathlessly waiting to hit the ground.

He had to do something. He couldn't leave it alone. If he didn't examine all aspects of . . . whatever this feeling was that plagued him, he might forever look back and wonder if he'd let something precious slip through his fingers. It was a big step. One he'd never considered taking. If something came of it, there would have to be changes made in his life. Changes he wasn't sure he could make. But he'd go crazy not knowing, wondering for the rest of his days if he'd made a big mistake. Dammit, no one had ever made him feel this way. No one. Straightening, he repositioned his hat. He was used to taking risks. He'd do just what he'd always done. Jump in feet first, then deal with the consequences as they came.

Zach checked the river ahead. He hadn't had any tingly feelings for several days after they'd left the mission. He was fairly certain they'd given their tracker friend the slip, at least for the time being. The current was calm and would carry them without his aid for a while. Glancing back at Alena, he decided this was as good a time as any.

On his side of the blanket he'd hung to allow Alena privacy, he rummaged through his gear. His fingers stopped briefly on his silver flask, then quickly moved on about their business. Finding his cleanest shirt, he did his best to smooth out the wrinkles. Before he slipped it on, he doused himself thoroughly with cologne. He buttoned up and tucked his shirttail in, deciding he should endeavor to stay as rational as possible during this procedure. From experience, he knew an experiment could get out of control if you didn't keep a handle on things.

Combing his hair, he checked his smile in the small shaving mirror tacked to the tarpaulin pole, and tried to recall what little he knew about courting. Finally giving up on the unruly lock that fell across his forehead, he leaned back a tad to inspect his efforts. "You handsome devil, you," he murmured beneath his breath, then clicked his tongue, winked, and headed purposefully toward the back of the boat.

Alena glanced up from her book as he approached, then did a double take. Good heavens. He'd combed his hair and buttoned his shirt. Her gaze shifted from the hat held properly in hand, to his spit-shined boots. What on earth had possessed the man to spruce up so in the middle of nowhere?

"Good afternoon, Miss Sutton. Do you mind if I join you?"

In shock, she could only nod and gesture toward the crate next to her.

He settled beside her with a smile brighter than the noonday sun. "Beautiful day, isn't it?" he asked, as cordially as if they sat among palms in a parlor.

Alena eyed him askance. Perhaps he was having another one of his fits. "Are you all right, sir?"

"I'm feeling very well, thank you. And you?"

Half-inclined to feel his forehead, Alena quirked one corner of her mouth. Sunstroke. It had to be sunstroke. "Are you quite sure you're not ill, sir?"

"I've never felt better in my life." He leaned forward and made his brows jump as if he'd just told her some great confidence.

While Alena looked on, completely baffled now, he lowered his lids to half-mast and produced that special fixation with his eyes. Yet there was something distinctly different about it this time. It wasn't forced. It was more natural ... genuine. She searched his face, wondering what he was up to, but she saw no signs of taunting or teasing. If she didn't know better, she might think—merciful Mary—was he trying to win her affections?

She fixed her gaze on his pulse-stopping smile and her heart began to thump against her rib cage. Once, much too long ago, she'd dreamed of the attentions of a gentleman caller. She had never imagined one quite so handsome, so bold, so daring as Zach. Yet, the way he was behaving, one could almost fancy they sat in a proper drawing room while she served him jam cakes and tea.

If he was not wooing her, then she had totally misconstrued his intentions. In which case, nevertheless, she dearly hoped the illusion might drag on a few minutes more. Actually, she rather enjoyed the attention after being snubbed for so long.

"Alena, I'd like to start all over."

A slight breeze ruffled his sable hair and swayed the lock across his forehead. His spicy scent fluttered her way, and she suddenly wished she'd pinned her hair up this morning instead of stuffing it under her hat. "Start over, sir?"

"Well, I know I haven't exactly been a joy to be around." Zach fiddled with the brim of his hat. "I guess we've been at odds from the very beginning, but I'd like that to change."

"Change, sir?"

"Please stop calling me 'sir.' It makes me sound old." He flashed a lazy smile. "I'm not really that old, you know."

Had he said "Please"? Alena couldn't believe her ears.

"You did suggest we should try to get along," Zach went on. "Maybe we could start by being friends, and my friends don't call me 'sir.'"

Alena stared for a moment at the hand he offered in friendship, then lifted her eyes to his. Regardless of his motive, there could be no harm in being comrades. Gingerly, she placed her fingers in his open palm. "Very well . . . Zach." She smiled at their joined hands. "We'll start all over. We shall be the best of friends, you and I, shan't we?"

"We will," Zach whispered hoarsely. God, he loved the way she said his name, as if she announced royalty at court. He took in every detail of her face, attempting to see beyond her shy smile, trying to look inside. "Alena . . . I . . . I've been a fool."

She laughed a little. "You are many things, Zach, but a fool you are not."

"How can you say that after everything I've done? I did all I could to keep you from coming here. I wasn't very tactful about it, either."

, "Indeed, and with good reason, I now realize. You were merely trying to protect me." She gave his hand a slight squeeze. "Zach, I quite understand why you attempted to dissuade me from this journey. I only hope you understand why I had to come. I must find my father. It is imperative that I do so. I have to know why he deserted me. I have to know why—"

"Alena," Zach interrupted. A pain stabbed his chest and he tightened his grasp on her hand. "Sweetheart, Howard's—"

She pressed the fingers of her free hand to his lips. "No, please don't say it. If you do, I might believe you. I can't give it up yet, don't you see?

I must keep believing that I'll find him."

Her eyes glistened with unshed tears, then softened with some other emotion. Zach paid no heed to the fluorescent sunset that lit the sky behind them or the gentle evening cries of the jungle. He lost all desire to keep things on a scientific basis as her eyes conveyed unspoken words akin to silent pledges. Without thought or hesitation, he said as much with his.

Pulled together by an invisible force, they leaned forward from the waist in unison. Making no other contact than his hand wrapped tightly around hers, Zach touched her lips in a kiss as soft as a summer breeze . . . and magic bolted between them.

They parted but a breadth, and Zach saw his alarm reflected in her face. A kiss to this woman was like a promise to any other. Yet he was drawn to take her lips again, rationalizing as he did that he was used to jumping feet first into the fire and would face the consequences later.

The kiss became fierce and Zach maneuvered her onto his lap, his hands roving sensuously up and down her back. She clung to him as his mouth moved hungrily over hers. Matching his own moves, her tongue teased and tantalized until he was sure she would drive him mad.

Alena gave in to the blissful dizziness that swirled in her head. He did care. He could no longer deny it, and neither could she. Wanting to give him everything, wanting to tell him all that was in her heart, she whispered against his lips, "I feel as if I'm floating on air."

"So do I, Angelface, so do I," he confessed, then claimed her mouth again.

Something warm and miraculous glowed

within Alena when he stretched his long legs out and stiffened until she lay molded against the hard muscled plane of his body. Sparks of pleasure ignited low in her abdomen as his hips rotated . . . and hers followed suit.

It was a wondrous sensation, this freedom from propriety. She felt at liberty to touch and be touched in a way that had always been forbidden. *Letting go.* Dear Lord, she was actually letting go. And it was rapturous. "Gracious," she murmured, "I hear a roaring in my ears."

"So do I, Angelface, so do—" Zach broke away from her mouth and froze, giving her a startled look.

"Zach? What—"

"Shh. Listen."

The heretofore imagined roaring grew louder . . . and louder. Jumping up, Zach swung her off of him so fast she stumbled, her bottom almost missing the crate. His head snapped to the bow of the boat and the color drained from his face as his eyes widened on the river ahead. "Oh, sh—"

His voice was drowned out by a thunderous rumbling sound and he tumbled Alena to the floor of the dugout, covering her body with his.

"What is it?" she screamed, trying to make herself heard above the roar.

"Rapids!" He attempted a reassuring smile. "I don't suppose you've ever ridden a bucking bronc—"

The front of the boat flew up till it was almost vertical, and slammed down with a ferocity that jarred Alena's bones. Water slapped against the side of the boat, splashing over to drench them. With unbelievable speed, they rushed down the turbulent river, bumping, bucking, swirling, tilting.

Zach pried her fingers from his shirt and wrapped them around the log that held up the tarpaulin. "Hold tight," he yelled. "I'm going up front to see if I can hold the nose down over the crests." He kissed the protest from her mouth, quick and hard, then scrambled toward the bow.

For what seemed like an eternity, she clung to the pole with all her might as the dugout was tossed about like a toy. Water showered over her in bucketfuls. She squeezed her eyes tight, fearing the angry river would swallow them at any moment.

Suddenly, as swiftly as it had begun, it was over. Waterlogged and exhausted, Alena lay relishing the calmness that gently rocked the boat.

A few minutes later, she raised her head and noticed that the roar had faded into the distance. "Zach?" she called, pushing soggy strands of hair from her face. Battered and bruised, she came to her knees. Looking to the front of the dugout, her heart stopped for several beats.

Unmoving, Zach hung half over the bow.

She scrambled across the deck as fast as her legs would carry her, and laid a trembling hand upon his back.

Thank God, she could feel a shallow breathing. His heart beat beneath her palm and relief washed over her. He'd open his eyes any moment and smile at her. She was sure of it.

The moment stretched into almost half an hour and his damp thick lashes stayed closed. Panic scaled Alena's spine. The sky was darkening to a deep purple.

"Zach? Please, please, open your eyes." She

brushed the wet curls from his forehead. "Zach?" She leaned closer and her hand stilled. The last of the day's dim light illuminated an ugly magenta swelling at his temple.

Next to maneuvering Zach onto the deck, poling the dugout to the bank had been the hardest thing Alena had ever done. She didn't know where her strength had come from. Nor did she know how long they'd drifted before she'd realized that her attention could not be evenly divided between Zach and the blooming boat.

Her hands were blistered. Her throat was raspy from trying to coax Zach back into the world. To make matters worse, once she tied them to the shore, weariness had overcome her. In a state of complete exhaustion, she had rested her head against Zach's chest and dozed off. She'd awakened to find the rope had slipped, and they were drifting again . . . to God knew where.

She had endured loneliness before, but *being* alone was quite a different matter. Though she'd somehow survived the night, the bright morning brought her no solace. Gazing forlornly at Zach's somnolent face again, a held-back tear escaped down her cheek. *Please, wake up. Please, Zach. I'm frightened.*

A terrible shriek came from the shore, intensifying her fear and resentment and frustration. The thing screamed again. Willing the current to carry them further and faster downstream, Alena gripped the front of Zach's shirt and leaned into him. "Zachariah Summerfield! Blast you, if you leave me here in this desolation alone, I shall *never, ever* forgive you. Do you hear me? Never,

ever." She gave him a vicious shake, then tears she couldn't stop trickled down her cheeks. "Oh, Zach, please . . . please come back to me. I need you."

Warm raindrops on his face made Zach flinch. His eyes moved behind his lids and pain split his brain. Slowly . . . with great agony, he opened his eyes. He squinted against the brightness that haloed the silhouette above him. His gaze focused, adjusted to the sunlight, and he reached up and touched Alena's wet cheeks.

She gasped, then laughed, her tears coming full force.

Zach tried to speak.

"Shh, now," she said, gaining control of her emotions. "Don't try to talk just yet. You received a nasty bump on your head when we went through the rapids yesterday." She laid a wet rag against his temple, and his eyes slid closed.

Seconds later, his eyes shot back open with the sharpness of a man who slept with danger. "Yesterday? How long have—" Raising his head, he winced, and lowered it again. His lids closed once more and he tightened his jaw. "Jeez almighty, I feel like I've been on a three-day drunk. How long have I been out?"

"All night and the better part of the morning." She placed another cool compress against his bruise. "Oh, Zach, I was so worried—"

"All nigh—aaah!" He groaned as he sat straight up, then grimaced. "I take it back. I feel more like I was on a five-day drunk and someone threw me in a pen with ten Texas longhorns."

Alena furrowed her brow. "Perhaps you should lie back down a bit."

Zach smiled at her concerned expression and grazed her jaw with his knuckles. "Nah, I'll be fine as soon as my head quits waltzing and I get this kink out of my back." He started to roll his shoulder, then stopped and frowned, crooking two fingers beneath her chin. "Jeez, no offense, sweetheart, but you look like hell. You okay?"

"I am now." She smiled and lowered her lashes, his touch evoking the remembrance of their intimacy. "I'm simply tired, that's all."

Her shyness sparked a memory in him, too. A memory of how things had been between them before the rapids interrupted them. He'd come close to ... He swallowed hard, grimaced, and dropped his hand. That wasn't the way he wanted it. If and when it came to that, he wanted it to be respectable. That was what she'd want. He didn't want her to cringe in shame when the deed was done. And no matter how willing she'd been in his arms, there was no doubt in his mind that that was exactly what she'd do. She was bound by convention. Propriety wouldn't allow her any other route. Then again, if this thing between them turned out to be no more than fascination, he'd be damned if he'd send her soiled to another man. She was too proud, too priceless, and he was too weak to carry that burden for the rest of his life.

He glanced at the surroundings, wincing at the effort it took to move his throbbing head. "How far have we drifted?"

"I don't know. I daresay I didn't keep track," she said, following his gaze. "I did get us to shore once but we broke away, and between you and the dugout—"

"*You* got us to shore?"

"I did." She lifted her chin in response to his disbelieving expression.

"You got us to shore?"

"I *did*. I have the blisters to prove it." She held up her hands. "You were certainly no help. I couldn't let us drift off the end of the earth, could I?"

Zach chuckled. "Okay, if you say you did, I believe you."

Admiration shone from his eyes, and pride filled Alena.

Clearing his throat, he looked away. "Get the map Slim drew for me out of my bag, will you? I'll see if I can't figure out where we are."

She did as he asked, and he slipped his glasses on and spread the map before him. Tracing a curved line that represented the river, he pointed to a certain spot. "If my calculation of time is accurate, we should have come to a fork in the river sometime last night right about here."

"Where are we on the map then?" Alena asked and knelt beside him.

"Somewhere in this area, I think," he said, making a small circle with his finger. "But I'm not sure, exactly. We could have drifted—"

"You're not sure?" Alena widened her eyes. "You mean we're lost?"

"Of course we're not lost." Zach picked up his hat, stood to a hunched-back position, then scowled as he straightened, bracing a hand on his spine. "I just don't happen to know *exactly* where we are at this precise moment. I'm pretty sure we're in the Amazon. It's hard to tell where because the Orinoco branches off at several points. You didn't happen to notice which way the boat veered last night—to the left or to the right?"

"No," Alena said quietly with a slow shake of her head. "I'm sorry. I didn't realize it would be important. I . . . I fell asleep."

"Ah, well, we'll get our bearings soon." Zach gave her a wink as he stood and tugged her to her feet. Keeping hold of her fingertips, he stared at her for a long moment. Suddenly uncomfortable, he dropped her hands and stuffed his in his pockets. "You should get some rest," he said, setting his sight on something in the distance.

Alena took a step closer to him and laid her palm against his chest, bringing his gaze back to her. She wanted him to kiss her, needed him to kiss her and assure her the worst was behind them—especially because, for some strange reason, she was afraid their perils had only just begun. She saw a movement at the base of Zach's throat. He was going to kiss her. She could tell by the look in his eyes.

"You've had a rough time of it, Angelface. Get some sleep." Dropping a quick, chaste kiss on her forehead, Zach spun her around. "Go on," he said with a smack to her bottom.

Shocked into moving, she headed toward the tarpaulin, rather disappointed that he hadn't kissed her on the mouth. By the time she reached her pallet, he seemed absorbed in Slim's map and the jungle ahead of them. Just looking at him set a wind under the wings of her heart. It was good to have him back and in charge of the world again. With a smile, she snuggled on her mat and watched him until exhaustion overwhelmed her and her lids slid closed.

It was several hours later that she awoke to see Zach at the bow. She rose, straightened herself as best she could, then joined him.

He glanced at her as she came to stand beside him, then scanned the region. "Take a good look, Angelface. This is the Amazon." He nodded ahead to where the river narrowed into a dark tunnel of overgrowth. "There's no other place on earth quite like it. It's as much alive with challenge as it is with untamed vegetation."

Entering the verdant, canopied tract, sunlight faded, peeking through the sparse gaps in the leaves above at rare intervals. There was an eeriness about the area that made Alena shiver. She thought perhaps she was being foolish, until Zach leaned down and slowly, very carefully picked up his rifle and cocked it.

"Zach, what is it?"

He shrugged, his gaze never wavering from his hard study of their surroundings. "Just a gut feeling. Something's not right. It's too quiet... too—" His eyes froze on an object on the shore.

Following his gaze, Alena's gasp was muffled by his hand, and he pulled her down, crouching beside her.

"Painted monkey skulls," he whispered in answer to the question in her eyes. Releasing her, he rested his shoulders against the boat, and nudged his hat up. "Damn, looks like we've wandered into unfriendly territory. They generally don't stake those god-awful things along the banks unless they're hostile."

Alena swallowed. She couldn't quite grasp the full meaning of what he'd said, but she connected those horrid things on the shore to... "Indians," she rasped and glanced at him askance. "Do you truly think they're *savage* Indians, Zach?"

"I'm not familiar with the tribes this far south,

Angel. From what I've heard, no white men have lived long enough to find out much about them." Zach furrowed his brows and continued as if talking to himself. "Yori did mention we might be having to weave around a tribe of headhunters as we journeyed deeper into the Amazon. We could have drifted further south than I assumed, I suppose. God, I hope they aren't anthropophagous."

"Anthro—what?" Alena asked.

"Cannibals," Zach murmured in deep thought, then looked at her as if just awaking. "Ah . . . there's nothing really to worry about, Angelface." He slipped an arm around her and nuzzled her temple. "I'm just thinking out loud. I'm not an anthropologist. I don't really know the first thing about it. Besides, we'll probably just float right by without them ever knowing we were—"

Swoosh. A long spear pierced the deck with a thud and stood vertical, not six inches from the toe of Zach's boot.

"Stay down!" he commanded, hurling Alena to the deck. He threw his rifle over the side and fired into the brush, dodging the shower of spears and arrows that flew from every direction.

Alena lay paralyzed, her eyes squeezed tight. Through covered ears, she heard the thunderous crack of Zach's gun, and the sizzle of spears piercing the deck all around them.

Zach had slipped back behind cover and was reloading, when an earth-shattering cry overhead turned his attention skyward. At the same time the artillery from the jungle ceased. Nothing more than a few hushed murmurs came from the banks, then total silence.

Alena lifted her head, pushed her hat back on her crown, and gazed at the sky.

A huge black bird with motionless, enormous wings floated in airy circles above them.

"A condor," Zach informed her. "It's highly revered here." He peeked over the side of the boat. The natives lining the banks stared in awe at the vulture. "I think they've taken it as a sign of some sort," he said, sitting beside Alena again. "Though of what, I'm not sure."

Alena rose to her haunches and touched his sleeve. "Zach, perhaps now that they've settled down, we could talk to them . . . tell them we're only passing through and we mean them no harm."

"Just like that, huh?" Zach half-snickered, half-sighed. "I wish it was that easy, Angel. Unfortunately, these savages aren't from the same school of etiquette we are. We've trespassed on their territory. That's an unpardonable sin. Other tribes in the area don't even set foot on each oth—"

Another bloodcurdling screech brought both their heads up in time to see the creature above diving straight toward them. They jumped to their feet. Zach swung the butt of his rifle. Alena flung her arms up, knocking off her hat. The bird dipped within a few feet of them, then soared upward and disappeared into the clouds.

"*Incaro!*" shouted a voice from the shore. "*Mahrakimba! Incaro!*"

Zach lifted his rifle, aiming at the warrior who'd spoken, then eased his finger off the trigger as the man fell to his knees, to be followed by the others.

"*Incaro,*" the man proclaimed again, raising

She dropped her head and nodded. "But I don't even know how to converse with them. And I certainly have no desire whatsoever to sup with them." She turned solemn eyes to his. "I'm frightened, Zach. I'm horribly frightened."

"I know, sweetheart," he said, brushing a finger along her jaw. "But right now we don't have a choice. I'll come up with a way out of this soon, I promise."

Before she could assure him that she had every faith in him, he was jerked roughly away from her. Several natives prodded him with spears off the boat.

"Stop that!" she screamed, anger momentarily replacing her fear. She started forward, but stopped cold when two of the savages, one on either side of her, took hold of her arms.

"Ah, don't rile them, Angelface," Zach pleaded, glancing at the point of the spear braced against his chest. "Just smile, nod your head, and agree with everything they say."

Alena's heart vanished into the vegetation with him as his captors took him away. Handled with considerably more care, she was led off the boat and down the trail far behind them.

"Smile, *princess*," she heard Zach yell out from somewhere ahead. "Be brave!"

His faraway command touched something deep inside. *Be brave*. She didn't feel very courageous without him beside her. And she certainly didn't feel inclined to smile. Indeed, she felt embarrassingly close to being ill. Her stomach churned. Her heart thumped furiously. Her palms were damp, and she swayed slightly with dizziness.

But she did smile. Completely ignoring the brutes on either side of her, she stared straight ahead, lifted her chin, and just for Zach, she smiled as best she could—although she was a bit afraid she looked more like she'd just eaten a lemon.

Chapter 12

Alena's feigned smiled faltered as she was led into the village. A sea of gaping brown faces greeted her, emerging in droves from the cluster of grass huts. Brown hands reached out at her from every angle as her escorts shuffled her through the crowd. The curious onlookers grabbed at her clothes, touched her skin, her hair, making her flesh crawl. Half-paralyzed, she frantically tried to see beyond them. *Zach. Dear God, where was Zach?*

She was halted before a dome-shaped grass hut, larger than the numerous others. The savages circled her, thankfully standing back far enough for her to breathe. They murmured amongst themselves in hushed tones and stared at her, nodding. Her two attendants let go of her arms, but remained by her side. No other native made a move toward her until a sturdy young warrior plowed his way through the gathering. Alena flinched when he grabbed her wrist. She widened her eyes on his unfriendly features. Scared motionless, she could do naught but watch as he turned her palm up, wet his finger on his tongue, and rubbed it hard against the inside of her wrist.

251

Her head sank between her rising shoulders. She wanted to scream, but no such sound would move past her throat. She could only stare into the heathen's black, soul-boring eyes.

At last he stopped the proceeding, apparently satisfied with whatever result he'd hoped to achieve. Frowning, he studied his finger, then turned a softened gaze back to Alena. His mouth quirked into the vague resemblance of a smile and he burst out laughing. Then he lifted his finger in the air, showing it to the assemblage. They all started laughing.

Bewildered, Alena glanced between her arm and his finger several times before it dawned on her that he must have thought . . . oh, but that was preposterous. Looking about at the others, she noted some of them had painted their arms, legs, or faces white.

Alena was aware that the laughter that slipped out of her mouth stemmed partially from hysteria. Yet the situation struck her as hugely funny. He'd thought her skin was painted white.

Her mirth was short-lived, however, for everyone's laughter ceased abruptly when the flap of the large hut was thrown back. From the depths of the dark entrance emerged a man of obvious importance. He stood a full head taller than the others and, though heavier and very old, was magnificently built. Bright feathers adorned his straight black hair and his person. The villagers parted in great reverence as he stalked toward Alena, carrying a spear draped with dangling, shrunken heads. He stopped before her and, in silence, assessed her from head to toe with granite eyes.

Alena fidgeted a little, unsure of what she

should do. The man was clearly in authority and might possibly be persuaded to release them if she acted in suitable manner. But how did one properly greet the leader of an Amazonian tribe?

Smile, Angelface, she could almost hear Zach say. So she did. By the time the insolent old Indian brought his cold expressionless gaze back to hers, she'd pasted a perfectly charming smile upon her lips. For endless moments, they stared at one another. Then his harshness vanished and the corners of his mouth curved up ever so slightly. Taking her hand, he lifted it into the air, turned to his people, and declared, "Mahrakimba!"

"Mahrakimba!" they chanted. "Mahrakimba!"

Alena was completely unprepared for what happened next. She was ushered through the cheering natives like a queen to a private hut. There, she was given fruit and clear, cool water. Maidens filed in to brush her hair, spread a bed of fresh palms, and sprinkle flowers about the dirt floor.

The day continued in such a fashion. She was pampered sinfully and, while she no longer feared for her own safety, her anxiety about what they'd done with Zach grew steadily. She tried to question the young women who fluttered around her. Not understanding a word she said, they simply giggled, nodded, and shook their heads. Alena's frustration and ire rose until she finally shooed the girls all out the door.

She paced back and forth, glaring at the two guards whose crossed spears blocked her exit. They made her feel like a white dove in a cage.

It wasn't until she'd been summoned to the chief's hut that evening and was crossing the grounds that she saw Zach. He was bound to a vertical pole not far from the great hut. Breaking away from her escorts, she ran and threw her arms around him.

"Here now, what's all this?" He teasingly lifted a corner of his mouth. "It must be true what I heard about doomed men. Women just can't resist them."

In no mood for humor, Alena pressed her cheek against his chest, and, after a moment's hesitation, he laid the side of his face on the top of her head.

"They haven't hurt you, have they?" he asked, his voice soft and serious.

"No." She looked up into his eyes, absorbing the sight, scent, and feel of him. "You were jesting when you said they might eat you, weren't you, Zach? They haven't harmed you, either, have they?"

Zach smiled at the concern glistening in her green eyes. *You, woman, you harm me . . . you alarm me*, he wanted to say. But "Don't worry, I'm fine" was all he could manage before she was pulled away from him.

Once again the chief made a regal exit from his hut, evoking a deathly silence. He scowled at Zach, then came to Alena and made some loud proclamation she couldn't begin to comprehend.

"I don't understand!" she asserted, interrupting his speech. She shook her head vigorously. "I can't understand—"

He stopped her cold with a vicious narrowing of his eyes. He glowered at her for some time, then, in a booming voice that nearly shook the ground beneath her, he shouted, "Sengali!"

A small wiry man made his way through the

wall of spectators. He inclined his head toward the chief. The chief, in turn, nodded toward Alena and the man pivoted to her.

Soberly, he glanced at his leader and said, "I am Sengali. I would be honored to tell Chief Chato, great *morbicha* of the Jaquaras, your words. And you, his words. I am very good to speak your language."

Alena's spirits lifted. At last, a *civilized* person. "That's very kind of you, Mr. Sen . . . Sen—"

"Sengali."

"Yes, Mr. Sen-gali. As I was saying, this is very kind. Now please tell His Majesty to make those men take their spears away from Zach." She gestured to where Zach was being held some twenty feet away.

"Zach? Do you speak of the man you came here with?"

"Yes. Now please tell His Majesty, Chief . . . oh, what is his name again?"

"Chief Chato, but—"

"Yes, Chief Chato. Tell Chief Chato to have Zach released."

The Indian ducked his head.

"Well?" Alena grew impatient as the seconds ticked by. "What are you waiting for, good man?"

Sengali eyed her warily. "I don't think Chief Chato will very much like your words."

"I don't care what His Majesty likes." She lowered her brows. "Tell him this instant or I shall . . . I shall—" *What would Mahrakimba do?* Zach had said she possessed great powers. "I shall turn you into a frog," she finished with a lift of her chin.

Sengali blinked, then turned to the chief and

translated Alena's request in rapid succession. The expression that crossed the bigger man's face made it quite apparent that he was indeed displeased.

At the chief's thunderous reply, Sengali squeezed his eyes tight. Yet, when he faced Alena, his features were sternly controlled again. "That is not possible."

"Not possible?" Alena looked from Sengali to the chief and back again. "Not possible? What does he mean it's not possible?"

"Chief Chato say you must not be with this man. He say this man will steal your powers. He say you must marry one of your own. When it is time, Chief Chato will choose a worthy husband for you."

Alena's mouth gaped but she couldn't utter a word. She could only stare, aghast, as the Indian continued on in a matter-of-fact manner.

"This one"—he indicated Zach—"must die within the rising of three suns. The shaman says so."

"No!" The protest broke from Alena's throat, resounding through the village. "No! You can't kill him!" She charged toward the chief and was jerked to a standstill by the two natives on either side of her.

"Alena!"

Zach's voice turned her head in time to see a crude knife hoisted to the base of his throat. He didn't speak another word. But his eyes conveyed an imploring message. *Don't start trouble. I'll think of something. Trust me . . . trust me . . . trust me . . .*

His silent plea restored her composure, and she nodded. Yet, she couldn't leave it alone. She shrugged her arms from the men's grasp. Perhaps she should be more diplomatic. She smoothed her waistband, then presented His Majesty with a reserved expression. "Sengali," she said calmly, keeping her gaze riveted to the chief's, "tell him that course of action is not acceptable." Without looking at the interpreter, she sensed his reluctance. "Tell him," she repeated firmly.

The chief's face turned black with rage upon hearing her argument. Not about to cringe, Alena returned his glare, though the hair on her nape stood straight out.

With a suddenness that made her jump in spite of herself, he ground out his response, waved a hand, and ducked back into his hut.

Sengali dropped his head, glancing up at her. "He say . . . your conduct is most shameful for a princess. You should leave him now for he tires of your angry tongue. He say, when this one"— he pointed at Zach again—"is gone, the spell the white man placed on you will be broken."

Alena's anguished gaze met Zach's. She struggled against the impulse to cry out his name and close the distance between them. *This couldn't be happening. It couldn't.*

Yet she knew indeed it was, when the two braves caught her arms and turned her toward the hut. Zach's handsome face gravely repeated his earlier message. His eyes held hers over her shoulder as she was led away.

Alena ran her fingers lightly over the brittle wilted flowers on the hat clutched against her breast. She closed her eyes and conjured up the essence of its previous owner. Pipe tobacco, spice, rum, an outdoors scent . . . Zach.

Her eyes opened on the crossed spears still blocking the doorway of the hut. Beyond the guards, dusk had turned the sky sienna. Zach would find a way out of this. He would. He'd promised.

Combing a hand through her hair, she tried to remember Sengali's exact words. *This one must die within . . . the rising of three suns*. Three sunrises. Three days. Tomorrow would be the last day before the third sunrise.

Tonight. They had to escape tonight.

But what if Zach couldn't think of a plan, or was hurt, or, dear God, what if they'd already—Unable to bear the thought, she curled into a ball on the palm mat and hugged her ribs. No matter how hard she tried to be optimistic, visions of the horrible methods these heathens might use to kill a man preyed heavily on her mind.

Please, please, God, she prayed, *help us. Zach's not a bad fellow. I know he's bullheaded and swears and acts heartless at times, but beneath his coarseness, he's gentle and kind and I love him.*

I love him.

The words had slipped unexpectedly into her mind. The thought, she suspected, had been there hiding for quite some time. "I love him," she whispered aloud. Saying it instead of keeping it locked away in her heart was strangely comforting. "I love you . . . I love you, Zach," she repeated over and over until her eyes slid closed and exhaustion eclipsed the bitterness of reality.

Alena ran in her fitful dreams. Through the winding paths of the jungle, she ran as fast as she could, pushing broad leaves out of her way. The bushes rustled behind her and her breath came in spurts.

Looking over her shoulder, she saw the vicious-looking savage that continued to stalk her. While he barreled toward her, her flight lagged into slow motion.

With a bloodcurdling cry the warrior leaped, knocking her to the ground. His face moved closer . . . and closer to hers.

"*Zach!*" she screamed. The name echoed around her. The heathen clamped a hand over her mouth and a cruel smile curved his lips. "The white man," he said, his eyes cold and glittering, "lives no longer."

She shook her head frantically and clawed at his hand.

"Ouch. Dammit, Alena, wake up! It's me!"

The urgent whisper made her open her eyes. She stared disbelievingly at the dark shadow above her, closed her eyes, and prayed she wasn't still dreaming, then opened them again.

Zach. It was Zach . . . Zach's hand covering her mouth! Prying his fingers away, she sat up, threw her arms around his neck, and kissed him.

He returned her kiss briefly, then pulled away. "I've missed you, too, Angelface. But we can do this later. Right now we need to get the hell out of here. There's some kind of hullabaloo going on out there," he said, glancing nervously at the entrance of the hut. "The guards have stepped away from the door." He clasped her hand and tugged her to her feet. "I worked the ropes loose hours ago but had to wait until they were distracted to make a break. It won't be long before they notice I'm gone. Don't forget your hat."

Alena picked up her hat and set it on her head, gazing at him from beneath the brim. "Zach, I realized the most wonderful thing about you today."

"Huh?" His attention was on the door and the goings-on outside. He cocked his eyes her way and his expression turned quizzical. "Alena, what's wrong with you? You look all moony. Aw, gads. You didn't drink anything that tasted fruity, did you?"

Alena looked toward the sound of wildly played drums and chanting outside. In all probability, they'd never make it past the celebrating Jaquaras. She had to tell Zach how she felt about him. She had to tell him now before they left the hut and met their fate, whatever that might be.

"Alena!" Zach took her arms and turned her to him. "Come on, Angel, take some deep breaths and clear your head."

Alena caressed his features with her gaze, her heart swelling. The low torchlight flickering across his bronze skin illuminated the puzzlement and concern in his silver-blue eyes. That wayward strand of hair he could never tame spilled over his forehead. Even tired and worried-looking, he was beautiful. She parted her lips to profess her love and . . . nothing came out. Simply nothing. She'd held such a tight rein on her emotions for so long that she hadn't considered how difficult it might be to express them. Since acknowledging her feelings about Zach that afternoon, she had expected the three little words to be spoken quite easily.

"Sorry, sweetheart, but whatever you want to say, you'll have to say later." Slipping an arm around her shoulders, Zach started to move them both toward the exit. "Stay close and in the shadows. Don't make a peep and—"

Time and her vocal chords giving her no other choice, Alena hurled herself in front of him. Determined to show him what she could not say, she caught his face and brought his mouth down to hers. She kissed him passionately, desperately, applying the same, sweet techniques he'd used on her.

Zach responded after a moment of apparent shock and he clasped her waist, pulling her to him. Knowing this kiss could be their last farewell, she arched her body against him until they fit together like matching pieces of a puzzle.

Just as Alena was feeling light-headed and short of breath, Zach lifted his head and stared down at her with knitted brows. He took a deep shuddering breath and whispered, "Good Lord, woman. What kind of magic did they work on you?" Then he slanted his mouth over hers again. Tightening his grip around her waist, he swept one hand up her spine and cradled her head. His tongue glided over her parted lips and delved deeper with a fierce urgency.

Alena clutched his tattered shirt, soaring with a glorious, unidentifiable need as his hand spanned her ribs and began a slow move upward.

"Morbicha! Morbicha!"

Zach whirled, shoving Alena behind him. The witch doctor, standing just inside the entrance of the hut, rattled a conglomeration of gourds at them. *"Morbicha!"* he yelled again.

Alena peeked around and gasped at the horrid mask the shaman wore. Zach covered her eyes and pushed her head back. She ducked, peering beneath his outstretched arm.

The witch doctor stepped aside as Chato stomped through the door in his usual arrogant manner, followed timidly by Sengali. Pointing at

Alena and Zach, the shaman hissed a litany of complaints.

Zach could only understand a few words, one of which was *Mahrakimba*. Another was equivalent to . . . "lover"?

The chief threw his head back and roared at the roof. His gaze returned with a killing look to the two accused. He slammed his staff down, stirring up dust, and blasted out a declaration. With an angry nod of his head, he indicated that Sengali should translate.

Sengali, his brown face unreadable, moved before Zach. "Chief Chato say you shame Mahrakimba before the gods and her people. He say you have destroyed her power and her honor. He say—" Sengali shifted his gaze to Alena, then dropped it to the floor. "He say you must marry her now . . . and take her with you to your death."

Zach looked disbelievingly from the interpreter to the chief. "Whoa now, just hold up there a minute." A nervous laugh escaped him as he ran a hand through his hair. "We were only kissing. That's all. We didn't . . . we didn't . . . do . . . what he thinks we did. Damn. Tell him that. Tell him we were only kissing."

Sengali hung his head and shook it slowly. "He will not listen. The shaman saw you. The shaman say you were—"

"Okay, okay." Zach stopped him with a hand. He looked at Alena. She appeared so small and wan in the dim light. He tried a smile, hoping to soothe the panic from her eyes.

A pitiful excuse for a smile, Alena thought, though she knew the reason for his unwarranted expression. It was neither the place, nor the time for a smile, yet leave it to Zach to try.

She lifted the corners of her mouth, imitating his forlorn attempt. At that precise moment, she loved the blue-eyed madman more than life itself. The world beyond the two of them ceasing to matter, she clutched his waist and clung to him with all her might.

All rationality fled when they were pried apart. Alena made a wild lunge for Zach. But viselike grips banded her arms to hold her back.

Likewise, Zach bucked against the four men who tore him away. A dozen or more spears pinned his body, halting his struggle. He stood like a stone statue, save for the heaving of his chest. His eyes sought her in a way that wrenched Alena's heart. "It's not over as long as we're still breathing, Angelface," he ground out as they prodded him from the hut. "Do you hear me? It's not over yet, dammit!"

Throughout the next day, Alena teetered on the brink of what was real . . . and what was not.

Her aloofness to the maidens that hovered about her wavered with each sip of something they called *cauin*. The giggling girls pressed the fruit-flavored drink into her hands at every opportunity. At last, half-dazed, she allowed them to bathe her.

Lying on the mat, she drifted in and out of consciousness while her body was glazed with palm oil. She swayed when she was helped to stand and wrapped in a soft, white doeskin *tanga*. They brushed her hair to a lustrous shine and wove orchids through the silver strands. Her scalp tingled and her head lolled back. Inside, she glowed with the same wonderful warmth

Zach's rum had produced, a lifetime ago.

The world outside the hut tilted when she stepped into the misty darkness. She was led toward the huge bonfire, her feet floating inches off the ground. She wasn't the least afraid. This was a dream. It wasn't really happening.

Zach stiffened and stared into the fire. The shaman danced around him, shaking his rattles, reciting incantations. Zach ignored him until the hideously masked witch doctor tossed something into the blaze. The illusion of thunder and lightning brought Zach's forearm up to shield his eyes from the smoky flare.

Slowly, the haze cleared and he sensed someone beside him. Looking down at Alena, his heart was captured by her adoring green gaze. She beamed a smile at him, and he returned the best he could give under the circumstances. She was breathtakingly beautiful with her lion's mane of hair spilling over her bare, glistening shoulders.

. . . Bare shoulders?

The corners of his mouth fell as he pinpointed her scarcely covered breasts swelling above the scanty *tanga*. He lowered his gaze, halting on the brazen amount of slender thigh the garment displayed, then let it slide down her legs to her bare feet. Gads, she was standing there half-naked . . . and smiling.

He jerked his eyes to her face again. She glowed a little too brightly, he thought. Her cheeks were too flushed. Good God, what had they done to her? She was walking to her death like a lamb to slaughter . . . and smiling.

Zach caught her as she swayed toward him but before he could question her, he was seized from behind. In a blur, Chief Chato grabbed Zach's left hand and nicked the palm with a knife. Seeing the chief take Alena's wrist and turn it palm up, he struggled against the men who held him. "Damn you, Chato. You leave her alone. Mahrakimba will leave her wrath upon this village. She will..."

Ignoring the outburst, Chato pricked Alena's unflinching palm, placed it in Zach's, and tied their hands together with a strip of hide. Throwing his arms to the heavens, the chief proclaimed the two before him were now one in spirit. That much, at least, Zach understood.

What he couldn't understand was why they were then separated again, blindfolded, and taken on a trek through the jungle. Furthermore, he wondered why their execution was being forestalled. From all he'd heard, it wasn't customary procedure for the natives in these parts.

Stumbling over the bumpy, slick trail, he worked at the ropes that bound his hands behind his back. They were being taken somewhere else. But where? A secret ceremonial ground? Damn. If he could just get loose. Maybe an opportunity for escape would present itself. Still, he couldn't move until he knew where Alena was.

Out of frustration he concentrated on sounds and smells, trying to get his bearings. He was almost certain they were moving south. How long had it been since they'd left the Jaquara camp? Two hours? The air was cool and moist. By calculation, he would guess they were headed for the rain forest.

A rush of distant water came from ahead. Rapids? No...a waterfall? Definitely a waterfall.

The roaring of the water grew louder and

louder as he was prodded up a steep slippery incline. A fine mist covered him. Sweet Jesus, were they going to throw them off the top of a waterfall? His footsteps halted with a sudden realization. His fear of death was minimal compared to the fear that gripped him when he thought of never seeing Alena again. A sharp jab between his shoulder blades moved him forward.

The air closed off around him, smelling stale and musty. He was shoved with a force that sent him tumbling onto a cold hard surface. He broke the fall with his shoulder, tugging the last knot free from his wrists. Lying still, he kept his hands behind his back and listened. Other than the rush of the falls, he could hear only the hollow, steady drip of water somewhere in the distance. Satisfied he was alone, he jerked his blindfold off and stood, verifying the theory that he was in a cave hidden behind the waterfall.

"Zach?"

He whirled at the softly spoken question, his gaze assessing the eerie surroundings. All he saw was an empty palm mat in the corner. There was no one, save himself, in the immediate cavern, though without a torch there was no way to tell how far back the cave stretched.

Jeez almighty, this place reminded him of the tombs in Egypt. It gave him that same case of the willies.

He must've imagined he'd heard Alena's voice. Wishful thinking, he told himself, then stalked to the entrance to see what was going on outside. Tugging down his hat, he marked that escape route off his list. The path was lined with torch-bearing natives. Alena was nowhere in sight. Drumming his fingers against the cold stone, he reluctantly looked over his shoulder toward the dark recesses of the cave. There had to be another way out.

He headed for the pitch blackness, his abhorrence of the childhood game of blindman's bluff crossing his mind. Gads, he'd hated being "it." He hated feeling around in the dark, dammit. The last time he'd rummaged through a cave and his torch had gone out he'd fallen into a blasted hole and broken his leg. It had taken Slim three days to find him. He paused as the darkness at the rear of the cavern engulfed him, then, grimacing, moved forward at a cautious pace until he felt an opening.

As he made his slow progression down the passage, a small, wiggly creature landed on his shoulder. He jumped and slapped it off. "Aw, jeez," he mumbled with a shiver. "Damn creepy-crawlies all over the place. Can't even see my frigging hand in front of my fa—"

Zach stood paralyzed, his palms frozen against the cool wall. A faint sobbing echoed through the funnel of darkness. But where was it coming from? His right or left? He listened intently. It was impossible to distinguish which direction. Sliding his hands against the side of the corridor, he made a split second decision and veered left. Soon, a dim light glowed ahead and the muffled crying grew more distinct.

Cautiously, he crept toward the light. It shone from an opening barely large enough for him to squeeze through. Ducking down, he peeked beneath a jutting boulder. A single torch illuminated the burrow and cast a flickering shadow against the low rock ceiling. He shifted his gaze to follow the path of the shadow. A small, familiar form was huddled in the rear. Immediately, he maneuvered his way through the hole and crouched beside the figure. "Alena?"

Alena raised her head slowly, pushing the hair from her swollen eyes. "Zach?" Hesitantly, she reached up and traced his face with her fingertips. "Zach, is it really you this time?"

He gathered her into his arms and she nearly toppled him, clinging to his neck. "It is you! It is," she cried, half-laughing and soaking his shirt with tears.

"Shh, now," he whispered against her temple. "It's me. I'm here, Angel. Don't cry."

Leaning back, she cupped his jaw. "Zach, please . . . please take me away from this place. I can't stand it. It's so small. I can't breathe here. I . . . told them. I told them but . . . they wouldn't—"

"Follow me." He grabbed the torch and crawled into the corridor, then turned to help her through the narrow opening. "Can you walk?" he asked as he tugged her to her feet. She nodded, but he slipped his arm around her waist just the same, averting his gaze from the soft mounds above her *tanga*.

Zach guided them through the winding passageway toward the main cavern. It took half the time with a torch to lead the way.

They emerged from the darkness into the spaciousness at the mouth of the cave where moonlight beamed through the curtained veil of water. Zach directed her to the pallet of palms in the corner and wedged the torch in a crevice nearby. He smiled over his shoulder. "Much better, wouldn't you say? All we need is to hang a

'Home Sweet Home' plaque right about here."
Home sweet home? *Fool. Quit staring at her legs
like that.*

Zach looked away at nothing in particular and
nudged his hat back. "You'll be okay here for a
minute or so, Angelface, won't you? I need to
check on our not-so-nice neighbors. I'll be right
back."

"I'll be fine . . . now that you're here." Alena
noted he clenched his jaw and stood there a moment longer than he needed to. She assessed him
boldly. His profile was unreadable, but he was
weary, she could tell. His hard-set chin was
shadowed with a few days' growth of stubble.
His tattered shirt, one sleeve torn, was damp,
and clung to his broad shoulders.

Suddenly, he rammed his hands into his pockets, pulling his britches taut across his hips, and
sauntered off. The sleek muscles of his thighs
jarred slightly as he walked. He was all mascu-
line, all man. And Alena was overwhelmed with
love for him.

She supposed she'd loved him long before she
had admitted it to herself. Perhaps he'd been
right all along. Perhaps she had fallen head over
heels in love with the man the very day he'd
burst into Mr. Dalton's office, his blue eyes blazing.

She'd had lots of time to think about those
things while they'd dragged her through the jungle to this unknown destination. She'd thought
of nothing else when the heathens had deposited
her in that hellhole.

All her life she'd feared this emotion . . . this
warm fuzzy feeling that encased her heart and
soul. She'd always feared it would make her vul-

nerable. Yet, because of it, because of Zach, she could face anything now. These savages could do what they would. They could take her life. Her love for Zachariah Summerfield was one thing that no one could destroy.

Her only fear was that she might die never knowing what it was like to give the full extent of her love. She knew nothing about the goings-on between a man and a woman, but Zach's ardent kisses had awakened some great need in her . . . a need that had to be fulfilled before she left this earth.

Zach's long shadow preceded him as he started back. Alena stood, hugging her ribs, and wondered how to broach the subject. What if he refused her?

"They're still guarding the trail. It looks like they're getting ready for some kind of festivity, though. Maybe we—" He halted a few feet away. "Alena, what's the matter?" He furrowed his brows. "Aw, jeez. Did they give you something to drink called *cauin*? Here, let me get you some water."

"I don't want any water, Zach. The effects of the drink wore off hours ago." Alena's gaze skittered from his quizzical expression and landed on his chest. "I . . . want something else."

Zach rubbed the back of his neck. "Well, we're a little limited on food. I guess I could try to catch a rat or something. We do have fire to cook—"

"That's not at at all what I mean." Alena stared down at her hands. "I don't know quite how to put this. Actually, I want you to do something . . . to me."

"Ah. I think I understand." Zach smiled. "You want me to kiss you again, right?"

"No."

His face fell. "No?"

"No . . . well, not just . . . kiss me." Her gaze flickered to his, then dropped to his throat.

Zach cocked his head and closed his eyes. Good Lord. She couldn't be asking what he thought she was asking. He took his hat off, ran a hand through his hair, and saw that she was trembling. She was probably just cold. "You want me to hold you?"

Alena shook her head. "Not just hold me and kiss me." She wished she could simply look him in the eye and tell him. But her eyes wouldn't move from his throat and she wasn't exactly sure how to tactfully explain what she wanted. She tried again. "Zach . . . I want you to . . . I want you to—" She sighed and dropped her head. "I don't know how to say it."

Shifting his weight, Zach propped a hand on his hip and glanced at the ceiling. "Alena, you're not asking me . . . I mean, we're not talking about . . . about making love . . . are we?"

Alena ran her tongue over her lips, swallowed, then nodded.

Zach's mouth fell open, his gaze roving over her curves. He must have imagined a hundred times what it would be like to have her beneath him, all soft and warm and giving. He felt himself tighten and start to ache. All he had to do was take three steps and pull her into his arms. He attempted a step forward yet his damnable feet refused his command.

The conscience he thought he didn't have was suddenly nagging at him. *Leave her be, Zach. She's not for you. You're a drifter. She needs a full-time husband, a home, children. All of the things you can't* give. *This time next year you could be six feet under a cave-in . . . or in an explosion like in Egypt. Then where would she be?*

Zach set his jaw firm and shook his head. "Alena, I don't think—"

"You like me. You said so on the beach that night. You said that you liked me and I liked you and—"

"I know what I said, dammit!" He slapped his hat against his thigh, then sighed deeply. "Alena, look at me." Her gaze wavered several times before it settled on his. "I was drunk that night. I was fooling around—"

"Are you saying you don't care for me in the least?"

Her broken voice cinched his heart. "No, that's not what I'm saying. On the contrary, I care too much to let you throw yourself away on the likes of me. Look, I pushed you into that situation on the beach—"

"And on the boat before we entered the rapids?"

"I let that get out of hand." Zach glanced at the cavern floor. "Alena, you don't want this. Not from me. Someday, you'll want to marry. What would you tell your husband?"

"That I was married before in the jungles of the Amazon. Chief Chato married us tonight, or have you forgotten?" She lifted her chin, knowing full well that neither of them truly acknowledged the marriage. She felt a bit deceitful for using it as an excuse, though she wasn't about to let it show. "I'm twenty-one years old, Zach, and I've never intimately known a man. It's something I'd very much like to experience before I pass on. Might I remind you our lives are due to end before tomorrow's dawn? Don't you hear the drums?"

The thrumming from beyond the cave pulsated in Zach's head. He raised his face to the ceiling. "Alena . . . don't. Don't do this to me," he rasped. "For the first time in my life, I'm trying to be noble. Don't make it any harder than it already is." He lowered his eyes to hers, pleading for understanding. "I can't make you any promises. I haven't sorted out this thing between us yet. I've been too busy concentrating on how to save our necks."

Tears gathered behind Alena's closed lids before she turned away. The ancient rhythm of the drums outside filled the silence as the world seemed to topple around her. On the morrow she would die, never having found her father, never knowing why he'd abandoned her. She'd never know what it was like to lie beside Zach and give him her love completely. She bit down hard on her quivering lower lip. There were so many things she'd never see, or do, or know.

Chapter 13

Zach could have handled a kick in the teeth. It was watching her turn from him and seeing her shoulders tremble that he didn't know how to cope with. Any other time he might have tried to hold her, but he couldn't take the chance of touching her—not now, not after she'd offered herself to him.

He ran a hand over his face, feeling as if someone had just sprayed his gut with buckshot. He had to say something, do something, to comfort her. Hell, she wasn't accustomed to life-or-death situations. She must be frightened out of her wits to have come up with the suggestion she just had.

"Alena," he said at last, "I know you're scared. That's why you asked me for what you did, isn't it?"

Without looking at him, Alena slowly shook her head.

"Yes, it is," he contradicted with a nod of his own. "It's okay, sweetheart. In a predicament like this we all say a lot of crazy things. I know it's not much consolation, but I'm scared, too." He dropped his gaze briefly to the small of her back, noticing how the *tanga* she wore cinched her tiny waist and accented the curve of her hips. "I'm scared of a lot of things," he whispered hoarsely, and focused on the back of her head ... her hair, her beautiful, long, silky— He cleared his throat.

"Listen to me, Angel. I don't believe in the finality of things. Fate can take a different course at the last minute. Destiny can be changed. Sometimes, you have to wait and watch for vulnerable spots, cracks in a wall that appears to be solid. When you see an opportunity, you have to be ready to take a chance. But you don't give up. You don't just give up, Alena . . . at least not until what's done is done, and over."

The tone of his voice, his words, and the way he said them, seeped into Alena's mind, warming her, fortifying her. His stubbornness was one of the very reasons she loved him so: he never gave up.

Alena focused on a shower of water that splashed onto the ledge. The cool, inviting spray beckoned her and an idea brewed in her head. A small smile curved her lips. Zach never gave up—neither would she. Swiping a wrist across her tear-damp lashes, she squared her shoulders, then walked toward the shower in a slow, seductive stroll, swaying her hips like Carmelita.

Her heart thrummed with a rush of excitement as she neared the ledge. With shaking hands she reached to the side of her breast and gave the *tanga* a tug. The doeskin fell around her feet and she stepped into the stream of water. Turning, she ran her fingers through her hair and waited for Zach's reaction.

A choking sound broke from Zach's throat,

though for the life of him, he couldn't utter a word. He felt as if the oxygen to his brain was being cut off. Paralyzed, he watched her comb through her thick wet tresses. The orchids fell from her hair into the shallow pool and floated around her ankles. His gaze, no matter how hard he tried to focus on the orchids, roved slowly upward, from shapely calves to slender thighs, the soft triangle between, over rounded hips, along the curved waist to full, proud breasts. Then he made the mistake of looking into her eyes.

The witchery of those clover-green orbs summoned him, lured him. His head began to spin and he closed his lids, attempting to regain some perspective. Beads of sweat popped on his brow when he tried to recall the reasons he had denied her offer. All his convictions were fading fast, losing their meaning. He couldn't think, couldn't analyze the situation—not while he labored for breath . . . not when he felt himself bulging against his seams.

He opened his eyes on the dreamworld before him and his last shred of resistance shattered like glass thrown against stone. The silver backdrop of the falls framed Alena's exquisite form, her skin gleaming in the ice-blue moonlight. God, she was beautiful.

His footsteps were wooden and halting at first, then they matched the pace of his heartbeat. As he strode purposefully toward the curtain of water, he jerked his shirt open and buttons flew, popping against the hard cavern floor. Dragging the toilworn garment from his shoulders, he entered the forceful spray.

Water cascaded between them to fill the space

that neither made an immediate move to close. Alena stared at the droplets of water clinging to the stubble on his chin and smiled. Hesitantly, she lifted her hands, and his fingers intertwined with hers. "I'm glad you came to me, Zach."

"You made it impossible to do otherwise and you damn well know it." His gaze devoured her as he brought her hands to his mouth, kissed them, then turned them over and nibbled her palms. "Damn you, Alena," he whispered achingly, and pulled her forward, guiding her arms around his neck.

The contact of his bare, wet chest against her breasts jarred Alena, then quickly sent a warmth like summer sunshine oozing throughout her spirit. She should have been embarrassed or ashamed about what she was doing, yet she wasn't. It seemed a quite natural thing to do with someone you loved. She raised her face for his kiss, her elation lending to the sensation of being magically lifted off the ground.

This kiss was different from all the others, perhaps because they both knew where it would lead. It was more demanding, more intense, full of tremulous emotion. With his fingers laced through her hair, Zach took her parted lips fiercely, and she reciprocated with unleashed passion. His hands raced over her shoulders, down her spine, past her waist, to cup the fullness below, pressing her against the buttons of his trousers. White-hot, tiny bubbles popped inside Alena's abdomen and she clung to him as if he, alone, was her life source.

Zach pulled away from her lips abruptly, though his hold didn't slacken. He threw his head back, faced the full force of the water a moment, then lowered a heavy-lidded gaze to hers. "Alena, are you sure . . . absolutely sure? God . . . be sure, Angel, because I'm not certain I can stop if we go much further."

Feeling his heart pounding against hers with the fury of the distant drums, Alena took the full measure of his silver, searching eyes. Strands of drenched hair tumbled over his furrowed brows and water trickled down his forehead. Reaching up, she traced his lower lip. "I'm sure," she whispered, and lifted her gaze from his mouth to his eyes. "I've never wanted anything as much as I want you. Now, stop fighting it and kiss me, Zach. We may not have much time."

Zach's mouth met hers like a bolt of lightning. He scooped her into his arms, cradling her against his chest, and stepped from the spray. Cool air stung her skin as he moved in swift strides across the cavern, his lips never leaving hers. He laid her gently on the mat. Releasing her reluctantly, he stood and staggered backwards a few feet.

Stretched out on the bed of palms, Alena marveled at his tall, powerful form silhouetted against the waterfall. His chest rising with shuddering breaths, he shook sprinkles of water from his hair. He raked the wet strands back, revealing eyes that roved over her, and when they met hers, held. Then he reached down to unfasten his breeches.

Unable to look away, Alena watched as he stood on the brink of the shadows and peeled the trousers from his hips. The drums outside the cave beat faster, more furiously, and so did her heart when Zach glided forward into the torchlight. He was magnificent . . . like the statues of ancient Greek mythology.

A hesitant smile flashed across his face as he eased down beside her. Alena was charmed by the mixture of tenderness and concern in his expression and was deeply touched that this bold adventurer, who had no doubt confronted scores of catastrophes, appeared to be a little skittish at the moment.

Yet when she pressed her body to his, he clutched her tightly. All lines of tension in his features fled, vanquished by the fire in his eyes. The potency in those crystal-blue orbs mesmerized Alena, made her feel suspended in time, as if this place, this man, weren't quite real.

A power greater than both of them drew their lips together in a kiss so sweet, so intoxicating, that Alena thought she might die from the sheer ecstasy of it. Zach's lips coasted over hers, gently, teasingly at first, then his tongue delved deeper inside her mouth with a raw hunger. One calloused hand spanned her back, pulling her closer, molding her soft body against his hard, muscled form, while his other hand worked its magic on her hip and thigh. Tingling from his touch, she tunneled her fingers through his damp hair and arched into him.

"Easy, little one," Zach whispered, prying her away from him and rolling her onto her back. "Let's make this last forever and a day." His slight smile wavered as his gaze dipped and turned smoky.

His palm came up, warm against her swelling breast, tenderly caressing, tickling. He brushed his lips along her cheek to her ear, then languorously trailed kisses down her neck and across her collarbone. Dropping his head, he nuzzled between her breasts, his hot breath and darting tongue scorching her skin.

Like leather on silk, his hand glided down her torso and fanned over her stomach . . . Alena flinched when he touched her most private place. Surfacing into reality, she instinctively pressed her knees together. Zach froze, yet kept his hand where it was. Slowly, his fingers began to tease her. Heat spread agonizingly through her abdomen and down her legs. Her body writhed with abandon. Soon, very soon, she was floating once more on a raft of pleasure.

Possessing her lips again, Zach took her in his arms and edged atop her. His hips swiveled sensually against hers, until Alena thought she would surely go mad. She dug her nails into his broad shoulders, pulling him to her, and arched her back with a need . . . an unknown longing that overflowed in her heart.

Zach lifted his chest from hers and braced himself above her. She opened her eyes on his smoldering gaze.

"Alena—"

"No, Zach," she murmured, pressing her fingertips against his lips. "Please, don't say anything. Don't. Just love me . . . *now*."

Something warm and precious consumed Zach as he looked down at her and saw the unmistakable devotion gleaming in her eyes. It was devotion he hadn't earned, devotion he didn't deserve, yet it was there, bright and shining just the same, and it made him glow with a desire that shook him to his inner core.

He clamped his jaw tightly, determined not to take her with the urgency he felt. He had to be gentle. Torn between the carnal craving that burned within him, and abhorrence at the thought of hurting her, his breath came hard and ragged. Sweat drenched him as he stiffened, willing his body to be still while he searched his brain for some way to alleviate the discomfort he was about to cause her.

She squirmed impatiently beneath him. Eagerness charged through him like wildfire and his self-control splintered into a thousand tiny pieces. Aching with his need for her, he hung his head and closed his eyes. A tightness gripped his chest as he slid his hands up her arms, raising them above her head. He entwined his fingers in hers and pinned her hands against the mat. "Forgive me, Angelface. God . . . I'm sorry," he whispered. Then he covered her mouth with his, and took her swiftly with one long thrust.

Alena's frame tensed with the sudden sharpness that shot from her abdomen, down her legs. Zach drowned the whimper in her throat, scattering tender kisses over her face. His breath came warm against her skin as he murmured sweet endearments, soothing her.

The pain subsided with the start of his slow lazy strokes. In its wake a glow . . . a wondrous glow circulated like some life-giving force throughout her body. Amazed by this extraordinary sensation, she lifted her hips to meet him. He drew a short, quick breath, and she gasped. "Zach, did I hurt you?"

"God . . . no," he replied with a small, husky chuckle. "Quite the contrary, Angel. Just don't move. Please . . . for the love of Pete, be still . . . just for a moment."

Alena smiled with the awareness that her movement had caused his sweet agony. Knowing she could torment his senses the same way he did hers made her feverish. Unable to stop herself, she wiggled a bit more, testing this new talent.

His eyes grew dark and he groaned, then began gliding within her again, inspiring her to do the same. He buried his face in her hair and picked up his pace, plunging deeper, closer to her soul. "*Alena . . . Alena . . . Alena,*" he whispered over and over again as softly as a lover's sonnet.

Alena spiraled endlessly, climbing ever higher, reaching for some nameless zenith. A release from the torturous bliss had to exist beyond the horizon. She raked Zach's back, pleading for him to take her there. Somewhere far away, frenzied drums pounded. Louder and louder, building violently, they seemed to cast an ancient spell of pagan desire. Alena's heart, attuned to Zach's, throbbed with the tempo while their bodies, polished by perspiration, moved with the rhythm of primitive passion.

An unexpected cry escaped Alena as pulsating pleasure rippled from her to Zach . . . and back again. For a brief but glorious moment, they were suspended somewhere high above the earth, in a sacred place where the two of them existed as one.

The drums calmed to a slow exotic beat, eventually stabilizing their pulse rates. Zach rolled to his side, keeping Alena enfolded in his embrace. They lay entwined like wilted flowers, Alena cuddled against his broad, furry chest, drifting on the border of heaven.

After a long period of serene silence, Zach tipped her chin, peering deep into her eyes. "Alena . . . are you all right?"

"Mmm . . . am I supposed to feel all fuzzy and warm?"

Zach chuckled softly. "Yes, I suppose so."

"Well, I do." Alena dropped her eyes to the hollow of his throat. "Zach . . . I never imagined it could be like that. I felt so needed, so cherished. You made me feel so . . . so . . . *beautiful*."

"You *are* beautiful, Angelface," he murmured, stroking her cheek tenderly. "Look at me, Alena. You are beautiful."

Alena's soul soared as she viewed his radiant expression. He did love her. Though he hadn't spoken the words, it was undoubtedly there in his eyes . . . there, in the way he said her name, in the way he touched her. "I love you, Zach," she whispered without any qualms at all. "I love you so."

Zach stared at her incredulously, then his lids closed. God, what had he done? He swallowed hard, trying to collect his thoughts. He cared for her, more than he ever had cared for anyone. He longed to tell her exactly that, yet telling someone you cared for them seemed a trifle weak, in reply to what she'd just said.

Her soft confession had wrapped around his heart, filling him with a sense of value he didn't deserve. He wanted more than anything to give her that priceless gift in return. He wanted to explain how she made him feel, how he felt about her.

But love? He wasn't sure he knew what the word meant. Was it love to want her with him for the rest of eternity? How could he love her and expose her to the dangers that were part of his daily life? He opened his eyes slowly, dying a little at the emotion etched on her face. "Alena . . . people sometimes feel that way after . . . after . . . *afterwards*."

"But I felt this way before."

"Alena . . ." Zach expelled a deep shuddering sigh, yearning to say so much more than he could. "It's been a long day, Angel." He pressed her head against his shoulder and gently kissed her temple. "Try to get some rest now," he said, then closed his eyes, praying that sleep would take him swiftly and end his misery.

Long after Zach's chest rose and fell in slumber beneath her cheek, Alena lay awake. The drums outside still pounded, each thumping note a threat. Yet Alena felt strangely at peace as she listened to Zach's steady heartbeat beneath her ear. She'd always felt as if something vital was missing from her life. Now she felt complete. Here in Zach's arms, at last, she felt complete.

Zach *did* love her. Perhaps he simply didn't know it yet. But he did. And nothing else mattered anymore. Everything that had been important before paled in comparison to the elation she now felt.

Careful not to wake him, she raised on her elbow to admire him while he slept. He was indeed the most handsome man she'd ever seen. The golden glow of the torchlight accentuated his fine features. His dark fringed lashes grazed his high cheekbones. They were lashes any woman would envy.

What would it be like, she wondered, to wake up with him every morning . . . to see every day as a new challenge, as he did? Life with him would most certainly be an adventure. One would never know what to expect on the morrow.

Suddenly solemn, Alena brushed a strand of hair from his forehead. There would be no more tomorrows for them. No more tomorrows. No more—

She jerked her eyes to the cave entrance, and listened intently.

No more drums . . . *there were no more drums*.

She started shaking Zach even before her gaze returned to him. "Zach!" she whispered urgently. "Zach, wake up!"

"Hmm?" His lids fluttered open, he smiled, growled, and grabbed for her.

"Zach! Stop it!" she said, and wrestled from his amorous hold. "The drums . . . listen . . . they've stopped!"

His head shot up. "Damn," he muttered, scrambling to his feet. "Get your clothes on, Angelface." He retrieved his shirt and trousers, slipped them on, and fastened them with lightning speed. Running a hand through his hair, he donned his hat, then headed for the entrance, only to stop dead in his tracks.

He turned slowly, and watched her secure her *tanga*. With three long strides and a grim look, he took her face in his hands. He kissed her hard, then pulled away, his thumbs fanning her cheeks. "Whatever happens, trust me. Keep your eyes and ears open for any opportunity to get away. I'll signal you and start a diversion or something. When I do, run like hell. Do you understand? Follow the river north to the mission and—"

"I'm not leaving you," Alena broke in. She slipped her arms around his lean waist and laid her cheek against his chest.

Zach smoothed her hair, then clasped her arms and set her away from him. "Alena, for God's sake, don't argue with me. Not now. There isn't—"

"I'm not leaving you," she repeated with a lift of her chin.

He flexed his jaw. "You're a stubborn woman, Alena Sutton . . . and a foolish one."

"Perhaps I am, but I'm still not leaving without you."

He tilted his head and studied the rock ceiling a moment before pinning her with his gaze again. "All right, dammit. If there's a chance for a break, we'll go together." His eyes turned smoky and he clutched her against him in a crushing embrace. "If not," he murmured brokenly into her hair, "if not . . . just remember—"

The shuffling of feet across the hard granite brought both their heads up. Chief Chato and his procession stood at the mouth of the cave, outlined against the rushing falls.

Zach moved Alena behind him and counted the guards. How many were there? A dozen or more. Too many. Even if he rushed them, Alena would never make it past the natives outside. Sweet Jesus, they needed a miracle to get out of this one.

Chief Chato bellowed a command and slammed his staff on the floor so hard the shrunken heads clacked together. The savage sentries started forward.

Zach's heart pounded. He wrenched his arm from Alena's grasp and shoved her farther back. Crouching, he waited for the first warrior to approach. The native came closer and closer, jabbing a long spear until the weapon was within inches of Zach.

In a flash, Zach grabbed the end of the spear, jerked the Indian forward, backhanded the side of his head, and sent him sprawling. That quick, he planted a foot into the ribs of another who charged him, while clubbing still another with the spear. Two more barreled toward him. One he rammed in the stomach, the other went down with a blow to the jaw.

Alena pressed her spine against the cold stone, digging her nails into her palms. Zach fought a futile battle. He wasn't the kind to go down without a brawl. It was in his blood: he never gave up. She knew that, but, even knowing, even understanding, didn't ease the pressure in her chest or the sting of tears.

Five . . . six . . . seven of them fell around him before the rest overpowered him, wrestling him, beating him to the damp cavern floor.

"Stop it! Stop it!" Alena's scream echoed eerily in the cave. She twisted and struggled between the two warriors who held her, scratching and kicking them every chance she got.

Zach lay rigid, face-down as they bound his hands behind him. When they jerked him to his feet, a silent rage dwelled in his eyes.

Alena broke from her captors and ran to him. "Oh . . . oh, you're bleeding." She reached to wipe the blood that trickled from the corner of his mouth.

Zach avoided her touch and wiped his mouth on his shoulder. "Not to worry, sweetheart. It's just another occupational hazard." Though his words were tinged with humor, his expression held no mirth.

Chato issued another order and two torch-bearers moved ahead of the chief into the dark tunnel. Alena and Zach were shoved along behind him, followed by the rest of the guards and the shaman.

Slipping her arm through Zach's, Alena regarded his narrowed, watchful eyes. Following his gaze toward their destination, she noted they veered off into the opposite tunnel than the one they'd taken before. She looked past the chief, on past the warriors who led the way. There was nothing ahead but a dead end. The party stopped where the tunnel did.

Chief Chato gave a nod and several of the guards moved forward.

Zach nudged her, and when she looked up, smiled. "Hey, Angel," he whispered, "it's not over yet, remember?"

A scraping sound caught their attention. Prying a huge rock away from the wall at the end of the tunnel, the guards pushed and shoved until they rolled it to one side, exposing an opening about three feet in diameter.

At another command from Chato, Alena and Zach were shoved to the cavern floor. On hands and knees, they were forced to accompany the rest of the party through the dark hole. When they were tugged to their feet on the other side, they found themselves in a secret passageway.

As they were ushered along the corridor, the torches the natives carried illuminated a series of ancient symbols painted along the walls. Zach squinted at the pictures they passed. "Alena, my glasses," he whispered urgently, wrestling with the ropes that bound his wrists. "Get my glasses out of my pocket and put them on me. Hurry."

Not too long ago, Alena would have thought he was having one of his fits, but by now, she had learned there were times when his madness held some method. Reaching into his shirt pocket, she pulled out the spectacles and tried to straighten the wire earpiece.

"Never mind that." Zach ducked his head. "Just put them on me." He barely allowed her to position the eyeglasses on his nose and hook them behind his ears before his concentration returned to the archaic writings.

His steps slowing, his gaze roved intensely over the wall. "Jeez almighty. Look at this, Angelface."

Alena threw a wary glance at the natives who brought up the rear, then peeked around Zach's shoulder. With a nod he indicated a particular drawing. "Does this look familiar?"

"It's . . . why, it's the same—"

"The same symbols that were on the map," Zach cut in. "Alena, the Jaquaras are direct descendants of the lost tribe. This proves it. Mahrakimba was a Jaquara. I had an inkling she might be when they called you her name, and revered you. But, according to our research, all the tribes in this area have heard the legend and worship the mighty Mah . . . raah—" Zach straightened with the jab of a spear to his back. Glaring at the Indian who'd prodded him, he nudged Alena forward.

"I know now," he said in a low voice as they continued through the corridor. "I know where they're taking us and how they plan to get rid of us." Alena's wide eyes shot to his. "They're taking us to the crypt."

"The . . . crypt?"

"Mahrakimba's tomb . . . the treasure chamber. I can't believe I didn't figure it out before. They plan to dispose of us the same way their ancestors did Mahrakimba."

Alena stared unseeingly in front of her. A tightness in her jaw crept down her throat and seeped into her chest. "Zach . . . do you mean, they're . . . they're going to bury us alive?"

"No, Angel," Zach said soothingly. "They're not going to bury us. Actually, they're going to seal us in the chamber. But don't you see," he rushed on, "that could give us a chance. I intend to watch every move they make when they open the vault. Maybe I can figure out how it works. Alena, look at me."

She did.

"Now, give me a smile. I need one."

She did, though it wasn't very sincere.

"That's my girl." Smiling back, he winked, then turned his full attention to the wall where the chief had halted. "Amazing," Zach muttered beneath his breath.

Alena looked in the same direction and her mouth gaped. The painting of the woman on the stone surface held an uncanny resemblance to herself.

Half of the natives fell to their knees, chanting, while the others, under Chato's direction, struggled with a large boulder that was wrapped with several sturdy vines. It appeared they were trying to push it off a small ledge.

Glancing at Zach, Alena followed his intense gaze. He studied the thick braided vine connected to the boulder. His eyes rose upward to where the vine was attached to the painted wall and extended across the top of Mahrakimba's portrait.

Of a sudden, the wall rumbled . . . creaked in protest . . . then slowly, slowly began to ascend.

Alena gagged from the foul odor that drifted into the corridor. Covering her mouth, her other hand closed around Zach's arm.

He tightened his biceps, squeezing her fingers against his ribs. "Gads, I hate the smell of tombs when they're first opened."

Chief Chato faced them, his black eyes as cold as the stale air. A sharp gesture of his staff indicated they were to enter the dark room beyond.

Neither Zach nor Alena moved until they felt the points of spears pressed against their backs.

Zach started forward and Alena stumbled alongside him, her knees growing weaker by the second. The rancid smell increased as darkness closed in around them. The door behind them whined, reverberated, then gave a hollow roar. The last glimpse of light fading, the wall grated shut, and they were sealed in a chilly, black void.

Chapter 14

❧⁓⁓❧

Alena shivered in the blackness that hovered about them like a frigid shroud. She could see not a thing, save the demons of her mind. She knew Zach was right beside her for she still clutched his arm. His presence, the sound of his steady breathing, should have reassured her. Yet her tattered nerves needed more. She needed to hear his voice. "Zach?"

"Hmm?"

"Well?"

"Well?" he answered as if his thoughts were elsewhere.

"Did you see how the door works?"

"Oh, that." There was a long moment of silence. "It's a very simple mechanism actually. A primitive version of a huge counterbalance—a counterweight. They were also used in ancient Egypt, and I saw one similar in Delhi a few years ago. At the time, it was really rather clever of them to—"

"Zach."

"Hmm?"

"Zachariah!" Alena found his rib and gave it a sharp pinch.

"Ouch! Dammit, that hurt."

"Do you know how it works, or not?"

"Of course I know how it works. You see, they connected the vines that were attached to the boulder to the door and opposed, that is, balanced, the rock with an equal weight and—"

"Yes, yes, that's very good. Now, hurry and get us out of this dreadful place. I don't like it."

"Yeah, well, I can't say I'm all that fond of being here either. Gives me the willies. However, there's a slight problem, Angelface." He cleared his throat. "The device that operates the door is only accessible from the other side."

"What?" She twisted the front of his shirt. "You mean we're trapped? What are we going to do, Zach? What are we going to do?"

"Now don't get hysterical. I'm thinking." Hearing her labored breathing, he rubbed his arm against hers. "While I'm thinking," he whispered, "why don't you make yourself useful and finish untying me. I've already loosened the ropes a little."

Alena let her hands slide down his chest, smoothing his shirt as best she could. Making herself useful was exactly what she needed to be doing at the moment. Panicking wasn't going to help the situation. She stepped behind him and groped for his wrists. When she found them, she propped his fists against her waist and went to work on disengaging the knots.

He wiggled his fingers, tickling her abdomen through the *tanga*, and she jumped. "Stop that and hold still," she scolded. "You're supposed to be thinking, remember?"

"There's no rule that says a man can't have a little fun while he's thinking." Zach's fingers made a sensuous trail back and forth across her stomach. "You weren't so mean last night."

Tiny, warm sparks burst within Alena and she was grateful the darkness hid her blush. "Hush," she said, trying to ignore what was going on inside her and concentrate on her task. "How can you possibly think properly while you're chattering so. And stand still, blast you, or I shall keep you tied up and . . . and do terribly wicked things to you."

"Promise?" His voice was breathy, just on the edge of teasing.

Alena smiled, but tugged the rope tightly. She paid his yelp no mind as the binding fell away from his wrists.

"Ah, you're an angel. Thanks," Zach said, flexing his hands until the circulation returned. "I thought I saw a torch over by the door before the lights went out." He reached into his pocket for a match. Gads, he hoped they were dry enough to strike. "Stay here, I'll see if I can get it lit."

A chill gripped Alena when he moved away. "Zach?"

"What is it?"

"Nothing." She heard a thump, a clatter, and a muttered curse. Then a soft flickering glow illuminated the chamber.

"Jeez almighty, will you look at this?"

The yellow halo of torchlight revealed a vast variety of obviously treasured articles: masks, statues, urns, jewelry, gilded shields and breast-plates, and what appeared to be a collection of drums. Some of the dusty prizes were stacked against the carved walls, others placed on ornate columns.

Alena watched Zach travel around the room like a child in a toy store, examining one artifact after another. He whistled through his teeth at each object he handled. "A gold mine," he muttered. "This place is a virtual gold mine. There's a whole exhibit here. Even a surplus I could sell to the Smithsonian to pay off the museum debts." Stripping off his shirt, he started bundling selected items in it.

A slight movement high in the corner caught Alena's eye. She cringed at the sight of a huge black spider crawling toward a web. Rubbing the gooseflesh that rose on her arms, she glanced around again.

The drums of various sizes and shapes captured her attention. One in particular lured her closer. It was the smallest of the group, no more than six inches tall. Something about it fascinated her. Hesitantly, she picked it up, blew off the dust, and studied it. Heavier than it looked, the little drum rattled as she lifted it. She stared at it for a long time before it came to her that it was the black bird painted on it that attracted her so. A condor, Zach had called it.

"Holy Moses! This is it!"

Alena spun, the forgotten drum clutched to her waist.

Zach knelt in the corner, cradling a tall golden crown of some sort. His blue eyes glazed as he turned to her and whispered, "This is it, Angelface. Mahrakimba's ceremonial headdress."

Bright green gems embedded in the headpiece winked like cat's eyes in the muted light. Alena moved nearer and a dreadful foreboding flooded through her with every step she took. "Zach, you're not truly going to take these things . . . are you?"

Zach looked at her as if she'd gone quite mad, then frowned severely. "You're damned right I'm taking them. I've been through hell and back to get here and I'm not leaving empty-handed." Turning from her, he placed the headdress with the rest of the loot. After a moment, he expelled a deep sigh and glanced over his shoulder without meeting her gaze. "Alena, look, Mahrakimba is dead. Long gone. She's not going to care."

Alena stared at him, a peculiar thought racing through her head. Something wasn't right. Furrowing her brows, she viewed the contents of the chamber thoroughly. "Zach, if Mahrakimba died here, wouldn't there be...remains... some trace of her?"

Zach stood, scanned the room for a second, and slowly smiled. He grabbed Alena so fast, she almost toppled backwards.

"Do you know what I like best about you, Angelface?" He planted a kiss on her nose. "You're not just cute and cuddly—you're smart."

Alena grimaced. "Zach, you're not having one of your fits...not here, not now, *please*." His expression went blank temporarily, as if he hadn't the foggiest notion what she was talking about. Then his gleefulness returned and he abruptly freed her.

Good heavens, he was. He was having another fit. She pressed her fingers to her lips and watched him turn a slow full circle, arms widespread. Apparently, he was searching for something. He came back around with a lopsided grin.

"Don't you see? You're right. You're absolutely right, Angel. Mahrakimba *isn't* here. She must have escaped. That can only mean there has to be another way out. And if she found it, so can we." He grabbed the torch, proceeded to the nearest wall, and began running his hand over the rough surface.

Alena ventured closer and watched him examine two walls before moving to the next.

"It has to be here some—wait a minute. What's this?" Rolling a gold shield aside, Zach stepped in front of an eight-foot idol, pressed his ear to it, and knocked. "Solid," he muttered, then traced his finger along the carved statue where it met the wall. "Still, there could very easily be an opening behind it. In Cairo we found a hidden passageway behind a mummy case. If I remember correctly there was a latch right about . . . aha! Found it. Ah, damn. I can't budge it." He looked up at Alena and nudged his hat. "It's timeworn, probably hasn't been used for centuries. I'll have to pry it with something," he said, and glanced around. "Hand me that spear."

Zach stuck the torch in a sconce by the statue. His hand closed over hers as Alena handed him the weapon. "Stand back and wait until I tell you to, before you go through. When I do, you move and move fast. Sometimes the blasted things are booby-trapped. You ready?"

More than ready to leave the ghastly crypt, Alena gave him a quick nod.

Zach wedged the spear in the crack and heaved. The statue screeched and began to vibrate. Dust and crumbled stone trickled down the wall around it. He braced his shoulder against it and his face contorted as he pushed with all his might. After his third groan, the tall idol started to grate sideways across the rock floor, exposing a narrow, arched opening.

Zach stood aside, and, catching his breath, gave the crude door an intense appraisal. He ran the tip of the spear along the frame and base, then tossed it through. When nothing happened, he rolled the heavy shield across the exit floor and into the darkness beyond. The statue shuddered and slid sideways a little. "Uh huh," he muttered, running a hand over his stubbled chin. "This thing was probably rigged at one time to close on whoever passed through it, but it looks like it's no longer in working order. Better let me go first though." He picked up his bundle, turned to Alena, and brushed his knuckles across her cheek. "Don't move until I say," he said, then winked and started forward.

Just as he stepped into the archway, the statue rumbled and tipped. Rocks began to fall from above the opening. Zach reacted quickly, propping his back against the toppling idol. "Go!" he yelled. "Hurry!"

Alena ducked swiftly beneath his body into the musty dark void. A gust of howling wind met her, whipping her hair wildly. She whirled around to see debris rapidly filling the exit. The dim orange light from the chamber was fading behind a cloud of dust. A sudden constriction in her chest imprisoned her voice.

Then the bundle wrapped in Zach's shirt flew into the dreary tunnel and landed at Alena's feet. A split second later, Zach bolted from the rubble, the torch he carried leaving a white trail behind him. As he passed Alena, he caught her with his free arm, pushing her further into the funnel of darkness, away from the vapors of the crumbling ruins.

As the dust and rocks settled, Zach released her from the awkward position in which he'd pressed her against the stale, damp wall. Dusting his hat, he searched the cavern floor until he found his bundle. He stooped to pick it up, then turned to her with the most ill-timed glee.

"Cheer up, Angelface, you look a little pale. Aw, come on. It wasn't that bad. Didn't you feel it? That rush of blood soaring through your veins?" He cocked his head. "Come here," he whispered softly, and stuffed the torch into a crevice on the cavern wall. "You just need a hug, that's all. Well, maybe a kiss, too. I know I could use one." His smile brightened. "In fact, I think I deserve a kiss, don't you?"

"A kiss?" Alena backed away, her pulse still pounding. "Whatever for? For scaring me half to death?"

"Hey, I got us out, didn't I?"

Alena closed her eyes, then opened them, looking down to see what it was she clutched against her waist. Her knuckles were white from the grip she had on the little drum. Glancing back at Zach, she prayed for the return of a regular heartbeat. He *was* insane. He thrived on danger: "living on the edge," he'd termed it. Close calls with death thrilled him. He'd been beaming when he shot through that door. God in heaven, of all the men to fall in love with, why him?

Of course, without a second thought, she knew why. He was sauntering toward her, oozing charm as usual, doing that thing with his eyes. In spite of herself, she chuckled. Perhaps his infernal lunacy was part of what made him so endearing. With a sigh, she stood on her tiptoes as he reached her, and pecked him on the cheek. Before she could evade him, he caught her waist.

"You call that a kiss? Put your arms around me and kiss me right or we can stay here forever." He raised a brow. "I've got all the time in the world."

"I daresay, Zachariah," she murmured, slipping her hands, drum and all, over his broad shoulders, "you find the oddest times to get playfu—"

He cut her off, possessing her mouth gently, running his tongue along her lower lip, his palms up and down her spine, over her *tanga*. That need, that fire, simmered within her again. Her knees went weak and she leaned into him. She filled her senses with his essence, with the security of his arms. Somehow, all the problems, all the fear, all their differences shrank. The dark walls that surrounded them fell away as he stirred a sweet remembrance of what had passed between them.

Alena met the thrusts of his tongue and the movement of his hips with her own, and his arms tightened around her. The kiss increased in fervor until both broke away, gasping for air.

"Now that, my dear, was a kiss," Zach said, breathing raggedly. With a light whack to her bottom, he set her a proper distance from him. "Let's get going. You're just too tempting in that cute little skimpy outfit you're wearing. We'd better leave now." He grabbed the torch, threw his bundle over his shoulder, and winked. "Or else we'll be here forever, making wild passionate love."

Zach turned and lifted the torch, illuminating cobwebs ahead. "Doesn't look like it's been used in a while, huh?"

Alena stayed close behind him as they moved into the darkness, unable to see more than a few feet in front of them. She recoiled from the sticky tendrils that dangled overhead and brushed against her.

For the better part of an hour the tunnel twisted and turned. Finally, a misty gray haze became visible from some sort of chamber in the foreground.

They stepped into the entry of the massive room. A film of daylight poured through a small hole in the high cathedral ceiling supported by ornate pillars.

Zach stopped Alena with a raise of his hand. "Hold it. I don't like the looks of this place."

Alena peered around him. Her gaze drifted over huge stone carvings of demigods and demons, half-animal, half-human, then traveled to what appeared to be a sacrificial altar. On either side of the slab, two archways were covered by tattered curtains.

"We'll try that way first," Zach whispered, pointing to the door on the right.

Alena nodded toward the patch of sky showing through the hole in the ceiling. "But Zach, there's an opening up there. Couldn't we just climb out that way?"

"We could if we had a rope. Unfortunately, those heathens took my bag, my gun, and my knife." He set his mouth in a grim line. "One of those doors has got to lead to a way out. Come on. Stay behind me and make sure you step exactly where I step. These old temples sometimes have tricky devices planted in the floor."

Alena kept her eyes riveted on Zach's feet, placing her own in the exact same spot. Wind howled out of the passageways as they crossed the room. It created a hollow melody that rose and fell in pitch, and echoed resonantly against the granite walls. Though Alena tried to ignore the eerie music, it seemed to sing through her bones with a warning. Nevertheless, in a slow, cautious procession, they moved ever nearer to the archway.

When at last they reached their destination, Zach expelled a long-held breath and looked over his shoulder. "You okay?"

Not really, Alena thought, but nodded. She glanced at the faint burst of daylight, loath to leave it behind and enter the gloominess beyond the hide-covered doorway.

Zach touched her, and she flinched. "It can't be much farther." He smiled reassuringly, then reached up and jerked the curtain aside.

Something lunged forward. With lightning reflexes, Zach struck out and the phantom clattered to the floor.

Alena's shriek reverberated through the tunnel as she leaped onto Zach's back, drew her knees up, and buried her face in his shoulder.

"Shh, Angel. It's all right. It's all right," Zach soothed her, his eyes trained on the dark, decaying bones at his feet.

"But . . . it's a . . . a—"

"A skeleton."

"Is it hu-hu—" Her voice was muffled in his shoulder blade.

"Human? I'm afraid so." He bent backwards and lowered her to the ground. "Open your eyes, Angelface. Look at it. This poor soul can't hurt you. Just step over it. We need to be on our way. Somebody could have heard you scream."

Alena squeezed the little drum and raised her lashes. Her few attempts to do as Zach bid were in vain. She couldn't look at the dreadful thing on the floor again. Giving up, she focused her eyes elsewhere, lifted her legs as high as she could, and moved past the pitiful creature as quickly as possible.

The route beyond reeked with the smell of mildew, making breathing near impossible. Threads of debris fluttered like maidenhair from the low beams and couldn't be avoided. Alena quivered with every brush of it against her face.

They'd woven their way some distance along the musty path when Zach halted abruptly. "I've got that uneasy feeling again," he muttered. "Follow my footsteps like before." He proceeded slowly, holding the torch at arm's length in front of him and waving it.

Alena tread on his heels, doing her best to keep her balance as she tried to match his wide stride. Yet it became harder and harder to do so when the passage narrowed. Tension teased the hair at her nape. A strand dangling from the ceiling grazed her cheek. She flinched. She teetered.

The next instant was a blur. She grasped the wall for support. The moss-covered stone beneath her palm sank into the rock. In a flash, a slew of sharpened sticks attached to a log swung toward them from the beam overhead. Zach sprang backwards. The torch flew from his grasp as he slammed Alena against the moldy damp floor, mere moments before the razor-edged snare whizzed above their flattened bodies.

When the ambush mechanism slowed to a sway, Zach reached up and carefully stopped it.

He tugged Alena to her feet. "Jeez, what the hell did you do?" he ground out, dusting his hat on his britches.

"I . . . I simply braced my hand against the wall." Tears puddled in her eyes. She was cold. She was hungry. She was frightened, and ashamed of being so. And she wanted to go home. *Dear God in heaven, how she wanted to go home*.

"Aw, Angel. Don't start crying."

Alena squeezed her eyes shut to hold the tears at bay, and cleared her throat. "I'm not crying," she insisted.

Zach surveyed her stern profile, partially lit by the hazy glow of the torch. A quiver of her tilted chin went straight to his heart. Lowering his bundle, he put an arm around her and pressed her head to his chest. "I'm sorry I yelled. Hell, I'm surprised I made it through that dinky space without my shoulder setting that thing off." He stroked her hair absently. "I'm some big lug, huh? Here I tell you not to get hysterical, then I blow my stack. I never thought too much about it before, but I guess I get a little cantankerous when I see blades coming toward me." He cradled her face, lifting her gaze to his. "Think you can put up with me for a while longer? You'll have to, you know, if we're going to get out of here and find Howard."

"Zach, do you truly believe there's a chance we'll find him? How can we be certain we're on the right trail?"

"He was here, Angelface. I'm as sure of that as I am there's another way out of this place." He scanned the passage ahead. "There has to be. The map Howie found didn't show a waterfall. That alone makes me think it was drawn from some other point of entry." His gaze came back to hers and he smiled. "Now, what do you say we get out of this dungeon, huh? It's beginning to make me nervous." He stooped to retrieve the torch and his bundle. The drum caught his eye and he picked it up. "What's this?"

"I . . . uh, it's a drum."

"I can see that." Zach grinned. "Ah. Why, Miss Sutton—" He feigned indignation. "You didn't *take* this from the treasure chamber, did you?"

"I didn't intend to. I only wanted to look at it. But when I rushed into the corridor, I found myself still holding it." She bit her bottom lip, glancing at him. "You may have it for your museum, if you like."

Zach rolled the drum over in his hand. "It's a very nice piece of workmanship and in excellent condition for as old as it is. However, I think you should keep it as a memento. It might inspire you to think twice the next time you get the urge to go tearing off into the unknown. Here, take it. Who knows, maybe it's a good-luck charm in your hands. After all, we've made it this far, haven't—" Zach's head turned with a snap to the darkness beyond. "Listen. Do you hear that?"

Alena cocked her ear. In the distance, there was a hollow padding sound. Running footsteps?

"Looks like we're going to have company." Zach took her arm, positioning her behind a protruding rock where she could peek down the passage. He listened again. "It sounds like only one person. A man, I think. You stand right here.

While his attention is on you, I'll surprise him. Got it?''

Alena nodded. Her heart picked up its pace as she watched Zach move across the way and hide behind the ledge. He gave her a quick wink before he ground the torch out on the cavern floor.

Blackness engulfed them. Alena stood ramrod-straight. The pitter-patter came closer and closer. Her own labored breathing was amplified in her head. She wanted so desperately to whisper Zach's name . . . to hear his voice in the dark void. Yet she didn't dare. He was there. Though she couldn't see him, couldn't hear him, she knew he was there, just a few feet away.

A soft yellow glow filled the tunnel ahead. What sounded like bare feet slapping the rough stone surface drew nearer and nearer. Then the outline of a torch-bearing man came into view. He was running at a steady pace straight for Alena. Light illuminated the immediate area. Her eyes shifted to Zach. His hands were clasped into one large fist and raised above his shoulder.

Alena focused then on the man's brown features coming toward her. Her gaze shot back to Zach as he lifted his hands higher. "Zach, wait!" she cried.

Zach's fist stopped within inches of the Indian's shocked face. "Yori! Jeez almighty. You scared the devil out of us. I almost knocked your head off.''

Yori glanced from Zach to Alena and back again, and smiled. "I am glad to find you, Doctu. And you also, missy. Sengali say you were dead. But I say, no! Doctu is great *mair*. He would not die so easily.''

"Sengali told you where we were?" Alena asked, stepping from behind the rock.

"Sengali is friend to Yori. He was at mission school when I was boy. Early this morning I find the dugout with Jaquara spears in it. I signaled Sengali. When he told me Mahrakimba had returned and had brought a tall white warrior with her, I put . . . I put . . . how you say, Doctu?"

"Two and two together?"

"I put two plus two together." The Indian's grin broadened.

"How is Slim?" Zach asked anxiously.

"John-sen is well. He say to tell you to 'mind your manners.' He say you will know what this means."

Zach glanced at Alena and cleared his throat. "Sounds like he's faring well enough. As for me, next to a hot epsom-salt bath, I'd like nothing better than to get the hell out of this place."

"You follow Yori, Doctu. I know way out through mouth of old shrine. Come. Come, missy."

Yori led them through the winding maze so fast they had trouble keeping up with him. The last musty aisle yawned out into a cavern. It was flooded with filmy daylight from the opening beyond. A sacrificial altar shrouded with cobwebs dominated the chamber. Huge, dusty caldrons were scattered throughout.

Alena averted her gaze from the ghastly sight. Barring her thoughts from what might have once taken place on the premises, she looked to the blinding sunshine at the mouth of the cave. Overanxious to fill her lungs with sweet fresh air, she ran toward it.

"Alena, wait," Zach called, then shifted his bundle and took off after her.

She froze at the entrance. Hundreds of black eyes outside the shrine widened on her.

Sensing the reason for her abrupt halt, Zach slipped to one side of her and hid himself. "Alena, how many are there?" he asked quietly as Yori crouched next to him. "No. Don't answer. And don't look at me. Keep your eyes straight ahead. Just stand there looking regal until I figure out what to do." He leaned back and slid down the cold stone until he met the floor. Grimacing, he turned to the little man who sat beside him. "Yori, what in the hell is going on?"

Yori shrugged. "On the last day of the full moon, the villagers come to pay homage to the shrine of Delgami, giver of life. They were not there when I entered."

"Great," Zach muttered, nudging up his hat. "It would be our rotten luck to time our escape with the last day of the full moon. How long will it take them to pay their respects?"

"Two, maybe three days."

Zach sighed deeply and glanced at Alena's stiff, trembling form. It was obvious she couldn't stand there like that for three days. He joined his hands loosely between his knees and studied them a moment. "Yori, do you know the Jaquara word for 'go' or 'leave'?"

"I know the word, Doctu."

"Good. Okay, here's what we're going to do . . ."

Zach picked up the unlit torch and waited, measuring the minutes it would take Yori to return to the mouth of the corridor. On cue, he crouched in the shadows directly behind Alena. "Don't turn around, Angelface. When I tell you to, raise your arms and look angry."

A horrendous howling broke into the cavern and echoed eerily through the opening. Like clockwork, Zach set the torch aflame to produce an uncanny glow behind Alena. "Now!" he said in a fierce whisper. "Raise your arms, now!"

Alena furrowed her brows, doing her best to produce a scowl, though under the circumstances, it wasn't easy. She lifted her arms slowly for effect. At the same time, the howl rang out again, followed by what Alena suspected was a string of Jaquara.

The shock that had covered the brown faces before her turned to terror. Mumbles and shrieks blended, rumbling through the crowd. Then, nearly knocking one another over, the villagers ran in every direction.

As the last of the congregation disappeared into the thick of the jungle, Alena's taut nerves gave way. She turned to Zach in a fit of nervous giggles. "We did it! They're gone!"

His laughter joined hers. "We did, didn't we?" Moving beside her, he slipped an arm about her shoulders and surveyed the emptied grounds. "And, if I'm not mistaken, you've just become a living legend, Angelface. To be sure, the happenings of this day will be passed on for generations."

Yori came to stand beside them. "This good trick. Is it not, Doctu?"

"It was indeed." Zach smiled at his friend and slapped him on the back. "You did an excellent job. Hell, you had the hair raising on my neck."

Yori beamed, then looked pensive. "We must go now, Doctu. They may come back."

"My thoughts exactly, old friend." Zach

tossed the torch aside and gathered his things. "I'm ready whenever you are."

Outside the cave, they stood for a moment, in awe of the shrine they'd just exited. The cavern's opening formed the mouth of a huge face carved into the stone. Weather-cracked through the centuries, the gargoyle features were partially overgrown with vines. The same face had been crudely sketched on Alena's section of the map, though the drawing hadn't looked nearly as ominous.

Alena had the oddest feeling that the creature watched them all the way across the ceremonial grounds. She was greatly relieved when the dense greenery of the jungle hid them from view.

"This way, Doctu. There is something here for you." Yori broke into a trot down the path.

"Jeez, Yori, not so fast." Zach braced a hand against his bruised rib and caught the broad leaves that flapped back into his face. "For Pete's sake, slow down. The lady and I haven't been on holiday, you know."

Yori halted just ahead. "It is here. This will make you a happy man. You'll see."

Alena and Zach looked on while Yori stooped to retrieve a large bundle from beneath the shrubbery. The Indian glanced up with a wide grin before he spread the bounty on the ground and carefully unwrapped it.

"My rifle!" Zach ran a hand over the stock. "Thanks, Yori."

"It is all here, Doctu. I give Sengali things to trade for your belongings. And missy's, too." He pulled Alena's book of Elizabeth Barrett Browning from the bundle and handed it to her.

"Oh, Yori." Alena hugged the book to her breast.

"And this too, missy," he said, holding out her hat and clothes.

Alena took the hat and ran a hand lovingly over the wilted flowers, then dropped a chaste kiss on Yori's cheek. "I shall be forever grateful."

The Indian smiled shyly.

Zach knelt and rummaged through his pack. "Bullets, too? And my knife. Yori, you're a gem. By the way," he said, continuing to take inventory, "you haven't heard of any other white men being in the area lately, have you?"

"Only *bandeirantes*, men who do what you do."

Zach sat back on his heels and shaded his eyes to look up at Yori. "Men who do . . . ? Archeologists? You mean . . . an expedition?"

Yori nodded, and Zach frowned pensively.

"I ask about the white man you look for also, Doctu, like you say."

Zach's expression turned hopeful. Abandoning his previous thoughts, he came to his feet. "And?"

"There was such a man found by outcasts just before the rains came. Their village is not far. Sengali say the man was badly beaten. The outcasts cared for him, but Sengali does not know if the man still lives."

Zach noted the way the color drained from Alena's face as she glanced between him and Yori.

"My father," she whispered. Her eyes widened on Zach for confirmation. "It could be him, Zach . . . couldn't it?"

Chapter 15

66 A lena." Zach laid a hand on her shoulder.
"We don't know anything for sure. A lot
of white men disappear in this region and are
never seen again. I still have my doubts that
Howard could've survived—" Pressing his lips
tightly together, he glanced to the side, then
sighed. "It could be a wild goose chase . . . but I
do think it's worth investigating."

Alena stared at the slight smile she knew Zach
had fixed upon his face just to please her. The
ground seemed to shift beneath her. For as long
as she could remember, her single greatest desire
had been to confront Howard Sutton. Now,
when she was closer to the possible end of her
pursuit than she would have ever imagined she
would be, she wanted to cleave to Zach and beg
time to stop.

She gazed deeply into his blue eyes, closing
off the sound around her until all she heard was
the palpitation of her own heart. Her quest for
her father had led her straight into Zach's arms.
Within those strong arms, within the circle of
warmth and security they provided, she'd found
love. This bold adventurer had forced her to let

go of her childhood vow, forced her to feel the blood pumping through her veins. He had reminded her that she was human and made her give in to the reality of having very human emotions. He had made her laugh again, made her live again. She had come to this wild untamed land in search of her father . . . and found love. A love that could never last outside the boundaries of this jungle.

The vortex in which she now stood was a fantasy-world—a storybook place where paradise could change to purgatory with a blink of the eye. Through all their perils, something magical had bound she and Zach . . . a wondrous, magical, mystical spell that would be broken once she found her father and returned to civilization.

Alena reached for Zach's face without quite being able to see him through the tears that blurred her vision. His features faded as if in a dream. If she found her father, she would have to face losing Zach. Once again, as fate would have it, she would have to lose someone precious.

Zach caught her as she swayed forward. "Aw, sweetheart," he whispered, scooping her into his arms. "Poor little thing. Had all you can take for one day, haven't you? Yori, spread out her bedroll. She's got to rest. We'll leave for the outcast camp first thing in the morning."

Alena transferred her bag to the other hand and dabbed her brow with a handkerchief. The thick moss and wet, deteriorating leaves that lined the jungle floor made the ground slick. At least she could be thankful for one thing this morning: Yori's gift of her belongings. Despite

the added warmth of her old clothes and boots,
they were much more suitable than the skimpy
tanga for the arduous trek.

Since waking, she had attempted to push spec-
ulation aside about the man they were going to
see. Whenever she succeeded, troubled thoughts
of Zach filled the void. Reality loomed harsh and
solid in broad daylight. She found she was
hugely embarrassed for taunting Zach into taking her virtue. He had tried to dissuade her, yet
she knew he would not extend his scruples as
far as an offer of marriage—nor would she want
him to. He was like a will-o'-the-wisp. Elusive.
Free. Wild. He had made his views on matrimony clear from the beginning. She expected no
undying vows from him.

Yet even while mortification at how she'd
wickedly enticed Zach unsettled her stomach
and made her cheeks burn, she did not regret
what she'd done. She loved him. She would always love him, long after they had parted ways.
She would forever cherish the memory of their
one, blissful night together; she would never forget the fire in his eyes, in his touch.

Alena pushed back her hat, wiping another
trickle of sweat from her forehead. There were
some who would call her a fool. And perhaps,
indeed, she was one, for it occurred to her now
that the look of love she had imagined on his
face that night might have been no more than
common lust. She had seen what she'd wanted
to see. It didn't matter, however. She could keep
the illusion.

An old, familiar stiffness crept up her spine as
she continued down the trail, shoving and nudging the dense foliage from her path. She would

persevere. She had survived for years without her father's love. She would survive without Zach's. When all this was over, she would return to England, resume her teaching position, and life would go on. For the time being, she would avoid any further intimate contact with Zach. It could do naught but intensify the pain when they parted.

A slight breeze brought the sound of distant drums. Alena looked in the direction that the exotic rhythm seemed to be coming from. She halted her footsteps as Yori and Zach did, and the three of them listened intently.

"Yori, what do they say?" Zach asked.

"It is death song, Doctu. Someone is dying."

The death song grew louder as they progressed in the direction of the percussion, and entered the outcast village late that afternoon. A wild dog yelped, darting from their path. Though the haunting drums proved otherwise, the small, untidy camp looked deserted.

Faces started to appear at the shaded entrances of the huts. Only one old man ventured forth. He assessed the trio warily while he answered Yori's questions with nods and gestures of his hands.

"The white man lives," Yori told Zach. "He is there in the last hut. But he is not well, *mair*. The drums beat for him."

Zach narrowed his gaze on the grass structure and tugged down the brim of his hat. "Alena, wait here," he said in a tone that brooked no argument. Taking a few long strides toward the hut, he threw the flap back and ducked inside.

Alena's pulse quickened with each passing minute that he did not return. Her nails dug into her palms. She wished she had never come here. No. That wasn't true. If Howard Sutton was the man inside the hut, she had to see him. He had questions to answer. She had to speak with him . . . but he was *dying* . . . *dying* . . . *dying*. The word echoed hollow against her sternum with every beat of the drums.

After what seemed like an eternity, Zach emerged. And she knew. As he approached, the grimness of his paled features spoke before he did. The man inside was indeed her father.

Zach took her hands in his and stared at them, rubbing his thumbs over her knuckles. "He has malaria, Alena. It's not a pretty sight. I hardly recognized him. But it's Howie, all right." He paused, struggling with his own emotions. "He . . . he may not know you. It's the fever. He's drifting in and out of coherency. I've seen the symptoms before, sweetheart. The malaria is in the last stages."

Zach lifted grief-stricken eyes and his arms wrapped around her like a warm cocoon, shielding her from the world. Burying herself in his chest, Alena wept tears she couldn't stop until her sobs turned to short rasps that jerked her body. "Oh . . . Zach, I'm s-so . . . afraid, so . . . afraid he'll . . . t-t-turn me . . . away."

"Aw, come on, sweetheart, who wouldn't love that face?" Zach cupped her jaw and lifted her gaze to his. "Even with smudges, it's irresistible."

He was smiling again. There was something so insanely soothing about his ill-timed smiles. The smile, the sunshine, the kiss he pressed upon her damp cheek all combined to calm her.

"Here," he said, setting her gently from

him. He tugged a handkerchief from his hip pocket. "Blow your nose and make yourself presentable. You're a damn fine woman, Alena Sutton." He reached out and straightened her hat, adding, "Any man would be proud to call you his daughter. So hold your head high when you go in there. You hear me?"

Alena nodded, automatically squaring her shoulders.

"Would you like me to go with you?" Zach asked.

The love Alena felt for him in that moment could have filled the ocean. Of course she wanted him to go with her. She wanted him *forever* with her. He fortified her, gave her strength and courage when hers failed. He made her smile when there was nothing to smile about. She ached for him to take her hand and be at her side when she faced her father. Yet she couldn't accept his offer. "I'm afraid this is something I must do alone," she said, and caressed his stubbled cheek. "But thank you for asking."

With a deep breath, she turned to the door and ducked into the hut before she lost her nerve. She stopped just inside, adjusting her eyes to the filtered light of the cool shade. Soft murmuring drew her attention to a dark corner. An old woman, apparently oblivious to her presence, sat on her heels, rocking to and fro, chanting.

A sudden movement across the way diverted Alena's gaze to a frail, shadowed figure thrashing about on a mat. She took an abrupt step backwards.

This was not her father. It *couldn't* be. Her father was a much larger man.

As the poor soul turned his head toward her, he suddenly fell still. His features were veiled by the darkness, yet Alena felt his inspection. He started to quiver, and she had the strongest urge to flee. This was a dreadful mistake. This man simply could not be her father. But her feet stayed anchored to the spot, ignoring her command to run.

"Marion? Marion . . . is that you?"

The earth floor wobbled beneath her at the sound of her mother's name. The room spun. The hauntingly familiar whisper—a ghost of the deep-timbred tone it had once been—sliced into Alena's memory. Her heart thumped furiously in her breast. Even disguised with pain, the voice was unmistakable. It belonged to Howard Sutton . . . her father.

Alena moved toward the man in a trance, believing, disbelieving, denying the truth. She'd only imagined the utterance. The man was too thin. His cheeks were too hollow. His eyes were too sunken . . . his eyes . . .

Kneeling beside him, she looked hard into the glazed green eyes. The circles beneath them did not diminish their brightness. The eyes mirrored her own. They *were* her own.

"P-Papa?"

He stared at her for a long moment. Then his lips quivered into a flickering smile, and a teardrop rolled down the side of his face. After several shaky tries, his withered hand raised and hovered near her cheek.

"D-dear God, it's my little Alena." Sobs broke from his throat in full force, jarring his body. "Alena . . ." He choked out her name again. "Praise be to God, it is you, isn't it? My sweet, sweet . . . little Alena."

Alena's tears joined his. She gathered him into her arms. "Shh . . . Papa. It's me. I'm here." She wanted so much to embrace him with all her might, yet fear of crushing his fragile frame stopped her from doing so.

Gently, she pressed him onto the mat and laid a palm against his fevered brow. "Oh, Papa, you're burning up." She spied a bowl of water at the head of the pallet, picked it up, and started to bathe his face.

"How can you ever . . . forgive me, girl?" he rasped, stopping her hand, clasping it in his own. "After all I've done, how can you forgive me?"

Alena focused on the blue veins in his hand and traced them with her thumb. "It doesn't matter any longer, Papa." Her gaze met his and tears rimmed her eyes once again. "All that matters is that we're together now and you must get better. I don't care why you left me. I don't need an explanation anymore. I just want you to get well."

"But I have to give you one, don't you see? I have to tell you why—" A spasm shook him. "I have to tell you before I can go in peace."

"Hush, Papa. You're not going anywhere. You're going to live a long while yet. You'll see, I'll take care of you and you'll get better and we can—"

"Alena, don't. Don't fill your head with illusions. You were always such a practical child." He attempted to smile, though his face constricted with some other emotion. "Look at me. I am dying. I'm a damned old fool who's done everything wrong. What I've done to you can't be justified. It was inexcusable. I don't deserve your understanding. I don't expect redemption. But please, grant me one last favor and let me try to explain."

Unable to speak, Alena nodded, and the motion spilled an endless trail of tears down her face. Her heart wrenched as she took a full account of the damage life had done to him. This once strong, robust, handsome man was now a shell of the image she'd held in her mind. She had never considered the fact that the years would have aged him. She hadn't expected the weariness, the vulnerability she saw. It was so hard to watch him struggle for each word, each breath. Pain, helplessness, bitterness at lost hopes and lost dreams, all flowed with the steady stream of her tears.

"Your mother . . . was the light of my life, Alena. I did love her so." His faraway eyes brightened as if he drifted through time. "I was a young rakehell when I met her, wild as a March hare. But there was a gentleness in her that tamed me. For eight blissful years she filled my days with more love than most men know in a lifetime." His fingers brushed Alena's cheek and he swallowed. "She gave me you . . . such a precious gift . . . a child molded from her likeness, yet with eyes the color of my own . . . a symbol . . . of our love, our unity. My happiness was complete. All the wealth I could ever seek was there in your mother's heart, in her smile . . . in your smile. I suppose I took it for granted that those days would never end. Do you remember when we used to cuddle before the fireplace and I would tell you all my adventures?"

Alena wiped her cheek and smiled. "I remember," she whispered.

"Most of those tales were exaggerated, you know. But they made you and Marion laugh. And the laughter that came from you was music to my ears; it filled me with joy. Sometimes, when I shut my eyes, I can almost hear it again." His lids closed.

Alena thought him sleeping until he shuddered and his eyes flew open. "Rest now, Papa," she urged, smoothing cool water across his brow.

"No ... no, I mustn't ... not until I've finished."

"We can talk later, Papa."

"No ... please ... let me finish," he beseeched in a quaking voice. "I have to tell you why. Alena, all I ever wanted was what was best for you. You must believe that ... you must ... you must believe—"

A racked cough seized him, and agony gripped her as she tilted his head. "I know, Papa. I believe you. Please, don't exert yourself." The spell passed and she laid him back upon the mat.

He grasped her hands as if he thought she might run away. "You're so like her ... so like your mother ... so lovely," he said hoarsely, giving her fingers a feeble squeeze. "Dear God, Alena, when she died, I nearly went mad with grief. I turned to the bottle to ease the pain. I drank until a numbness took my heart, until blackness engulfed me and I didn't have to think anymore ... until I didn't have to *feel* anymore. With each day that passed I became more despondent, more dependent on the crutch of liquor. It became unbearable ... *unbearable* to look at you, child. Every time I did, I saw Marion's face, that b-beautiful, beautiful face, and the agony of losing her struck me anew. It was a sickness, Alena. A sickness that grew daily. Even in my befuddled state, I loved you so dearly. I was terrified something would happen to you because of my negligence. I finally had to come to grips with the reality that I was unfit to raise a child.

"Alena, believe me, leaving you at that school was the h-hardest th-thing I've ever had to do. The h-hardest—"

"Oh, please, Papa, don't." Alena caressed his face. "Don't say any more. Please, please don't. You have to rest."

Calmed by her touch, he reached up and traced her features, his gaze adoring her. "I swear, girl . . . by all that's holy, at the time I had every intention of straightening myself out and returning for you. I dove into my work. But at night, God, at night, the loneliness was there waiting for me in my tent . . . and so was the bottle. You have no idea how many letters I wrote you and never posted . . . how many times I've wanted to see you . . . how often I longed to tell you how much I love you. But I feared the years between us had filled you with bitterness. You were just a child . . . just a child when I left. You couldn't have understood, and I couldn't blame you if you'd learned to hate me through the years. I was so afraid to face you. I . . . couldn't . . . bear . . . the thought of you . . . rejecting me."

Alena's tears came in full force. She brought his hands to her lips, kissed them, then laid them against her cheek. "I love you, Papa. I didn't want to. It h-hurt so much to think you didn't want me. I tried to hate you, Papa, I tried. But

I couldn't. I couldn't. I have always loved you and I always will."

His chin quivered and he closed his eyes. "Oh, Alena . . . my sweet . . . little Alena. Your forgiveness . . . was . . . an old fool's . . . last wish. You can't possibly know . . . how happy you've just made me."

They shared the silence for a moment before his eyes opened again. They were glassy and he appeared to see something that wasn't there. "The tomb . . . Mahrakimba's tomb . . . the headdress . . ."

Alena furrowed her brows, trying to make sense of his delirious ravings. "Shh, Papa. It's all right. Zach has the headdress."

He grasped her sleeve frantically. "The drums . . . did you . . . it's the least . . . the drum . . . the drum . . ." His voice trailed to a whisper, then broke off.

"Yes, Papa, I hear the drums. Shh now, rest. Rest." She pressed a kiss to his cheek and brushed the silver hair from his forehead. "I won't leave you. I will never ever— Papa?"

Alena looked into his glazed eyes and terror swept over her like a dark shroud. "Papa? Wake up." She shook his frail shoulders. "Papa, can you hear me? Oh, Papa . . . not yet . . . not yet . . . it's too soon."

He didn't move. He didn't blink. She wrapped her arms around him and held him close. "No!" she wailed. "No . . . no, you can't go yet . . . not yet . . . it's too soon. Papa, please . . . please wake up."

"Alena?" Zach said softly. He'd been halfway across the hut when his old friend's blank stare interrupted his stride. "Alena, come with me.

There's nothing more you can do. He's gone, love." Kneeling beside her, he pried her from Howard's form and pulled the cover over the dead man's face.

Alena turned shock-glazed eyes to Zach. "Shh, I must take care of Papa. He's . . . only sleeping."

"Alena—"

"Oh, Zach, he's s-so . . . v-very . . . ill."

Zach clutched her shoulders and when she tried to shrug free, pulled her to him in a crushing embrace.

"Let me go!" she whimpered, beating her fists against his chest. "Papa needs me, Papa . . . needs . . . me . . ."

Zach locked his arms around her, tilted his head back, and stared at the grass ceiling until her blows slowed and finally ceased. When she wilted against him, expelling harsh bursts of air, he loosened his hold. "Alena," he murmured, and gently brushed the damp curls from her face. "I'm sorry. I'm so sorry."

"It isn't fair, Zach. It just isn't fair. There were so many w-wasted years between us. It isn't *fair* that I should find him only t-to . . . lose . . . him . . . again. I can't *bear* losing him again," she sobbed. "Not again . . . not so soon."

"Life isn't always fair, Angelface." Zach rubbed his jaw across the top of her head. "We aren't given any guarantees. We have to latch on to what happiness we can. Just try to be thankful for the time you were given to make peace with your father. I never had that opportunity. Howie was more of a father to me than my own ever was. God, Alena—" His voice cracked. "I . . . loved him, too."

Alena looked up to find Zach's throat working convulsively, his eyes bright with a sadness he fought to conceal. Consumed by her own grief, she hadn't considered Zach's loss. Wanting to console him, she reached out and touched his cheek. He caught her hand, kissed it, and tucked it through his arm.

For a long moment, they stood over the shrouded figure that lay on the ground, silently sharing their sorrow. Then Zach turned her toward the exit.

Alena paused at the doorway and looked back. The bitterness she'd clung to for so many years had vanished. Pain numbed her body, heart, and soul, yet a peacefulness . . . a blessed tranquility had blossomed where bitterness had once dwelled. "Good-bye, Papa," she whispered, then ducked from the dark hut into the blinding white sunshine beyond.

Chapter 16

⌒ᴏᏏᏏᴏ⌒

Morning dawned an appropriate gray. Thunder rumbled overhead as Alena knelt to lay a cluster of orchids atop the freshly turned mound of earth. She straightened the crudely fashioned cross Zach had wedged between a pair of stones, and a single tear rolled down her cheek. "I love you, Papa," she said quietly. "I always have, and I always will."

Zach stood at her side, hat in hand, his long shadow falling across her. His mere presence was a great source of consolation. He had held her, simply held her, all through the night, stroking her hair with whispered words of comfort. Through those dark hours, between the spasms of grief for her father, another sorrow had claimed her. Soon she would lose Zach, too. It was time to go home.

Alena focused on the battered boots beside her. The man who filled them would never rush her. Zach would give her as long as she needed to pay her last respects. Yet she knew it *was* time to go. It was time to return to civilization. With a reticent expression, she rose and turned to him. "I'm ready."

"Are you sure?" he asked, fiddling with the brim of his hat. "We can spare a few more minutes, if you'd like. It will only take us a day or so to catch up with Yori. He left yesterday to fix the boat. He'll bring it around to the far side of the ridge and wait for us there."

Alena looked away from him, scanning the vast, green wilderness she had grown to respect and admire. It was a mystical, magical place where anything could happen. Her days spent here had convinced her that the jungle was a living, breathing entity, with a thousand eyes, a thousand voices. It was ages old and gave no impression of ever dying. Desolation, danger, and immense beauty thrived side by side in this exotic region hidden from the rest of the world. Alena would forever cling to the lessons she'd learned within the heart of the tall, emerald canopies they called the Amazon.

Dropping her lids a moment, Alena inhaled the fragrance of the jungle flowers, trying to retain the sweet scent as if she pressed the blossoms between the pages of a book. "I should like to go home now," she said at last when, in truth, she wished she never had to leave. "I think ... we should be on our way. We've both found what we were searching for."

Placing his hand on the small of her back, Zach ushered her a few feet away and picked up their waiting gear.

Alena turned once more to the grave. "It's beautiful here, isn't it, Zach?"

Zach followed her gaze and took a deep, shuddering breath. "I think Howie would be very pleased with the spot you chose, Angel. Very pleased."

* * *

Alena stared hard into the flickering campfire. Zach and she had hardly spoken since they'd left the glen where they had buried her father. She had purposely seated herself across the way from Zach. The emptiness that engulfed her made her vulnerable. She feared she might crumble if Zach touched her once more . . . feared she might cling to him and beg him to never leave her.

Raising her gaze above the golden flames, she caught him contemplating her with great concern.

"I'm sorry, Alena," he said softly. "I really am very sorry." He lowered his eyes by degrees to the fire. "Howie was the best. He'll be sorely missed in the field of archeology."

Alena swallowed the swelling in her throat, and the brittle wood crackled in the silence.

"I'm going to find out who attacked him," Zach went on as if talking to himself. "I swear I will. From what Howie said, the bastard never gave him a chance. Came up behind him and clubbed him. Howie suspected someone was following him. That's why he sent the map. Dammit, I told him not to take off without me. He was always doing that . . . just taking off on his own. I've told him a hundred times . . . a hundred times . . ."

Zach's voice trailed off and he looked at Alena abruptly. He wanted to take her in his arms, ease her pain . . . and his. But she'd made it clear by keeping her distance all day that she didn't want him to hold her, didn't want him to touch her. She had recoiled every time he'd tried to help her up an incline or over a rock or fallen tree. Maybe she was feeling exactly the way he had feared she would—ashamed of what had happened between them that night in the cave. Maybe she'd had come to her own conclusions where he was concerned. Maybe she had made up her mind that they were all wrong for each other.

But he was right for her, dammit. And she was right for him.

Strange, Zach thought, but tragedies often left you with something valuable. Howie's death had reminded him that no one was immortal. Eventually, everything passed away. Howie's passing had made him realize that on the rare occasions when you found someone you treasured, you'd better hang onto them. While he had dug the grave early that morning, Zach had viewed his own life in retrospect. Looking back, his existence had appeared shallow and bland, boring in fact, until Alena had come along. As he had laid Howard's frail body in its final resting place, it had become evident to him that you don't close any doors on your future that can't be reopened. Zach focused on Alena. She was no longer looking his way, rather staring into the fire again. He pressed his lips into a determined line. If you wanted something bad enough, there was always a way to make it work. It was imperative that he talk to Alena, made her understand how he felt. But she was dealing with her grief in her own way and he had to respect that. He needed to give her a decent amount of time to mourn.

Zach ran a hand over the thick bristles on his chin and the next time Alena's gaze met his, he gave her a smile instead of the hug he wanted to give. Then, instead of saying all he yearned to, he said, "You look tired, Angelface. What do you say we call it a night? If we get an early start, we can meet Yori by late tomorrow afternoon."

The heat was unbearable by mid-morning. Zach had considerately slowed his pace. He even suggested they stop for a short rest when they came upon a shallow stream.

Wading ankle-deep into the water, Alena stooped to bathe her face. Zach sidled next to her and, having removed his shirt, splashed himself liberally. When Alena straightened, his movement stilled, and she met the gaze of his rippled reflection in the water.

"Alena, we have to talk," he said quietly. "I know this is bad timing, but I can't hold back any longer. We have to talk about what happened between us in the cave."

Alena closed her eyes, unable to look at him and keep her voice convincing. "There is nothing to discuss. I . . . I apologize for my forwardness. I cannot imagine what possessed me to goad you into doing something you had plainly stated you had no wish to do. It must have been the drink those native girls gave—"

"God, you still don't understand, do you? It wasn't that I didn't want you. I was afraid, dammit. Afraid you'd feel exactly as you do." Zach sighed. "Alena, I don't want you to hate me."

Alena searched his face for a split second, then swiftly focused on a group of monkeys chattering in a tree across the stream. "I don't hate you. I don't." Her eyes stung and she blinked. "Please, Zach, I . . . can't go on with this discussion. It was a mistake. *My* mistake. I take full blame for what happened. Truly, I don't hate you, so there's no need to continue this conversation. There's nothing more to say." She pivoted, intending to put as much space between them as possible.

"I have more to say, dammit," Zach said, catching her arm. He didn't turn her around to face him, but bent to her ear. "I have plenty more to say. And you're not going anywhere until you hear me out. You don't have to look at me. Just listen. Promise me you'll listen and I'll turn you loose."

Alena nodded, and he guided her to the grassy bank before letting go of her arm. She watched him jerk his shirt on as he started to pace.

"I tried to wait to talk to you about this. I really did. But I can't stand you treating me like I have the plague. I can't take it all the way back to the States. Not after—" He stopped his pacing, raked his hand through his hair, then looked at her with what Alena could only describe as an overwrought expression.

"Alena . . . I realize you have no previous experience in . . . in . . . doing what we did. But I do. I have . . . er . . . many times with many different women." He glanced to the side and cleared his throat. "What I'm trying to say is that it was never like that before for me . . . not with anyone . . . *ever*. Don't you see? It was something special. What happened between us was special. Like . . . like . . . fireworks on the fourth of July."

Alena stared at him as if in a daze. She'd never seen him look so flustered. He shrugged his shoulders, spreading his arms wide. His mouth opened and closed several times as if he strove for the right words to explain himself.

As she stood staring at him, a sudden thought made her heart beat like a bird caged within her breast. Could he possibly be struggling for the courage to say—

A shot cracked, resounding hollowly through the air.

Zach stumbled. His eyes, fixed on Alena, momentarily vacillated between blank confusion and pain, then took on a vacant glaze, and he fell.

Alena ran toward him through a grotesque nightmare that pushed him farther and farther away. She moved faster, ran harder until she broke through the barrier of horror and dropped beside him.

Dear God, blood was seeping through the front of his shirt. His eyes were closed. He wasn't moving. Was he breathing?

He was. He was. He had to be.

Holding her hand to his mouth and nose, she expelled a sigh when his warm breath grazed her skin. With relief, she felt her blessed practicality take hold of her. She had to stop the bleeding. She swiftly tore the sleeves from her blouse and pressed them against Zach's chest. She scooped water from the stream's edge into her hat, then positioned his head in her lap.

"Don't give up, Zach," she urged while she mopped his brow and sponged the blood. "Fight this with me . . . help me, Zach." She found the bullet hole . . . too near the heart. Her own constricted in her chest. Pressing the wadded cloth against the wound, she wrapped the makeshift bandage tight, winding it around his shoulder. Tears welled inside her as she continued washing his pale face. "Fight! Blast you, Zach! Fight!"

Zach's eyes half-opened, raising Alena's hopes. He murmured something inaudible.

"Don't try to talk, my love," she said, and smoothed his brow. "The bleeding will stop soon and I'll take the bullet out. Rest. Rest now."

He shook his head frantically and tried to speak again, and Alena bent closer.

"Get out ... Alena ... get the hell out ... of here ... hurry ... before ... before ..." His voice faded. His eyes rolled back, then his face lolled to the side.

Alena cradled his head tightly against her breast. Her own life force seemed to drain as the desolate world closed in on her. Dazed and disoriented, she ran a hand through his thick hair. "Zach? Oh, Zach, no. Please ... don't leave me. You can't leave me, Zach. You see, I love you. I ... love you ... s-so ... d-dearly, so ... very ... very dearly...."

"Good God! Miss Sutton? What on earth has happened here?"

Alena raised a blurry gaze and lifted her hand to shade her eyes. A dark form silhouetted against the bright yellow sun stood above her. Both the voice, with its distinctly British accent, and his slight frame were vaguely familiar.

The man immediately crouched beside her. "Miss Sutton? Dear heaven, you're in shock." He lifted her chin. "Look at me. Don't you remember? We met in Philadelphia. I'm a friend."

Alena concentrated on his face. Recognition flickered in the back of her brain. She *did* know him.

"I introduced myself at the restaurant in Philadelphia. Nigel Flemming, remember? With the British Museum of Antiquities. You do remember now, don't you?"

"Help me," Alena rasped and tears gushed

forth. "Oh . . . Mr. F-Flemming . . . p-please . . .
help Zach."

"Oh, Miss Sutton. Dear me. I . . . I don't know
a farthing about medical remedies. I—"

"Please." The word stuck in Alena's throat.

"Oh . . . well," Nigel stammered, "if you insist, I . . . I suppose it would do no harm to take
a look at the poor chap. You'll have to let go of
him, my dear."

Alena reluctantly let the man take Zach from
her arms yet she stayed where she was.

"Good Lord, Summerfield. What have you
gotten yourself into?" Flemming muttered.
Poised above Zach, he lifted the injured man's
lids, then felt his chest. Nigel's expression was
grave as he checked for a pulse, first in Zach's
throat, then on his wrist. Thorns twisted around
Alena's heart. The Englishman repeated the procedure again and again, before his sympathetic
gaze lifted and he slowly shook his head. "I'm
sorry, Miss Sutton. I simply don't know. Perhaps
I'm doing it wrong. I fear I can't feel a pulse."

"*No* . . . he just spoke to me. No!" Alena dove
for Zach, but Nigel caught her shoulders and
pulled her to her feet. When she struggled, he
tightened his grip, giving her a violent shake.

"Here now, Miss Sutton, stop that! We should
go for help. Miss Sutton, please, calm yourself!"
The sharp sting of his hand to her cheek turned
Alena's head to the side, and she froze.

"Oh . . . oh, forgive me, my dear." Nigel Flemming hesitantly drew her limp form against him.
"There, there," he said, patting her on the back.
"You were becoming hysterical. If you think
you're up to it, I really do believe we should see
to getting the poor fellow some help. Come now,

we shall return in all haste to camp. You can rest there, and I will bring someone out here to—"

"You go," Alena said, pulling herself free of his embrace. She focused on Zach's motionless form and swiped the tears from her cheeks. "I'm staying with him."

Flemming glanced between her and Zach. "Oh, dear, Miss Sutton. I'm afraid that won't do. No. It won't do at all." He gripped her arm. "I simply can't leave you here unattended. I must insist you—"

"Nigel?" Another voice came from behind them, priming Alena's memory, and she looked over her shoulder to see Richard Blythe emerging from the thick greenery. Breaking away from Flemming's grasp, she ran toward the other man.

"Why, Miss Sutton." Richard caught both her hands in his as she reached him. "What a pleasant . . . here now, what's all this?" His gaze landed briefly on Zach, then shot back to her. "Lord. What's gone on here? Summerfield, is he—?"

Alena stopped him with a frantic shake of her head.

"Richard. Thank God you're here, old man." Flemming stepped forward. "Have a look at him, will you? I'm afraid I'm not much good at such things."

"I'll see what I can do." Richard patted Alena's wrist, then released it and moved to kneel beside Zach.

Alena clutched her hands against her waist, her heart beating in the base of her throat. Breath held, she watched Mr. Blythe conduct an examination similar to the one Nigel Flemming had performed earlier.

Minutes seemed like hours until Richard rose and turned to Alena, his face pale and distressed beneath the brim of his hunter's hat. "Miss Sutton . . . Alena, I'm terribly sorry." He shook his head slowly. "I'm afraid he's gone, my dear. He's—"

"No," Alena whispered, fiercely at first, then sobbingly. "No." Her knees liquified. Gravity pulled her toward the ground. Everything went bright white.

Richard caught her shoulders and guided her to a fallen log. "There now, Miss Sutton. Sit here and collect yourself. I'm sure this whole thing has been quite an ordeal." He bent over her and brushed a strand of damp hair from her cheek. "I need to talk with Mr. Flemming a moment. We'll decide what's best and see to it. Everything will be all right, my dear. I promise."

Though she gave him a slight, automatic nod, Alena wasn't listening. With her gaze fixed on Zach, she barely noticed when Richard moved away.

"Poor chap," Nigel commented as Richard drew near. "I wonder who could have done such a deed."

"Summerfield made his share of enemies. It could have been any of them."

Nigel sighed deeply, and averted his attention from Dr. Summerfield to his countryman. "Well, at least it's good to know you've come to no harm. Where on earth have you been? We put a search party out first thing this morning when you didn't return to camp last night. I say, old man, I had been looking for you for hours when I heard the shot." He scanned the area. "Can't imagine where the others are. Surely they heard it, too."

"You hired me to locate the treasure, didn't you?" Richard glanced at Alena, then motioned Flemming to accompany him out of her hearing range. "How do you expect me to do my job unless I explore?"

"You could have taken some men with you."

Blythe hooked his thumbs through the belt of his safari shirt. "I work alone, Nigel. I do things my own way. I told you that before we left Philadelphia."

"Yes, yes, of course, I remember. And I never said a word about you insisting to arrange your own passage and meet us here, did I? But going off like that. Really, old boy. You might have informed someone you were leaving. We all thought you might have met up with those heathens we had a run-in with."

"You're not paying me to inform you of my every move, Nigel. You're paying me to find Mahrakimba's tomb, and I'm certain we're close to doing just that." Both of their gazes shifted to Alena. "Do you think she knows anything?"

"I haven't had time to find out. Haven't even thought of asking her, actually. She might, I suppose. Poor little thing. Look at her. Pitiful sight, isn't she? Hardly the pretty young lady I met in the States." Nigel quirked a brow at his colleague. "What are we going to do with her?"

"There's a mission not far from here. She needs medical attention. She's in shock. I shall take her there. The good sisters will see to her, I'm sure."

"Yes." Nigel nodded. "I suppose that's best. I'll return to camp and roust some men to help me with Summerfield's remains."

"That's not necessary." Richard adjusted his

rifle strap over his shoulder. "I can handle things here. You should go back to camp and let the others know I've come to no harm. Wait for me there. I'll be along shortly. The mission is no more than a day or so from here."

"Well, if you're certain you can manage . . ." Nigel said hesitantly.

Blythe was already walking away from him. Pausing in his stride, he looked over his shoulder and tugged the brim of his hat down. "I'm certain," he said. "See you in a couple of days, my good man."

From her stiff perch on the log, Alena had vaguely noticed Mr. Blythe rummaging around the weeded bank, gathering her things, gathering Zach's. She had the sensation of awakening from a bad dream only to find herself in a nightmare when Richard covered Zach's body with a blanket. The action was significantly final and brought her to her feet.

Her movement drew Richard's attention. "Ah, Miss Sutton. Feeling a tad better, I hope. Good. We must go then. Whoever did this awful thing may still be lurking about. Is this your bag?"

"We cannot leave him here like this," Alena heard herself say in a faraway voice.

Richard started toward her. "Miss Sutton— Alena—I assure you everything will be taken care of. Mr. Flemming and I discussed it thoroughly. I give you my word Zach will be given a proper burial." He bestowed a patient smile on her. "*Is* this your bag?"

She nodded and let him press it into her numb hands, then watched him sling Zach's rifle over his shoulder. She took a step forward. "That is

Zach's gun," she stated boldly. "You may not take it."

"But I only thought—"

"It is Zach's rifle and it shall stay with him."

"Very well." With a jerk he broke open the stock, emptied the gun of ammunition, and laid it on the ground next to the shrouded body. "I'm afraid it wouldn't do at all for some savage to get hold of an armed weapon."

Uneasiness at the way his smile failed to reach his eyes spiraled through Alena. She quickly dismissed it. She was distraught, wary of everything at the moment. The man was simply trying to help her.

"I trust you will not disapprove of my taking this." He lifted Zach's bundle containing the golden headdress. "I'm sure Zach would want us to see that it reaches the museum. After all, it's the least we can do for the poor fellow. Now, we really must be on our way, my dear."

"A moment, please," Alena said, and, kneeling beside Zach, uncovered his face. "Just give me a moment." She pressed a light kiss upon his forehead. His skin was still warm. He appeared to be merely sleeping. Alena fancied he would open his eyes any second as she laid her cheek alongside his and whispered ever so softly, "I love you."

Forever. She wanted to stay where she was forever. She wanted to die at his side, meet him in whatever realm he was in now.

She might have done so, had Richard not touched her shoulder. "Miss Sutton. Come now," he said, catching her arm and pulling her upright. "I'm certain he's in a better place."

Alena let him help her to a standing position.

She placed her hat on her head, her eyes caressing Zach's face one last time before Richard hid it from view beneath the blanket.

"Miss Sutton, we *must* go," Richard insisted again as he filled his arms with their gear.

Alena turned and as she did, her foot bumped the little drum. She stooped to pick it up and hugged it to her breast. *No more adventures, Zachariah Summerfield. There shall be no more adventures for me without you. Every time I look at the drum . . . I'll remember . . . I'll remember.*

Richard took her arm and steered her away through the broad leaves that flanked the trodden path.

Alena moved mechanically down the trail in a haze of confusion and agony. She seemed destined to have everything her heart reached out for taken from her. She fought the nagging voice that accused Zach of deserting her. Through her clouded reasoning she knew it was by no fault of his own. But he had abandoned her, the voice persisted.

Every other moment, she was consumed with the same desolate, childish anger that she had felt when her father had left her on the steps of Mistress Stephens' School for Young Ladies.

Why had this happened? She couldn't comprehend any of it. All she could grasp was that the two people she had opened her heart to, after so many solitary years, were now forever lost to her. And part of her had gone with them. She knew, no matter where she went or what she did, that that certain part of her . . . the part that made her whole would always remain in the untamed jungles of the Amazon. The hollow void left within could never be filled.

It might have been minutes or hours before Richard Blythe touched her arm and said, "We'll rest here a bit, Miss Sutton. Would you like a drink?" He handed her the canteen.

Alena took a sip and returned it. Lowering herself to the ground, she took off her hat and glanced about. They were on the edge of a cliff above the river. She had no idea how far they'd come or in what direction they were moving.

Tossing his gear a few feet away, Richard Blythe settled beside her. He propped an arm across his knee and scrutinized her for some time before he attempted conversation. "You poor dear." He reached out to brush her hair behind her ear, letting his fingers linger on her cheek. "You've been through quite a lot, haven't you?"

When Alena lowered her head, disengaging his touch, he withdrew his hand and cleared his throat.

"Tell me, Miss Sutton, were you successful in locating any news of your father?"

Alena raised her gaze to his. His concern appeared genuine, yet there was something she couldn't identify about him that bothered her. "I found my father, Mr. Blythe. Unfortunately, he passed away shortly after."

"What a pity. My condolences, Miss Sutton. Howard was a good chap." He lowered his lids and picked a blade of grass. "How . . . long did he live?"

"Not long." That strange feeling swept over Alena again, making her shiver. The nonchalance of his tone and mannerism struck her as being odd for someone who was as supposedly fond of her father as Richard Blythe claimed to be.

"Did he . . . say anything . . . about me?"

"I'm afraid he was in no condition for idle chatter, sir." Alena watched the man carefully. Had his lips curved slightly? "Mr. Blythe, may I ask what you were doing in the area when Zach was shot?"

Richard angled his head her way and blinked. "I was looking for ceremonial grounds, old shrines, anything that might have been connected to Mahrakimba's tomb. You can imagine my surprise when I came across the headdress while going through Zach's things. I take it you found the tomb. Tell me, my dear, you wouldn't happen to recall the vicinity, would you?"

It was Alena's turn to avert her eyes. "The treasure chamber was destroyed, Mr. Blythe. Even if it hadn't been, I certainly couldn't lead you to it. After we left there, I was distraught, and became even more so as we journeyed to the outcast camp in search of my father."

"I truly am sorry about Howard. I can't imagine who on earth could have beaten that poor old man so severely. It must have been one of those heathens he was forever fraternizing with. If I told him once, I told him . . ."

Alena looked at him in disbelief as he spoke. All the pieces of the puzzle began to fall into place. Alarm tingled in her veins. The foreboding she'd felt in context with this man at the stream had been a warning . . . a warning to which she'd paid no heed. Nothing more than a seed of doubt that he'd had something to do with all the sordid goings-on pushed her to test him. "Mr. Blythe, my father died from malaria." She studied his reaction. "I don't recall saying anything about an attack on his person."

"Well . . . certainly you did. You must have mentioned it. How else would I—"

"Exactly, Mr. Blythe."

His world-weary expression was transfigured into a cold, hard glare, his eyes glittering like black marbles. A sinister smile distorted his pleasant face.

True fear crept up Alena's spine. Her lungs begged for air as she stared at Blythe and saw unmasked evil. Cautiously, she started to scoot away from him, but he caught her wrist in a vicious grip.

"Just where do you think you're going, my dear? Why, we've not yet become properly acquainted. It would be rude of you to leave so soon."

He twisted her wrist into a position that sent an excruciating jolt up her arm and stopped her attempts to wriggle free. "It was you," she whispered pitifully. "*You* hurt my father. And Zach . . . oh, dear God, you . . . you murdered Zach, didn't you?"

"You're such a clever young woman, now aren't you?" His brows lifted with a deranged sort of pride.

"But why? *Why?*"

"Why?" He moved closer, forcing her back on her heels. "I'll tell you why. Your father was an old fool, that's why. I tried to be reasonable with him. I told him I had a buyer for the headdress. A private collector willing to pay three times what it was worth. I even offered him a cut. He would have none of it. So I followed him. But when I found him, he didn't have the map on him. I gathered he must have sent it somewhere safe. It didn't take much to find out he had a daughter." He gave Alena a sickly-sweet smile that made her stomach churn. "I truly did think he was dead when I left him, you know."

"You beast!" she spat, swinging her free hand toward his face. He caught it, folding it within his palm tightly.

"That wasn't very nice, Miss Sutton. We will play later. Right now, I'm rather enjoying listing my accomplishments. I think even you will appreciate my cunning. I pride myself on it, you know. Now where were we? Ah, yes . . . Summerfield." Blythe narrowed his eyes. "I've always abhorred the man. Somehow he always got there first . . . always obtained the very object I sought . . . always won. Only he didn't win this time, did he? I must admit a certain thrill rushed through me when I sighted down the barrel, aiming for his heart, and pulled the trigger. His size made him impossible to miss, standing out in the open as he was.

"Oh, I've made you cry. Are the tears for Summerfield or yourself, Miss Sutton? Tell me, my dear, did he whisper sweet nothings in your ear? Did he say you were the only one? I'm sure he told the others the same before he galloped off into the sunset."

Alena turned her face but Richard's fingers dug into her jaw and jerked it back. "Let me tell you about your precious Summerfield. Perhaps then you can appreciate me as the better man. I set off an explosion in Egypt. I do have extravagant tastes and the tidy little sum I received for my part in that raid kept me very comfortable for quite some time. Oh, it was a brilliant plan. Summerfield himself hired me. I am somewhat of an authority on Egyptian artifacts. Your learned archeologist never suspected a thing until it was all over and done with. Even then, he couldn't prove it. You see, I was very careful not to leave any evidence behind. The only other man who knew I was involved conveniently died in the blast. I had rather hoped Summerfield would get caught, too. He's had investigators hounding me ever since the raid. I'd have taken him out a few weeks ago if that damned-fool Texan hadn't stepped in front of him. With good old Zach out of the way, I could have taken his place."

Alena stared at him in disbelief and horror. Slim. He'd shot Slim, too. The man was ruthless. The fact that he actually took pleasure in boasting about his violence terrified her all the more.

Blythe rolled his eyes, taking a deep breath. "It does the soul good to confess, don't you agree? No? Well, it doesn't really matter whether you answer or not. Your face is one of those that reveals everything you're thinking." He pressed a kiss to her cheek. "For instance, right now I can see you're shocked . . . and perhaps . . . frightened? Ah, yes, definitely frightened. Would you care to scream, Miss Sutton? It might make you feel better."

Alena glared at him with disgust. "I'll not scream for you, you snake."

"Oh, but you will, my dear, you will. They all do eventually. But out here, you see, no one will hear you."

Alena held her chin steady, resisting the urge to quiver. Yet her bravado died a little as his fingers began to play torturously up and down her bare arm.

"I'll make you scream, all right," he promised.

"First, however, I'm curious to know what happened to Hawkins . . . the man I had on the freighter."

The memory of the surly fellow that had attacked her on the boat made Alena's skin crawl and she shivered involuntarily.

"Ah, I see you met him. Very cordial fellow, wasn't he? I was really quite worried when he missed our appointment in Caracas. I'm sure he didn't jump ship. He was being paid too well. What's the matter, Miss Sutton? Cat got your tongue? Oh, come now, we'll have no secrets between us. I've told you most of mine. Tell me now, did Summerfield do away with him?"

At her hesitation, he gathered her wrists with one hand in a painful grip while the other twisted into her hair, jerking her head back. "Miss Sutton, I asked you a question."

"He . . . fell on his knife. He was chasing me . . . and he fell." She hated her helplessness. In frustration, tears misted her vision.

"He fell," Blythe repeated thoughtfully. "Well, what a pity. He always was rather clumsy, though it will be a chore to find a replacement for him. He was the sort who would do anything if the price was right. Yes, I believe I shall sorely miss poor Hawkins."

Pensive, Blythe seemed to have forgotten Alena for the moment, yet he still imprisoned her wrists and she could only pray his preoccupation would last long enough for her to think.

His attention came back to her sooner than she'd hoped. He stood, dragging her to her feet with him.

"I'll have to kill you. I must," he said in a voice filled with soft, sick agony. He tunneled his fingers through her hair, brushing it over her shoulder. Abruptly he caught her waist and crushed her against him. "You do understand, don't you? You know too much." He caressed the side of her face, then his hand slid down the side of her neck and closed around her throat. "I was right about Summerfield, wasn't I? He's already spoiled you for me, hasn't he? That was a very touching little scene back there on the bank."

Wide-eyed, Alena stared at the crazed man, feeling the pulse in her throat beat against his thumb.

"Well, it doesn't matter. He may have had you first, my dear, but I shall have you last." His eyes glazed as he looked into hers. "Yes. I shall be your last lover, Miss Sutton . . . and have the last laugh on Summerfield yet."

A well of pity, anger, terror, and sorrow overflowed within Alena . . . for herself . . . for Zach . . . for her father, and tears streamed down her face.

"You want to strike me, don't you?" Blythe asked with a raise of his brow. "Go ahead. Strike me, Alena. I do so enjoy resistance."

Slowly, she shook her head. "No," she whispered. "I won't give you a reason to hurt me. Please . . . don't do this. You don't have to do this. I won't tell, I promise. If you let me go, I won't tell anyone anythi—"

Chapter 17

"Liar!" Blythe's fingers tightened around Alena's neck, cutting off her air supply. He brought his face within a hairsbreadth of hers and wildly searched her eyes. "You little liar. You'd say anything to save your neck."

Alena coughed, gasping for breath as he loosened his grip and drew small circles with his thumb against her throat.

"Don't tell fibs, Alena. Don't make me angry. I don't wish to do away with you . . . not yet. Not before we have our bit of fun."

He moved his mouth toward hers and Alena turned her face, but that didn't stop him. His kisses drooled down the side of her neck. His hands roved freely over her body. "P-please," she choked out.

"Please?" Blythe stilled and raised his head. "Don't plead, my dear, it doesn't become you. There's no one left to save you but yourself. By all means, try to salvage your virtue, if you wish. Of course you could never win, but I'd find immense pleasure in the struggle. Would you like me to provoke you?"

Alena bit the inside of her lip so hard she broke

the skin. He wanted her to scream, wanted her to fight. She wouldn't. She wouldn't give him what he wanted.

Suddenly his hand delved beneath the fabric of her blouse, his fingers biting hard into the soft flesh there, and she lost all restraint. Wrenching her arms free, she raked her nails across his face.

In a flash, he captured both her wrists and pinned them behind her with one hand. The glint in his cold dark eyes petrified her. A slow, demented grin curved his lips while he traced the scratches on his cheek. He glanced at the blood on his fingertips, then stared into Alena's eyes. Watching her reaction closely, he raised his hand and, emphasizing each move, curled it into a fist.

Alena closed her eyes and braced herself for the blow.

"Blythe! Hold it right there, unless you relish having a hole blown through your belly. Let the girl go."

Alena melted at the sound of the deep, resonant voice. *God in heaven, was she imagining it?*

At the click of a gun cocking, Blythe whirled, swinging her in front of him. She opened her eyes and there was Zach. He was swaying slightly and looked as if he'd just crawled from the pits of hell. But it was him. He was there.

Tucked under Zach's arm was the rifle Richard had left behind. He held the stock braced against his rib with his elbow, while his other arm hung limply from the shoulder Alena had bandaged. Only sheer will could be keeping him upright, thought Alena. She strained toward him, but Blythe's grip confined her movement.

"Damn you, Summerfield. I should have put another bullet in you on the bank."

"Yeah, well, you missed your chance, Richard, old boy." Zach's steel-blue glower transmitted a warning, yet one corner of his mouth quirked into a smile. "Lucky for me you're a lousy shot and not too bright, huh?" Losing the smile, he nodded toward Alena. "Like I said, let her go."

Richard laughed. "Give it up, Zach. You haven't any bullets. I emptied your rifle on the riverbank."

"Wrong again. This gun is loaded. Obviously, you forgot to check my pants pockets. Another mistake, Richard. How many mistakes can you afford to make?"

Richard chuckled again, this time not so assuredly. "You're bluffing. You wouldn't dare fire. You might miss me and hit our little friend here."

"Don't play any games with me, Blythe. I'm not in the mood. Believe me, even one-handed, I'm a far better shot than you are. I don't miss my target."

Alena felt Richard tense behind her. The rise and fall of his chest increased against her back. His breath came hot against her head. "Go ahead," he blared in the tone of a man who had lost all touch with reality. "Shoot." Shielding himself with her, he lurched to the edge of the cliff. "But first, tell Miss Sutton good-bye."

"Blythe!" Zach took a step forward, then stopped. "Blythe, so help me God," he said, struggling to keep his voice easy, "if you hurt her, I'll see you in hell before this day is out. And mark my word, eternity in Hades will seem like a holiday when I'm done with you."

"Why, Zach." Blythe nuzzled Alena's neck, making her cringe. "I do believe you actually care for the little twit."

"She doesn't mean a thing to me," Zach said flatly. "In fact, she's been nothing but a thorn in my side since the first day I laid eyes on her. I brought her here. I'm responsible for her, that's all." Zach shifted his weight. "Look, it's me you want, not her. Let her go."

"Put the gun down, Summerfield. Put it down and back off." At Zach's reluctance, Blythe rushed on. "Do what I say, Zach, or it's one good shove and she's over the cliff." He jerked Alena closer to the ledge. Loose stones tumbled over the edge and vanished from view before they reached the raging water and jagged rocks below.

"Okay, Blythe." Zach held the rifle away from him. "I'm laying it down. See?" His gaze met Alena's, telegraphing a silent message.

Alena's lungs stopped working. *Merciful heavens.* He was going to do something. She could tell. He had that look. She watched his every move, waiting, praying that whatever it was would work.

Very slowly, very carefully, Zach crouched and laid the loaded gun on the grass. Then in one quick motion, he rolled, grabbed the bundle containing the headdress, and suspended it over the side of the cliff. "I have a deal for you, Blythe. You want this lovely showpiece. I want the girl. Either we do business, or *you* say good-bye to the headdress."

Richard stiffened against Alena, then relaxed. He laughed cynically. "Don't take me for a fool, Zach. I know you too well. You'd never destroy such a priceless artifact."

"At the moment, I'm a man with a mission to see the lady released. If any harm comes to her, you have my solemn promise I'll drop this thing so fast it'll make your head swim. Then, by God, I won't hesitate to tear you into alligator food and toss you over, too." The hard glint in Zach's eyes belied his sudden smile. "Care to try me?"

"Come now, Zach, you can barely stay on your feet now. You're already bleeding again, or hadn't you noticed? I only have to wait for you to fall."

"Oh, I can stay on my feet." Zach struggled to an upright position. "Hell, even with a bullet in me, I can give a weasel like you a run for your money. You're a coward, Blythe . . . a weakling who leaves a man to die in the jungle because he doesn't have the guts to finish him off, a depraved worm that gets a thrill out of hurting defenseless women half your size. Tell me, Richard, does that make you feel like a big man?"

"Shut up!" Blythe's arms constricted around Alena's ribs. "Shut up! Shut up, Summerfield. I'm warning—"

"Why don't you come over here and shut me up? What's the matter? Don't you think you can take me? Hell, look at me. I'm wounded. You said so yourself, I can barely stand—"

Alena shrieked as she was slung to the ground. As she tumbled toward the ledge, she grabbed frantically at grass, rocks, *anything* that would stop the world from spinning. At the instant her fingers closed around a thick vine, the earth dissolved beneath her. The lower half of her body dangled off the cliff. She dug her hands into the thick moss and looked up.

Zach barreled toward her like a freight train. Richard charged him. The two collided dangerously close to the edge of the cliff.

"Hold on, Alena!" Zach cried out, trying to shove the crazed man from his path. "Damn you, Blythe." Zach swung the headdress, delivering a blow to the side of Richard's head. "Get the hell out of my way!"

Completely unhinged, Richard fought with the strength of a madman to hold him back. A wild punch plowed into Zach's injured shoulder. In reflex, Zach turned the headdress loose to clutch his wound.

Blythe lunged for the prize.

A horrifying howl mingled with Alena's scream as Richard flew over her and off the cliff. For a long, ghastly moment, he seemed to float in midair, still clutching the headdress. Then he plummeted, spiraling downward until he crashed against the rocks that jutted from the turbulent water.

Kneeling above her, Zach caught her arm. "Come on, Angel. Come on, climb. That's it."

His face flickering with pain, Zach attempted to pull her up using his one good hand. To help lighten his burden, Alena swung her legs to the side until she gained a foothold. When she crawled onto the ledge, Zach collapsed beside her.

Reaching out, she wiped the beads of sweat from his forehead. "Zach?"

He angled his head her way. His eyes were ghostly pale, the color of life draining from them.

"Oh, Zach . . . I . . . he told me you were dead."

He tried an impossible grin. "Well, he probably wasn't too far . . . from right. Get . . . the gun, Alena."

"What?"

"Yori . . . is bound to be within earshot. Get the . . . rifle."

Alena glanced about. Locating the weapon a few feet away, she retrieved it.

"Careful . . . it's cocked and loaded," Zach cautioned. His breath was labored. "Sit down. Point the barrel . . . in the air. It's . . . it's going . . . to kick . . . so brace the butt . . . against the ground before . . . you fire."

A jolt shot through Alena as she pulled the trigger. The bullet cracked, momentarily deafening her. She couldn't lay the contraption down fast enough. Grabbing the nearest article of clothing from her bag, she scrambled back to Zach to soak the blood that oozed through the bandage.

"Take . . . good care of me, Angel," he stammered. "We . . . have . . . unfinished business to discuss."

"That, dear sir, will have to wait." Alena's heart ricocheted off her sternum as her gaze met his. *Love* seemed too inadequate a word to describe her feelings for him. "You stay quiet now and rest."

"No problem." A hint of a smile touched his lips. "Since the adrenaline quit flowing . . . I don't have it in me . . . to do much else but rest." His lids lowered a fraction. "Alena, did . . . it really happen? The headdress . . . Blythe, are they . . . gone?"

"They're gone, love," Alena said, brushing her fingertips across his furrowed brow. "I'm sorry. I know you had hoped the headdress—"

"It doesn't . . . matter. You're safe. That's all . . . that matters. There will be . . . another time . . . another place . . . another treasure." He made a feeble effort to raise his hand. Alena caught it, raising it to her lips, and his eyes slid closed. "I

...need some...sleep, Angelface. I...don't feel so good."

A stirring of leaves turned Alena's head toward the brush. "Yori! Thank God, you're here! Help me. Help me, Yori. He's been shot."

Chapter 18

A lena sat on the edge of the hotel bed, running her hand over what was left of the flowers on the old hat Zach had given her. Since arriving in New York, the Amazon seemed far, far away, like a dream of long ago.

It seemed incredible now that she and Yori had managed to get Zach back to the coast. Infection had already set in when they boarded the freighter. Yori's potions had been a godsend for keeping the fever down. At least they had calmed Zach, helping him sleep most of the voyage.

The hardest part of all had been waiting for two days on the wooden bench in the hospital hall until the doctor had confirmed that Zach would live. A blessed relief had washed over Alena when she'd heard he would live to journey to some other place the world had forgotten.

Zach would live. It was the news she had waited to hear. While she'd worried on that hard bench, her reaction when she'd thought Zach dead had come back to her over and over again. That awful, empty feeling of being deserted. And something else had emerged whilst she'd sat there, something she had dismissed for a short, but sweet time in the Amazon. A life together was impossible. Zachariah Summerfield would never stay with her. He would never bind himself to anyone. He'd said as much.

She had made up her mind yesterday to leave quietly rather than have Zach tell her good-bye. There would be no parting between them then. No farewells to mar her remembrance of their adventure together.

Alena smoothed the weathered brim of her beloved hand-me-down hat. Carefully wrapping it in tissue, she placed it in her bag. She was going to miss her train to Philadelphia if she dallied any longer. With a sigh, she rose and glanced about the room for anything she might have overlooked. Her gaze settled on the tiny drum she'd left atop the bureau.

The drum. If she hurried, she could drop it off by the hospital for Zach. Perhaps he would exhibit it in his museum. The thought that he might think of her when he looked at it, somehow gave her courage to do what she must.

Swiftly closing her valise, she walked over and picked up the drum. She hadn't planned on going back to the hospital. Zach had been unconscious when she'd left. He could very well still be, but she couldn't take the chance of facing him. She wouldn't be able to look into those blue eyes and simply walk away. She couldn't bear any spoken words of parting: the paper-thin shell around her heart would surely crumble.

Alena rolled the drum over in her hand and bit her bottom lip. She could give the drum to that nice nurse who had been so very kind. The nurse would see to it that the relic was delivered to Zach.

* * *

Zach faded in and out, drifting between lush green jungles and the luxury of a soft warm bed. A bright, hot pain behind his eyes was his first response when he forced his lids open. The second was confusion.

A rosy-cheeked woman in a long white veil stood by his bed with a tray. "Good morning, sir," she said, setting the tray on the nightstand. She gestured to the meal and smiled. "Tea and broth for you today, perhaps something a little more filling tomorrow. You're to finish it off, sir. Dr. Mallory's orders."

Zach glanced from her to the tray and back again. Furrowing his brows, he lifted the covers and briefly inspected the stiffly starched white gown he wore. "A hospital. I'm in a hospital?"

"Yes, sir."

He started to lift his head and felt a series of sharp stabs between his ears. "Ahh," he groaned, easing back on the pillow. "Dear lady, would you be kind enough to tell me why my head feels like someone's playing billiards inside? I may be disoriented, but I only recall being shot in the chest."

"It's the aftereffect of the laudanum, sir. The doctor said you would have a fine headache when you first woke. Will you be needing anything else, sir?"

Zach flung an arm across his brow. "No ... yes!" He propped up on his elbows, swallowed down the rising nausea, then opened his eyes wide at the nurse. "Alena ... Miss Sutton, is she here? Is she all right?"

"Miss Sutton, sir?" The nurse appeared thoughtful for a moment, then smiled. "Oh, you must be speaking of the pretty young English-woman. The poor little thing slept on the bench just outside your door for two nights. I brought her a blanket."

"Where is she now?" Zach asked with a bit more urgency than he'd intended.

The nurse shrugged her shoulders slightly. "Why, I don't know, sir. She left shortly after the doctor assured her you would recover. We didn't see her for a day or so, then this morning she rushed up to me downstairs, asked me to give you that thing, and rushed right out."

Zach followed her pointed finger to the little drum on a small table across the room. "She didn't leave a note?"

"No, sir. I told her you might be waking soon, if she'd like to wait, but she said she had to hurry to catch her train."

"Train?" Zach threw back the covers and sat up, grabbing his head to keep his ears from ringing. "What train?"

"Oh, sir." The nurse caught his shoulders and attempted to press him backwards. "You mustn't. Dr. Mallory says—"

"Blast the doctor!" Zach pried her hands from him, keeping a grip on one of her wrists. "What train, dammit?"

"I don't know, sir. I truly don't. Please, sir, you're hurting me."

Zach looked at his fingers wrapped around her wrist. He was holding her so tight his knuckles were white. He released her instantly, and raked a hand through his hair. "I'm sorry," he said as she stumbled away from him. "I'm sorry, miss." He studied her aghast expression a moment, then sighed. "Look, Nurse . . . what is your name?"

"Emma, sir. Emma Dawson." Eying him warily, she retreated a step.

Zach put on one of his best smiles. "Nurse Dawson, I'm sure you attend to your duties very efficiently. I mean, you minister to your patients' every need. Am I correct?"

"Oh, yes, sir," Nurse Dawson said with a lift of her chin. "I'm a very good nurse, if I say so myself."

"Excellent. Then get me my pants." Zach pushed up from the bed and came to his feet swaying.

"Oh! Oh, sir, you're not to be out of bed yet." Nurse Dawson started forward.

Zach stopped her with a hand. "I don't need you to help me back to bed, woman! If you truly want to help me, get . . . my . . . pants!"

"But, sir, I can't. It's against regulations."

Gaining his equilibrium, Zach straightened to his full height, all traces of his former smile gone. "Nurse Dawson, I don't have time for this. Now, I'm not going to hurt you. I promise. But I don't intend to leave this hospital wearing this damn gown." He took a step toward her. "I need my pants," he gritted between his teeth.

The woman paled and began a slow shake of her head. "Sir, you're not well. I'm going to have to call the doctor." Glancing at the door, she eased in that direction.

"Dad-blast it!" Zach blocked her escape.

Backing away, she covered her mouth, tears gathering in her eyes.

"Nurse Dawson, I want my pants and I want them now," Zach said, continuing to stalk her around the room. "I *need* my pants. Do you understand? The only woman I've ever loved has just walked out on me and I don't even know why. She's left me, dammit. She's left me." Passing the table, he grabbed the drum and shook it in the air. "And all she's left me with is this lousy little drum. That's all. Just this lousy, stinking little—" His throat working convulsively, he glared at the drum, then hurled it against the wall with all his might.

An explosion of bright green crystals showered from the drum as it shattered into pieces. While the nurse ran screaming from the room, Zach stood mesmerized by the tiny emerald lights ricocheting off the wall and floor.

Chapter 19

The incoming train whistle blew. Steam billowed through the Philadelphia station, blanketing everything with immense, white puffs.

Alena stood alone in the dense fog, waiting for the train to New York. She tightened her grip on her valise handle, feeling very out of place amidst the strangers that bustled around her. She watched passengers disembark and board, watched them embrace loved ones . . . kiss hello . . . kiss good-bye . . . and a knot formed in her throat.

She had returned to Philadelphia and gathered her belongings from Mr. Dalton's office and settled her father's affairs. She had her ticket for the next train. The day after tomorrow, she would board the ship and sail for England. All the arrangements had been made. It was a simple enough procedure. She only had to convince her feet to cooperate and stop dragging.

No more tears, she reminded herself. Zach was incapable of making a commitment. She had accepted that. His spirit was as free as the wind. He could not be bridled or confined. She would consider it no less than sacrilege to attempt to tame him. A future together was simply not meant to be.

From now on, she would love him in the same way she did sunshine, blue skies, the moon, and the stars . . . from afar: always untouchable, yet always treasured. To want any more of him would be selfish.

It wasn't as if she couldn't keep Zach in her heart. Dream about him, think about him, remember, and smile. He would forever be the love of her life. Nothing—neither time nor distance—could change that.

On rainy days, she could bar her door and conjure up his memory. She could sit in her chair by the window, sipping tea, and relive each moment, cherish each moment spent with him. Someday, perhaps when she was old and gray, she would write about her great adventure in the Amazon, *and* the man who touched her soul.

"Alena! Alena, wait!"

Alena swirled, half-believing her mind was playing a cruel trick. Yet as she scanned the crowd, Zach emerged from the mist of white fog.

She hardly recognized him, dressed as he was. Hat held in hand, he was clean-shaven and wore the same suit he had worn the night he had taken her to Pierre's.

Heaven help her, he still took her breath away.

"Alena, wait!" Zach nudged his way toward her through the hordes of people. "Wait for me," he yelled again, waving a bunch of flowers.

The whistle blew. "All aboard!" called the conductor.

Alena glanced from Zach to the train. *What was he doing here?* Of course. He'd come to see her off. Clouds of white steam formed alongside the puffing locomotive.

Move, Alena's logic ordered. *Hurry. Get on the train and don't look back. He's too tempting. You could stay on another day, another week, but he can't make you any promises. And you're too vulnerable right now to refuse him anything. Hurry, before he gets any closer.* She closed her lids momentarily, then forced herself to turn, and commanded her legs to move toward the train.

"Alena! No! Stop!"

Biting her bottom lip so hard she could taste blood, she prayed the whistle would blow again so she couldn't hear his pleas.

"Alena Sutton! Damn you, woman! You hold it right there! By the laws of the Jaquara tribe, you are my wife!"

Alena's steps faltered.

"The marriage was consummated!" Zach bellowed at the top of his lungs. A hushed silence fell over the station. "The marriage *was* consummated," he repeated in a quieter tone, yet the words echoed loud and clear into the stillness.

Alena felt the blood drain from her face. She whirled to find Zach no more than ten feet behind her and surrounded by curious onlookers.

His face broke into a grin. "And you loved every minute of it, Angelface." He turned to an older, gray-haired gentleman nearby and commented conversationally, "Why, she was purring like a—"

Storming up to Zach, Alena clapped her hand over his mouth. "Zachariah Summerfield," she hissed under her breath. Glancing from side to side as more bystanders gathered round, she lowered her speech to a murmur. "Keep your voice down!"

Above her hand, his amused gaze clashed with

her glare. She felt his mouth twitch beneath her palm. Long before he tugged her hand away, she knew he'd be wearing one of his idiotic smiles. Zach handed her the flowers.

Flustered by the spectators, she passed the bouquet to a lady who stood near, then leaned forward. "How *dare* you," she whispered fiercely. "How dare you speak of such delicate matters in public!"

"I *dare*, my dear, because you gave me no choice." He narrowed his eyes and all but a trace of his smile faded. "You heard me calling you. You saw me, dammit. You looked straight at me and deliberately turned around and started walking the other way." With his smile now gone completely, his expression displayed so much sorrow. "Why, Alena? Why did you leave without a word?"

"All aboard! Last call!" barked the conductor. "All aboard!"

"Zach . . . there's no point in discussing this," she said, absorbing every detail of his face, dying to touch him . . . to kiss him just one last time . . . but knowing she mustn't. "I have to go. My train—"

Zach caught her hands. "Go? Go where, Alena? Back to that dreary school? Back to that old witch, Mistress Stephens? What will you do there? Spend the rest of your life locked away in your drab little room, reading about other people's adventures?"

Tears misted Alena's vision. An unbearable pressure built behind her breastbone and she dropped her head. "Zach, why are you doing this to me?"

Zach crooked two fingers beneath her chin,

lifting her face to his. Once again, she was captured by the magic of his ice-blue eyes. He raised her hand and pressed it against his chest. "Do you feel that, Alena? I have a heart. I never believed such a thing existed inside me before. You ... *you*, Angelface, brought it to life ... made it rumble until I could no longer ignore it."

Alena's chin quivered. His touch, his words, the pumping beneath her palm, enveloped her in sweet agony. She squeezed her eyes shut and a single tear escaped, trickling down her cheek. "Oh, Zach, we're so different, you and I."

"In some ways. But that's the beauty of it. I can teach you how to soar beyond those self-imposed restrictions you've shackled yourself with, Angel ... how to enjoy life ... find pleasure in simple things. I can show you the world. You can show me how to be gentle and loving. Help me tame my temper. I need you to keep me in line. I need you to save me from myself. Don't you see? You're my salvation. Open your eyes, Alena. Don't shut me out. Don't be afraid to live. Don't be afraid to love."

Alena hesitantly raised her damp lashes.

"You love me, Angelface. I can see it when you look at me."

She couldn't deny he spoke the truth. From the second she'd seen his face among the crowd at the station, she had feared this moment. She knew, without a doubt now, she would go anywhere with him, be anything he wanted her to be. He had only to ask.

Zach cupped her face, brushing the tears from her cheeks with his thumbs. "Alena ... God knows I have my faults, one of which is my inability to express myself. It has never been as important to me as it is right now to explain my feelings. I don't know where to begin . . . how to tell you . . . all I can say is that I want to wake up every morning and see your face on the pillow next to mine. I . . . want you beside me to watch each sunset," he whispered. "I want to grow old with you, Angelface. When your hair turns silver and mine turns gray, and our children have grown and gone, I want to hold hands on the veranda every evening, talking, laughing, sharing fond memories."

"Children," Alena murmured, suddenly becoming terrified of the prospect. She pushed away from Zach and met his gaze. "Oh, Zach. I hadn't thought of that. But children would be a very real possibility, wouldn't they?"

He gave her a puzzled frown. "Well . . . I assumed . . . Alena, don't you want children?"

"Of course, I do, but . . . oh, Zach, what if something happened to me?"

"Nothing's going to happen to you, sweetheart. I won't let it."

"But what if it does?" she asked, gripping his lapel. "What if it does and there's a child and—"

"Alena, I would never abandon a child of ours." Zach's voice was edged with the same hurt his eyes displayed. "Never. I know the scars the desertion of a parent can leave. I've worn them a long time. My father was physically present sometimes, but he was never really there for me at all. I know the agony of feeling unloved. I swear, by everything holy, Alena, no child of mine will ever have to contend with those feelings." He pulled her to him and nuzzled her temple, expelling a warm breath that fluttered against her hair. "I intend to spend the rest of my life proving that to you, if you'll let me. I need you, Alena. God, I love you so much it hurts. Please . . . please don't leave me.''

Bright colors burst inside Alena's head, inside her heart. Tearfully, she tilted her head and looked up at the man responsible for the warm, wonderful sensation that enveloped her. "Did you just say . . . that you *loved* me?"

"I said it, all right." Zach grinned and slipped his arms around her waist. "I said it and I meant it. Lord, woman, do you think I would be here making a fool of myself if I didn't love you?"

Laughter bubbled from Alena. "Then you wouldn't mind saying it again, would you?"

"I love you, Alena Sutton," he murmured, then promptly turned toward the bewildered gentleman next to him and announced in a booming voice, "I love this woman, by God, and I want her to marry me." The poor man raised his brows and looked the other way, and Zach turned an adoring gaze on Alena. "That is," he added softly, "if she'll have me."

Alena opened her mouth, closed it, then opened it again. "If I'll have you?"

"Jeez almighty, woman, do I have to go down on bended knees?" he asked, starting to kneel.

Alena caught his arm. "Stop being ridiculous, you madman. Of course I'll have you."

"You will?"

"I will," she said with a smile.

Zach flashed a grin, then tapped the portly fellow beside him. "She said yes," he informed the gentleman.

This time the man returned the smile. "Congratulations," he said, and tipped his hat to the bride-to-be.

Alena reached up and turned Zach's face back to hers. "I love you, Zachariah Summerfield . . . as insane as you are, I love you."

"I *knew* you did," Zach said with a wink, then, catching her off guard, lowered his mouth to hers.

An all-consuming passion devoured Alena, leaving her weak and wanting in Zach's embrace. She forgot all about his cocky self-assurance. She slipped her arms around his neck and most audaciously leaned against him.

Applause and cheers from onlookers broke the kiss, shattering the lovers' illusion that only the two of them existed.

Alena blushed the color of summer-red roses. She wrapped her fingers around the arm Zach offered and accepted the good wishes tendered them as he ushered her through the crowd.

Zach clasped one extended hand after another, smiled, and nodded politely while they made their way to the exit. Between a pat on the back and a handshake, he leaned toward Alena. "I've wired Slim in Texas and asked him to be our witness. I hope you don't object."

"Of course not." Alena beamed up at him. "You know how fond I am of Slim. But when—"

"I have a coach waiting," he injected. "We have a lot to do before Saturday."

"Saturday?"

"I mentioned I've reserved Trinity Church in New York for Saturday, didn't I?"

Alena smiled at another well-wisher, then looked at Zach in astonishment. "You most certainly did not." Halting, she swung around in front of him. "Zach, that is only three days away—"

The final whistle blew, drowning her out. Her gaze snapped to the train. "Heavens, Zach, my baggage! I forgot—"

Zach patted her hand. "Now, now, don't fret, Angelface. Your bags aren't aboard. I had the porter load them on my coach."

Releasing his arm, Alena pressed her lips together and stared at him. "When exactly did you reserve the church?"

"Ah . . . I believe it was yesterday before I left New York."

"Yesterday. I see. And you had my things loaded on your coach *before* you proposed to me? Am I correct?"

"Ah . . . so far, yes."

Alena folded her arms across her chest and her foot began tapping against the hard pavement. "Do you not think that was rather presumptuous of you?"

Zach ran a hand over the nape of his neck and peeked at her beneath his brows. "Well, I suppose it was . . . but you see, I had no intention of letting you say no. I was prepared to go down on my knees and start spouting poetry if I had to. I even brushed up on Elizabeth Barrett Browning."

"Zachariah, you are the most arrogant, most conceited man I should ever hope to know."

Zach nodded in agreement, then bent to her ear. "That's because I'm so good-looking."

Alena rolled her eyes. She couldn't keep from smiling when he wiggled his brows that way. "Whatever am I going to do with you?"

"Love me." Zach turned her toward the door and tucked her hand in the crook of his arm once more. "And do your best to keep me on the straight and narrow. I have this gut feeling a chore like that might just take you the rest of your life."

Zach stopped outside the coach and looked up and down the street.

"Are you expecting someone?" Alena asked.

"A delivery. Ah, there's James now. Wait here, I'll only be a moment."

Curiously Alena watched Zach hand the young man several coins in exchange for a small wrapped package. He returned wearing a Cheshire-cat grin, yet merely gestured to the open coach door.

"After you, Angelface," he said, helping her into the coach, then climbed in beside her. His eyes twinkled like a child's at Christmastime as he handed her the box. "It's a wedding gift."

With furrowed brows, Alena untied the string. She peeled off the brown paper from a black velvet case and glanced at Zach. He gave her a nudge. "Open it."

She flipped the lid up and gasped aloud as a large rectangular emerald surrounded by sparkling diamonds sent a spectrum of tiny lights bursting throughout the dark coach. "Oh . . . Oh, Zach . . . it's beautiful."

"The color of your eyes, Angel," he said as he took the ring from its velvet container and slipped it on her finger. "Ah, good. It fits. I had to rush the order, but it just so happened an excellent jeweler in New York owed me a favor. He should have the necklace completed in time for the wedding."

Alena held her hand out in front of her. A ray of sunshine from the window touched the stone, making it shine all the brighter. "Zach . . . I've never dreamed of a ring this lovely . . . but . . . but . . . wasn't it too . . . too—"

"Expensive?"

"Exactly."

"It's worth a fortune. A goodly portion of my savings went for the diamonds and toward having the center stone cut and set. Though I must confess, it was you, my dear, who provided the emerald. In fact, you can afford an abundance of jewels of far greater value, if you wish."

Alena stared at him in blank confusion. "Zach, what in heaven's name are you talking about?" Frowning, she reached up and felt his forehead. "Oh, gracious, you haven't fully recovered yet, have you?"

"I feel splendid." Zach pulled her hand from his head, enveloping it between his two. "Let me explain. You are now considered a wealthy woman by any standards. You own over five hundred thousand dollars' worth of similar high-grade stones. I've insured them and placed them in a safety deposit box in your name at my bank in New—"

"Oh, Zach. My poor darling." Alena caressed his cheek worriedly. "You really must see a physician about these fits."

"Fits?" Zach frowned. "What fits? Alena, listen to me. The drum, the little drum you brought back with you, was filled with emeralds . . . high-grade, flawless emeralds."

Alena blinked twice, then examined her ring once more. "Emeralds?"

Zach raised his brows and nodded. "That particular stone is the pick of the litter."

Alena stared unseeingly in front of her for a long moment, oblivious to the swaying jar of the coach. "Zach . . . Papa said something about a drum just before he passed away. Could he have possibly known one of the drums in Mahra-kimba's tomb was filled with emeralds?"

"He could have, I guess. Howard was famous for finding out things no one else knew." Zach slipped an arm around her and she laid her head against his chest. "I suppose we'll never really know for sure, Angelface."

"Zach?"

"Hmm?"

"Have you ever wondered if Papa meant for this to happen—between you and me, I mean? I've thought about it and thought about it and I can think of no logical reason for him to separate the map the way he did. Surely he couldn't have foreseen things turning out this way, could he?"

"Howie was full of wisdom, Angelface. I wouldn't put anything past him. If you want my opinion, the old rascal knew exactly what he was doing when he threw us together." Zach lifted Alena's chin and smiled down at her. "In any event, I'll be forever in his debt. I've spent years searching for treasures, but the excitement of finding priceless relics always fades. The glory that fills me when I look into your eyes is an everlasting treasure. Long after all the other treasures on earth are gone, it will be there shining like a star in the sky. Howie's ended my search. I don't need it anymore—any of it. You will keep my heart pumping."

His lips met hers with such tenderness that the blood sang in her veins. Sliding her arms around his neck, she was on the brink of euphoria when his words echoed back into her head. *I don't need it anymore—any of it.*

Alena pulled away from him abruptly and searched his face. "Zach, you're not saying you intend to end your career in archeology . . . are you?"

"I'm getting old, Alena," Zach said, fixing his attention on something out the window. "I'm starting to feel aches and pains from every old injury I've had. Besides, if I'm going to be a proper family man—"

Alena turned his face to hers. "Stop talking such nonsense, Zach. You're not old. Banged up a bit, but certainly not old. All you need is a long holiday with a loving, caring wife and you'll soon be as good as new." She concentrated on straightening his tie. "You mustn't give up your life's work . . . not for me . . . not for anyone. Can't you see it's part of what makes you the man you are . . . the man I love. You could never be completely happy if your life lacked the thrill of living . . . the adventure you've become accustomed to." She lifted her eyes to his. "I don't want to change your life, Zach. I want to share it."

Zach stared back at her, his heart feeling full and whole for the first time ever. "Would you really do that for me? Follow me to the ends of the earth? Could you be content living in a tent? Camping beneath the stars for months at a time? Would you really do that for me?"

Alena smiled. "I think I caught a fever for excitement in the Amazon. Perhaps I've always had it. I know, without a doubt, I would go anywhere with you. I learned to trust you with my life; I will trust you with my happiness. I can help you with your work, Zach. I can keep accurate accounts of the artifacts you discover. Together . . . *together*, Zach, I don't believe there's any place we can't go or anything we can't do."

Zach wrapped his arms around her, lifting her onto his lap, and leaned his forehead against hers. "Alena Sutton, you are indeed a treasure. My very own angel," he added, dropping a kiss on her nose. "It would only be for a while. Of course, we'll settle down when we have children."

"Of course we will. But we can wait a while to have children. I'm rather looking forward to a few years of camping under the stars with you . . . among other things."

"Why, Miss Sutton," Zach murmured, "how very brazen of you to bring up such an indelicate subject."

Alena gazed into the depths of his too-blue eyes, her heart unbound, filled with serenity, and free, free at last to follow love's destiny. Life with Zach might not always be this peaceful. But it would most certainly never be dull.

"Ah, Angelface, you're going to love Crete." Zach gave her a little squeeze. "The islands are beautiful this time of year. Arthur Evans has asked me to continue my work on the Minoan ruins. Of course, I haven't given him an answer yet. I'll write him we're coming as soon as we get to New York. Oh, and you remember that Nigel Flemming who said he was with the British Museum? Arthur informs me he is the curator's new son-in-law. You know, I think we ought to display the drum in our museum. I have someone piecing it back togeth—"

"Zachariah," Alena whispered, tunneling her fingers through his thick dark hair.

"Hmm?"

"Do be quiet, you madman, and kiss me."

*If you enjoyed this book, take advantage
of this special offer. Subscribe now and . . .*

GET A *FREE*
HISTORICAL ROMANCE
——— NO OBLIGATION (a $3.95 value) ———

Each month the editors of True Value will select the four best historical
romance novels from America's leading publishers. Preview them in
your home Free for 10 days. And we'll send you a FREE book as our
introductory gift. No obligation. If for any reason you decide not to keep
them, just return them and owe nothing. But if you like them you'll pay
just $3.50 each and save at least $.45 each off the cover price. (Your
savings are a minimum of $1.80 a month.) There is no shipping and
handling or other hidden charges. There are no minimum number of
books to buy and you may cancel at any time.

send in the coupon below